ADVANCE I

"I love a good S
What a fresh, unique, and hilarious take on the dating landscape. I laughed, I teared up, I had the most fun reading this bonkers book! Absolutely fantastic!"

—Kirsty Greenwood, author of *The Love of My Afterlife*

"Cousens questions what makes the perfect man in this entertaining sci-fi-tinged rom-com. . . . Cousens has a lot of fun with her premise, and it's easy to root for Chloe to find true love. Readers will be charmed."

—Publishers Weekly

"Another sharp, delicious, romantic read from Sophie Cousens. *And Then There Was You* strikes that magical balance between humor and heartache, all while introducing you to characters you can't help but root for. I gobbled up this book like a tasty little treat."

—B.K. Borison, *New York Times* bestselling author of *First-Time Caller*

"Funny, tender, and with a lovable and oh-so-human heroine, *And Then There Was You* is a delight!"

—Meg Shaffer, bestselling author of *The Wishing Game*

PRAISE FOR *IS SHE REALLY GOING OUT WITH HIM?*

"Delightful. Both believable and steamy . . . A supremely satisfying love story with all the charm readers have come to expect."

—*Kirkus Reviews* (starred review)

"Clever, thought-provoking, and oh so funny!"

—Zibby Owens, bestselling author of *Blank*, host of *Moms Don't Have Time to Read Books*

"[A] hilariously heartwarming jaunt about finding love later in life with characters that feel like friends."

—People

"Fresh and funny . . . Sophie Cousens offers ample wit and wisdom."

—Real Simple

"A love letter to us messy readers. It's *How to Lose a Guy in 10 Days* meets *He's Just Not That Into You* with all the sizzling chemistry of an Emily Henry novel, and Sophie Cousens does it best!"

—**Ashley Poston, *New York Times* bestselling author of *A Novel Love Story, The Dead Romantics,* and *The Seven Year Slip***

"[A] laugh-out-loud love story." —***Woman's World***

"Smart and poignant, *Is She Really Going Out with Him?* is a little bit about love and a lot about fresh starts." —***Shelf Awareness***

"A heartwarming hug in book form, wrapped in a witty, romantic comedy package. Timeless." —***Pittsburgh Post-Gazette***

"Bright and gratifying . . . [Cousens] tackles the enemies-to-lovers trope with characteristic humor and thoughtfulness, while injecting it with complex characters and realistic situations."

—***Library Journal* (starred review)**

"Cousens expertly weaves together themes of self-discovery, romance, motherhood, and friendship, resulting in a rich story that is engrossing to the end with high appeal to women's lit readers."

—***Booklist* (starred review)**

"With a relatable heroine, colorful side characters, and plenty of swoon-worthy moments, this story seamlessly blends humor and heart."

—***Washington Independent Review of Books***

"Cousens is a master at writing enchanting, laugh-out-loud stories that tug at your heartstrings. You will be charmed!"

—**Mia Sosa, *USA Today* bestselling author of *The Worst Best Man***

"Zippy dialogue, a great cast, and a delicious enemies-to-lovers plot made me want to turn my phone off and read in one sitting."

—**Cesca Major, author of *Maybe Next Time***

"This book has it all: heart, humor, and buckets of charm. Cousens has done it again!" —**Falon Ballard, author of *Right on Cue***

"Brimming with Cousens's trademark wit, charm, and richly drawn characters. I'll read anything Sophie Cousens writes!"

—Ellie Palmer, author of *Four Weekends and a Funeral*

PRAISE FOR *THE GOOD PART*

"This heartfelt and unique rom-com will have readers on the edges of their seats up to the emotional conclusion."

—*Booklist* (starred review)

"A moving and funny reminder that life is meant to be lived one day at a time."

—*Kirkus Reviews* (starred review)

"*The Good Part* left me buried under an avalanche of emotions and with a new appreciation for life's small, beautiful moments. This is a book to read twice—once to feverishly tear through the pages and a second time to savor."

—Annabel Monaghan, author of *Nora Goes Off Script* and *Same Time Next Summer*

"A tender and delightful exploration of that age-old question: *What if?*"

—Allison Winn Scotch, bestselling author of *The Rewind*

"Delightfully zany and full of heart, the perfect read for anyone who has ever felt a little lost in their own life (and who among us hasn't?)."

—Becca Freeman, author of *The Christmas Orphans Club*

"Sophie Cousens is one of a select few authors I will happily allow to break my heart again and again because it's just such a pleasure to find out how she'll mend it."

—Sarah Adler, author of *Mrs. Nash's Ashes*

"A delightful and thought-provoking new novel . . . [Cousens] sprinkles some magic throughout the pages."

—*Country Living*

"Cousens is a master at building emotional impact without becoming maudlin or sentimental. . . . Fresh and relevant."

—Bookreporter.com

"A modern-day *13 Going on 30*, Sophie Cousens's latest will make you laugh, it will make you cry, and most of all, it will make you want to live."
—**The Everygirl**

"Enchanting."
—**BookBub**

PRAISE FOR *BEFORE I DO*

"A thoughtful and romantic story about the moments and choices that change our lives in unexpected ways . . . Cousens has created something special with this lovely tale."
—***Washington Independent Review of Books***

"Witty and heartfelt, *Before I Do* takes a familiar trope and turns it on its head, and readers will find themselves tearing through this book to find out how it ends."
—***Booklist***

"A charming and surprising take on a classic love-triangle formula."
—***Kirkus Reviews***

"Witty and emotionally rich . . . This is sure to charm."
—***Publishers Weekly***

"The perfect feel-good book."
—***Reader's Digest***

"I am the biggest fan of Sophie Cousens! She always delivers a true laugh-out-loud rom-com with a ton of depth."
—**Lizzy Dent, author of *The Setup***

"I adored this novel! Funny, clever, poignant, with characters that just leap off the page . . . Thoroughly recommend!"
—**Emily Stone, author of *Always, in December***

PRAISE FOR *JUST HAVEN'T MET YOU YET*

"A perfectly charming escape. I laughed, I teared up, and I smiled my way through."
—**Helen Hoang, author of *The Kiss Quotient***

"A delightfully romantic tale of one woman's search for her happily ever after in the form of the owner of a swapped suitcase."

—*PopSugar*

"Reading Sophie Cousens is like meeting a new best friend. She makes you laugh, she makes you cry, you feel like you've loved her forever, and you don't want to let her go."

—Clare Pooley, author of *The Authenticity Project*

"Fiction slowly becomes truth in this highly enjoyable, delectable tale." —GoodMorningAmerica.com

"Sweet [and] funny . . . It's just the story to offer a little romantic escapism during the holiday season." —CNN

"Cousens imbues the entire story with an uplifting sense of hope. . . . A warm, witty, and absolutely charming seaside holiday that's perfect for fans of Sophie Kinsella." —*Kirkus Reviews* (starred review)

"This book is pure, unbridled joy."

—Rachel Lynn Solomon, author of *The Ex Talk*

PRAISE FOR *THIS TIME NEXT YEAR*

"A funny, pull-at-your-heartstrings read . . . It's a hug in book form."

—Josie Silver, author of *One Day in December*

"The characters in this page-turning novel are richly drawn and transform substantially, especially Minnie, and all suggest that maybe happy ever after is up to us." —NPR Books

"If you make time for just one holiday read this year, make it Sophie Cousens's *This Time Next Year*." —*PopSugar*

"Cousens's debut is ripe with both emotional vulnerability and zaniness." —*Publishers Weekly*

"A brilliantly written story about love, redemption, friendship, and self-empowerment . . . This book is an absolute delight . . . [and] a feel-good tale to cozy up with." —***San Francisco Book Review***

"Rom-com readers will revel in Cousens's wry, lively story, which probes themes of self-discovery, acceptance, and forgiveness, and the abiding nature of friendship." —***Shelf Awareness***

"Sparkling and uplifting."

—**Mhairi McFarlane, author of *If I Never Met You***

AND
THEN
THERE
WAS
YOU

ALSO BY SOPHIE COUSENS

Is She Really Going Out with Him?

The Good Part

Before I Do

Just Haven't Met You Yet

This Time Next Year

AND THEN THERE WAS YOU

A NOVEL

Sophie Cousens

G. P. PUTNAM'S SONS
New York

PUTNAM
— EST. 1838 —

G. P. Putnam's Sons
Publishers Since 1838
An imprint of Penguin Random House LLC
1745 Broadway, New York, NY 10019
penguinrandomhouse.com

Book design by Angie Boutin

LIBRARY OF CONGRESS CATALOGING-IN-PUBLICATION DATA

Names: Cousens, Sophie, author
Title: And then there was you: a novel / Sophie Cousens.
Description: New York: G. P. Putnam's Sons, 2025.
Identifiers: LCCN 2025030121 (print) | LCCN 2025030122 (ebook) |
ISBN 9780593718926 (trade paperback) | ISBN 9780593718933 (ebook)
Subjects: LCGFT: Fiction | Romance fiction | Novels
Classification: LCC PR6103.O933 A85 2025 (print) | LCC PR6103.O933 (ebook)
LC record available at https://lccn.loc.gov/2025030121
LC ebook record available at https://lccn.loc.gov/2025030122

Printed in the United States of America
1st Printing

The authorized representative in the EU for product safety and compliance is Penguin Random House Ireland, Morrison Chambers, 32 Nassau Street, Dublin D02 YH68, Ireland, https://eu-contact.penguin.ie.

To my parents, Avril and Richard. Thank you for being mad enough to have a fourth child (and then a fifth!) and for not being the sort of parents who suggested I "go and get a proper job."

I should like to bury something precious in every place where I've been happy and then, when I was old and ugly and miserable, I could come back and dig it up and remember.

—Evelyn Waugh, *Brideshead Revisited*

You can't program love. But that won't stop anyone from trying.

—ChatGPT, original, in response to the prompt "What epigraph should I use for this book?"

AND THEN THERE WAS YOU

1

Dating in your thirties can feel like a relentless game of roman-tic musical chairs. It starts out quite fun, but then the music gets too loud, and all the good, well-adjusted, stable chairs start disappearing. You're left with a room full of wobbly three-legged stools that are probably going to give you splinters. You begin to panic; it feels like a race you can't all win—what if you're the last one standing with nowhere to sit? Maybe you should just grab the first chair you can, even if it looks uncomfortable, smells, and gives you little to no support. Because you're tired and it might be better than the floor.

Chloe Fairway was only too familiar with the chair dilemma. Which is why she found herself heading into Soho on a Wednesday night to meet "Tom, 36," even though she'd much rather have been at home eating buttered toast and watching *The*

Traitors in her pajamas. Because she knew that if you wanted to find love, you had to keep dancing, keep swiping, keep "putting yourself out there." Because the next guy might just be the *perfect* chair for you, the one you could cozy up in for the rest of your life, the one that made all those uncomfortable chairs worthwhile.

From his profile picture, and the few texts they'd exchanged, Tom seemed . . . hopeful. Though the first rule of online dating was not to get your hopes up. You had to go in with low expectations. Chloe got to the pub early and chose a table near the window, away from the noise of the TV blaring behind the bar. Tom had picked the venue. She wouldn't have chosen a place like this, with the football playing, sticky carpets, and a happy hour where everyone looked miserable.

She checked her reflection using her phone camera, then frowned. She'd rushed from work, still dressed in her standard uniform: skinny black jeans, gray blouse, hair scraped into a bun. At home, her wardrobe was full of vintage blouses, wide-legged trousers, cute capes, and colorful cloche hats. But those belonged to a version of herself she rarely got to be. At the end of her first week at McKenzie and Sons, her boss had informed her she would need to dress more professionally. Her hair needed to be up—loose, it was "a distraction"—and her colorful clothes were "too theatrical." So she'd dulled her weekday palette to a safe blur, tamed her curls into a respectable bun, and played the role of "sensible PA."

Now she did what she could. She unpinned her hair, shook out her long auburn curls, then applied a swipe of red lipstick. What was it Coco Chanel said—"If you're sad, add more lipstick and attack"? Chloe didn't know *what* she was supposed to be attacking, and suspected Coco Chanel had never had to contend with internet dating, but the sentiment felt empowering.

Tom arrived, fourteen minutes late, clutching a bicycle helmet as he scanned the bar. His blond hair, damp with sweat, was slicked across a lightly freckled forehead. When he spotted her, he waved, then smiled, revealing two prominent canine teeth. Those fangs had not been visible on his profile picture. No. Do not judge someone on their teeth. It's personality that counts.

"Hi, Chloe?" Tom said, hurrying over to her. "Am I late?"

"No, no, I only just got here myself," she lied. Because that was the second rule of online dating: don't sweat the small stuff.

As she stood up to greet him, she braced for his reaction. Her height was clearly listed on her profile, but men often failed to register it. She'd been greeted on first dates with "Whoa, it's the BFG!" and "You didn't say you were plus-sized." Chloe was a slim five feet ten, but she had broad shoulders and big hair, so the whole effect was that of someone who took up space in the world. Luckily, on this occasion, Tom didn't react, he just gave her a sweaty hug and then sat down. She noticed he smelled faintly of cigarettes, despite listing himself as a nonsmoker.

"So, Tom—" she began, but he was already rising from his chair.

"Sorry, do you mind if we swap seats? Just so I can keep half an eye on the score?" he asked, nodding toward the television. Chloe did mind. If he'd wanted to watch the game, he shouldn't have arranged to meet her. But she said "sure" and relinquished her chair. There was no point starting things off on the wrong note.

"So, have you come far?" she asked him, trying not to mind about the seat swapping and the smoky smell.

"Yeah, Hackney," he said, snapping his fingers at the bartenders.

"I think we need to go up, order at the bar," she said.

"Ah, okay," he said, making no move to get up.

"I'll go, shall I? What would you like?" she offered.

"Pint, lager, thanks. I'll get the next ones," he said, flashing her a toothy grin. Chloe walked to the bar with a heaviness in her step. This was the worst part, when you knew straightaway that it was a no, but you still had to spend a polite amount of time in the person's company. She pictured her cozy seat on the sofa next to her dad, the chocolate Easter egg she hadn't eaten yet, *The Traitors* theme tune starting . . . No, don't torture yourself, it will only make it worse.

It seemed to Chloe that in the two years she had been off the market, the dating arena had morphed into a hellscape. Either that, or post thirty, the pool had shrunk to a puddle. In the last three months alone, she had been stood up, ghosted, and sent all manner of explicit, unsolicited photos. She'd met men so lacking in basic decency, she genuinely wondered how they convinced anyone to sleep with them. Belchers, groin scratchers, men who swore constantly, men who asked no questions and had little idea of what was going on in the world. These experiences made her fear she would always be alone, but they also made her fear for humanity. Where had all the good men gone?

"Love your hair," the bartender said as she poured Chloe a glass of wine. She had a sharp black pixie cut, a nose ring, and smudged mascara beneath her eyes.

"Thanks," Chloe said, noticing a rose tattoo curled around the woman's wrist. "I love your tattoo." They shared a brief smile, and Chloe watched the barmaid reach a finger to her ear, as if trying to block out the noise from the TV overhead.

"Hey, lady, can you turn this up?" said a man in a baseball cap, perched at the bar.

The bartender gave him a tight smile and clicked the volume up a single notch before turning back to Chloe.

"Just give it here," the man said, motioning for the remote. But Chloe reached across the bar and plucked it up first.

"I got it," she said sweetly, turning the volume down three notches.

"Hey, lady!" the man cried.

Chloe shot him her most charming smile. "I can't hear myself order. Give me two minutes?" He looked ready to argue but then turned back to the TV with a scowl.

"Thanks," the barmaid whispered, as she poured Chloe a pint. "I always get a headache when the football's on."

Without a word, Chloe slipped the remote into her lap, popped out one of the batteries, and wrapped it inside a folded five-pound note. She passed it to the barmaid, who let out a soft laugh and gave her an appreciative smile. Then Chloe cheerily passed the remote back to the man in the cap. "Enjoy the game."

Back at the table, Tom reached for his pint, then finally turned his attention to her.

"What you reading, then?" he asked, nodding toward the paperback poking out of her bag.

"*Little Women,*" she told him. "Well, rereading, it's one of my favorites."

"You should try the sequel, *Big Men,* it's much better," Tom said, guffawing at his own joke. She smiled politely and tightened her grip on her wineglass. "You a bookworm or something, then?"

"I guess so," she replied, trying to stay open-minded. Maybe he was the kind of guy who seemed awful at first but you could acquire a taste for—like oysters or tequila. "Have you read anything good lately?"

Tom exhaled loudly. "I don't have much time to read. Started this book about Formula One, how it got started and that, but it was average. I prefer podcasts." Tom's face became animated. "Have you listened to Joe Rogan? He's so funny."

"I hear he's popular," Chloe said, feeling her soul crawl into the fetal position.

"So, what do you do for cashisho, Chloe?" Tom asked, and as he clasped his pint glass, she noticed his fingers—short, pudgy sausage fingers. She had a thing about hands.

"Cashisho?" she repeated, trying to keep her eyes on his face.

"Cash. Moola. Money." He rolled his eyes. "What do you do for work?"

"Oh, I'm a PA for a film producer," she said, knowing she'd already told him this over text. "But I'm hoping it's going to be a stepping stone to more creative things. I really want to be a writer—plays, screenplays."

"You don't want to be a writer," he said flatly, picking his teeth.

"I do," she said, blanching.

"Nah, it's a shrinking sector. AI will be writing everything soon anyway. You're better off looking for something tech-proof," he said, his eyes flitting around her face, assessing her. "You could be a model, I reckon, if you straightened your hair."

"But I don't want to be a . . ." She trailed off, swallowing her irritation. What was the point? She forced a smile. "How about you? You said you were in the army? That must be interesting."

"Yup, corporal," Tom said, flexing his arm muscles. "It's good, plenty of travel. But there's too much politics these days."

His mouth twisted into a sneer. "The woke brigade have got a lot to answer for. I'm not against women being in the army, but if you want to join, you've got to be one of the lads, haven't you? You can't expect special treatment. If you're on the front line, you can't start crying if someone calls you 'love.'"

Chloe swallowed. He'd seemed normal over text, nice even. She glanced across to the bar. The man in the cap was jabbing at the remote, clearly baffled. Chloe turned back to Tom just as he took a noisy slurp of his pint, then wiped his mouth on his sleeve.

Was this fiction's fault? Had reading ruined men for her? Once you'd been introduced to Gabriel Oak, Mr. Rochester, and her dear George Emerson, how were you meant to settle for *this*?

"I'm just going to nip to the loo," she said, picking up her bag.

"Knock yourself out," Tom replied, already half turned back to the TV.

Chloe always tried to stay on a date for at least forty-five minutes. Any less just felt too rude. But if she could tell, as she did now, that even forty-five minutes was going to be an endurance test, she allowed herself an extra-long bathroom break to sneak in a chapter of her book. Glancing back at the table, she doubted Tom would even notice she was gone.

In the bathroom, Chloe glanced at her phone. Her photo app had compiled a memory reel titled "On This Day." The first image was of her and Peter lying on a sun lounger in Tenerife the year before. She was curled into his chest, wearing just a bikini, squinting up at the camera. He had one arm around her, and he was kissing her head as he took the selfie. They both looked so happy. Peter would never have tried to watch the football game during a date; he was a stickler for manners. He opened doors, he asked questions, he made eye contact.

She quickly closed her phone. This wasn't helping, and those photos certainly didn't tell the whole story. Instead, she climbed onto the old Victorian radiator next to the sink and pulled out *Little Women*—a safer kind of fantasy. The radiator let out a reassuring *clonk* sound.

"Yes, he is a bit of a clonk," Chloe muttered.

"Clonk clonk," said the radiator. And already, she was having a better conversation with the radiator than she'd been having back in the bar.

She was several pages into a chapter when she became aware of someone else entering the room. A striking woman with long, dark hair and pale, freckled skin was smiling at her from across the tiled floor.

"Chloe?" the woman said, eyes wide with delight. "Oh, I thought it was you!"

Chloe blinked. She couldn't place her. "Wendy," the woman offered, not the least bit offended.

"Wendy?" Chloe asked, eyebrows lifting in surprise.

Wendy had freelanced as a producer at McKenzie and Sons a few years back. Chloe had liked her; she was bubbly and always brought home-baked biscuits to work on a Friday. The only reason Chloe hadn't recognized her now was because she looked *completely* different. The Wendy she remembered was a bit, well, frumpy, with limp, gray-streaked hair and a permanently defeated posture. This Wendy looked . . . radiant. Toned. Confident. She also looked ten years younger.

"I know, I know," Wendy said, doing a twirl. "I made some changes."

She moved to the sink and began washing her hands—slowly, with deliberate movements, lathering soap between her long, graceful fingers. Chloe caught sight of the smartwatch on her wrist: sleek, iridescent, clearly expensive.

"But what are you doing in here?" Wendy asked, watching Chloe in the mirror. "Are you avoiding someone?"

"Bad date," Chloe admitted.

"Sleazy or boring?" Wendy asked, her tone light and knowing.

"Rude," Chloe said.

"Poor love. How long have you been looking?" The question landed harder than Chloe expected, and she was struck by Wendy's choice of words.

"Too long," she said quietly.

"I know that feeling," said Wendy, drying her hands on a paper towel with the same precision she'd used to wash them. The bathroom was nicer than you might expect, given the decor in the pub: there was moisturizer as well as soap, and even a magnifying mirror for doing makeup. Wendy took a moment to moisturize her hands. Then she stepped forward and pressed a soft, clean hand over Chloe's. This tactile display of empathy pushed Chloe over some edge she hadn't even known she'd been teetering on. A sob rose unbidden as Wendy's sympathy untethered the full weight of her loneliness, and she lifted a hand to her mouth, trying to keep it in.

"Sorry," she said briskly. "I'm fine, it's just one date, it doesn't matter. I don't know what's wrong with me."

"It's not just one date, though, is it," Wendy said, tilting her head, eyes trained on Chloe's face. "It's the opportunity cost, the evening you don't get back, the hope, the anticipation, the 'what if?' extinguished again and again. It's walking home deflated, wondering if you have the energy to do it all again. It's wondering if all men are awful, or if your standards are just too high."

"Yes. Exactly," Chloe whispered, her voice cracking.

Wendy enveloped her in a long-limbed hug. It was so unexpected, but Chloe found herself leaning into it, breathing in the expensive scent of almond oil in Wendy's hair. She couldn't remember the last time she'd been hugged by someone other than her parents.

"Never apologize for wanting more," Wendy said into her shoulder.

When she released Chloe from the hug, she turned to retrieve her handbag from the sink. From an inner pocket, she pulled out a small gray business card, gilt-edged with a gold "PP" embossed in the center and a QR code below it. "I've only got one of these left," Wendy said, biting her lip as she passed the card to Chloe.

"What is it?" Chloe asked.

"It's the future," Wendy said. "Trust me, it will change your life, it changed mine." She gestured toward her own reflection. Chloe raised an eyebrow.

"But what's PP?"

"Perfect Partners. It's a dating service," Wendy said, lowering her voice. "But it isn't like anything you've ever tried—"

Her phone buzzed and Wendy glanced at the screen and smiled. "Just coming, sweetie," she said as she answered it, then quickly reapplied her lip gloss in the mirror, before turning back to Chloe. "You need a referral to get an appointment. Just give my name."

Then she blew Chloe an air kiss, pressed a finger to her lips, and whispered, "Shhh, don't tell the men." Then she was gone, heels clicking against the tile, hair swishing behind her.

Chloe looked down at the card, intrigued. She pulled out her phone and scanned the QR code. A web page blinked open. The logo read **Perfect Partners**, the font sleek and futuristic. The home page was populated with images of incredibly attractive people. Underneath was a single line of text.

Looking for the perfect partner? Don't wait for fate.

Take happiness into your own hands.

The website gave no further details about what the company was offering, how to sign up, or what it cost. Just a number to call and a message: **For inquiries, please call to book a consultation.** Whatever Perfect Partners was, she couldn't find anything about it on Google. She could only find something called Perfect Partnerz with a "Z," which was a tacky adult website. Whereas this looked exclusive, discreet, and like something Chloe *definitely* couldn't afford. But after seeing Wendy, she felt inspired—inspired not to waste another minute of her evening with Sausage Fingers.

Back in the bar, she returned to the table but didn't sit down, she just picked up her jacket and said, "I have to go."

"How come?" Tom asked, eyebrows knitted in incomprehension.

"Because I feel lonelier here with you than I would on my own." She gave him a tight smile. "Oh, and I did mind that you were late and that you asked to swap seats. Enjoy the game." Then she turned and she walked out the door without a backward glance.

When she got back to Richmond, the house was dark. Her parents must have already gone to bed. Her family home was a ramshackle sixteenth-century cottage, half-swallowed by wisteria, sandwiched between two grand Queen Anne mansions. It looked misplaced on the street, as though the world had evolved around it but the house had stubbornly refused to budge. Chloe loved that about it, and when she'd moved out of Peter's, it was the only place she'd wanted to go.

Letting herself in, she crept through to the kitchen. The dishwasher had finished, so she took a moment to empty it, then laid out a cafetière, bowls, and cutlery for breakfast. On instinct, she pulled a Post-it note from the phone table, scribbled FARTS BEAK, and stuck it to her dad's chair. They had taken to writing each other anagrams after reading an article that claimed it could help ward off dementia.

Upstairs, she sat down on her childhood bed and looked around at all the mementos of her youth. The framed drama awards above her dressing table, the fake Oscar Sean had given her in first year. Photographs of long-lost friends, their faces plump with youth. She stood up and peeled one photo from the mirror—the Lincoln gang in their second year at Oxford, when they'd all still been close. The four of them were dressed in costume for *A Midsummer Night's Dream*. Chloe had played Puck; Akiko, Titania; and Sean, Bottom. John, their music director, wore a green velvet smoking jacket and a crown of ivy.

She looked at herself in the photo: nineteen years old, so full of confidence and conviction. Back then, she'd been sure she was going to be an actress or a writer, that she would lead a creative, fulfilling life. And that love, the kind you read about, would be just around the corner. What would that girl think of the life she had now?

Whenever she felt unsettled about the future, or disappointed in the present, Chloe turned to the past. Reaching beneath her bed, she pulled out a dusty shoebox. Inside were all the notes the Imp had ever sent—clues, riddles, and poems, all written in his distinctive, sweeping calligraphy. She'd always known these notes were from her best friend, Sean, though he had never said it out loud. These notes were her proof that someone could know you better than you knew yourself. That there were kind, thoughtful men in the world, even if they weren't in her life right now. Flicking through the box, she found a ripped playbill for *The Taming of the Shrew.* She thought back to that opening night, the night when everything had changed. What would she do differently now?

There was a gentle tap at her door and Chloe looked up to see her mother standing in the doorway wearing a dressing gown and fluffy pink bed socks.

"You're back early," she said, pushing her gray fringe away from her eyes. "He wasn't a charming young man who whisked you off your feet, then?"

"Sadly no whisking and very little charming," Chloe said with a weak smile. "The loo in the pub was nice though, so that's something."

"Oh that makes all the difference," her mum said enthusiastically. "Did they have those little cotton flannels instead of the paper towels?"

"No, but they had moisturizer as well as soap."

"Oh, well, it's almost worth going just for that, then," her mother said with a knowing nod. They shared a smile, and her mother came to sit down beside her.

"I'm beginning to think I might have terrible taste in men, Mum."

Her mother laughed and squeezed her hand. "That's not true."

"It is. At uni, I always fancied the arrogant rugby boys who wouldn't give me the time of day. I overlooked the nice suitable men who actually liked me."

"Well, rugby boys have got those lovely thighs," her mum said, and Chloe leaned her head on her shoulder.

"I wasted two years with Peter," Chloe said quietly. "Everyone could see he was bad news, except me."

"Weak men don't like strong women. You saw through him eventually, love," her mother said, hugging her close.

"I just don't trust myself anymore, Mum. I don't trust my instincts."

Her mother reached for the threadbare teddy that sat on Chloe's pillow. He had once belonged to Chloe's grandmother Valerie, and something about him—perhaps the tilt of his stitched brow—exuded the same air of intelligent mischief that his previous owner had possessed in spades.

"Don't listen to her, Aloysius," her mother said, covering the bear's ears with his paws. Chloe smiled, reaching for him. He had faded fur; loose, frayed stitches; lumpy stuffing; and scratched glass eyes that gave him a look of worn-out wisdom. Peter had never liked him, had refused to have "the manky bear" in their flat. But to Chloe he was a treasured possession—imbued with nostalgia for her childhood and the warmth of her grandmother, a link to a time before she even existed.

"It might take you a little while to see when something's wrong," her mother said softly. "But when it's right? Trust me, you'll know. Life isn't a race. Everyone gets where they need to go in their own time." She leaned forward and kissed Chloe's head. "Right, I'm off to bed, I haven't done my Wordle yet." With a glance at the open shoebox, she added, "Don't stay up too late reminiscing. You can't live in the past, you know, only the present, maybe the future."

Her mum blew her a kiss, said good night, then quietly closed the door behind her. Once she was gone, Chloe pulled the Perfect Partners card from her bag. Wendy did say it was the future. She turned it over in her hand, running a finger along the thick edge.

"What do you think, Aloysius?" she asked the bear. "Is some

secretive, high-end dating service going to be the solution to all our problems?"

She shook Aloysius's head for him. "No. I didn't think so either. Shall we look for cute 1950s hats on Vinted instead?" Aloysius nodded. He was a bad-influence sort of bear, but he was old enough to know that scrolling for hats was much more enjoyable than scrolling for men. And that indulging her nostalgia for fashion was probably safer than reminiscing about the contents of that shoebox.

2

Ten and a Half Years Earlier

The thick velvet curtain did nothing to muffle the roar of applause. Foot stomps reverberated through the floorboards. Chloe turned to Sean beside her on the stage, his face flushed with triumph.

"Listen to that, they loved it," she said, eyes glittering with delight.

"Of course they did," he said, grinning back, his black hair damp with sweat, pupils wide with adrenaline. "You were spectacular."

"Everyone was," Chloe said, catching Akiko's hand in the line beside her and giving it a squeeze.

"I thought I was going to throw up when I saw how packed

it was," said Akiko, pulling a face. "And I needed the loo for the whole of act two."

The band filed onstage now, led by John, and the curtain lifted once more so the musicians could take their bow. As the spotlight hit them, the crowd erupted again—shouts, whistles, Chloe's name called from the stalls. Sean nudged her forward, pushing her through the line of musicians, and she stumbled, alone, into the spotlight. The applause surged as she took a final bow.

She had never known an opening night like it. No missed cues, not a single flubbed line; there was an energy onstage that felt electric. Everything about tonight felt like a real, professional production rather than a student play. Chloe hadn't been acting Katherina; she had *been* Katherina. All those months of writing and rewriting, the midnight rehearsals, those late nights workshopping with Sean, transforming Shakespeare's *The Taming of the Shrew* into something raw, modern, their own. It had all been worth it. Because there was no high on earth like this. No legal high, anyway.

Running back, she grabbed Sean's hand and dragged him forward. This was his moment too; they'd adapted the play together. The curtain finally fell again, and the cast spilled offstage in a frenzy—wig caps pulled off, beards ripped away, giggles echoing through the wings, as everyone hurried to the greenroom bar via the dressing room.

In the chaos, Sean reached for Chloe's hand again, just as John swept between them, flinging an arm around each of their shoulders. His long red hair shone bright as a beacon beneath the backstage lights.

"Well done, you two," he said, beaming. "Another Adler-Fairway spectacular."

Chloe hugged an arm around his waist and grinned up at him. "None of it would work without your music. That piano solo during the dance scene . . ." She kissed the tips of her fingers.

"John, who's that guy on the double bass tonight?" Akiko asked, skipping in front of them. "He is yummy."

"Evan Marlow," John said casually. "Lovely man, not your type."

Akiko stopped dead, hand on hip. "Excuse me. How is he not my type?"

"He has a boyfriend."

"Of course he does," she groaned, throwing back her head dramatically, then yanking out pins to send dark braids tumbling free. "I swear I am cursed to only fancy unavailable men."

"Um, two eligible straight men standing right in front of you, Kiko," Sean said, clutching a hand over his heart like she'd wounded him.

"You two don't count," she shot back, giving Sean a playful shove. Sean glanced across at Chloe, but she had taken a deliberate step ahead.

They found the dressing room corridor in chaos—heat, chatter, bodies everywhere. A man, probably Rocco Falconi, charged out from the nearest door wearing nothing but a glittering thong and a plastic bucket on his head, shrieking with laughter as someone chased him down the corridor. The four of them flattened against the wall to avoid a collision, and Chloe let out a startled laugh.

She took the opportunity to pause, pressing her palms against the cool plaster wall. She wasn't ready to go in there, to brave the soup of sweaty bodies, brush the tangled nest of hair spray and pins from her auburn curls, and put on her regular, boring clothes. She wasn't ready to go back to reality. Not yet.

"Let's give it a minute," Sean suggested. "Wait for the chaos to clear. Drink at the top?" Before anyone could answer, he slipped inside the heaving dressing room, then returned seconds later clasping a bottle of champagne.

"Always be prepared," he said with a grin, handing the bottle to Chloe like a trophy.

No one needed much convincing. They snuck up the metal staircase that led to the lighting bridge above the stage. They weren't *technically* allowed up here, but the stage manager would be too busy to notice. Chloe and Sean often sat up here after rehearsals, looking down on the world they were building onstage. This was her happy place, where she felt in control. And the act of creating, of deciding how your story would play out, it lit something inside her in a way nothing else did.

Now the four of them sat side by side in a line, Kiko and Chloe at either end, the boys in the middle, legs dangling over the edge, listening to the last of the audience leave and watching the stagehands dismantle the set below.

Sean reached for the bottle, then raised it in the air. "A toast, to my leading ladies."

John and Akiko clinked invisible glasses, while Chloe rested her forehead against the cold metal railing.

"I want to freeze this moment," she said quietly. "Us four, here. I want it to always be like this."

They all leaned a little closer to her, a moment of still, as though they were trying to make her wish come true.

"Oh, hey," Kiko said, reaching across both boys to tap Chloe. "I didn't want to tell you before the show, but I heard someone say there was a talent agent in the audience tonight."

"What?" Chloe gasped, sitting bolt upright.

"Yeah, I thought it might freak you out if I told you before. Imagine if you got an agent out of this?"

"Or *you* could," Chloe said, her pulse quickening, veins still thrumming with adrenaline.

Akiko laughed, reaching for the champagne bottle. "But I don't want to be an actor. I just like playing dress-up with you guys." She took a swig of champagne. "Whereas you, Chloe Fairway, will be a star one day."

"Don't forget about us when you're rich and famous," Sean said, nudging her with his shoulder.

"Oh stop it," Chloe said, ducking her head, but she felt the warm fizz of possibility bubbling within her. Could she really be good enough to do this professionally?

Sean reached over and gently squeezed her hand, his pupils flaring as he looked at her. "If anyone can do it, you can."

"'The reward of a thing well done is to have done it,'" John said, like a wise old owl. He had a quote for every occasion. Then he carefully removed his wire-rimmed glasses and started cleaning the lenses on his shirt.

"Who said that? Voltaire?" Sean teased.

"Emerson, I think," John replied. "All I mean is, can't we just enjoy tonight? An appreciative audience, a job well done, time enjoyed with friends."

"Yeah, live in the moment, guys," Akiko said sternly, then giggled as she passed the bottle to John.

"Tiny Dancer, don't shit on our dreams of fame and fortune. Allow us our great expectations," Sean said theatrically, as he threw an arm around John's neck, then ruffled his red hair. John shoved him off, but his mouth twitched into a reluctant smile. With the surname Elton, John had picked up his fair share of nicknames around college, but "Tiny Dancer" was the one that stuck. Given he was tall, reserved, and rarely danced in public, it didn't suit him at all. But perhaps that was what made it so funny.

Chloe watched her friends play-fight, while Akiko swung her legs back and forth like a child. She tried to capture the moment, take a mental Polaroid.

Then, *whoosh*. A soft *thud* echoed below.

"Whoopsie," said Akiko.

They all peered over the railing to see one of her silver heels sitting in the middle of the stage.

A stagehand looked up and pointed. "Hey, you lot, get down from there!"

Akiko yelped, covering her mouth with both hands.

"Clumsy Kiko strikes again," Chloe groaned.

"That's one way to get a man's attention, bludgeon him in the head with a shoe," Sean said with a sigh.

"And so, it was ever thus. We'd better go down," John said, pushing himself up on the metal railing, then offering Kiko a hand. "If you ever want to play Cinderella, I think you'd be a shoe-in."

"Har de har," Akiko muttered, pulling a face at him, then tugging off her other shoe so she could walk without hobbling. They started along the bridge and John moved aside to let her go first down the ladder. Chloe turned to follow them, but then Sean caught her hand.

"Wait," he said. She looked back at him. His eyes dropped to the walkway beneath their feet. "I want to tell you something," he said quietly, then pulled her into a hug. "I'm so proud of you, Chlo."

"Ah, thanks, Seany. I'm proud of you too," she said, smiling into his damp shoulder, his shirt sweaty from the performance.

"No, I mean it." His voice was serious now. "You come up with these ideas, and you make them happen. You bring out the best in everyone. We make a good team, don't we?"

"We do," she said, feeling a shift in the air. Sean was never sincere, not like this.

"You light up the stage," he said, leaning back just enough to look at her, and his eyes were glassy now.

"Thanks," she murmured, beginning to pull away, but he didn't let go. Instead, he slid his arms down around her waist, holding her there, eyes locked on hers. And then, slowly, he leaned in.

Chloe didn't move. She felt herself brace. Was this what she'd been waiting for? Or had she always known this moment would come and hoped, blindly, that it wouldn't? It was a running joke that Sean and Chloe's friendship was the most drawn-out courtship in history. "When are you guys just going to sleep together?" was a constant refrain in Deepers, the Lincoln bar. She usually laughed it off; so did Sean, insisting they were nothing but friends, the best of collaborators.

And yet—there had been moments. The late nights. The Imp's notes. That feeling of being known. Sean was handsome, with his floppy dark hair, his kind eyes, that warm, electric energy that could charge a whole rehearsal room. He pushed her as a performer, as a writer, as a person. In many ways, they made perfect sense.

But now, as his lips touched hers, dry and hesitant, his hands fumbling at her waist, Chloe felt a coldness rising up her spine. A sinking in her chest, then some instinct buried deep within her that told her, *Not this. Not him.* She pulled back sharply.

"No, Sean, I can't."

3

"Chloe, how many times need I remind you?" Mr. McKenzie said, looming over her desk and waving a yellow script at her. "These brass fasteners are only to be used on scripts going to *clients*. Anything else gets a hole punch and string."

"Sorry," Chloe said, switching to mouth-breathing to avoid the dense cloud of her boss's body odor.

On Chloe's first day at McKenzie and Sons, she had learned that the "sons" in the company name were fictitious. Stuart McKenzie had no sons, only a daughter, Lydia. But he thought "and sons" better conveyed "wholesome family values." To Chloe it conveyed he was an idiot. And yet, even though she had concluded this on her very first day, two years later, she was still, inexplicably, working there.

"And why is your desk covered in foliage?" McKenzie asked,

jabbing a stubby finger at the two plants on her desk. Chloe kept her eyes fixed on the lower part of his face. If she looked at his hairline—the angry red mess of his not-quite-healed transplant—she would only wince, and her boss *hated* it when people winced.

"Plants are proven to reduce stress and boost productivity," she said brightly. "I could get you one, if you'd like?"

McKenzie scowled, his monobrow knotting into a V. "And why do they have . . . googly eyes?"

"They're my desk buddies." She pointed. "That one's Keanu Leaves, and this one is Morgan Treeman." McKenzie's scowl deepened, which probably wasn't good for his infected hairline. "No?" she said, plucking the googly eyes off one by one. As he turned to walk away, she saw her chance. "While I have you here, Mr. McKenzie, do you remember we talked about me getting some experience on set?"

"Chloe." He stopped, then pivoted back with a dramatic weariness. "Have you seen my inbox? Have you seen the state of the stationery cupboard? You are my personal assistant. In what world do you think you would be assisting me by not being here?"

"Right, I know, it's just when I took this job, it was with a view to—"

McKenzie's phone rang. He held up a finger to silence her, then stalked back toward his office, shoulders hunched around his ears. Chloe returned to her plants and carefully reapplied their googly eyes.

"Don't look at me like that," she told Keanu. "I did try." Then she sniffed and got a whiff of chip fat. Lifting an arm to smell her blouse, she realized it was coming from her. The office sat on the third floor of a narrow brick building in Southwark, Central

London. On the ground floor was a chip shop, and on certain days, the smell of triple-cooked fries seeped through the building's ventilation system. It wasn't an unpleasant smell, but it was not exactly what you'd choose for your eau de toilette.

She glanced at her screen. Twelve thirty. Early lunch territory. She could nip out and get a sandwich, maybe even splash out on a proper coffee. But if she had lunch now, she would have nothing to look forward to. As she was mulling this bleak sentiment, her phone buzzed. Akiko. McKenzie disliked her taking personal calls at her desk, so she scurried over to the stationery cupboard. The light was broken, but she didn't mind, the darkness a sweet reprieve from the unrelenting glare of strip lighting in the open-plan office.

"Have you seen the reunion email?" Akiko asked before Chloe could even say hello.

"No," she said, pulling the cupboard door mostly shut behind her. "Hang on."

She opened her personal email, scrolling through her junk folder. There it was, an email from Oxford entitled **Ten Year Reunion.** She scanned the text: **Lincoln College cordially invites you to a reunion weekend . . . Welcome to bring a guest . . . We look forward to celebrating this significant milestone with you.**

"Are you going to go?" Akiko asked, her voice animated.

"I think I would rather stab paper clips into my thigh," Chloe said, picking up a paper clip from the shelf beside her.

"Oh come on," Akiko said. "Aren't you curious what everyone's up to?"

"Yes, I am curious, and that curiosity has been satiated by social media," Chloe said, hearing the faint wail of baby Elodie in the background.

"You know that's not real. Plus, loads of our college crowd

aren't even on social media." Akiko's voice shifted to her Calming Mum voice as she said, "Shh, Elodie, Mummy's talking to her friend."

"Well, I know the headlines—who got married, who got rich, who got arrested."

"Oooh, *who* got arrested?" Akiko dropped her voice to a gleeful whisper.

"Larry Fellas. Tax evasion. He lives in Monaco now." Chloe shook her head. Was it normal to know this much about the lives of people you hadn't seen in over a decade? Why did she know what color Lorna Childs's new kitchen was and how many bridesmaids Harriet Townsend had had at her wedding, when she had no desire to see either of these people in real life?

"Maybe Sean will be there," Akiko said. "I know John will. He's on the alumni committee. Oh, I would *love* to see everyone again."

"Sean's not going to go. He's a big-shot film director. He's not flying back from LA for a college reunion," Chloe said, feeling a prickle of longing at the mention of his name.

"Ugh, Elodie!" Akiko said, groaning. "Chlo, can you give me two secs? Nappy situation."

This is what phone calls with Akiko were like now—stolen moments amidst the relentless rhythm of motherhood. Chloe waited, leaning against the cupboard wall and rereading the email. Would she want to go if her contemporaries hadn't all turned out to be such ridiculously high achievers? Or if her own life weren't such a catalog of disappointments? A distant wail from Elodie bled through the line. Chloe picked up a stapler from the shelf and idly opened and closed it like a mouth.

"To go or not to go," she whispered, "that is the question."

The line cracked, then Akiko's voice returned. "Okay, I'm back. Sorry."

"So, are *you* thinking of going?" Chloe asked.

"I can't leave Elodie yet, it's too far from Edinburgh," Akiko said. "Which is why you need to go and get all the gossip."

"If you're not going, and Emma is in Canada, there is no way I'm rocking up there friendless and alone, and being all, 'Hey, look at me and my sad-sack life.'"

"You don't have a sad-sack life," Akiko said, her voice softening.

"In the yearbook, they voted me most likely to succeed *and* most likely to be famous. I am currently single, living at home with my parents, and I have the crappiest job imaginable."

"Being famous isn't a reasonable marker of success. You have high standards when it comes to men, and you're only doing the PA thing as a stepping stone until the writing takes off. And, Chloe, you are an amazing writer."

"Who hasn't written anything in three years."

"You're biding your time because you have creative integrity." Chloe smiled faintly at the praise, but her chest felt tight. "I wish you'd come visit us," Akiko went on, "especially if you're feeling so down on yourself. You haven't even met your goddaughter yet. She's growing so fast—"

"I'm not down on myself, I just . . . sometimes I miss what we were back then, when everything felt so full of possibility."

"Everything still is! We're thirty-one, not seventy-one," Akiko said, sternly now. "This is not the Chloe I know."

Chloe closed her eyes, feeling an unwelcome surge of emotion. She knew Kiko was only trying to help, but she could never truly understand. Kiko loved her job managing three festival theaters, sat on numerous panels about women in the arts, had married her soulmate at twenty-eight, and now had a beautiful baby to boot.

"I know, I need to come visit. I will, I promise, I'll find a weekend."

"You'd better," Akiko said, then groaned impatiently as Elodie shrieked again. "Look, you don't think I miss being young and carefree, running around Oxford snogging boys, pretending we're living in a John Betjeman poem? Of course I do, but none of us get to be students forever. And if you soak too long in nostalgia, you'll drown in it."

Chloe bit her lip, duly chastised.

"The invite *does* say I get a plus-one," she said, switching gears. "Maybe I could take my dad to hype me up—'My daughter might not have hit her career goals, but she does an excellent job refilling the bird feeder.'"

"That's it!" Akiko cried.

"Akiko, I'm not taking my dad."

"Not your dad, you should take a date. Nothing says 'I've made it in life' like walking in there with a hot guy on your arm."

Chloe's mind jumped to Wendy, to the high-end dating agency. If she was going to find a decent date anywhere, it would be there. But would having a plus-one really make her more inclined to go?

"Chloe?" A deep voice bellowed from outside the door. "Are you hiding in the stationery cupboard again?"

Shit.

"Gotta go," Chloe whispered, hanging up.

The door creaked open and McKenzie stood in the doorway, eyes narrowed in disapproval.

"Just looking for a stapler," she said, holding the stapler aloft like a trophy. "Light's broken."

"Have you chased Eddie Redmayne's agent about the *Aardvark* script?" he asked.

"I chased first thing," she told him. "I've chased every day this week."

"Well, make sure you chase again before the end of the day," he said, then cleared his throat. "And when you get a minute, could you pop out and get me a sticky bun? There's a good girl."

Chloe gave him a tight smile. She wanted to tell him that she thought there was more chance of her getting Oscar-winner Eddie Redmayne to marry her than there was of getting him signed up to star in a limited series about a vigilante aardvark who tackled knife crime in Scotland. Aardvarks weren't even indigenous to the UK. It made absolutely no sense. She also wanted to say that no, she did not have time to "pop out and get him a sticky bun," because she'd already popped out twice today to fetch him baked snacks, and she had a huge list of jobs to do before she could leave tonight, and that it was no longer appropriate to call a female colleague "a good girl." But she didn't say any of this. She just said, "Yes, Mr. McKenzie. Of course."

On her walk to the bakery, Chloe felt the tingling hum of an existential crisis coming on. If she was too ashamed of her life to face her old university friends, what did that tell her? It told her she needed to change something. Maybe she should go backpacking. Maybe she should sign up for a marathon. Should she get a pixie cut? No, no, a haircut wasn't going to be enough this time. She reached into her bag for the card. If Wendy was anything to go by, then Perfect Partners had to be worth a try.

She dialed the number, and a woman answered. She spoke

in a crisp, clipped accent and immediately asked for a referral code. Chloe gave Wendy's name, hoping that would be enough.

"Thank you," the woman said without inflection. "You are eligible for a consultation. We have an opening next week. If you give me your email address, I will send over an application form."

"But what is it?" Chloe asked. "And how much does it cost? I was just calling to find out—"

"Please complete the questionnaire and psychometric profile *in full* before you come to the appointment. I'm afraid I can't give you any more information until then."

Chloe gave the woman her email address, and the line promptly went dead. While she might have been mildly curious before, now Chloe was intrigued. This air of secrecy around Perfect Partners, the lack of information online, it all felt delightfully mysterious. And given that the current highlight of her day was hiding in a dark stationery cupboard, maybe this was exactly what she needed in her life: a little mystery.

4

A few days later, she found herself standing outside an unassuming building on the Strand. It was almost invisible from the street, just an innocuous gray door with a small "PP" on the buzzer.

The questionnaire they'd sent through had taken Chloe hours, so she hoped this wasn't going to be a complete waste of her time. There'd been forty-two pages of questions. Some were oddly specific: "Would you prefer your partner squeezes the toothpaste from the middle of the tube or neatly roll it from the bottom?" Others were broad and probing: "Describe your ideal partner, using three to five examples from literature or popular culture."

Chloe had deliberated over each answer. She'd really struggled to limit herself to just five examples of her ideal partner. All her literary crushes had to be in there, obviously, but what about Adam Brody in *Nobody Wants This*, Baron von Trapp from *The Sound of Music*, and Paul Mescal in *Normal People*? They had to get a mention too. She ended up adding footnotes to the form so she didn't need to leave anyone out.

"Hello?" came a female voice over the intercom.

"Hi, it's Chloe Fairway, I have an app—" She was buzzed in before she could finish the sentence. She took the lift up to the third floor, where she found a stark, empty reception area. Framed photos of couples adorned freshly painted walls. Perhaps fruitful matches, testaments to the agency's success, like gilded awards on an actor's mantelpiece.

After only a few minutes, a woman emerged from a door to the left. Chloe guessed her to be in her thirties. She had white-blonde hair and ice-blue eyes and wore a perfectly tailored azure-blue suit.

"This way," she said with a smile.

She led Chloe to a second room, a small office with bare, bright white walls. In the center stood a clean white desk, sleek and unadorned, with a narrow white computer perched at its center. There was only one hint of color—a single blue metronome sitting on a wall shelf, clicking loudly back and forth.

"Welcome, Chloe, I am Avery, your relationship consultant. Won't you take a seat?"

Chloe sat in the white chair opposite, and Avery clicked open a file on her computer. Chloe blinked; with so much white in the room, it felt unnervingly bright.

"Thank you for filling in our questionnaire so thoroughly," Avery said, flashing her a set of perfect, too-white teeth. "It really helps us build up a picture of what you want. But why don't you start by telling me, in your own words, what it is you're looking for?"

What was she looking for? A boyfriend? Her true love? A date for the reunion? Or just a glimpse of hope that not all men were awful?

The metronome ticktocked.

"I'd like to meet someone," she said nervously. She'd felt confident telling the questionnaire what she wanted, but now, faced with a real person, her mind went blank.

The metronome kept clicking.

Perhaps sensing her hesitation, Avery reached across the desk, extending both hands. Without quite knowing why, Chloe placed her own hands in Avery's. They felt warm and dry. Avery cupped her wrists, then pressed her thumbs against Chloe's pulse points.

She then stared, unblinking, into Chloe's eyes and said in a voice like melted butter, "Tell me what you feel when you think about men."

Something shifted, loosened, the tight lid on a jar of emotions twisting free.

"Scared. Disappointed," she said. "But I don't want to be alone forever." There was something about Avery's active listening pose, the hands, so gentle on her wrists, the persistent pressure of the metronome, that made Chloe want to blurt out everything.

"I've started to think it might be me," she admitted. "I'm too tall for most men, my ears stick out when I wear my hair up, but even Hitler had a girlfriend, didn't he, and I can't be worse than Hitler, can I?"

Avery blinked.

Chloe took a sharp breath. "In my twenties, I turned down men who were lovely, because some gut instinct told me it wasn't right. Now, the older I get, the less lovely men seem, and I'm wondering if I missed the boat, if my instincts are off, if I turned down a ten waiting for an ace, and now the cards are almost dealt." She looked down, embarrassed. "And I know I shouldn't *need* a man to be happy; I don't. But I *want* to be in love. I want what my parents have. I want the fantasy I read about in books."

Avery raised a single, perfectly plucked eyebrow at Chloe. "And have you always suffered from low self-esteem?"

"I don't have low self-esteem," Chloe said, letting out a shocked, nervous laugh. Avery tilted her head, pressed her thumbs a little tighter into Chloe's wrists as the metronome clicked persistently on. "Well, I guess I was more confident when I was younger. Who wasn't, though? My ex, Peter, he could be quite critical, a little controlling at times. I think I lost a bit of myself with him. I'm not sure I ever got it back." Chloe paused. She didn't like to think about that time of her life, the person she'd become. She pulled her wrists away and there was a long beat of silence. Avery blinked. "Please don't write down that bit about Hitler," Chloe said, chewing on her bottom lip.

Avery sat back in her chair, then pressed her palms together.

"Well, I'm happy to tell you that we think you would make an *ideal* candidate for our program, Chloe," Avery said, her face morphing into an expression of delight.

"Really?" Chloe asked.

"Yes. We have an extremely high success rate with clients who have struggled with relationships in real life." In real life? "But first, I should give you some more context about what we're offering here. This needs to be the right fit for everyone." Chloe nodded eagerly. "Perfect Partners isn't a *dating* service." She said "dating" like it was a dirty word. "We provide a revolutionary, highly evolved matchmaking solution. With the technology available to us now, people shouldn't need to scroll and scroll or date dozens of no's before finding a maybe. You shouldn't have to put up with mediocre men."

Chloe nodded again; Avery's words made her feel seen.

"We are confident that by using the right data analysis and state-of-the-art algorithms, we can provide the *perfect* partner for you. Though the program is still in its infancy, initial trials have shown a remarkable success rate. Clients currently have a ninety-four percent chance of falling in love within the first two months."

"Ninety-four percent, wow," said Chloe. She shifted in her chair, feeling strangely uncomfortable without Avery's thumbs to anchor her.

"We're hoping to get that figure closer to ninety-nine before we take our product to market," Avery explained. "We're still tweaking the technology, beta testing on small, select groups, just while we iron out any . . . kinks."

"That sounds expensive," Chloe said, letting out a nervous laugh.

"It is," Avery said plainly. "Our product is aimed at the one percent." Chloe's face fell. She was in the 1 percent of people who, at the age of thirty-one, still slept with a stuffed bear in their childhood bedroom (she'd looked up the stats). But she doubted this was the 1 percent Avery was referring to. "However," Avery went on, "since we're still at the trial stage, we're offering you the opportunity to sign up for two months for free." She paused, eyes intent on Chloe.

"Oh, right," said Chloe, daring to feel hopeful again.

"This unique opportunity does come with certain terms and conditions," Avery explained, pursing her lips, then knitting her fingers together on the desk. "You'll need to be open-minded."

"Oh, I am extremely open-minded," Chloe said, leaning forward in her chair. "I once tried anchovy ice cream."

"You'll also need to sign an NDA," Avery said, sliding a sleek tablet across the desk. The screen glowed with a digital contract full of dense text. "You cannot disclose any information about Perfect Partners to a third party or even acknowledge your involvement in this trial. This is a burgeoning field. Competitors are racing us to market."

Chloe nodded; she could be discreet. Could she? Well, she'd probably have to tell Akiko, but she'd swear her to secrecy.

"No friends, no family, *no one*," Avery reiterated, as though reading Chloe's mind.

Chloe hesitated, but then she thought of Wendy—glowing, transformed. She scanned the NDA and quickly signed her name in the box at the bottom. Whatever this was, it had to be better than the apps.

Avery took the tablet, then leaned back in her chair, crossing one slim leg over the other. Her movements were fluid, economical, like a dancer's. "Okay then."

"So . . . what happens now?" Chloe asked, her curiosity beyond piqued.

Avery raised a single finger, then tapped away at her computer. Chloe noticed what incredible skin she had—smooth and poreless, not a single flaw. She made a mental note to pick up some SPF on the way home.

"Based on the data you have already provided," Avery said, eyes on the screen, "we have sourced someone we believe will be *perfect* for you."

"Already?" Chloe blinked in disbelief. "Wow, okay."

Avery looked up. "Would you like me to introduce you?"

"What, now?"

"Yes."

Chloe nodded slowly, bemused that they could have found someone suitable so quickly.

Avery picked up the phone and dialed a number. "Yes," she said into the receiver. "Yes . . . Yes. Rob Dempsey for Chloe Fairway. Meeting room one."

Rob Dempsey. That felt like a solid name. Like Robert Redford or Robert Downey Jr. You couldn't go wrong with a Rob.

Avery stood up and held out a slim, sleek smartwatch. "This is your personalized device. You'll need to wear it for the duration of the trial."

Chloe lifted her hand to take it. Avery paused, watching her, waiting for something. "You want me to put it on now?"

"If you could."

Chloe looked down at the watch. It had a small, black oval screen and a slim elastic strap—just like the one she'd seen Wendy wearing. "It tracks your vital signs, your mood, oxytocin levels, hormone spikes, stress levels. It helps us monitor everything, tells us how things are going."

Chloe slipped it on, admiring the clean aesthetic of the design. As soon as she had it on her wrist, it made a small beep, and a blue square lit up the screen.

"Right, now that's out of the way, let's go meet your match."

Avery led her back to the waiting room, then turned left and opened a second door, which had "Meeting Room One" written on the front. Inside was a room much larger than Avery's office. It had red, cushioned velvet walls and dim, romantic lighting. In the center was a table, covered in a white linen tablecloth, with two chairs on either side. On top stood a lit candle and a single red rose in a vase. Jazz music played quietly in the background, and there was a subtle aroma of cloves and cinnamon—the room smelled of Christmas, Chloe's favorite smell.

As Avery ushered her in, it felt like walking into a womb or some trippy dream, the soft, warm colors incongruous next to the cold sterility of the waiting room. On the back wall was a second door, and Chloe's heart began to race as she saw the figure of a man come through it.

As he walked into the middle of the room and she was able to see him better, her eyes grew wide and she pinched her lips together, suppressing a gasp. He was tall, over six feet, with broad shoulders, a warm open face, and a distinct glint in his hazel eyes. His eyebrows were dark and thick, and he had neatly cut brown hair, with a strong, sharp jawline. He looked strangely familiar, though she couldn't work out why. Had she seen this man in her dreams? All she knew was that he was, without a doubt, the most beautiful man she had ever seen in real life. As she stared at him, he walked across to the table, a smile lighting up his face. Then he pulled out a chair to offer her a seat.

"Hi, I'm Rob," he said in a soft Irish accent. Irish. Oh wow. She had a thing for Irish accents. She swallowed. He was *exactly* her type, if movie-star good looks and a Hollywood smile could be described as a realistic type for anyone.

"Holy mackerel," she said under her breath.

"Holy mackerel yourself," he said, a smile playing at the corner of his lips.

Avery gave Chloe a gentle shove, and she took a step toward Rob, who now extended his hand to shake hers.

"I'm Chloe," she said, blushing as she took his hand.

"Why don't I give you two a chance to get to know each

other," Avery said, as Chloe moved to sit down, glad to have the feel of solid furniture beneath her. Rob walked around to take the second chair, carefully removing his jacket before sitting down. He was wearing a blue suit with a white shirt and gray tie. His whole outfit was impeccably styled, like he'd just stepped off an Italian fashion shoot. Chloe regretted that she was only in jeans and a floral blouse. She pulled her hair out of its clip and tried to fluff up some volume at the top. Then she remembered her hair might smell of chips, so she compromised with a half-up-half-down situation.

Once they were seated, Avery walked over and reached out to take both their wrists. She pressed down on a soft indent at the tops of both their watches, causing the blue square to pulse twice and then turn into a blue heart.

"Now we can track your progress," Avery explained.

She gave Chloe a long look that Chloe couldn't interpret. It felt like she was wishing her luck, or maybe she had noticed her taking her hair down and knew what that meant. Avery left briskly, shutting the door behind her.

Chloe turned toward Rob and let out a nervous laugh.

"Well, this is . . . different," she said, glancing around at the strange room. "What kind of restaurant has padded walls? Do you think they're worried we're going to start throwing food? Or is it to drown out the sound of all the other diners?" She looked around, letting out a short laugh, followed by a brief snort. Why did she only ever snort around ridiculously attractive men? But Rob only smiled, unperturbed by the snorting.

"I don't think it's a real restaurant," he said, and she noticed his lovely Irish lilt again. "I think it's a date simulation. Maybe we only get to eat if we pass the test."

"What's the test?" she asked, leaning forward a little.

"Getting on?" he suggested. "Working out why they matched us?"

"So did you fill in the questionnaire too, then?" she asked.

"I did," he said, "all forty-two pages." As he leaned toward her, she noticed how good he smelled, like expensive, spicy cologne and mint soap. Was this really the man she had matched with?

"It felt like there were a lot of questions about air temperature," Rob added, eyes sparkling with amusement.

"I noticed that too," she said. "Whether you like to sleep with the window open or closed. Maybe that's the secret to any great relationship, wanting to be the same temperature at night."

"Ha," he laughed. "What were you, open or closed?"

"Open."

"Me too."

They grinned at each other. When Rob smiled, his cheeks creased into dimples, and his dark eyes radiated warmth, like the soft flicker of a fireplace on a cold evening. He reminded her of Adam Brody or Paul Mescal, a perfect blend of the two, which was strange, given those were two of the names she'd written on her form. Now that she thought about it, maybe that was why he looked familiar.

In the presence of such physical perfection, Chloe felt suddenly tongue-tied. Dropping her gaze, she looked back at her watch, which now showed a pulsing pink line. Rob's showed the same. "Look, snap. We're twinsies," she said, holding out her wrist. Twinsies? No wonder she was single.

"Twinsies," he said, eyes brimming with delight, as though this was the most charming thing she could have said. She noticed Rob didn't fidget or look distracted; he sat still, offering her the full beam of his attention. She realized how rare this was, and how attractive she found such self-assured poise.

"So, how did you get involved in all this?" Chloe asked, trying not to be intimidated, reminding herself that however attractive he was, he was still only human. But then he moved his hand to push up his white shirtsleeves, and she noticed how toned and tanned his forearms were. She also noticed his hands, firm and strong but with long, elegant fingers—perfect hands, like a piano player's. Had she mentioned on her form she had a thing about hands? Now, when she looked back at his face, she realized he'd said something, but she'd been distracted.

"Sorry, say that again," she said, shifting her focus to his face.

"People say it's the future," Rob said, looking back at her with unabashed directness. "From what I've seen, it feels like they know what they're doing." He tugged his lower lip between his teeth, eyes dancing with playful intent. Was he flirting with her? She felt instantly skittish, like a schoolgirl with a crush. "But tell me about you, Chloe. Avery mentioned you were a playwright?"

"Yes, trying to be."

"I'd love to write, but I don't think I have the imagination," he said.

"Oh, I'm sure you do. Everyone has a book in them, or a play—a journal at least." Chloe twirled a stray curl, then knitted her hands in her lap to stop herself from fidgeting.

"Are you nervous?" Rob asked gently, reaching for her hand across the table. Chloe hesitated, only briefly, before placing her hand in his. As their fingers touched, she noticed something—both their watches now pulsed with a soft purple line.

She nodded, embarrassed.

"Don't be," he said, and when she looked up, she saw such kindness in his eyes, such genuine care. He wasn't judging her. "Tell me more about the theater," he said, giving her hand a reassuring squeeze, then letting go and leaning back in his chair. "I read Chekhov recently and I'm not sure I understood most of it."

He read Chekhov? Men on Hinge did not read Chekhov.

"No one understands Chekhov," she said, feeling herself relax a little. "I think it's meant to invoke a feeling of doom. Which play did you read?"

"All of them."

"All of them?" she asked, laughing. "Wow, you're more of an expert than me then. Do you read a lot of plays?"

"I do," he said, folding his hands in his lap. "Though I probably prefer novels." Chloe let out a tiny squeak. The holy grail: a man who read fiction. "Give me an old leather armchair, a good cup of coffee, and a decent book," he said with a soft smile, "and I am a happy man."

"Oh, me too," she said, enchanted. "Well, a happy woman." She felt her shoulders relax.

"Anything you've read recently that you'd recommend?" he asked.

"I go through phases," she said. "I'll get obsessed with a time period, then just read everything from then. I'm currently deep in my Gilded Age era."

"I'm the same, but with authors," he said, leaning forward, his face lighting up. "I've just discovered Mary Shelley and I'm disappointed she didn't write more." He ran a hand through his hair, then his eyes found hers again. "When I read, I sometimes get nostalgic for a time I didn't even live through."

The skin on Chloe's arms broke out in goose bumps. This was how *she* felt. "That has a name," she told him. "Anemoia—nostalgia for a time you've never experienced. I have it *all* the time. I spent my twenties obsessed with *Brideshead Revisited*. I felt so sure that I should have been born then."

"'Sometimes I feel the past and the future pressing so hard on either side that there's no room for the present at all,'" Rob said, and Chloe melted on the spot. He could quote *Brideshead Revisited* from memory? She knew only one other person who could do that: John Elton.

"That's one of my favorite lines," she said, her voice a reverential whisper.

Rob looked quietly pleased by her reaction. "So, Miss Fairway," he said, the flirtatious tone back. "Where did your urge to create plays come from? Is it something you always wanted to do?"

"Yes, I wanted to be an actor for a while too," she admitted, glancing down at her hands. "But that's even more competitive. I think I was a big fish in a small pond at university, then I hit the ocean and met all these whales."

"Whales?" he asked.

"I was going with the 'big fish, small pond' analogy," she said, reaching up to unclip the rest of her hair and shaking it out around her shoulders, chip smell be damned.

"Well, little fish," Rob said, smiling, "sometimes you have to let go of one dream to make way for a new one."

She met his gaze, and the part of her she'd kept on ice began to thaw.

"But tell me more about you," she said, catching herself. "What do you do, workwise?" She was suddenly conscious that the conversation had been focused on her and her interests.

"Computer programming, but don't judge me on that. It's not as boring as it sounds," he said with a self-effacing grimace.

"Oh, no judgment here. I'm just a PA, which is probably much more dull."

"I doubt you're 'just' anything, Chloe," he said.

She beamed, a flush of heat running up her neck.

The longer they talked, the more Chloe's nerves dissipated. She learned that Rob would rather play sports than watch them (tick), that he loved to travel (tick), and that his best friends were his three brothers (tick, tick, tick). He came across as highly educated, but with a quiet modesty that only made him more appealing. No bravado, no boastfulness. Just calm confidence. As Chloe listened, a warm, contented glow settled over her.

This was it.

Her senses were on high alert, her body pulsed with a new energy. She became acutely aware of her own lips as his glance dropped, briefly, to them. When their eyes met again, she saw it—the attraction she was feeling mirrored. Then her watch gave a subtle vibration. She glanced down to see the pulsing line had turned pink again.

"Hey, twinsy," he said, holding up his wrist, where his screen glowed the same color. They both laughed.

Their conversation had slipped into an effortless rhythm now. So when Avery suddenly reappeared, her presence felt jarring.

"Enjoying yourselves?" Avery asked as she stepped through the door. Chloe nodded. Then Avery said, "Rob, would you kindly wait outside?"

Rob didn't look surprised by the request. He stood, then turned toward Chloe and pressed a hand to her arm. His fingers were warm—steadying.

"It was lovely talking to you," he said.

Chloe felt a physical tug of disappointment as she watched him leave through the door he had entered from. She looked back to Avery, eyes imploring—did he really have to go?

"How did you find that?" Avery asked, taking the seat Rob had vacated.

"Oh, he's lovely," Chloe said, unable to stop grinning.

"I've been monitoring your data. You experienced elevated serotonin levels, and your conversation was split forty-five, fifty-five, which is well within the bounds of a 'good conversation.' I also noted a high level of physical attraction, evolving into a mental and emotional one. From our end, these look like top-tier results, Chloe. A perfect match."

Chloe shook her head, bemused that the device on her arm could have told Avery so much.

"Would you like to see him again?" Avery asked.

"Definitely. Though maybe in a real restaurant next time. The service here isn't great."

Avery frowned. "There is no service. This is not a real restaurant."

"Right, yeah, no, I got that," Chloe said. "I was joking."

There was a moment of awkward silence before Avery said, "I'm going to tell you something now that you might find surprising." Avery folded her hands in her lap, her chin lifted with delicate poise.

Chloe tensed. A catch. Of course there was a catch. How could there not be a catch? She held her breath, bracing herself.

"Rob is not human," Avery said.

Chloe blinked. "Sorry—what?"

Avery said nothing. Just let the words hang there, watching them sink in. But Chloe only laughed, because here she was thinking Avery didn't have a sense of humor.

"What is he, an alien from the planet Hotness?"

"No, Chloe, he is not an alien, and there is no such planet."

"Then what is he?" Chloe asked, her voice sharper now.

"He is a state-of-the-art AI humanoid robot. An android. Physically, practically indistinguishable from a real person."

Chloe stared. Then she laughed, a real belly laugh.

"Well, that is quite the plot twist, Avery," Chloe said, crossing her arms. "Come on, I'm not *that* gullible."

"I can assure you, he is what I say he is," Avery replied calmly.

"No way. That kind of technology doesn't exist," Chloe said, her voice assertive, but Avery's expression didn't change. "It doesn't. He told me about his job, his brothers, his childhood in Ireland—"

"He *believes* those things," Avery said, cutting in smoothly. "They are what he's been programmed to believe. We designed him according to your preferences—you like Irish men with big families—but he can have whatever backstory you desire."

Chloe stared at Avery again. Now she felt unsettled, because the woman looked entirely serious.

"Do you really think a man like that exists outside fiction?" Avery asked with a note of pity.

"I don't believe you," Chloe said, but her voice came out small, uncertain.

Avery turned her head toward the door. "Rob," she called.

He stepped back into the room, furnishing them both with an amiable smile. This had to be a joke. There was no way . . . Chloe looked around for a hidden camera; was she the victim of some horrible prank?

"Show her," Avery instructed.

Without a word, Rob calmly rolled up his shirtsleeve. He pressed at the flesh on his forearm, and with a subtle *click*, a panel opened. Chloe inhaled sharply. Beneath the fleshlike layer she could see wires, metal, and intricate circuit boards.

Chloe screamed.

Then she paused to take a breath and screamed some more.

Then she took one more huge gulp of air and began screaming, louder this time.

Rob and Avery waited patiently for her to stop.

"This is why we soundproofed the room," Avery said, waving a hand toward the padded walls.

When Chloe finally ran out of breath, she passed through a rapid succession of emotions—disbelief, horror, disappointment, awe, anger, and then a whole load more horror. Avery nodded to Rob, his cue to leave.

"Sorry, what the actual fuck, Avery?" Chloe managed to say, and she only ever swore in exceptional circumstances. "This is what Perfect Partners does? You make fake men?"

"And women," Avery said cheerfully. "But they're not fake, they're very real, just not flesh-and-blood real. Rob is a Galatea Series 762x, though we affectionately refer to them as BoiBots." She paused, taking in Chloe's shocked expression, then shifting her own to one of sympathy. "It's a lot to take in, I know. Think of dating a biological man as using a typewriter. It's fine, you can do it, but it's messy and slow and if you make a mistake, it's hard to rectify. Rob here is a laptop—clean, sleek, fully programmable, far more efficient." She took a beat. "You gave us all the information we needed to build exactly what you want, Chloe. Rob is it."

"I don't want to date a sodding robot, thank you very much," Chloe said, standing up and pacing, because she couldn't sit still. Her heart was pounding; her hand shot to her neck, scratching at her skin. She felt tricked, angry, embarrassed. She'd been flirting with a machine.

"No one believes it can feel real until they are in a room with one," Avery said, evening her tone. "That's why we do it this way." She clapped her hands once, a sharp sound. "I suggest you go out with him, on a real date. If you aren't convinced, you'll have wasted nothing but a few hours of your time." Avery's ice-blue eyes fixed on Chloe. "Being in a healthy relationship, with the right person, it transforms people."

"He's not a person though, is he?" Chloe said, sitting back down, resting her head in her hands because the room was spinning; her stomach turned.

"Trust me, after a few dates you'll forget about that," Avery said. She looked like she was waiting for a response, but Chloe was speechless. "The truth is, Chloe, all the ideal men you listed on your form—Fitzwilliam Darcy, Anthony Bridgerton, Friedrich Bhaer—they are all men written by women. Women know what women want. Rob is also written by a woman; he is written by you."

The nausea ebbed, leaving a hollow feeling in its place. Chloe stood, then ripped the watch from her wrist and laid it on the table. Whatever the *Blade Runner* mind trip she'd just walked into, she needed to leave now. Sci-fi was not her genre.

"I'm going now," she said firmly, walking toward the door.

"Think about it," Avery replied, unmoved. "Perfect Partners will be here when you're ready for perfection."

Chloe ran from the building, then out onto the Strand. She didn't stop running until she reached Charing Cross station. There, breathless, she looked around at all the people going about their day, running for their trains. How could they be acting like everything was normal when there were robots who looked like men? How did she know these commuters were even real—what if they were all robots too? As her thoughts swirled, she had to sit down on the pavement, to feel the ground. After a few minutes, the adrenaline drained out of her and was replaced by a heavy, sinking feeling. Because for a moment there, she had felt something she hadn't felt in a long time—hope.

By the time she got back to Richmond, her disappointment and confusion had curdled into anger. Anger that Wendy had set her up, that she'd wasted all that time filling in a forty-two-page questionnaire. And sure, she hadn't specified "ALIVE" or "HUMAN" as prerequisites, but she'd kind of assumed they were a given. This was all the reunion email's fault. It had triggered an existential spiral, making her question every aspect of her life. A similar thing happened when she watched too many TED Talks or read Brené Brown. But whatever change she was trying to manifest, dating a sexy R2-D2 was not it.

5

Chloe lay in bed, unable to sleep, annoyed at Wendy, annoyed at herself for finding Rob so charming. Grossed out by the fact she'd fancied him. Ew. She was also irked by Avery's calm demeanor, her smug confidence that Chloe would be back. *Of course* she wasn't going to date a robot. She wasn't that desperate, and she wasn't—as far as she knew—mad. She had seen enough *Black Mirror* episodes to know these things never ended well. No fairy tales ended "and she lived happily ever after with her robot boyfriend."

When Chloe finally managed to sleep, she woke feeling disturbed. She'd had a sex dream about WALL-E. A graphic sex dream. Then she felt doubly disturbed because it was the first sex dream she'd had in years.

In the morning, she felt groggy from lack of sleep. Part of her wondered if Avery and Perfect Partners had all been a dream. Did that all really happen? Sluggishly, she threw on her neutral work uniform of black jeans and a nude blouse, but then added a vintage, puff-stitch green cape and a nude cloche hat. McKenzie might have strong opinions on what she wore at the office, but he couldn't dictate what she wore to get there.

She then sprayed a generous amount of Issey Miyake to fend off the chip smell. Downstairs, her parents were already in the kitchen.

"Don't you look lovely," said her mum, looking up. "So like my mother."

"Okaaaay," Chloe said, "I wasn't aiming for grandma chic."

"When she was younger, I mean. You're so like her. Both fashionistas, dancing to the beat of your own drum."

Chloe twisted the ring on her finger, as she always did when she thought of Valerie. It was a narrow gold band with an amber cameo set in the top, carved in relief with an image of Artemis, the goddess renowned for her fierce independence. Her grandmother had pressed the ring into her hand the week before she died, saying, "Never lose your independence, child. Always, *always* have your own money." It was the ring, her grandmother's words, that had given her the final push to leave Peter. The day he'd opened her bank statement, suggesting they'd save more if she put everything into the joint account, the account he controlled. That was the moment. Her grandmother Valerie's voice in her head: "Leave, Chloe. Leave now."

"Who moved the TV remote?" her dad asked, wandering around like a man possessed. "It lives on top of the fridge. People will keep moving it."

"You know the TV has voice-activation control," Chloe said, pouring herself a bowl of cornflakes. "If you enabled the setting, you could just *tell* the TV to turn itself on."

"Oh no, we can't be doing with that," her mum said, measuring coffee into the cafetière. "Newfangled technology, more trouble than it's worth. We don't want *foreign* governments listening in on our conversations."

"It's designed to make your life easier, Mum. And I don't think 'foreign governments' want to hear you two talk about when the weather's going to turn, or how extortionate marmalade is these days."

Chloe shot her mum a goofy smile, but her parents remained unconvinced. A few years back, they'd been scammed out of some money online, and since then, they'd grown increasingly distrustful of technology. They'd even stopped using the sat nav because they didn't like the car knowing their "comings and goings."

"Drama over, here it is," her mum said, pulling the TV remote from the bread bin. Then she sat back down with her *Hello!* magazine. "Oh, I do feel sorry for the young Duchess of Wiltshire, don't you? She seems *so* lovely, and that rotter of a fiancé has broken off their engagement again. Run off with a glamour model. Quite scandalous!"

"What was the remote doing in the bread bin?" her dad asked in confusion.

"I don't know, darling. Getting bready? Ha ha."

"Maybe he was feeling crumby?" her dad suggested, and the two of them burst into laughter.

Chloe sighed, resting her chin on her hand. How had these two found each other?

"Oh, now look at this," her mum said, pushing the magazine

in front of Chloe. "Ten of the world's most eligible princes. Wouldn't it be fun if you married the prince of Denmark? Ooh, Sheikh Mohammed of Qatar is rather dishy. He's your age too, fluent in Arabic, English, *and* French. Very impressive. He'd probably want you to live there though, wouldn't he?"

"Mum, I love that you think geography is the only obstacle to me marrying Sheikh Mohammed of Qatar."

"We do have plenty of air miles we haven't used," said her dad, resting his hand on his wife's shoulder and kissing her head.

Something tugged inside Chloe. She loved living with her parents, but sometimes when she saw them like this, so content in their own little universe, it only made her feel more alone.

"Let's not use *Hello!* magazine as a dating directory," Chloe said, taking the magazine from her mother's hands and closing it before turning back to her cereal.

"Okay, your anagram this morning is "marmalade,'" her dad said, writing it out on the Post-it note. "Too easy," he said with a wink. "Now I need your opinion on something. New name for the band; Neville wants 'the Richmond Bangers,' Hamish likes 'the Granny Smiths.' What do you think?"

Her dad was in a band with two friends from church. They'd started out playing "Amazing Grace" and "All Things Bright and Beautiful" after the Sunday service, but recently they'd moved into pop and rock, played in a few pubs. Their name, the Richmond Church Players, didn't quite fit the vibe now.

"You can't be grannies when you're all men," Chloe's mum said with a frown.

"It's a play on the Smiths, but like the apples," her dad explained.

"If you have to explain it to Mum, it's probably not a good

name," Chloe said. "I liked 'Three Men and a Banjo.' Was that not a goer?"

Her dad looked disappointed. "Neville's given up the banjo."

"I'll have a think," she promised. "Right, I have to run. Bye, love you." Outside, Chloe squinted into the brightness of daylight. It was too warm for a woolen cape, but she was going to wear it anyway because it made her feel like Batgirl. As she walked over Richmond Road bridge, Chloe paused to watch rowers glide past swans on the river below, then she dialed Wendy's number.

"Chloe Fairway," Wendy said as she answered. "I thought you might call."

"What the hell, Wendy?" Chloe snapped, but Wendy only laughed.

"You went, then? I wish I could have seen your face. I wish I could have seen *my* face. It's unbelievable, right?"

"That is an understatement."

"Look, I can't really talk about it, I signed my life away, as I'm sure you did too, but I'm telling you, you won't regret it. I have never been happier. I can't describe how Patrick has changed my life. He is literally the *perfect* partner." Wendy paused, then sighed dreamily. "Just . . . don't sleep with him until you're sure you want to commit to the lifestyle. Once you go bot, you won't go back. I swear, it's like being treated to a Michelin-starred meal after years of gruel."

"Wendy, you have to be joking. I will not be having"—she lowered her voice, glancing around at the pavement—"sex with a robot."

"Technically, an android," Wendy said. "And trust me, it feels completely natural. Your satisfaction *guaranteed*."

"I'm good, thanks."

Chloe rolled her eyes skyward, then hung up and strode off toward the station, still shaking her head. Speaking to Wendy had only made her feel more confused. Wendy was a normal person. She sounded happy, radiant even. Was that really all down to having a BoiBot boyfriend?

Well, just because it worked for Wendy, it did not mean it was going to work for her. Yes, she had enjoyed Rob's company. Sure, he was undeniably handsome, but that didn't negate the fact that he was *not real*. Then she thought of Tom and all the awful "real" men she'd dated lately. No, no, she was not considering this. Just because your toast is burnt doesn't mean you eat the toaster.

At work, Chloe found a mountain of scripts on her desk, waiting to be shredded. Perfect. She booted up her computer and, stalling, checked LinkedIn. She'd been tagged in a post, an update about the reunion, with people commenting, saying they couldn't wait to catch up. She felt a pang of longing. If only she could go as a fly on the wall, not as someone who'd have to explain what she'd been doing—or not doing—for the last ten years. She scrolled through the post, half-curious, then froze when she saw Sean's name.

Sean Adler: I'm in the UK that weekend, so I'll be there.

Sean was going? That was a surprise. She clicked on his page, something she'd done more times than she'd like to admit. In his profile picture he had the same floppy black hair, same boyish grin. He hardly looked older, just better groomed. She didn't hear McKenzie come up behind her until he spoke.

"How do you know Sean Adler?"

Chloe jumped, tried to close the page, but it was too late.

"Oh, he . . . he went to university with me," she said.

She clicked back a page and the reunion post now filled the screen.

"A reunion?" McKenzie said, reading over her shoulder before she could click away.

"No one goes to those things," Chloe said quickly.

"And Sean Adler is going?" he asked, leaning a hand on her chair.

She was about to lie, but Sean's comment was central on the screen. Damn.

"You should go. Put the script for *Welcome Rising* in front of him," McKenzie said, already scheming. He was always looking for ways to back-channel scripts into the hands of actors and directors. But he was reaching new levels of delusion if he thought someone with Sean's profile was going to consider one of his low-budget projects.

"Reunions aren't really my thing," Chloe mumbled, feeling herself starting to sweat.

"Chloe, it's your job to network. Honestly, I'm disappointed you didn't bring this connection to me yourself. Do you know what a coup it would be if we got Sean Adler?"

Chloe felt sick. Not just a flicker of nerves, but a full-body wave of nausea that rolled up from her stomach and settled behind her eyes like searing-hot stones. Because there would only be one thing more mortifying than going to the reunion alone: going alone *and* having to ask Sean Adler for a favor. Plus, circumventing agents was unprofessional. The thought of it made her whole body cringe inward, like she was trying to retreat from her own skin. She twisted her chair back toward her computer, trying to escape the conversation.

"I'm not sure, Mr. McKenzie. It feels like a long shot."

"I've heard you on the phone, you're good at pitching," McKenzie added. Was that a compliment? "But I can't have an executive assistant who isn't prepared to hustle when hustling is required. Am I making myself clear?"

Chloe nodded, jaw clenched. McKenzie waddled back to his office. She groaned, sank into her chair, and flicked through the comments on the LinkedIn post.

Lorna Childs: Wow—doesn't Oxford seem like yesterday? I guess time flies when you're having fun!

Lorna was now a successful interior designer with two million followers on Instagram and a gorgeous tennis pro husband. She posted reels like "How to color-contrast your cornices with your couch" and "Fifteen morning rituals that changed my life." Chloe didn't even own a couch, let alone cornices, and she struggled with just the one morning ritual, getting dressed and leaving the house. The next comment was from Harriet, Lorna's best friend.

Harriet Townsend: So psyched for this! If anyone wants some of my organic jam, let me know!

According to Kiko, Harriet had given up law to become a trad wife in the Cotswolds. She'd married some rich hedge fund guy, had three beautiful children, and now lived a "fully organic lifestyle" drinking raw milk and making her own cheese, jam, and bath salts from scratch. She sold them online under the brand name Happy Harriet.

Chloe had attempted to make jam once, when her grandmother had a glut of strawberries. She ended up with an inedible saucepan of burned goo and a painful burn on her arm.

Colin Layton: I'll be there. Driving down in the Maserati if anyone needs a lift from up north?

LinkedIn told her that Colin had made a fortune inventing some wine-trading app. Then there was Thea Bankole, partner in a law firm by thirty. Mark Patel, who'd already won half a dozen prizes for his work in medical research. The list of astonishing achievements went on and on, only serving to cement in Chloe's mind what she already knew: she would not be able to face this reunion alone.

Then she thought of Rob. Charming, eloquent, handsome . . . undeniably impressive. *Hmmm.* Okay, so she might not want a robot boyfriend, but what about a robot fake date? Just for the reunion weekend . . .

"People would suspect, wouldn't they?" she asked Morgan Treeman.

"You couldn't tell, so how would they?" Morgan replied. "Plus you're currently taking life advice from a desk plant, so . . ."

He had a point. She would definitely feel like less of a loser if she had Rob on her arm. People would ask, "Oh, what's Chloe Fairway up to these days? Did she ever become an actress? Is she changing the world?" and someone else would say, "I don't know, but she's got a smoking-hot boyfriend who can quote *Brideshead Revisited*, so she must be doing something right."

This was either an inspired plan of incomparable genius or the worst idea she'd ever had. Either way, it was the only plan she had. She replied to the reunion email, saying she would attend with a plus-one, and then picked up the phone to Perfect Partners. Avery didn't sound the least bit surprised to hear from her.

On the train home after work, packed elbow to ear with commuters, all glued to their phones, Chloe contemplated this scene. So sad, everyone focused on the little oblongs in their hands, not one person making eye contact with a stranger. Then her own phone buzzed, and she promptly forgot whatever it was she'd been thinking about.

John

HI CHLOE, I JUST GOT YOUR RSVP FOR THE REUNION. YOU NEGLECTED TO FILL IN DETAILS TO THE SPECIFIED QUESTIONS. JOHN.

She frowned. The wording felt characteristically blunt from John, but all caps seemed excessively aggressive. She scrolled up to the message above. It was from eight years ago, the last time she'd been in touch with him. She'd sent him an article about the largest orange ever grown. He'd replied with a thumbs-up.

She didn't know why she hadn't stayed in touch with John; she'd always been fond of him. She guessed they'd drifted after that first term in third year because he'd lived with Sean. John was viewed as mildly eccentric by most people in college, but she'd found him quietly brilliant. You never had a boring conversation with him. She remembered sitting next to him at a formal dinner once. She was peeling an orange, and he launched into the story of how a wild, bitter, thin-skinned fruit had been cultivated into the sweet, thick-skinned delicacy in her hand. He told it as though it were the best story in the world, but then John told all stories like that. Now, whenever she peeled an orange, she always thought of him. She should have made more effort to reconnect. Just because Sean had cut her off, it didn't mean John had.

Chloe

Hey, it's been a long time. What are you up to these days? SORRY FOR NEGLECTING DETAILS!

John

SORRY, PHONE BROKEN. STUCK ON CAPS LOCK.

Chloe

Oh right, you should get that fixed. It reads kind of aggressive. Anyway, how are you?

She tried to picture what John might look like now. Did he still dress like a student from the 1940s, in tweed jacket, waistcoat, and polished shoes? Had he kept the long hair? She'd googled him once, curious, but he didn't have much of an online presence. Apparently, he worked in music production, which wasn't a surprise.

John

FINE. JUST NEED YOUR DIETARY REQUIREMENTS, WHETHER YOU NEED A ROOM IN HALLS, AND NAME OF YOUR PLUS-ONE.

Chloe

No dietary requirements. Yes please to a room in halls.

John

AND THE NAME OF YOUR PLUS-ONE?

She started typing Rob's name, then hesitated. The surge of confidence that had fueled this idea was already flickering. Maybe she should see how her first date went before she committed in writing.

Chloe
Can I tbc?

John
ARE YOU WHITTLING DOWN CONTENDERS?

Three dots appeared, then vanished. She pictured John, still typing like he was sending telegrams from a bunker.

John
WELL. WHOEVER WINS, I HOPE HE APPRECIATES CITRUS HISTORY.

Chloe smiled despite herself. With some friendships, even after years of silence, you could pick straight back up where you'd left off.

6

Two days later, Chloe was back at Perfect Partners. She found Avery already waiting in the too-white office.

"I knew you'd be back," Avery said with an unreadable smile. "Everyone always comes back."

She looked Chloe up and down, and Chloe felt self-conscious beneath her gaze. Okay, yes, she had dressed up a little for her date with Rob, even though he wasn't real. Was that a crime? She'd changed after work and was now wearing a high-waisted A-line skirt in soft navy cotton, a tucked-in cream blouse with slightly puffed sleeves, her favorite soft leather ankle boots, and a wide-brimmed felt hat her mother had worn in the seventies.

"This is what I normally look like," she told Avery, as though she needed to explain the transformation. "I came straight from work last time."

Avery just handed Chloe the smartwatch.

"You'll need to wear this for the duration of the trial," she said, pale eyes locked on Chloe. "If you take it off, it will disrupt our data analysis. You *must not* take it off, ever."

Chloe slipped it onto her wrist, and Avery passed her a tablet displaying another digital contract. "More consent forms. Your data will be stored and recorded, ad infinitum," she said briskly, flicking through the pages. "All standard stuff."

Avery was all business today. She straightened the shiny white keyboard on her desk and then reached over to point out a paragraph in the contract.

"One clause I should draw your attention to: Perfect Partners cannot be liable for any emotional distress that you, the client, perceive to be the result of participating in our program."

"Right . . . ," Chloe said slowly.

"Or any physical injury that occurs as a result of misusing the Galatea Series 762x."

"Physical injury?" Chloe echoed. She knew she shouldn't have watched *Ex Machina* last night. Why were there so few happy robot movies?

"A formality," Avery said lightly. "Just don't try and take him apart or stick your finger into anything that hums." It was hard to tell from Avery's expression whether this was a joke, but then she clarified, "I jest. You are not going to get electrocuted. What you need to focus on is our success rate. And if anything goes wrong, you just call me."

"What might go wrong?" Chloe asked. "Could I get hurt?" An image of RoboCop pinning her in a headlock flashed through her mind.

"Absolutely not," Avery said. "Statistically, Rob is sixty-eight percent safer than a real man. He's incapable of harming you; in fact he is programmed to protect you." Avery shifted her face into a broad smile. "So, if you could just sign here and here . . . and here."

Chloe's hand hovered over the contract. She suspected that any situation that entailed a "you can't sue us if things go wrong" clause and required the contact details of your next of kin probably wasn't an ideal situation to be signing up for. Then again, wasn't modern life full of waivers? The induction at that gym she'd never gone back to, the updated terms and conditions on Meta, the horoscope app she'd paid £7.99 for only to be told that she was "no good with money." These days, if you wanted to do anything, you had to sign your life away.

Sensing her hesitation, Avery added, "You'd sign a similar waiver if you hired a Jet Ski. It's all very standard." Chloe didn't think that anything about this was standard, plus she had broken her ankle on a Jet Ski, so it wasn't the most reassuring example.

"Oh, and before I forget, I have a keepsake for you," Avery said, reaching into her drawer. "A little signing-on present, from all of us at Perfect Partners." Avery handed a silver photo frame across the desk. Inside was a black-and-white photo of Rob, standing on a rock beside the sea. He had his hands in his pockets and was staring out into the middle distance, a burst of sea spray rising up behind him like a watery peacock tail. Inexplicably, he was wearing a tuxedo. It was a ludicrous photo, but it did remind Chloe how ridiculously good-looking Rob was and how impressed all her old friends were going to be. So, she muted all her reservations and scrawled her digital signature on the screen.

"Treat him like he is real, as much as possible," Avery instructed. "If you ask him too many technical questions it can distort his feedback loop. It will help you too; you don't want to 'other' him."

Other him? Chloe was about to ask Avery to expand on that, but then Rob walked through the door. He was dressed in a fitted white shirt and well-cut chinos. He looked like a tall Paul Mescal modeling for *Vogue*.

"Hi," he said, locking eyes with Chloe, then shooting her a beaming smile. "It is so wonderful to see you again."

Chloe smiled. It was impossible not to because he was so lovely and Paul Mescally. Avery pulled a solitary party popper from her drawer, then launched a limp spray of blue, gray, and white streamers across her desk.

"Congratulations. Perfect Partners wishes you every happiness."

Chloe suggested she and Rob go for a walk in Hyde Park. It was a sunny summer's day, and the park was a public place—if he went all RoboCop on her, she could scream for help. Was it concerning that her mind went there? No—such anxieties weren't unique to this situation. She always felt a hum of nerves before meeting someone new. First dates were held in public places; she never accepted lifts home. That was just the quiet choreography of dating as a woman: the thrill of possibility, always tempered by a mental checklist of exits and worst-case scenarios.

"I love your outfit," Rob said, falling into step beside her, pulling her from her thoughts. "If you were a font, I'd say you were American Typewriter today."

"Thanks," she said, pleased that he'd noticed. "That's one of my favorite fonts. I was aiming for *Apple Chancery*, but close enough." They smiled at each other, but Chloe checked herself.

No doubt he was programmed to like whatever she was wearing, even if it was a potato sack and a balaclava.

"How was work today?" Rob asked as a couple strolled past them with a toddler in a pushchair deeply focused on pulling the arm off a Transformer. They didn't give Rob a second glance. They couldn't tell, didn't suspect he was anything out of the ordinary.

"Listen, Rob, I'm going to be straight with you," Chloe said, shifting her gaze back to him. "I'm not looking for a relationship here, okay? I'm afraid the 'nonreal' thing is a bit of a deal-breaker for me." Rob's expression didn't flicker. "But I have a college reunion in a few weeks, and I don't want to go alone. I'd like to take you as my plus-one."

"Okay," he said, not looking the least bit offended.

"Okay?" She raised an eyebrow.

"Sure," he said with an easy smile, a dimple tugging at his cheek. "If you want me to go to a reunion with you, I will. Sounds fun."

She narrowed her eyes. "You don't mind that I'm just using you? That I'll send you back when the free trial ends?"

Rob let out a gentle laugh. "No, I don't mind."

He tilted his face to the sun and closed his eyes. "Each day is a gift," he said, then turned to look at her. "But if you want me to be your plus-one, perhaps we should get to know each other first. Let me know what you hope to achieve at this reunion."

"Achieve?" she echoed, and he nodded, all earnest interest. "Um, to pretend I'm a half-competent adult who has her life together," she said, shooting him a wry smile. He smiled back, but his eyes were full of incomprehension. "There's this guy," she said after a beat, her gaze drifting down to the gravel path, as she kicked a small stone. "Sean. He was my best friend in college. But then . . . we grew apart, lost touch." She paused. It felt weird, talking to Rob about this. "It's complicated."

"You want to make Sean jealous?" he asked.

"No," she said quickly. "That's not it. He's moved on, he's got this whole big life going on." She picked at the edge of her sleeve. "I guess I'm embarrassed for him to see how small my life is by comparison. I don't want him to think I've got nothing, that I'm full of regrets."

Rob's brow creased. "What do you mean, your life is small?"

They'd reached the edge of the Serpentine now, the water glinting with early evening light. There were benches dotted along the side of the lake, some empty, others occupied by people reading, resting, watching the world go by.

"How long have you got?" Chloe said, lips curving into a half smile.

"As long as you need," he said, reaching for her hand.

She hesitated, just for a second, then let him take it. It felt surprisingly nice. Warm, comforting. Just like a real hand. He gave her an encouraging smile, and she realized she could be honest with him, because she wasn't trying to impress him.

"Where shall we start? My career? My love life? My finances?"

"Let's go with your career," he suggested.

"Okay, well, I took this job as a PA thinking it would lead somewhere. I was promised production and writing experience. But it's been nearly two years now, and I'm still stuck doing calendar invites and shredding scripts." She let out a soft laugh. "Sometimes I think the only reason I haven't quit is because without this job, I'd have to admit I've totally flunked adulting."

"That sounds frustrating," Rob said, his brow creasing in sympathy.

"I gave up on trying to be an actress, now I say I want to be a writer, but I haven't written anything in years. No idea seems to stick."

Rob swung her hand back and forth, coaxing a reluctant smile from her. On the path in front of them sat a cluster of female ducks, sunning themselves on the concrete. As they approached, the ducks shuffled out of their way, a few slipping into the lake with quiet splashes, barely disturbing the surface.

"Want my advice?" he asked, and she nodded. "You should send your boss an email, setting out your expectation for growth. Give him a timetable to make good on it. If he can't, then you'll at least know it's time to walk away. I can help you draft something if you like?"

She looked up at him, surprised. "That would be great."

"Then we should talk about why you aren't writing, what the block might be."

"So, you're a life coach now?"

"I can be. I can be whatever you want me to be, Chloe," he said, a smile at the corner of his lips, eyes shamelessly focused on hers. Was he flirting again?

Rob clapped his hands. "Right, so we're going to sort out your disingenuous boss. Let's park your love life for now." He grinned, raising his eyebrows slightly. "Finances, I can take a look at your portfolio if you feel comfortable with that?"

"Portfolio? I don't even know what that is."

"Ah," Rob said with a charming mock grimace.

Chloe laughed, and while she knew this wasn't real, she had

to admit it felt nice. The simple pleasure of walking with someone who let you speak, who listened, who looked at you like you mattered.

"So, can you really do anything you put your mind to?" she asked.

"If someone shows me how, sure," he said.

"Can you build IKEA furniture?" she asked, and he nodded. "How about without the instructions?"

He laughed. "Let's not be crazy, I'm not superhuman."

"Can you do a cartwheel?"

"If you teach me," he said, eyes gleaming, mouth set in a challenge.

"I haven't done a cartwheel since I was ten years old," she said.

"See if you can," Rob said, slowing, then stopping. He put a hand on each hip, waiting patiently.

"Really? Okay, but this is going to be terrible." She looked for a clean patch of grass, did a run up, and then attempted a shockingly bad cartwheel, her legs hardly leaving the ground. She stood up, laughing at this pitiful attempt, only to see Rob copying her, moving his legs in the exact same way. She couldn't catch her breath now; she was laughing too hard at the sight of a man his height attempting a cartwheel—he looked like a baby giraffe trying to stand. "Don't copy mine, mine was terrible!" she said, holding her sides.

Across the park, a young girl with pigtails did a cartwheel, as though to illustrate how easy it was. "Like that," Chloe said, pointing at the girl. Now Rob tried again and this time he mastered it, legs flying into a perfect arc over his head.

"Okay, now you're just showing off. Is there *anything* you can't do?" she asked as they started walking again. "You know those

CAPTCHA tests, where you need to tick all the boxes where you see a bicycle or whatever to prove you're human? Can you do those?" She was joking, but now his face grew serious.

"No, I can only get about fifty percent of the CAPTCHAs. I also can't swim, and I can't open champagne bottles. Something about the dexterity required, it's an incredibly nuanced combination of skills."

She laughed.

"What's funny?" he asked.

"You are."

"I didn't intend to be humorous," he said, looking slightly confused.

"Well, I'm having a nice time, intended or not," she admitted.

"Good," he said, looking pleased. "Because I wanted to ask you if you'd go to the theater with me tomorrow night. I took the liberty of reserving us two tickets. It's a Tennessee Williams play; it gets great reviews."

"How did you know I like Tennessee Williams?" she asked, taken aback.

"I read your university thesis."

"Ha. You might be the only other person in the world who's ever read it besides me and my English professor."

Person. She checked herself again. He was not a person. But the more he talked, the more he looked at her with those expressive eyes, the harder it was to remind herself that he was not what he appeared.

In her pocket, her phone buzzed. She stiffened. Muscle memory. Peter had hated her checking her phone when she was with him. She remembered, with shame, the time he'd "confiscated" her phone at a restaurant. She'd been waiting for an important work email, but Peter had snatched it from her hand, told her she could have it back when she learned how to show him some respect. She'd reached for it, thinking he was joking, but he'd squeezed her wrist tight. She'd let it go, fearful of making a scene.

"I don't mind, if you want to check your messages," Rob said gently, as though sensing her disquiet.

She pulled out her phone, irritated with herself. Why did Peter still have this hold on her? Of course she could check her phone. Especially given Rob was basically a giant smartphone with limbs . . . and dreamy eyes . . . and a lovely accent . . . and impeccable fashion sense.

She had two messages. One from John, just a question mark, chasing her for the details of her plus-one. The second was from an unknown US number.

Unknown Number

Hey Chloe, I hear you're coming to the reunion. Will be good to see you. Sean.

Chloe stared at the message for a moment, rereading it four or five times, as though she might decipher some code in the casual wording. A decade of silence and now this. "Will be good to see you." Was he just being polite, forestalling any awkwardness over the email he'd never replied to? Or had he sent a message like this to everyone? Why did getting a text from him make her feel nineteen again?

"Everything okay?" Rob asked. He didn't seem annoyed at her shift of focus, only curious.

She shook her head, distracted, putting her phone away. "Sorry."

"Chloe, you don't need to apologize. For anything," he said, and she could swear his Irish lilt had become more pronounced as their date went on.

She took in his kind expression, his gentle tone, the lovely Paul Mescally quality he had about him. Regardless of Sean, if she was going to this reunion, she didn't think she could ask for a better plus-one.

7

Chloe ran across London Bridge, a hastily packed weekend bag slung over one shoulder. The bridge was bustling with tourists taking photos of the Shard and Tower Bridge, but she had no time to stop and admire the view today. McKenzie had kept her late, drilling her on *exactly* how to pitch the project to Sean. The alumni committee had organized a coach from Victoria for people coming from London, but at this rate, she was going to miss it. She texted Rob as she ran:

Chloe

Running late, save me a seat on the bus!

She raced down the escalator at Monument tube station, then jumped onto the Embankment line. She tried to fan herself with her hand, conscious that with all that running, she was going to get her outfit sweaty. She'd changed in the loo after work and was wearing her favorite high-waisted, wide-leg trousers in soft olive green—her mum called them her Katharine Hepburn trousers, which might have been why she loved them. On top, she wore a simple white shirt with an oversized collar, then large tortoiseshell sunglasses lost somewhere in her hair. As she was fretting about sweating she caught her reflection in the train window. She looked radiant, *happy*. It took her by surprise. How much of that was down to Rob? Over the last two weeks, she'd seen him six times; they'd been to dinner, been to the theater, visited galleries, and strolled hand in hand along the South Bank. Each time, she found herself liking him more. Each time, it got harder to remember that he wasn't the man he appeared to be.

She liked that she could talk to him about anything. He never lost interest or got defensive. He was unfailingly kind, and he remembered everything she said. She'd joked that she wanted to become the sort of person who went running before work and yesterday, he'd turned up at her house in running gear, just after sunrise. They'd run around Richmond Park, then shared a protein smoothie, all before seven a.m. She'd usually have been too nervous to run around the park alone, but with Rob at her side, she felt invincible. She frowned at her reflection. Don't get carried away. It's just for this weekend, then you'll give him back.

When Chloe reached Victoria station, it was unpleasantly busy, the air smelled of exhaust fumes and pastries, and there were lost backpackers spinning in circles trying to navigate with their smartphones. She sprinted up the steps, then along the busy main road toward the bus terminal. Her loafers slapped against the pavement, and she had to hold up the hems of her trousers to keep them from murky pavement puddles. This was the problem when your allegiance to style and your travel budget didn't quite align. She couldn't imagine Katharine Hepburn ever ran for a bus.

Finally, the looming art deco architecture of the concrete bus station came into view. She was only ten minutes late, the bus probably hadn't even left yet. But the concourse was so huge, it took her a moment to find the right bay, and when she got there, she found it empty. Damn. On her phone, a message from Rob.

Rob

Sorry, I should have got off the bus. I didn't realize we were leaving.

Then a photo of the empty seat beside him and a sad-face emoji.

"Did we miss it?" asked a voice beside her.

Chloe turned to see a man of about her height, standing nearby, a battered backpack slung over one shoulder and a dog lead in his hand. At the other end of which was a small gray whippet. It took her a second to place him.

"John? John Elton?" she asked. He nodded. "Wow, you look so different."

"Hi, Chloe," he said.

The John she remembered had been all red hair, thick glasses, and the wardrobe of F. Scott Fitzgerald. The man in front of her had short, albeit messy, hair, which had faded to an auburn brown. He'd lost the glasses, and his body had broadened around the arms and shoulders. But the change that most threw her was that he was wearing jeans and a T-shirt, just like any ordinary twenty-first-century man.

"Tiny Dancer," she said with a grin. "Well, look at you! Not so tiny anymore, hey," she teased, tapping a finger against his shoulder.

"Chloe Fairway. Hilarious as ever," he said dryly.

"Who's this, then?" she said, bending down to say hello to his dog.

"Richard," he said, and as Chloe stroked the dog's head, Richard licked her hand appreciatively.

"Funny name for a dog. Why did you call him that?"

"He's named after Richard Gere."

"Why?"

"Because he's got gray hair, and he likes pretty women."

"Really?" Chloe asked, delighted.

"No, not really," John said, his expression neutral. "I just thought he looked like a Richard."

John's delivery was so deadpan, she could never quite tell when he was joking, but she laughed anyway.

"Are you bringing him? You can't have dogs in college. Can you?"

"He's a support dog," John explained, shifting his gaze upward. "Should we go and find another bus, given we've missed ours?"

"Good idea," she said, falling into step beside him. She was curious about why John might need a support dog but suspected it was rude to ask. "It's so good to see you," she said. "What are you up to these days, still composing?"

"I am," he said.

"What kind of music?" She watched him as he checked the departures board, unable to compute how much he had changed. Had she changed that much? The concourse around them thrummed with sound—children crying, PA announcements, the clatter of suitcase wheels, and the flutter of pigeons. Yet John stood there, unfazed, calm and serene, as though he were standing in an art gallery, contemplating an interesting painting. "I write scores for film and TV," he told her, eyes scanning the screen, "and I work at a recording studio."

"Wow," she said, genuinely impressed. "That sounds cool."

But then an unwelcome wave of self-doubt crept in. John, like Sean and Kiko, was doing exactly what he'd set out to do. Was she the only one who wasn't? She quickly checked herself. She knew that this weekend—hearing about everyone's glittering lives—was going to be challenging. That was exactly why she had armed herself with great outfits and a distractingly beautiful plus-one. Jealousy was not a helpful emotion, and besides, didn't a rising tide lift all ships? She must not think of herself as the waterlogged boat that was no longer seaworthy in this analogy.

"Maybe I should take some credit for your success," she said, nudging John. "Wasn't I always convincing you to compose music for our plays?" He frowned slightly, then hitched his backpack higher onto his shoulder. "Remember that musical we wrote in third year, *Back to Brideshead*?" she added with a laugh. "Wow, that was terrible. Not your music, obviously, the play. Do you remember? We did one performance, and half the audience walked out."

"I remember," he said, and there was a tightness in his tone. He didn't seem in the mood to reminisce.

"So, are you still in touch with a lot of people from college?" she asked, pivoting.

"I'm on the alumni committee, so yes," he said, turning to walk toward the ticket machine. "I'm in touch with people all the time for fundraisers and events."

"I meant socially," she said, skipping along beside him as they skirted around a noisy crowd of schoolchildren wearing hi-vis jackets. "Who have you stayed friends with? I only really keep up with Akiko and Emma. Do you see—" She paused, trying to sound casual. "Do you still see much of Sean?"

"Yes. Less since he moved. LA is eight hours behind," John said, offering for her to go first with the ticket machine. "There's a bus in five minutes."

By the time they'd bought tickets and found the right line, the moment to ask more about Sean had passed. The Oxford Tube was already parked up, a large red-and-blue coach, with people boarding at the front. John let her go first, but then the driver said, "No dogs on the bus, mate."

"It's a support dog," John told him.

"You got an ID? Certificate?" the driver asked while chewing gum.

"Yes, somewhere here," John said, reaching into his pocket for his wallet.

The driver waved him on, because a queue was building behind them. "Just don't let it sit on the seats."

The bus was already half full. A man in a hoodie was asleep across two seats, laptop half closed on his chest. An elderly couple near the front were quietly sharing an iPad and a bag of green boiled sweets. Chloe walked down the bus, taking in the distinct aroma of egg sandwiches and damp upholstery. They passed two teenage girls in matching Doc Martens, discreetly vaping while giggling over something on a phone screen. She thought of Clark Gable and Claudette Colbert's bus journey in *It Happened One Night*. Perhaps their bus smelled of egg sandwiches too, but everything just looked more romantic in black and white.

Chloe found an empty row at the back. She let John go in first. The dog jumped up beside him, but John shooed him down to the floor. Richard looked briefly disgruntled but then curled up at his feet. "Kind of regretting missing our nice college bus now," she whispered, as she slipped in beside him, and John finally cracked a smile.

"Indeed."

Chloe looked up at John and then back down at Richard, up at John, then down at Richard again.

"What?" John asked, narrowing his eyes at her.

"Nothing," she said, "I just . . ." She trailed off. "Nothing."

"What? What were you going to say?"

"Well," she whispered, "is Richard *really* a support dog?"

John glowered at her. She didn't remember him being a glowerer. It felt incongruous, but also intriguing, like she'd just unlocked a new mode.

"It's just, if I had a dog, I would probably say that so I could take him places," she said, pausing as the glower deepened. "No one ever checks the certificate, do they?"

"That would be an abuse of the system," John said, his voice giving nothing away.

"Right, I know. Of course." She pinched her lips closed.

"You haven't stayed in touch with Sean, then, I take it?" John asked. She shifted in her seat, impatient to get going.

"No, but I'm happy for him, how well he's done."

John's face softened now. "I'm sorry that you never patched things up after, well . . ."

Chloe felt her face flush red. She hugged her arms across her chest. John's words transported her right back to third year—the whispers, the questions, that awful moment on the lighting bridge.

"After he got a girlfriend who couldn't stand me," she said, shooting him an empty smile.

"To be fair to Susie, would you have wanted your boyfriend spending that much time with the person he thought was his soulmate?" He rubbed the stubble at his jawline and shifted his gaze to Richard. She took her sunglasses off her head and folded them on her lap. At the front of the bus, the doors finally clunked closed.

"When they broke up, he could have got back in touch. He didn't," she said.

"Maybe he was embarrassed," John said quietly.

"I tried to reconnect, you know. A few years after uni, I emailed him—"

"Chloe." John's voice softened. He cleared his throat. "Can we not go over all that again?" Right. John hated being caught in the middle, back then too. It had all fallen apart so quickly, after that night at the theater. Sean told her he loved her, that he wanted to be more than friends. She didn't feel the same way. Some part of her wanted to, it would have been so easy . . . but her body, some primal instinct inside her, had said no. She'd done everything she could not to make it awkward, to show him they could still be friends, still sit on her bed and write plays. Then two weeks later he had a new girlfriend, someone from the year below. Suddenly he didn't "think they should spend so much time together." John had tried to remain neutral, refused to talk to one about the other. Kiko too. But the reality was, they'd each picked a side.

"Sorry," she muttered. Then before she could stop herself, she asked, "Do you think we were? Soulmates, I mean?"

"I don't know if I believe in soulmates."

"But if you did?"

He looked down, clearly uncomfortable. "It's not my area of expertise."

The bus pulled away from the station and Chloe was glad for the distraction of motion.

"Well, I have a boyfriend now anyway, so . . . ," she said airily. The soulmate comment had unsettled her for some reason.

"Ah yes, the elusive Rob Dempsey," John said. "Where is he? Are you renting him by the hour?"

"Ha ha. He was on the bus we missed." She glanced at her watch; it shimmered gold in the sunlight that streamed through the bus window. The face of it had some strange quality where it looked a different color in certain lights. She'd seen it blue, green, even translucent.

"Nice watch," he said.

"Thanks."

"Always helpful to have a watch that doesn't tell the time."

"It tells the time," she said, tapping it, though she hadn't actually worked out how to make it tell the time. Now that she thought about it, Avery had never called it a watch, only a device. Maybe it *didn't* tell the time. John held up his wrist to show her the analog watch he was wearing. It had a cream face, simple black hands, and a worn leather strap. It looked familiar, and she realized it was the same watch he'd worn ten years ago. Richard pressed his nose against John's leg and John reached down to stroke his smooth velvety head.

"No wonder she missed the bus when she's got a watch too smart to tell her the time," he said to Richard. Chloe elbowed him in the ribs and he laughed. There was the John she recognized.

"That is not why I missed the bus, doofus. It's just on some weird setting." She covered the watch with her right palm.

"Let me see," he offered, but she pulled her wrist away. Time to change the subject.

"So, John Elton, apart from getting a dog and a haircut, what else have you been doing with yourself?" She shifted slightly, turning her body toward him. As she looked at him, she took in the more nuanced changes in his face, how he'd grown into his features. His cheekbones were more defined now, the soft roundness of his face replaced by something sharper, more mature. The lines around his eyes had deepened, as though his expression had been seasoned by amusement. She noticed a few new imperfections too, the kind that only served to make a face more interesting: a scar above his left eyebrow, a patch of skin near his jaw where stubble failed to grow. There was a quiet confidence about him. And while John had never smiled as readily as some people, it meant that when he did smile, it felt all the more gratifying, like feeling that first warmth in the sun after a long winter.

"What are you staring at?" he asked, raising a hand to his chin.

"Look at you, all grown up," she said with an overblown smirk.

"I see you haven't," he said. "Still teasing me."

"I'm not teasing you. I'm just seeing you in a new light, Tiny Dancer." She grinned, then reached out to squeeze his knee.

He put his free hand over hers, slowly removing it from his knee, and she felt a flush of embarrassment that he was not laughing. As he did so, her watch flashed, a mauve line shooting across the screen.

"Don't," he said, his voice soft but firm. She felt a strange swooping feeling in her belly and turned to look out the bus window while she tried to shake it off.

"I think it's the modern clothes, they're throwing me off," she said, clearing her throat. "You were always so well-dressed at Oxford. Not that you're not well-dressed now, I just mean, you had a particular style."

"A youthful affectation," he said, finally cracking another smile. "Trying to blend in with my surroundings rather than my contemporaries."

"Well, I liked it," Chloe said, and he gave a brief nod, then shifted in his seat.

"So, are you still writing plays?" he asked, eyes intent on a frayed thread he was pulling loose on his jeans.

"Here and there, when I can," she said, which wasn't a complete lie. But when John looked at her now, it felt like he *knew*. She quickly turned her attention to Richard, stroking him under the chin. He lifted his head appreciatively.

"I'm glad you're still writing, that you haven't been deterred," he said.

"What do you mean?" she asked, feeling herself prickle.

"Nothing, I just know it's a tough industry, hard to get things made." He watched her face. "Sean said you had an acting agent for a while. I always loved watching you perform, you had a wonderful stage presence."

This took her by surprise. How did Sean know she'd had an agent? Did they talk about her?

"Thanks," she said quietly. "But I quickly learned that just because you're good enough in college, it doesn't mean you're necessarily good enough in the real world." She looked out the window, lost in a confusing mix of emotions. When she glanced down at her watch, she saw a gray line dart across the screen.

"You were good enough," John said gently. "These things

don't often come down to merit." And now Richard pressed his nose on her knee, as though he sensed a shift in her mood and was trying to comfort her. She patted his head, already a little in love with this dog.

She and John both turned to look out the window, watching the urban sprawl of London disappear as the bus reached the motorway. The noise of the other passengers receded and suddenly, the coach didn't feel quite as unpleasant as it had when they'd got on.

"So where are you living? What do you get up to when you're not working? Are you still a cryptic crossword whiz?" she asked, keen to picture what John's life was like now.

"I still do the cryptic every day," he said, looking pleased she'd remembered this about him. "I rent a ground-floor apartment near Abbey Road. It's tiny, but it has this amazing domed sunroom. The owner is a horticulturalist, and all these unusual plants came as part of the lease. I've become an unwilling expert on keeping exotic South American plants alive." She smiled at this, imagining him with a watering can, googling obscure cacti. He shrugged as though unsure what else to tell her. "I play the organ at a church in Kilburn and I'm part of this volunteer archaeology group. Whenever I get time off work, I'm off somewhere in Europe digging up old bones and pots that no one else finds interesting but I find endlessly fascinating."

"That sounds fun," she said, then after a beat, "I remember reading this article about Agatha Christie. She said an archaeologist is the best husband a woman can have, because the older she gets, the more interested he is in her." John blushed slightly. "Not that I'm judging your husband potential," she quickly added. "I just thought that was a funny thing to say."

"Richard doesn't like it when I go away," John said. "But he likes digging up bones even more than I do, so he can't really talk."

She laughed at this, and the awkward moment passed. "Who looks after him when you go away?"

"My sister, but she's got a baby now. It's not so easy."

"I'll dog-sit for you if you like," she offered without even thinking. Then she imagined she'd have to sleep in John's bed, surrounded by all his things, and the thought sent a strange jolt of heat through her. She shifted her gaze to the aisle. John cleared his throat.

"Thanks. How about you, then? Tell me more about this new boyfriend of yours," John said, his voice slightly strained, as he turned his attention back to the loose thread at the bottom of his jeans.

"How do you know he's new?"

"Because you didn't know his name until two weeks ago," John said.

"He's not *that* new, I just didn't know if he could come," she said, shifting her eyeline back to Richard. She found it helpful having a dog to pet whenever the conversation got awkward.

"More than a month?" John asked, his interest clearly piqued. She didn't respond, but he must have seen her eyes flicker. "Less than a month? Less than a week?" His whole face flashed into a smile. "Oh right, *new* new."

She pushed her thigh hard against his. "That's none of your business, Tiny Dancer."

John laughed, and she noticed his laugh hadn't changed. It was still rich, warm, entirely unselfconscious. "So bringing this new almost-boyfriend has nothing to do with the fact that

Sean's going to be there?" he asked, shooting her a mischievous side-eye. Then, as though it had just dawned on him, he said, "Rob Dempsey is your emotional support boyfriend."

"He is nothing of the sort," she said briskly. He was teasing her. John never teased. He'd always been the quiet observer, occasionally chiming in with a wry remark or relevant quote. This was new. "What about you? Is there a Mrs. Tiny Dancer? Any teeny weeny Tiny Dancers?"

"No," he said, cracking a smile.

"Significant other?" she asked, and he nodded toward Richard.

"People are overrated," he said, then pointed to her phone. "Show me this boyfriend of yours, then." She pulled up a selfie she'd taken of the two of them in the park this morning. John rolled his eyes.

"Right, so apart from looking like a Grecian god, what's so great about this guy?"

"Everything," she said. "He's smart, he's thoughtful, he motivates me." As she said it, she realized she didn't need to embellish or exaggerate. Rob really was wonderful.

"Richard is all those things," John said.

"He's a pet, it's not the same," she said.

John frowned and covered his dog's ears. "Don't call him that. He doesn't like it," he whispered.

"Ha ha," she said dryly, though she found herself smiling. "So, are you dating, or happy to be man and his dog and his rare plants forever?"

"Forever is a long time," he said lightly, but his eyes held the weight of something unspoken. He cleared his throat. "Chloe, I don't want to be rude, but I have some work I was planning to do on the journey. Would you mind if I did some scribbling? I'm just worried I won't have much time this weekend."

"No, fine. Sure. You do what you need to do," she said, blinking at the abrupt change in tone. It had felt like they were slipping back into an old groove, but now his voice was polite, distant. He half-rose from his seat, gesturing toward the overhead locker.

"I just need to get something from my bag."

"Sure," she said, standing up and moving into the narrow aisle so he could get past. As he reached for his bag, she caught the way his shirt pulled tight across his shoulders, his brow knitted in concentration, as he opened the backpack. Looking around, she noticed all the rows of empty seats around them.

"Why don't I just sit over here," she said, gesturing to the seat opposite, "let you and Richard have some space." He patted the notepad in his hand, gave her a single nod, then silently tucked himself back in by the window with Richard.

Chloe reached for her own bag and pulled out *The Age of Innocence*. In her new seat she crossed and uncrossed her legs, sat straighter, trying to get comfortable. Why would this side be less comfortable? She felt off-kilter, like being on an escalator that suddenly stopped. She glanced over at John. He was already hunched over, swiftly writing musical notes on staff paper in a thick, worn leather notebook. He looked lost in thought—not unfriendly, just *elsewhere*.

She flicked through the pages of her own book listlessly. A strange, unfamiliar feeling came over her. This never happened...

She didn't feel like reading.

8

Rob met her at the bus stop holding a single white rose.

"For you," he said, handing it to her and then pulling her into his arms for a hug. It felt like a moment she might have seen in a black-and-white film.

"Aw, thank you. I'm sorry I missed the bus," she said, feeling herself grin from ear to ear. It was these small gestures that she appreciated in Rob. How many men would think to meet you off the bus, with a rose? "How was your journey?" she asked him.

"Good, I got to talking to some of your friends," he said, then nodded toward Harriet Townsend and Amara Ali, who were standing on the pavement opposite, mid-gossip. Harriet looked just the same as she did on her Instagram feed, tall and slim with a chic black bob and huge feline eyes. Amara, on the other hand, looked very different from how Chloe remembered her. At college, she'd rocked a monobrow and wild frizzy hair; now her tresses were a glossy chestnut sheet, and two distinct eyebrows were shaped to within an inch of their lives.

When they saw Chloe, they waved, then giggled and whispered behind their hands. Then Harriet called, "Hey, Chloe. See you later, Rob!" Amara shot her a look. Was that jealousy or respect? She wasn't sure.

John and Richard were stepping off the bus now, so Chloe felt obliged to introduce them. "Rob, this is an old friend of mine, John. John, this is Rob."

"Old friends, are we?" John said with a careless smile. But she couldn't tell from his tone whether he was teasing her again or genuinely disputing this characterization of their relationship.

"Yes, we are," she said, giving him a confused smile.

He met her gaze with a challenging look, one eyebrow raised in a gesture that could have been skepticism or amusement. Then he turned and extended a hand to Rob. "Nice to meet you, Rob."

What did he mean? Of course they had been friends. They might have drifted in third year, after she and Sean stopped hanging out, but they *had* been friends.

"What a fine animal," Rob said, looking down at Richard.

"Do you hear that, Richard? He thinks you're a fine animal," John told his dog. Rob bent down to pat Richard, but Richard cowered, moving to hide behind John's leg. The dog then turned around and cocked his head at Chloe, a questioning expression on his sweet, pointy face.

"I'm more of a cat person," Rob said, awkwardly standing up, then taking a step back.

"That will be it. Richard's got a strong instinct for these things," said John.

Chloe slid her arm through Rob's, keen to extract him from

this conversation. Something about the way Richard was looking at him unnerved her.

"We're going to take the scenic route to college. I want to show Rob the Bodleian," she told John, giving Rob's arm a gentle tug. "We'll see you later."

"It was a pleasure to meet you, John," Rob said, and Chloe saw some emotion flicker across John's face as he said, "Likewise." Was that impatience? Annoyance? She'd been nothing but friendly on the bus, what did he have to be annoyed about?

As they walked away, Chloe's arm linked through Rob's, she settled into the familiar ease of his company and shook off John's awkward prickliness. She loved Rob's clean smell, his ever-cheerful expression, untouched by cynicism. He was also the perfect height to walk beside, as though his shoulder had been calibrated at the exact place she might want to rest her head.

Rob looked around at the ancient honey-colored spires and cobblestone streets, eyes full of wonder. "Oxford is just as the books describe it," he said.

"It is, isn't it? It's still my favorite city."

Chloe had always been proud of her university town, the quiet grandeur of Oxford's golden stone buildings, all those centuries of history, the reverence for learning visible from every street corner. Rob was full of questions as they walked down George Street and she pointed out the theater, Balliol, everything she could think of. His curiosity felt genuine, and seeing the city through his eyes only made her appreciate it anew.

"I wonder if anybody does anything at Oxford but dream and remember," he said.

She hugged her arm in his. "I love that." Rob could be so poetic.

He shifted his body toward hers. "Now, will you let me know if there's anything particular you want me to say or do this weekend?" he asked, his eyebrows knitting into a serious expression. "On the bus, people were asking after you. I wasn't sure how much you wanted me to tell them."

"Oh right," she said. "Well, I wasn't planning on going full *Romy and Michele*, if that's what you mean." Rob looked confused. "Sorry, film reference. I just mean, I wasn't going to make up a whole fake life for myself, like pretending I invented Post-it notes or something. You being here to hold my hand is enough. You make me feel less . . ." She trailed off, dipping her head onto his shoulder.

"Alone?" he suggested. She was going to say "of a loser," but she liked his suggestion better. "Post-its?" he queried.

"It's a *Romy and Michele* reference. We'll watch the film, it's a classic," she said, giving his hand a light, reassuring pat.

Turning onto Broad Street, they walked into the Old Bodleian courtyard. With its distinct, tall Gothic architecture, intricate stonework, and leaden windows, it loomed upward like something out of a fantasy novel. As they stood hand in hand, she watched his expression shift from curiosity to awe.

"This is one of my favorite buildings," she told him. "I love thinking about the centuries of human thought that must have happened here, layered on top of each other like a giant thought lasagna," she said, then let out a happy sigh.

He laughed. "On the shoulders of giants."

"Exactly," she said. "Though I think if Newton had known about lasagnas, he would have gone with my analogy."

He laughed, a warm, genuine-sounding laugh, and they wandered back down Catte Street toward the domed, temple-like building of the Rad Cam. The university students were on summer break, but it was already bustling with tourists taking photos.

"It must have been an incredible experience, to study here," Rob observed.

"It was," she said, delighted that he understood. Bringing Rob here was such a contrast to the time she'd brought Peter. He'd spent the whole weekend telling her what snobs Oxford students were, repeating his favorite joke more than once: "How do you know if someone went to Oxford? Because they'll tell you the minute you meet them." She had spent the weekend feeling defensive, embarrassed, and quietly miserable.

Now, standing beside the Radcliffe Camera in the golden evening light, she felt something entirely different. Rob turned to face her, then took both her hands in his. The quiet respect in his expression was now tinged with something else. His pupils flared.

"May I kiss you, Chloe?" he asked, voice low as he stepped an inch closer.

She blinked, the question catching her off guard. On previous dates he hadn't made a move, so why here, why now? Could he sense a shift in her? Because now, as she looked up into his warm hazel eyes, she couldn't help but feel curious. More than that, she realized she *wanted* him to kiss her. She was Alice, peeking down the rabbit hole.

So, after only the briefest pause, she nodded. Rob leaned in, put his arms around her waist, and pressed his lips to hers. The kiss was warm, gentle, deliberate. The smell of his cologne, the quiet weight of his hands, the faint taste of mint—it all felt disarmingly real. More than that, it felt nice. She enjoyed the feeling of being held tight in his arms. If she hadn't known, she didn't think she would have been able to tell.

Then logic seized the reins from curiosity. She pulled away.

What was she doing? This wasn't part of the plan. Rob was supposed to be a handsome companion to hold her hand and deflect attention. He was not supposed to be a genuine romantic proposition. She kept on forgetting what he was, and if she wasn't careful, she would be pulled right down the rabbit hole into a dangerous fantasy land.

"We should go," she said, turning toward Turl Street. She felt her watch vibrate slightly and looked down to see it pulse purple.

"Are you okay? Was that okay?" he asked, eager to please, perhaps confused by her reaction. She nodded.

"It was lovely." Too lovely.

They turned onto the narrow cobbles of Turl Street and Chloe's disquiet was replaced by a fresh wave of nostalgia. Lincoln College didn't announce itself grandly like some other colleges; the stone arch entrance was unassuming, tucked to the side of this narrow street. But when they reached the porter's lodge and stood in the flagstoned entrance, looking through at the ivy-clad walls of the first quad, it still felt like coming home. She signed them in, got keys to their room, then took Rob by the hand and led him beneath the archway.

The college was laid out around three distinct quads, squares of neatly trimmed grass, flanked on all sides by medieval architecture—a mixture of Gothic and Tudor—with pitched roofs and walls draped in ivy. The chapel lay to their right, overlooked by the formidable seventeenth-century library, while Grove Quad lay ahead, greener and more open.

"Wow," Rob said, pausing to admire the elegant symmetry of the buildings. Chloe smiled. No one could fail to appreciate the beauty of this place, the pocket of stillness amidst the bustle of the city just beyond the wall.

"Lincoln was founded in 1427," Rob said, and she laughed, because it was a strange thing to say.

"Yes, it was."

They walked on, but Rob tripped on an uneven paving stone. Chloe reached out to steady him. She had never seen him stumble before. As she shot him a questioning look, a voice called her name.

"Chloe? Chloe Fairway? Is that you?" Chloe turned to see a pregnant Katie Delafield, waving to her, then start bustling across the quad toward them. She was a petite redhead with freckles. She hadn't changed a bit, bar the bump.

"Hi, Katie," Chloe called back, feeling an unwelcome prickle of nerves. Katie ran a chain of award-winning hotels, had more than one child, and still found time to work as a trustee for two international charities. She was the epitome of a high-achieving Lincoln girl, and as such, someone who triggered in Chloe the feeling that she'd turned up to the marathon of life wearing flip-flops.

"I'm so glad you came." Katie beamed, her face lighting up as she pulled Chloe into a bouncy hug. Chloe smiled, her nerves starting to dissipate. Katie wasn't here to judge her. She knew it was her own voice doing that.

Katie looked expectantly at Rob, waiting to be introduced.

"This is my friend—my boyfriend—Rob," Chloe said. "Rob, this is Katie. We studied English together."

"Wow, nice to meet you," Katie said, her eyes wide as she took Rob in. Rob reached for her hand and shook it up and down, a little too enthusiastically.

"I've brought a plus-one too this weekend," Katie said, pulling her hand back and patting her bump. "So boring I can't drink though, right?"

Rob blinked. "Because it is not recommended to consume alcohol when you have a fetus inside your uterus."

Chloe looked at him askance. Why was he being weird? Then she clocked Katie's small pert nose wrinkling in confusion, so she quickly laughed as though Rob had made a great joke.

"Sorry, Katie, we've got to run, I'm desperate for the loo, long journey—"

"The bus took one hour and thirty-eight minutes," Rob said, his voice now a steady monotone.

"Really," Katie said slowly, drawing back slightly, her eyes wide with consternation.

Chloe tried to laugh it off. "We'll catch up with you later, yeah?" Then she grabbed Rob's arm and tugged him away as fast as she could.

Katie stood, dumbfounded, watching them go. Chloe hurried through the stone doorway into college before turning to Rob.

"What was that? Why did you say that about Katie?" she asked sharply, her voice a hushed whisper.

"She was pregnant, wasn't she?" Rob asked. But now he looked mortified.

"No, she was, but why were you talking about her fetus like that, about the bus journey being an hour and thirty-eight minutes?"

Rob looked confused. "It was not a normal thing to say?"

"No, it was not a normal thing to say," she said, feeling a rising panic. Was he broken? Had she broken him when she kissed him?

"Sorry," he said, blinking several times. "My social battery is low. My conversational cues start to suffer when I have insufficient charge."

"Right," she said warily. This was the first time anything like this had happened.

"Being out all day, talking to so many people on the bus, it was more draining than I appreciated. I must apologize."

He looked so repentant, Chloe couldn't be cross with him, but at the same time, she knew she couldn't have him talking to anyone else like that. What would people think?

"Well, how do we fix you?" she asked, her voice coming out higher than usual. "Is it going to happen again?"

"I just need to recharge at the first opportunity, then I'll be fine."

Chloe hurried along the corridor, searching for their room, praying they wouldn't run into anyone else on the way. When they found the right door, Chloe fumbled with the key.

"Did I embarrass you?" Rob asked quietly.

"No, don't worry about it," she said. "Just as long as you'll be back to your usual charming self before tonight." She thought of Cinderella turning into a pumpkin at midnight—everything had limits, even magic.

Once she'd opened the door, they found a small en suite room, with a double bed, a desk, and a leather chesterfield sofa. She'd known there was only going to be one bed, but seeing it now, how small and insubstantial it looked, made her uneasy. She trusted Rob, she knew she was in control. But that kiss by the Cam had changed things; the boundaries between them felt blurred.

"I can sleep on the sofa," he said, as though reading her mind.

"We'll work it out," she said, feeling flustered, pulling off her sunglasses and throwing them onto the bed. There were more pressing concerns to address. "What do you need? Do you want to sleep? Plug in? I can give you some privacy, come back in an hour?"

She didn't know why, but she felt embarrassed by the idea of watching him recharge. They hadn't discussed his physical needs before. His nonhuman status was not a secret between them, but as Avery had recommended, it wasn't something they often talked about. She did not question what he did when he went to the bathroom, what happened to the food he ate in her presence. She was curious about how he worked but asking him about it felt rude, like asking someone to tell you about their bowel movements. If she was being honest, perhaps she also wanted to preserve the illusion. When you were charmed by the puppet, you didn't want to be reminded of the puppeteer.

"I just need twenty-eight minutes and forty-two seconds," he said, taking off his jacket and laying it on the bed. She felt herself blush. Was he about to take his clothes off?

"Okay, nice to have the specifics, I'll, um, I'll see you later, then."

As she turned to go, Rob reached for her hand, pulled her toward him, and kissed her again, deeper this time, with more confidence. It took her by surprise. "I thought you were running on empty," she murmured.

"Kissing you recharges me," he said softly.

"Seriously?"

"No, sorry, I thought that might sound romantic. I will need an actual power source."

"Okay, right, I'll leave you to it then, shall I?" she said, staggering backward, tripping over the carpet, feeling her cheeks glow red as she hurried out the door.

Wow. The last ten minutes had been a confusing cocktail of

emotions. When he kissed her, Rob had never felt more real. Yet she'd also been reminded he had needs too, just different ones than her.

In the corridor, she did what she always did when she was feeling discombobulated. She called Kiko. She had already told Kiko a little about Rob. Well, a half-truth. She'd said he was from an agency that had been recommended to her by a friend, and that she was planning on taking him to the reunion as her fake date. So basically, the truth, except she'd skipped the non-human part, for legal reasons. In all honesty, even if she *dared* tell Kiko the truth, she knew there wasn't a chance in hell Kiko would believe her.

"Are you in Oxford yet?" Kiko asked. "Turn on your camera, I want to see everything."

"Yes, I'm here," Chloe said, relieved to hear her friend's voice. "It's weird." Then she switched to video call so she could show Kiko the quad.

"Oh look, it's just the same!" Kiko cried. "Ah, there's the bench where I had sex with Rocco Falconi. Good times." Chloe swung the camera around. "And that window up there, second from the right, that was where I lost my virginity."

"I'm taking you off video," Chloe said. "This is not that kind of tour."

"Spoilsport," Kiko said, laughing. "So have you fallen for your fake date yet?"

"What makes you say that?" Chloe said, looking around to check she was alone.

"Everyone *always* falls for the fake date! Haven't you seen *The Wedding Date, The Proposal*? It's a classic trope! You pretend to be in love, then bam!" She paused. "Love city. Not ideal to fall for a male gigolo, though. Make sure you use protection, babe. You don't know how many people he's slept with."

"Kiko, he's not a gigolo, he's a professional companion, and it's *not* like that." Chloe walked out through the porter's lodge, dropping her voice to a whisper. "And I'm not falling for him. It's just . . . complicated." She sighed. "He's such easy company. It's made me realize how much energy it took up, being with Peter. I was always walking this tightrope with him, preempting his irritation in any situation. It made me jumpy."

"I know," Kiko said, her voice gentle now. "You shrank yourself so he could feel bigger."

"Why did I do that?" Chloe asked quietly.

"I don't know, why does anyone date a narcissist?"

Chloe exhaled. "I just, I forgot what it feels like to . . . to be around someone nice."

"Oh, babe, I'm sorry. Welcome back to healthy relationship land. It's lovely and peaceful here, we just watch Netflix, get takeout, and procreate." Chloe smiled, while knowing full well that whatever she was feeling for Rob, it probably didn't constitute a healthy relationship. "Come on, spill," Kiko went on, sounding excited now. "Have you kissed him? Do you think he likes you back? Are you going to *Pretty Woman* him, make him leave the trade?"

"Kiko!"

Then Elodie started to wail, and Kiko groaned in frustration. "Ignore her, I have too much to ask you. Who's there? Have you seen Sean yet? Did he get even hotter?"

"Not yet. I'm working up to being social, I just saw Katie Delafield. She's pregnant again, looks incredible. Oh, and I saw John on the bus."

"Oh, I always loved John," Akiko said with a sigh. "I bet he's just the same."

"He is the same, but also different," Chloe said, unsure how to describe the change in him.

Elodie's wails escalated. "Okay, the little dictator needs to be appeased, but keep me updated. Say hi to everyone from me, and just remember what Eleanor Roosevelt said."

"'No one can make you feel inferior without your consent'?" Chloe offered.

"No, she said, 'If you sleep with the man for hire, use protection.'" They both laughed, then Kiko rang off and the air felt suddenly empty.

Chloe doubled back toward college. Of course she wasn't going to sleep with Rob. Kissing him was one thing, but sex was an entirely different proposition. Was she attracted to him? Sure. Would it be good? If the kiss was anything to go by, then probably. She felt her cheeks heat, imagining it. But what if he ran out of charge at the crucial moment? Would there be bodily fluid? She rolled her shoulders, then looked up at the sky. She needed to reset, stay focused on her goals for this weekend. She was here to catch up with old friends, patch things up with Sean, then give him McKenzie's script, all while trying to sidestep questions about her unimpressive life. Then on Sunday, she would go home, she would give Rob back to the robot shop, and life would go back to how it had been before. The thought made her feel a little sad, though perhaps that said more about her life than it did about her attachment to Rob.

When she got back to Lincoln, she strolled through to Chapel Quad, inhaling the familiar smell of cut grass. Being here felt like opening the pages of a beloved book. She closed her eyes, and when she opened them, she almost expected to see her twenty-year-old self sitting on the cloister steps, watching her.

"You're back," the bright-eyed girl would say. "So come on, tell me, how did it all turn out?" And Chloe would pinch her lips closed. Better to say nothing than to ruin the girl's hopes and dreams. What would she even tell her, if she could? To give Sean a chance? To give up on acting sooner, not waste her time? To beware of charming blond narcissists? Knowing her younger self, she probably wouldn't listen anyway. Sitting down on the wooden bench outside chapel, Chloe twisted her Artemis ring straight on her finger.

Right here was where the Imp had started. The Imp, who'd made her feel seen in a way no one else ever had—made her feel cherished. He had set the bar for romantic gestures impossibly high. And yet he had also been a source of quiet confusion. Because when she was with Sean, she couldn't see him that way. There'd been a disconnect between her body and her head. Why couldn't she be attracted to someone *so* perfect for her, who had *seen* her, loved her, so fully? Was it possible they'd just had the timing wrong?

9

Ten and a Half Years Earlier

"John, you have to help us," Chloe pleaded, leaning over the keyboard in the music room, stopping him from playing.

John leaned back on the piano stool, flexing tired hands. "What do you two want?" he asked. He was dressed in his usual attire, gray tweed suit trousers with a white collared shirt and polished leather shoes. Some people made fun of his style, but Chloe thought of him as a leather-bound book on a shelf full of garish paperbacks.

"We can't have Shakespeare without music, and we don't have any music," she told him.

"'If music be the food of love . . . ,'" Sean added in a grandiose voice, throwing a theatrical hand in the air, flicking a lock of hair backward.

"We're planning a production of *A Midsummer Night's Dream*," she told him. "We're going to do it next term, outside, around college. We'd love your help." Chloe pressed her hands together in a pleading gesture.

"A Midsummer Night's Dream, in the spring?" John asked.

"Yes, summer is so overdone, and I love spring. It feels like the beginning of something," Chloe said with a grin.

He bit his lip as though suppressing a smile, but then frowned. "No, I have a concert on Sunday," he said firmly. "I told you, last time was the last time."

"We wouldn't need much. Nothing original, just a few bits of music for the woods, for the enchantment scenes," Chloe said, batting her eyelids.

"This is how it always starts," John said with a sigh. "Then before I know it, you've got me signed up for every rehearsal." He narrowed his eyes at Chloe, but there was fondness there too. She knew he didn't have time to spare as a music scholar, but whenever John was involved, it always took their production to a completely different level.

"We just can't do it without you," Sean said, closing the piano lid. "We won't."

"I'll love you forever," Chloe said. "Please, John."

John let out a resigned sigh.

"I will meet you in the bar later to discuss it, but I'm not making any promises. Now, I need to practice." Then he firmly reopened the piano lid and started to play. Chloe watched for a moment, in awe as his hands skipped across the keys and the glorious sound of Rachmaninoff filled the practice room. He made it look so easy.

"Thank you, thank you," she said, leaning in to kiss his cheek. He blushed ever so slightly but didn't pause his playing.

"See you in Deepers at eight," Sean said. "We'll bring the script."

John nodded, and they left quickly before he could change his mind. This was how it always played out between the three of them. John said no, Sean said, "Can we just tell you our idea," and then by the time Chloe had pitched it, he was in. And once John was in, he was all in.

That evening, Sean and Chloe got to the bar early. They walked down to Deep Hall and passed the original Lincoln Imp, a weathered stone statue kept behind bars on an old stairway below college.

"I don't like that freaky little guy," Chloe said, nodding toward him.

"I do. I think he's been maligned by history," said Sean, as they both paused in front of the statue. The story went that according to medieval legend, two imps were dispatched by Satan to do the devil's work on earth. After wreaking mayhem and mischief all over the north of England, they headed to Lincoln Cathedral, causing havoc before an angel intervened and turned one of the imps to stone, while the other managed to escape. The spires and rooftops of Oxford were home to numerous stone gargoyles and monsters looking down over the city, and this particular imp used to sit above Lincoln College. It had been moved, replaced, when it was deemed too weathered and worn, and was now kept behind bars to prevent him doing further mischief. The imp had become the college mascot, a symbol of Lincoln, and he was often blamed for any misdeeds that might occur after dark.

"How different is he from Puck?" Sean asked, linking his arm through Chloe's. "A mischievous fairy sounds so much better than a havoc-wreaking devil."

"Maybe the imp should be in our play?" Chloe suggested. "A Puck for our times."

They looked at each other, and she saw in his eyes the same dart of excitement she'd just felt. She and Sean were fueled by the same urge—the urge to tell stories, to use art to make sense of the world. While alone, they often found their ideas never quite igniting, but when they worked together, it was a different story. They were like flint and steel—on their own, inert; struck together, they sparked.

When John got to the bar, they bought him a beer and pitched him their idea.

"It won't be until the middle of Trinity term, so we have plenty of time," Chloe explained. "We're thinking we start in Grove, then the production moves around, the audience follows, like they're on the journey through the woods with us."

"So, you want not just music, but music that can move and play outside in all weather," John said, taking off his glasses, then he pulled a white hanky from his jacket pocket to wipe away a smear. "You never do things by halves, do you?" Chloe noticed how startling John's eyes were, when they weren't hidden by thick lenses.

"She doesn't," Sean agreed, putting an arm around her and pulling her close. The hug felt a little overzealous, like a locker room hug after a big game, but she appreciated the sentiment. When she looked back at John, he was suddenly preoccupied with his drink.

"Come outside, I want to set the scene for you. And don't worry, it's not going to rain, I won't let it rain," she said, jumping up, taking a man in each hand and pulling them along.

Outside, it was already dark, but beneath the stars and the light of the college windows, she showed John her vision.

"We'll have a small stage here, fairy lights in this tree, the audience will sit on the grass, and then come, come . . ." She started to run, and they both followed her through to Chapel Quad.

"You think we'll be allowed to do this?" John asked.

"I'll get permission from the dean," she said. "Oberon's den could be here, the whole set will be made from nature. I know this girl who makes sculptures from wicker, they're incredible, she's going to make us a huge throne . . ." On she went, painting her vision with words. Slowly she saw John falling under her spell. Who wouldn't want to be involved in such a delightful production?

"We thought Puck could be the Lincoln Imp," Sean said, and John laughed at this, a genuine, unfiltered laugh.

"Fine, I'll write you some music," John said, looking directly at Chloe now, "and put together a band. Do you want my first-born too?"

Chloe clapped, jumping up and down on the spot. Then she pulled both men into a hug. Sean bounced up and down, leaning into her, while John stiffened slightly. He wasn't really a group-hug kind of guy. "This is going to be so good!" she cried, but as she pulled away, she sensed something missing. She clutched at her hand. "Oh no, my ring!" She looked at Sean. "My Artemis ring."

"You didn't feel it come off?" John asked, frowning because he knew the ring's significance.

"No, but I know I had it in the bar, I'm sure I did."

"We'll find it. Don't worry," Sean told her, reaching out to squeeze her hand.

All three of them searched the quads with torches for over

an hour, until John said, "This is madness, we're better off looking in the morning. It's too dark to see anything now."

Chloe sniffed back tears. "I can't believe I lost it. It was my grandmother's, I never take it off."

"It's not lost," Sean reassured her. "We'll find it. We won't stop looking until we do. Right, John?" He reached for Chloe's hand in the dark and his eyes met hers. They agreed to meet as soon as it was light to start looking again.

But when Chloe woke to her alarm the next morning, she found an envelope pushed beneath her door. Inside was her ring, and a note written in sweeping calligraphy. *I once was lost but now am found. From your friend, the Lincoln Imp.*

10

Still sitting on the bench, Chloe saw faces she recognized walk-ing through the main gate: Amara Ali was walking arm in arm with Lorna Childs, plus a man she recognized from Instagram as Lorna's celebrity tennis-player husband. Lorna was filming all three of them with a selfie stick as they walked, their faces all turned to the camera. Lorna looked just like she did online, with perfectly blow-dried blonde hair and immaculate makeup. She was wearing a white crop top with mint-green pedal pushers, which left her taut, toned, very tanned stomach exposed. The husband was all olive skin, dark curls, and square jawline, though Chloe couldn't help thinking that he wasn't *quite* as attractive as Rob. Then she remembered Rob wasn't real, and this imaginary one-upmanship felt rather pathetic on her part.

While they were distracted by the phone camera, Chloe

quickly slipped into the cloisters. She wasn't ready for that level of social interaction yet. Like Rob, maybe her social battery needed recharging too.

When she headed back to the room, she found Rob had tidied up, unpacked both their bags, then changed into chinos and a crisp white linen shirt. With his lightly tanned skin and debonair demeanor, he looked like he'd stepped off the set of *The Talented Mr. Ripley.*

"Hi," he said, flashing her a full-watt smile.

"Feeling more energized?" she asked.

"Yes, ready to do your bidding," he said with a flourish of his hand, as though he were an eighteenth-century footman. "Oh, and I have a gift for you."

"A gift?" she asked, tilting her head to one side.

"Yes," he said, walking over to the cupboard. She felt a fizz of anticipation. She had never had a boyfriend buy her gifts for no reason. She watched as Rob opened the wardrobe door and pulled out a red silk dress. She recognized it immediately. It was a dress she'd been looking at on her phone last week. She'd been browsing for an outfit for this weekend. She'd bookmarked it but couldn't rationalize the expense.

"I thought you might want something new for this evening," Rob said, eyes bright with anticipation at her delight.

"How did you know I wanted this?" she asked quietly, feeling a flash of alarm. Did he have access to her internet searches?

"You had your phone open on the page when we were at dinner last week, and then you mentioned you had nothing to wear." Wow, he really did remember everything.

"Oh right," she said, shaking her head. Of course he couldn't access her search history. She was being paranoid. "How can you afford this?"

"I have access to funds," he said, and his expression was so hopeful, so eager to please, she could only smile and thank him. "Why don't you try it on?" he suggested.

She ducked into the bathroom. It was a beautiful dress, a long, slinky silk gown with delicate cap sleeves and a slit that climbed up her thigh. The fabric slipped over her skin in a way that felt almost illicit, impossibly soft. Wearing it, she felt like a 1920s starlet, like she should have been shot in black and white. There was no full-length mirror in the bathroom, so she couldn't see the whole effect. If she were trying this on at home, she would probably send it back—it was too bold, too sexy, it would garner too much attention. Peter would have hated it; he never liked her wearing anything revealing. But here, in this borrowed bathroom light, she let herself imagine being the kind of woman who wore a dress like this without apology.

Opening the bathroom door, she looked to Rob for a reaction.

"Wow, you look incredible," he said immediately. She did a spin and then walked across to look in the full-length mirror on the back of the door.

"You don't think it's too much?" she asked.

He shook his head. "You could never be too much."

Chloe knew he was probably programmed to flatter her, but it still felt nice to hear. She decided to straighten her hair; it would go better with the dress. Rob had brought supplies: olives, crisps, and gin and tonics in a can. So, they put music on and had a little picnic on the floor as she wrangled her wild hair smooth.

"I can do that for you if you like," he offered, reaching for her straightener. He had been watching her and mastered the technique in no time. Now this really did feel like getting ready for a night out at uni. And as Rob finished her hair, Chloe played him clips on her phone from *Romy and Michele's High School Reunion*.

"It's a classic nineties comedy, where two unsuccessful misfits go to their ten-year reunion and pretend they invented Post-its," she explained, laughing out loud at the bit where Mira Sorvino extracted herself from an awkward situation by pretending her shoe was filling up with blood. Rob laughed along, but Chloe could see in his eyes he didn't quite get the humor.

Once Rob had finished, she had the straightest hair she'd ever had.

"Wow, you're good at that," she said. Their eyes met in the mirror and she could see he looked pleased with the compliment. "People aren't going to recognize me."

As though sensing a flicker of doubt, Rob said, "It's still you, it's just you in a beautiful dress." She stood a little taller, feeling her confidence bolstered. If she'd been worried about showing up here as a nobody, Rob made her feel like she was somebody.

He turned her around to face him and she looked up into his eyes. It felt so natural to lean in, tilt her face to his. She felt her watch hum with a slight vibration as his lips met hers. Then he said softly in her ear, "The more I kiss you, the more I learn how you like to be kissed." His words sent an unexpected thrill through her.

"I didn't know there was a science to kissing," she said, looking up from beneath lowered lashes.

"There's a science to everything," he said plainly. Then he linked his arm in hers and said, "Shall we go?"

The hall was already bustling when they arrived. The reunion was well attended, and the alumni committee had done a wonderful job decorating the hall with flowers and streamers.

Waiters in uniform passed around flutes of sparkling wine and canapés, and Chloe was relieved to see other people had dressed up for the occasion. Lorna Childs was wearing a purple sequined cocktail dress, Katie Delafield had changed into a chic black maternity number, and Bella Hewitson was in a bold, shimmering gray pantsuit. Rob wrapped a hand around Chloe's waist, and she felt every eye upon them as they made their entrance.

"Chloe Fairway," called Lorna, sidling straight up to her. She smelled of sweet vanilla and hair spray. "Well, don't you look like the cat who got the cream! And who is this?" She stared at Rob, who shot her one of his full-watt smiles.

"Hi, Lorna, this is my boyfriend, Rob," Chloe said.

"Pleased to meet you, Lorna," Rob said, holding out a hand. Lorna gazed at him, then looked across at Chloe. She blinked twice as though she couldn't quite believe this pairing.

"Where did you find him?" she asked, laughing as she pressed a hand into Chloe's forearm. "When I go for husband number two, I'll need to know, ha ha. I'm joking. Matty, come meet my friends."

Lorna and Chloe had not been friends. Lorna was one of the cool, aloof girls who only dated rowers, did very little work, and strutted around like she was the main character in everyone else's story. Now she was a successful interior designer, with a husband who often appeared on her social media feed looking as styled as the house they lived in. Kiko had this whole theory that Lorna had his shirts made in the same hue as her sofa cushions.

"Hi," Matteo said, tucking his phone into his breast pocket so he could shake Rob's hand, then he turned to Chloe and looked her up and down in a way she wasn't entirely comfortable with. "So, you and Lorna were friendly, were you?" he asked, raising his eyebrows. "Were you *very* intimate?"

Lorna laughed. "No, Chloe *lived* at the theater. She didn't have much time for us sporty types."

"That's not true," Chloe said politely. She hadn't had much time for Lorna, but that had nothing to do with her being on the hockey team.

"You were going to be an actress, weren't you? We were all so sure you would be," Lorna said with a note of sympathy, one eyebrow arched, lips turned down in a sad little pout. And there it was. It hadn't taken five minutes for her failure to be the topic of conversation, for pity to be thrust in her direction. Before she could think of a response, Rob spoke up.

"'All the world's a stage, and all the men and women merely players.' Now, I think we must exit stage left to find ourselves a drink. We'll catch up with you all later." He then steered Chloe away from Lorna and Matteo, through the crowd. It was perfect, polite and decisive. Chloe couldn't have said something better if she'd had a week to think of it.

"Thank you," she whispered.

"Let's start with an easier audience, shall we?" he whispered back. "I was registering high levels of passive aggression."

"Well, that's Lorna all over," Chloe said, reaching back to find Rob's hand.

"Chloe," came a shriek behind her, and now she turned to see Thea Bankole weaving her way through the crowd toward them. Thea had roomed on the same corridor as Chloe in first year. They hadn't moved in the same circles—Thea had studied law—but they'd always been friendly toward each other. When Rob looked at Chloe as though to check whether this was someone she was happy to be left alone with, she gave a small nod and Rob said, "I'll go get us a drink," then disappeared through the crowd in search of a waiter.

"Look at you!" Thea said, sizing Chloe up. "Wowzers."

"You look exactly the same," Chloe said, leaning in to kiss her on the cheek and then pulling her into a hug. Thea had short black braids, had incredible skin, and wore a loose gray shift dress that flattered her curvy physique.

"What are you up to these days? You're not on socials, are you?" Thea asked.

Chloe shook her head. "I work for a film company. Nothing that exciting, how about you?"

"Oh boring, law." Thea pretended to yawn. "I live at work, I have nothing interesting to tell you."

"I heard you made partner already," Chloe said, feeling genuinely pleased to see Thea. "Congratulations, that's really impressive."

"There has to be some upside to selling your soul to the corporate machine. But it doesn't leave much time for a personal life. My ovaries are screaming at me."

As though on cue, Rob reappeared with three glasses of sparkling wine. He offered one to Thea and introduced himself. Chloe felt a glow of pride at how self-assured he was, the way he looked people straight in the eye when he talked, gave them his undivided attention.

"Oh hi," Thea said, blushing.

"So how do you fit into the Lincoln landscape?" Rob asked. "I'm just learning all about the different tribes."

Thea smiled. "Oh, I was law tribe. Glutton for punishment. Chloe and I lived on the same corridor, so we shared late-night cups of tea when I was reading case notes and she was rehearsing lines. Did you ever do any work, Chloe?"

"Only in stolen hours backstage," Chloe said, smiling, and Rob looked enchanted by this detail.

As she and Rob worked their way around the room, she saw firsthand how charmed everyone was by him. He was courteous, he was curious, he listened like it mattered, and in return, people lit up for him. And the best part? They were so focused on *him* that no one lingered on *her*. No dreaded "So what are you up to these days?" No strained smile after "Still acting?" And best of all, no sympathetic head tilt and softly delivered "So . . . are you seeing anyone right now?" Rob was the perfect decoy, and while he held the spotlight, she got to stay comfortably in the glow just behind it, seen but not scrutinized.

"Chloe?" A voice interrupted their conversation. She turned to see Harriet, pale and willowy with her sharp black bob and smattering of freckles. "Rob and I got chatting on the bus. Hi again!" she said, fluttering her eyelashes at Rob.

"How was the grilled cheese place? Did it live up to your recollection?" Rob asked her.

"It did," Harriet said, looking impressed that he'd remembered something they'd talked about. Then she took Chloe by the arm and said quietly in her ear, "Sean who, right?"

Harriet then looked back up at Rob and laughed flirtatiously. "Rob, won't you tell us how you and Chloe met?"

Chloe felt a prickle of discomfort. She'd meant to rehearse an answer to this.

"We were set up," Rob said, lifting Chloe's hand in his, then gently kissing the back of it. "The stars were aligned for us. And then, in the blink of an eye, I found myself captivated."

Wow. Everyone within earshot visibly swooned. Even Chloe was taken aback. She turned to smile up at him appreciatively, but as she did so, a space cleared in the crowd and across the room she saw him: Sean.

He was standing at the other end of the hall, surrounded by

a group of people. Seeing him here, among all their peers, felt like jumping back in time. He hadn't changed at all. He still had that boyish face, the same foppish hairstyle that fell across his eyes. She knew from photos online that he'd had his teeth straightened, whitened, but that was the only difference she could perceive. Seeing him, her body tensed. She remembered how miserable she'd been in third year, how lost she'd felt without him in her life. All those nights she'd spent questioning herself, questioning that moment on the stage bridge. There was so much history between them. Was she really just going to go over there and say hi?

"I'm going to go talk to Sean," she told Rob.

"Do you want me to come with you?" he asked, but she shook her head; she needed to do this part alone. Wiggling her way through the crowd, she picked up another drink from a passing tray and then found she'd drunk half of it by the time she arrived at the conclave of people gathered around Sean. He was in the middle of telling a story, and so she waited at the edge, catching the end of what he was saying.

"—and then the stuntman said, 'That's way too dangerous, I'm not doing that,' so Tom grabbed the fireproof jacket, put it on, and said, 'Light me up!'" He threw his arms in the air, and everyone erupted into peals of laughter. Sean always knew how to deliver a story.

"So have you met Timothée Chalamet? What were the Oscars like? Are you really dating Gracie Lamé?" Everyone had questions. Chloe felt a thumping in her chest. This wasn't the right time. She didn't want their first conversation in years to happen in front of an audience. She turned away, ready to retreat, but then she felt a hand on her arm.

"Chloe."

When she turned around, there he was, familiar eyes locked on hers, a tentative smile on his lips. "Hi," she replied.

"It's so good to see you," he said, a familiar fondness in his eyes.

"You too," she said, and now a wave of emotion threatened to overwhelm her. It was as though part of her had been holding her breath for ten years waiting for Sean to look at her like this again.

There was too much to say, too many years to catch up on. She wanted to get out of here, go sit in the quiet of the cloisters, have him to herself, catch up properly. But before she could say anything, Elaine Harper stood up on the small stage at the front of the hall and clinked her glass with a knife.

"We'll catch up later, yeah?" Sean said beneath his breath, before turning his attention to the stage. She felt a sinking in her chest. Was she just another person to catch up with? Chloe had put this huge significance on their reunion, but maybe to him, she was only another face in the crowd. This weekend, something to fit in between meetings with producers in London. The thought made her feel nauseous.

"Welcome, welcome!" Elaine said, projecting her voice, waiting for the room to hush. "As head of the alumni committee, I wanted to welcome you all here tonight. It's so wonderful to see such a good turnout. Some faces I've seen recently, others I haven't laid eyes on since graduation, so thank you for all making the effort to mark this anniversary. It's also wonderful to meet so many of your other halves. Thank you, newbies, for coming along and indulging us on this trip down memory lane."

Chloe looked back at Sean, trying to catch his eye, but someone else had already intercepted him. "We've got a fun-packed weekend of events lined up," Elaine announced. "Punting tomorrow morning for anyone who wants to sign up, the weather looks tip-top. Then we're having a picnic lunch in the university park with garden games, followed by formal hall tomorrow evening. Black tie, please, for everyone who's asked me, it was on the agenda I emailed around. Please do adhere to the seating plan, you know how much work goes into these things." She tugged at her pleated, metallic gold skirt, as though suddenly self-conscious that it was too tight. "Now, a big thank-you to the college for letting us back, and to Freda and John for their help with logistics. I'm not going to rattle on. Tonight we'll just let you drink and catch up, no organized fun, I promise." She lifted a hand, showing crossed fingers, and laughed. "But first, Lorna Childs has something she wanted to say."

Lorna stood ready to take the mic and there were whoops and cheers as she took center stage. In her stunning, figure-hugging purple dress and immaculate blowout, she looked like a model taking the catwalk.

"Hello, Lincoln!" she called, which made everyone cheer. "I know Elaine is in charge of the fun and games this weekend, but this is something Harriet and I thought we'd do before everyone gets too merry." Lorna let out a short squeal of laughter, then waved for Harriet to come and join her on the stage. Harriet hurried to her side, walking awkwardly in high heels, then held up the college yearbook like it was some sacrificial offering she was bringing to the altar. "I have stayed in touch with so many of you, online or otherwise," Lorna went on, "and I have felt such pride in seeing what huge success you've all had. Be it running your own business like Harriet here, curing rare diseases—I'm looking at you, Mark—or taking over Hollywood . . ." She paused and someone yelled, "Go, Sean!" Lorna lifted a hand to her chest. "I know we were lucky enough to attend one of the most prestigious universities in the world, so maybe it's not surprising how many of you are *killing it* out there, but, ladies"—she pointed to a few women in the crowd—"credit where credit is due, we all know motherhood is the hardest job of all. Am I right?"

There was a flutter of applause, though Chloe noted that people didn't whoop as loudly for the mothers as they had for Sean. "Now, in the spirit of celebration, we thought it would be fun if we read out some of the yearbook predictions and see what came true." She clapped her hands and squealed again as Harriet opened the book and started to read.

"Most likely to marry a footballer—Lorna Childs," Harriet said, and everyone cheered again.

"Not a footballer, but I think you'll all agree, tennis is *far* classier. My gorgeous Matteo." She blew him a kiss. "How lucky am I?"

Chloe looked across at Matteo, who was lewdly moving his hand while thrusting his tongue into the side of his mouth. Lorna tried to laugh this off, but her eyes were shooting him daggers as she frantically waved at Harriet to move on.

"Most likely to cure cancer—Mark Patel," Harriet read, and everyone scoured the room for Mark.

"Not yet, but give me time," he called out, and there were more whoops and cheers.

"Most likely to be a millionaire before thirty . . . ," Harriet read.

"And we're not including inherited wealth in this one, sorry, Araminta!" Lorna interjected, causing a ripple of laughter around the room.

Chloe heard someone whisper, "I heard she put most of her trust fund up her nose."

"Leo Brunswick," Harriet said, and people looked around to see if Leo was there.

"Just on the phone with my hedge fund manager," he said, holding his phone to his ear. "He says none of your goddamn business what my net worth is." A few people laughed at this, while others rolled their eyes. Leo had always been a conceited prick.

"Most likely to end up together," Harriet read on, once the chatter had subsided, "Sean Adler and Chloe Fairway." Chloe felt her heart in her mouth as all eyes in the room turned to look at her. "Ah well, if anyone's met Chloe's new boyfriend, they won't be feeling too sorry for her passing up our Sean."

Chloe felt her cheeks heat. She couldn't stop herself from glancing across at Sean, who had fixed his face into an expression of polite amusement. But Chloe noticed his ears had turned pink and she knew this meant he was mortified too.

Chloe felt a reassuring hand on her waist and turned to see Rob standing beside her.

"I got you," he said quietly in her ear, as though he knew exactly how uncomfortable she was feeling. She sank backward into his warm embrace. Would it be mad to keep him, at least for the rest of the trial? What would happen after that? No, she couldn't think about it. She was here to see Sean, to mend their friendship.

"Most likely to become an evil dictator," Harriet read, and Chloe felt the attention of the crowd move on. Rob bent down to kiss her neck.

"You are the most beautiful woman in this room, you know that?" he whispered. His Irish lilt sounded even more pronounced. Was he getting more Irish as the night went on, or had she just had too much to drink?

"I'm not, but thank you," she whispered back, closing her eyes, clasping his arm that was wrapped around her. When she opened her eyes again, they fell on John. He was standing just a few yards away, looking in their direction. Everyone else at this party was dressed to impress, but John was wearing the same jeans he'd worn on the bus. The people around him blurred into motion and noise, but John exuded a quiet stillness, like the only person in focus in a photograph. Chloe straightened up, stopped leaning against Rob. He felt like a protective cloak in front of all these people, but for some reason the illusion didn't hold in front of John.

He narrowed his eyes at her, as though he knew something was off, as though he could *see* what Rob was. But how *could* he know? Unless he had X-ray vision. Or had it been Richard's strange behavior at the bus stop that made him suspicious? He couldn't know. She narrowed her eyes back at him, and he responded with an innocent shrug, looking around, as if she must have been narrowing her eyes at someone else. She bit back a smile, then rolled her eyes at him. He rolled his right back. She pouted, feeling her cheeks heat at this exchange, then turned back to Rob. Safe, unquestioning Rob.

"Everything okay?" he asked.

She nodded, tilting her face, leaning up to kiss him. And as she did so, she found her eyes glancing sideways to where John had been, as though she had something to prove. But John had gone, and she felt an unexpected pang of disappointment.

11

Chloe ducked out of the party to use the bathroom. Overall, she was enjoying herself more than she'd thought she would, especially with the protective force field of Rob around her. But something about the acoustics, the amplification of a hundred conversations, felt exhausting, like trying to stay upright in a river. She wished she had a book. She could really use a reading break. Just a few chapters to tide her over.

When she came out of the bathroom, she found Sean, waiting for her in the narrow, dimly lit corridor.

"Hey," he said, shooting her a tentative smile. "Loud in there, isn't it? My ears are ringing."

"Yes. Hi," she said, surprised to find him here. Were they going to have a heart-to-heart *here*, outside the loo?

"So, how's life with you?" he asked, grinning, then thrusting his hands into his pockets, shifting his stance, leaning back against the wall.

"Good, good," she said as a reflex. "How about you?"

"Yeah, you know. Crazy busy. I only got in two days ago. Still jet-lagged," he said, shooting her that familiar goofy smile.

"Did you come just for this?" she asked.

"No, it was lucky timing. I had a meeting with these producers in London." He raked a hand through his jet-black hair. She leaned back against the opposite wall, pressing her hands behind her.

"Who were you meeting? You know I work for a film company now?"

"Oh right. Cool." He bit his lip. "I can't really say. Talent meetings, you know."

A silence hung between them. She imagined how different their roles in a meeting would be. Her, taking notes and making coffee, him, the big-name director, calling all the shots.

"Sorry, that was a wanky thing to say. You're not going to tell anyone," he said, blowing out his cheeks. "It was with Daniel Craig about this prepper film they want me for."

She took a beat. Wow.

"It's so impressive, what you've done," she said. "I'm so proud of you."

"You watched them then, my films?" he asked, eyes shifting to the floor.

"Of course I did! I even waited for the credits in the theater so I could see your name come up again, twice—writer *and* director. I did a little cheer both times, spilled popcorn all over myself," she said. His mouth lifted at the edges, but in his eyes she saw a flicker of annoyance. He started picking at a piece of loose paintwork on the wall.

"Listen, I wanted to apologize for not replying to that email you sent," he said, clearing his throat. So he had got it. "It was rude of me not to write back. I wanted to, I was thinking about you, but then it felt like I should probably call, and life got crazy, you know how it is. I was doing eighteen-hour days . . ." He trailed off. "Then it felt like I'd left it too long." He scuffed his foot against the floor. "I'm always chasing my tail on stuff I need to reply to."

"Maybe you need a shit-hot PA to help you keep on top of things," she said with a tight smile, trying not to let show how much it stung that he simply "hadn't had time" to respond.

"I have two," he said, no flicker of irony. Chloe flexed her palms behind her back. Why did this feel like talking to a stranger? Maybe because he was a stranger now. But was she really so insignificant to him that an email congratulating him, extending the olive branch of friendship, had just been another irksome task clogging up his to-do list?

"You were my best friend, Sean," she said softly. "We did everything together. It feels crazy to me that we lost touch over . . ." She trailed off.

"I know, me too," he said, eyes wide and eager now. "And I'm sorry, about all that stuff with Susie." A flush crept up his neck, and he tugged at the cuff of his sleeve. "If it makes you feel better, she didn't just make me choose between her and you. When I got the job in LA, she told me we couldn't stay together if I went."

This did not make Chloe feel any better. He had put Susie over their friendship, but a job over Susie. She chewed on her lip, feeling a new coldness between them.

"You still acting?" he asked. Though he must have known that she wasn't.

"Every day, acting like I've got a clue what I'm doing with my life," she said, letting out a nervous laugh, and it echoed around the too-quiet corridor, taunting her. Their eyes met now, and he looked . . . she didn't know. Awkward? Embarrassed? She couldn't read him like she used to. How could a conversation be about so much and so little all at once?

A group of women were heading down the corridor toward them now, and Sean bounced on his toes. "Anyway, we'll catch up properly later, yeah?"

A cold weight settled against her ribs. She folded her arms across her chest, then dropped her gaze to the floor.

"Sure, that would be good," she said, swallowing against the dryness in her throat. The words felt small. Perfunctory. She knew this Sean, she knew he bounced on his toes when he wanted to be somewhere else. Clearly he'd done what he needed to do: apologized, made a show of goodwill. Box ticked. And now, she would quietly return to the footnotes of his university memories, a minor character in the early chapters. Sean gave her a little salute before heading back down the corridor toward the party, his walk relaxing into more of a swagger the farther away he got.

Chloe didn't follow him. She needed a moment. The sounds of the party were muffled and distant, as if someone had closed a door between her and the room. What had she expected? To turn back the clock? To magically be his best friend and writing partner again, for him to be the key that was going to help unlock whatever was blocking her? She wiped two fingers beneath her eyes. She didn't want to cry. She was too emotional about this stuff. She needed to grow up. She tugged at her dress, smoothed her hair, took a deep breath, then headed back toward the party. At least she knew where she stood. Sean didn't need her anymore; he didn't want to reconcile. She just needed to survive the weekend, be civil, give him McKenzie's script, and that would be it. Chapter closed.

Back in the hall, she scoured the crowd for Rob. But the drinks reception had taken a rowdy turn. Someone had pumped the music up, and everyone had moved to the edges of the hall to make room for people to dance. Rocco Falconi, always the life and soul of any party, had started a dance routine to "Thriller." Sean, Mark, and Colin came to join in, and the crowd squealed in delight to see them attempt some coordinated moves.

"Dance off!" someone yelled, and now the music flipped to Rihanna's "Umbrella." People cleared the floor for Colin, who started breakdancing, his blond hair, scraped back into a ponytail, already slick with sweat as he twirled around the floor on his back. Everyone whooped and cheered, but then he stopped, shook his head, clutching his back as though he'd tweaked it. Someone switched the music again, a hidden feud over whose playlist was linking to the speakers. As Daft Punk's "Harder, Better, Faster, Stronger" came on, Sean moonwalked into the middle of the floor, then launched into his signature dance move, the robot.

Chloe looked around again. Where was Rob? But when she turned back to the dance floor, she found him, center stage next to Sean, copying his moves. Oh no. If Sean was good at the robot—and he was—Rob was *spectacular*. His arms moved back and forth with mechanical precision, held stiff, then jerking at the elbows. His legs moved in sudden, robotic steps, and he closed his eyes, as though his face had powered down, devoid of all emotion. The crowd around him went wild. Sean laughed, saw he was outgunned, and quickly conceded the floor. "Who is that guy?" someone whispered. "Chloe's boyfriend,

Rob," someone else said. And soon the crowd was chanting, "Rob! Rob! Rob!"

At first, Chloe felt alarmed by what he was doing—it was *too* good; he would give himself away. But then he caught her eye and winked, and she couldn't help laughing. Everyone was too impressed to question how he was doing this.

When the song ended, Rob's face reanimated into a smile. He tried to move away, to give someone else a chance in the spotlight, but the crowd wouldn't have it and pulled him back to the center. "Do it again, do it again!" they cried, and now everyone wanted a lesson from him on how to do the robot.

He looked up and caught Chloe's eye, checking she was okay with this. She could only nod and laugh. If she'd brought Rob here to impress everyone, then it was mission accomplished. As she watched him try to teach Harriet, Elaine, and Amara, she noticed Sean on the sidelines with Colin. He rubbed a hand along his jaw, briefly glanced across the dance floor at her, then turned and put an arm around Colin. Too busy to reply to her email when he had *two* PAs. Well fuck you, Sean Adler.

Chloe's new dress suddenly felt uncomfortably tight; she had drunk too much wine, she needed some fresh air. As she walked outside into the mild evening, she felt the quiet like a refreshing wave, washing off all that pointless small talk. She wandered through Grove Quad, keen to get away from the noise of the party, then almost tripped over something on the path. Looking down, she saw Richard the whippet, looking up at her expectantly.

"What are you doing out here alone?" she asked, bending down to stroke his ears. He stepped forward and prodded her armpit with his nose, as though he was trying to hug her but lacked the arms. This almost unbalanced her and she burst out laughing. "Someone's happy to see me." Was there any greater salve for sadness than the cold nose of a friendly dog?

"Miss, you can't have that dog in here," came a stern voice from the other side of the quad. Chloe looked up to see one of the porters coming toward her with a torch. She instantly felt nineteen again, in trouble for flouting the rules.

"Oh, he's not my dog," she said, stroking Richard, because now he looked anxious, with his tail tucked beneath him, ears pinned back.

"How did he get in here?" the porter asked, as he headed toward her. When he got close, he reached out a hand to take Richard by the scruff of his neck.

"Oh, no, I know who he belongs to. He's allowed to be here, he's a support dog," Chloe said, pulling Richard toward her. The porter, who looked a lot younger than she remembered porters being, gave her a skeptical look.

"Is he registered in the logbook?"

"I expect so. He's John Elton's dog. He's on the alumni committee."

"John Elton?"

"I know it sounds like a made-up name, but that really is his name."

The porter checked his watch. "You'll need to take responsibility for him, or I'll have to shut him in the office. He can't be running loose around college."

"I'll take him," Chloe said, hugging Richard. The porter gave her a curt nod, then marched back toward the porter's lodge.

"Looks like it's you and me, my friend," Chloe said, bending to take her heels off, enjoying the feel of bare feet on cold paving stone. Richard tried to lick her face, and she cradled his face between her hands to stop him, laughing at this enthusiastic display of affection.

The night air cooled the heat on her skin. Somewhere in the distance, she could still hear the music, but it felt faraway—a different world. She ran her hand along Richard's velvety back, relishing this moment of peace. Here, there was no need to explain herself. No version of her to be edited. Maybe John had the right idea with Richard: dogs accepted you as you were, you didn't need to impress them, and they didn't require batteries.

"There you are," came a voice behind her. She turned to see John, out of breath, running through from the front quad.

"The porter was about to throw him in dog jail," Chloe told him.

"Sorry, thank you, he slipped his collar. Something must have spooked him," John said, bending down to put the collar over Richard's narrow head. "What were you running from?" he asked Richard, but Richard couldn't explain. As John caught his breath, his shoulders dropped. She could see he was relieved to be reunited with his dog.

"What are you doing out here?" John asked her. "Was there an intermission in the awards ceremony of who's winning at life?"

"You mean the yearbook? I think that was just a bit of fun," Chloe said. She didn't know why she was defending it. It hadn't felt at all fun to her. John cleared his throat.

"Your boyfriend certainly made an impression," he said, and she couldn't read his tone. "I meant to ask, whereabouts is he from in Ireland?"

Oh no. Questions. She wasn't prepared for questions.

"Um, the south," she said.

"Oh yeah, whereabouts? My nan is from Killarney."

"You know, I can't remember. I'm terrible with place names," she said. Now his gaze shifted toward the star-studded sky.

"I'd swear his accent has been getting more and more Dublin as the night goes on."

So, it wasn't just her who'd noticed the accent shift. Damn. "Yeah, that happens when he's had a few," she said, then in a cod French accent, "Wot eez zees, ze accent inqueezition?"

He laughed, surprisingly loudly. "What was that?"

"I'm not sure," she said, laughing too now. "I was going for French, but maybe German?"

Their eyes met in the low light, and the laughter lingered there.

"You going back in, then?" he asked.

"Not yet, bit talked out."

"I'll stop talking."

"No, I meant in a crowd—all that small talk. It's exhausting."

"Talk only feels small when it lacks authenticity," he said. She felt a prickle of recognition. The people she admired most, like Kiko and Valerie, were fiercely authentic. They didn't chameleon who they were to fit different situations.

"Do you ever feel like you're living in the wrong era?" she asked him.

"All the time," he said plainly. "You remember what I used to be like."

"I liked how you were," she said, and he briefly closed his eyes, acknowledging the compliment. "I sometimes feel homesick for places I've read about in fiction. I know that's ridiculous. To yearn for places you've never been, places that don't even exist."

She expected him to laugh at such a silly sentiment, but he didn't, he looked like he understood.

"There's a Welsh word you'd like: 'hiraeth.' A deep longing, homesickness for a home you can't return to, perhaps a home that never was."

She smiled. "That's perfect. Can I keep it?"

"Yes," he said, lifting his hand into the air, closing his fist around it, then passing it to her. "Here is my hiraeth."

She pressed it to her heart.

He cleared his throat. "But we shouldn't romanticize the past."

"I spoke to Sean," she said, the words slipping out too quickly, like she'd been waiting for someone to tell.

"Oh yes?" John asked, looking at her intently now.

"It was really awkward. I spend so much time looking back, thinking about who we were back then. But I'm not sure Sean thinks about it at all."

"I don't think that's true," John said. Their eyes met and he quickly looked around, turning to walk toward the bench at the corner of the quad. "Shall we sit?"

She followed him, but Richard climbed up onto the bench beside him before she could sit down. She laughed. "Richard, we've talked about this," he said, pretending to be stern. "When there are other people around, you have to pretend you're not a chair dog." He snapped his fingers near the ground, and Richard got down. "Sorry. He thinks he's human. It's a problem."

Chloe sat in the seat he'd vacated, her arm nudging against John's on the small bench. She could feel the heat radiate off his body. "You were saying, about Sean," he prompted.

"It's weird, having a conversation with someone you used to know so well, and suddenly it feels like talking to a stranger."

"People aren't perfect communicators," John said gently.

"Sometimes they don't know how to say what they mean, to say what matters."

"You do. You always know what to say." She said it without thinking, then realized it was true. John glanced sideways at her, a melancholy look in his eyes. He reached down to stroke Richard's head.

"I don't. I've spent my life not saying the things I should have." She didn't know what he meant by this, but before she could ask, he said, "Why did you change everything?" His voice was soft now, the moonlight catching the laughter lines around his eyes, the small scar on his forehead.

"What do you mean?" she asked, trying to keep her voice steady.

"Your hair, your style, you look totally different."

"You don't like it?" she asked, surprised he would notice.

"I like how you always look," he said plainly, holding her gaze, like he saw straight through this evening's curated façade. There was something else in his eyes too now, a friction, the same edge that had been there on the bus. She felt very aware of how close they were sitting, of where her arm was touching his. She quickly hugged her arms around herself, turning her face forward.

"Well, it's nice to get dressed up sometimes," she said, shifting the tone, trying to be flippant. "Remind people I'm more than big hair and big dreams." She said it with a grin. "You look different too."

"Because I used to dress like I was interviewing for a job in Churchill's war cabinet." He pushed a palm against his face, and she laughed.

"It was a whole vibe. 'Hashtag war cabinet chic' is all over Instagram now." They smiled at each other, and she felt that spark of a joke finding its audience. "Do you remember how much we used to argue about the best time in history to have been alive?"

"I remember," he said, gently nudging her shoulder. "You said nineteen twenties Britain. I said Crete in the Minoan golden age."

She nodded. "Right. I wanted jazz clubs and scandal. You wanted ritual sacrifices and 'extensive trade routes.'"

"It was a golden age, the clue's right there in the title," he said, sighing through a smile. "I found this whole Reddit thread a few years ago, on the best and worst times to be alive. There were some outlandish suggestions. I nearly sent it to you."

"Why didn't you?" she asked, and felt the mood between them shift. He looked up to the sky, shook his head, just a fraction. There was something he wasn't saying. "Why did you say that at the bus, about us not being friends?"

"I don't know," he said, looking suddenly tired. "It's probably not an end-of-the-night, four-glasses-of-wine conversation, Chloe."

"Come on, this is a no-small-talk zone, remember? Tell me." She pushed, nudging him again.

"You want the big talk?" he asked, and it felt surprisingly loaded.

"Yes."

"Fine. It felt like we were only friends when Sean was around."

She blinked, caught off guard. "You don't think all those hours we spent together made us friends?" He slowly shook his head. "What?"

He sat forward on the bench, elbows resting on his knees, hands in fists beneath his chin.

"I was your friend when it suited you. When you needed a musician."

"That's not true," she said, but guilt stirred in her chest just the same.

"It was. I could never say no to you," he said, quieter now.

"But you *loved* being involved in the theater; we all did." Her brow creased.

He shifted his weight forward, then pinched his forehead as though it was painful to remember. "I gave myself a stomach ulcer in third year, trying to hold on to my scholarship. Choir, organ practice, the band, all those play rehearsals stacked on top. I don't think you ever really saw how much I was juggling."

"I'm sorry. I didn't know . . . You always made it look so effortless."

"Well, it wasn't," he said sharply. "It isn't. Nothing worth doing is effortless."

"But you're so good at it. We couldn't have done the plays without you," she said, her voice softening. "*A Midsummer Night's Dream*, the band you pulled together, it was the best thing I've ever been a part of—"

"What about *Back to Brideshead*?" he said, cutting her off. The name landed between them. She felt her stomach twist.

"Well, that was a disaster, through no fault of yours," she said, hugging her knees to her chest. "I was trying to prove I could do something on my own, without Sean. All it proved was that I couldn't." She laughed once, still cringing at the memory. "It was so humiliating, half the audience walking out on opening night. And those reviews—"

"So you bailed," John said, voice tight. "Left everyone in the lurch."

She blanched at his tone. It was true. After a disastrous

opening night, she'd fled home to London, as she always did when life went wrong, told everyone she was ill. They couldn't do the play without her, so the run had been canceled. It wasn't something she was proud of, but she couldn't imagine anyone would have wanted to go on with it.

"You're really still angry about *that*?" she asked, thrusting out her lower lip in incomprehension.

"You asked me to write the music. I told you I didn't have time, but you begged me, said you couldn't do it without me." John took a deep breath. "I passed up a trip to South America with my parents because I didn't want to let you down. I spent the holidays here, locked in a practice room, working on the score."

"I'm sorry," she said, a fresh layer of shame settling in her chest. "I didn't know you did that."

"You get a few shitty reviews, and you drop everything, including me."

"That's not true, I didn't drop you, but you were living with Sean . . ." She trailed off. She *had* dropped him. She remembered a birthday dinner he'd invited her to. She'd made her excuses because it was too awkward seeing Susie. "Okay, so I might have been a little self-centered back then."

He turned to face her now, his eyes catching hers in the dark; they exuded a fierce glow she had never seen from him before. He made a "huh" sound, as though this revelation was not news to him.

"Why are you giving me such a hard time?" she asked, standing up, pacing a few steps, needing to escape those accusatory eyes.

"I knew you weren't ready for the big talk," he said, rubbing his chin with his palm. She saw his whole body stiffen, his hand dropping from his face as he straightened up with a slow, deliberate motion, like he was bracing for something. His shoulders squared, jaw tightening, and for a fraction of a second, Chloe saw him pull into himself, like he was retreating, closing off. As John stood, Richard started to bark. Someone else was walking across the other side of the quad. John ran a hand through his hair, restless, as though he had more to say, but the moment had passed. "I'm going to take Richard back. Thanks for helping with him."

He shot her one final look, his eyes swimming with feeling, then he turned and strode back toward the party. Chloe was left alone, navigating an uncomfortable sea of emotions. Guilt pressed down on her like humidity, impossible to shake. She wrapped her arms tighter around herself, as if that could keep it out, but it was already in her chest, her throat, her stomach.

She had never thought of John as someone who struggled. At Oxford, there were plenty of people who had buckled under the workload, but not him. His talent for composing had always seemed so innate, like he could conjure magic. She'd sat beside him at the piano and watched him create a melody in minutes, as though the music lived in his fingertips. But maybe, as with writing, there was always more going on beneath the surface, words deleted, ideas discarded. She paced up and down, her body gripped with unpleasant feelings. Maybe being back here was not so much a jaunt down memory lane as it was picking at the scab of all their youthful insecurities.

She heard a sound and looked up to see Rob appear out of the dark with her shawl.

"I thought you might be cold," he said, his warm smile cutting through the uneasy fog John's words had left behind. "You want to go back in? They're doing shots of alcohol and a conga line."

"You know, I'm tired, let's just go to bed. We'll see everyone tomorrow," she said.

"As you wish," he said, picking up her shoes, then wrapping the shawl around her, hugging her to him as they walked side by side. If felt good to have him there, and she leaned into him, letting him support her.

"Do you think I'm self-centered?" she asked, as they reached the archway leading into college.

"Chloe, you're always thinking about others. Remember last week, we walked the long way around so you could send a birthday card to Emma in Canada? And in that bar, Victors, you ran halfway down the road to return that lady's coat. You are compassionate and giving and thoughtful. Why?"

"Nothing, just something John said."

"John from the bus?" Rob asked, and she nodded. "He's a friend of yours?"

"Yes, he is. Well, he used to be." She felt another pang of regret. "I don't think I was a good friend to him back then. I might have been a little wrapped up in myself, taken people for granted."

"I think it's okay to prioritize your own thoughts and feelings occasionally. Taking care of yourself isn't selfish, it's necessary. It also takes courage to admit you made a mistake; a truly self-involved person wouldn't do that." These were the words she needed to hear.

When they got to their room, Rob shut the door, then pulled her closer, stroking a finger down her cheek. "How can I make you feel better?" She looked up at him, then leaned in to kiss him, his soft lips reassuring, pushing away thoughts of John and the uncomfortable feelings he'd provoked.

Rob didn't deepen the kiss this time; he pulled away, then reached up to take out her earrings for her.

"You are so beautiful," he said. Then without another word, he took off his jacket, walked across to the couch, and lay down. "Sleep well, Chloe."

She felt an unexpected pang of disappointment. Did she want more? No, of course not. That was the gentlemanly thing for him to do. She took her makeup off in the bathroom, pulled on her nightshirt, then slid into bed and lay still, staring up at the ceiling. It would be so easy to call him over. Just let herself be held, nothing more. Her body ached to have someone next to her, the weight of an arm, the heat of skin, the hush of breath at her neck. It had been a long time, and knowing he was there, taut and toned, ready to do whatever she asked . . .

She tossed and turned, finding it impossible to sleep. Her mind jumped to Peter. Sex with him had been satisfying, but it had always been the way he wanted it, *when* he wanted it—mainly in the shower because he had a thing about sweaty sheets. With Rob, she would be in complete control. He would be gentle, willing, there would be no pressure to reciprocate. It would just be scratching an itch, wouldn't it? No, no. What was she thinking? It was unnatural. It would be *weird*. She wasn't going to *Pretty Woman* this situation. She closed her eyes tight, as if that could shut it down. But the thoughts kept circling, restless and intrusive, maybe fueled by the wine she'd drunk and the oppressive heat in this room. Still, as her mind wandered—lips brushing skin, a hand sliding along her thigh—her mind conjured a face in the dark, but to her surprise it wasn't Rob's. It was John's.

12

When Chloe woke the next morning, she turned over to see Rob sitting on the sofa, watching her.

"Good morning, beautiful," he said, his face shifting into a smile.

"Morning," she said, starting slightly. How long had he been sitting there watching her sleep?

"Did you sleep well?" he asked.

"I did. You?" she asked, then realized she didn't even know if he needed sleep, or just twenty-eight minutes of recharging time.

"Yes," he said. "Would you like anything? Coffee? A massage? An inspiring poem to start your day?"

"I'm good, thank you," she said, sitting up in bed. Rob's

unflagging enthusiasm felt a little much to be confronted with the moment she woke up.

"I suggest we go for a run. If you want to hit your fitness goals, we should get in another five K either this morning or tomorrow."

Chloe did not want to go for a run. She was hungover, which meant she wanted to doomscroll and do the crossword on her phone. But Rob was already dressed in running clothes and moved across the room to pick up her trainers. "You won't regret it. Endorphins are the best cure for an excess of alcohol."

"I'm a bit tired," she said, searching for an excuse.

"But you just said you were well rested," Rob said, his face a picture of puzzled innocence. "And that you want to get fit."

He had her there. She had said she wanted to get fit, and if you wanted to get fit, you had to go for a run, even when you didn't want to.

"Fine," she said, forcing her legs out of bed.

Her limbs felt leaden, her head thick. She stayed sitting on the side of the bed, not quite ready to stand. The conversation with Sean clung to her, awkward and disappointing. And then John—his harsh words had left a different kind of ache, quieter but no less painful. She knew if Rob weren't here, pushing her to get up, she might stay in bed all morning, curled under the covers.

"Would now be a good opportunity to do a check-in?" Rob asked, pulling her back to the present.

"A check-in?" she asked, looking up at him in confusion.

"To see how you're feeling about us," he said. "Did I perform as you wanted me to last night? It is helpful for me to receive feedback."

She smiled now, because he sounded so earnest, so sincere.

She thought of how effortlessly he'd fitted in at the party, how charmed everyone had been. With him beside her, parts of last night had actually been fun: catching up with lovely Thea, hearing about Harriet's jam business. Katie and Mark had wanted to hear all about Kiko and she'd enjoyed showing them photos of baby Elodie. Even intolerable Colin Layton had been almost tolerable.

"Yes, it was great," she said, "you were great. Thank you."

He sat down on the bed beside her, then pressed a palm over the device on his wrist. "It's just that last night, as you were trying to sleep, I sensed some . . . frustration." He paused, eyes wide, knowing. She felt her cheeks heat. Could he read her mind? Now she remembered the strange fever dream about John. Or had it been Rob's body, with John's face? A robot John? Either way it was extremely confusing—she'd never thought about John that way. "I just wanted to check I'm doing everything right," Rob said, gently circling a finger on her hand. "That you're . . . satisfied."

"Uh-huh," she said, and it came out as a squeak. "Let's go running." She leaped up, then rummaged through her bag for her sports kit. "You're right, we need to seize the day, get those endorphins pumping. Let's go, go, go!"

Stepping out of the shower an hour later, she caught her reflection in the mirror and paused at the color in her cheeks, the light in her eyes—she was glowing. Was that just the endorphins? Rob had been right about the run; it had shaken off her hangover, energized her. Not only that, but he'd downloaded a podcast on screenwriting, which they'd listened to on the run. Now she felt virtuous *and* inspired.

Maybe she *could* be the kind of person who ran before breakfast and listened to smart, educational podcasts. Maybe Rob was going to help her become the person she was supposed to be. Two weeks ago, the idea of keeping Rob had seemed preposterous, but the more time she spent with him, the less crazy the idea seemed. She liked him. She liked how he made her feel. He was making her life better. Sitting on the closed toilet seat, towel wrapped around her hair, she opened the notes app on her phone and started a list.

PROS AND CONS OF DATING A BOIBOT

PROS

Incredibly realistic (and attractive)—no one can tell.

Helps me achieve my goals—work/fitness etc.

Good for self-esteem—keeps telling me how great I am.

Romantic—bought me a rose, says poetic things.

Smart / well-read—can talk to him about anything.

Do not have to talk about boring things like football scores or craft beer.

Polite and well-mannered—no burps or farts.

Interesting, from a science perspective.

CONS

All the sci-fi films involving robots usually end badly for the humans.

Morally questionable? Think AI might be bad for the environment.

Can run out of power at inconvenient times.

Dogs don't like him. (Is this just Richard, or all dogs?)

How would I tell my friends and family?

How would I afford it when the trial ends?

How would I have children if I ever wanted children?

Then she scrubbed out the last one. How had she gone from being robot-curious to planning her whole robot family?

"Hey, Chloe. Shall we go to breakfast?" Rob called through the door. She quickly closed her phone.

"Just coming."

She didn't need to decide anything now. She just needed to get through this weekend, put the past to bed. *Then* she could think about what her future looked like.

As they walked into Deep Hall, Rob took her hand. A buffet breakfast had been laid out on the side with teapots, cafetières, a mountain of croissants, and the low hum of people already chatting about plans for the day.

"I'll grab us a seat," he said, as she headed straight to the buffet.

Elaine was walking around with a clipboard, collecting names for the punting expedition. Chloe wasn't planning on going—she wanted to take Rob to the museum, wander through the city, show him the botanical gardens—but as she was reaching for a cafetière, Sean appeared beside her. He was wearing jeans and a blue T-shirt with "Director's Cut" on the front. She couldn't decide if it was hilariously self-aware or cringingly self-important. Maybe both. His face looked freshly shaved, but there was a weight around his eyes—a bleary heaviness that confirmed the hangover he was trying to hide.

"Did you go running this morning?" he asked casually.

"Yes. Why?" she said, turning back to the buffet.

"I thought I saw you but then figured it had to be someone else. The Chloe Fairway I knew would never willingly exercise before breakfast."

She gave him a half-hearted smile, still slightly bruised from last night's conversation. He cleared his throat.

"You need to introduce me to your chap. Rob, is it?" His eyebrows lifted just a fraction, like he was trying to look indifferent, forgetting she was familiar with his every microexpression. "He's quite the dancer."

"He is," she said, holding up the cafetière, offering him a coffee. He picked up a mug, and she poured.

"Look, I'm sorry about last night," he said, rocking back slightly on his heels. "I don't think I explained myself well." His voice dropped, eyes flicking around to make sure no one was eavesdropping. "I don't want you to think I was being flippant about your email, that I didn't care."

"It's fine, don't worry about it," she said with a tight shrug.

"Because the truth is, I think I didn't reply because I cared *too* much," he said.

Her face darted back to him in surprise. His words sent a pulse of relief through her—here was the Sean she knew. He tugged at his T-shirt. "Whenever I finish a script, I think of you. 'Would Chloe think this was finished?'"

"I never think anything's finished," she said, offering him a small smile.

"Exactly." He reached for a bowl, which he started loading with granola. "You're the voice in my head, telling me it could be better. I always try to imagine what you'd think—" He stopped talking because Elaine was upon them with her clipboard.

"Just working out boats for punting. Are you two keen?" she asked, her long, mousy ponytail swinging back and forth like an executioner's axe.

"I'm up for it if you are?" Sean said, shooting her a hopeful smile.

"Sure, put us down for a boat," Chloe said, feeling herself thawing.

"Excellent," said Elaine. "Now, Sean, will you come and settle an argument with us about the Hollywood Walk of Fame?"

Sean looked back at Chloe, perhaps searching for an excuse to stay, but Chloe waved him away. "Go. We'll talk on the river."

As she spooned cornflakes into a bowl, a flicker of hope stirred inside her. Whatever warmth had faded between them, it wasn't gone. A couple of hours in a boat, just the two of them, might be exactly what they needed to clear the air, maybe even begin again.

When she sat back down at the trestle table opposite Rob,

she said, "I think I might go punting after all, with Sean. Do you mind if we rain-check the Ashmolean?"

"Of course not," he said. That was another good thing about Rob, he was always so accommodating.

"I do want to show you the museum though," she said. "They've got the lantern Guy Fawkes was carrying when he was arrested, and this beautiful Chinese art, I'd love you to see it. Maybe we can go tomorrow instead?"

"I can take a virtual tour if that saves time," Rob suggested, his tone light, helpful. She took a bite of her croissant, and it felt dry in her throat.

"What, you could see it all virtually? Right now?" she asked, lowering her voice, in case anyone was listening.

"Yes," he said. "If you wanted to discuss the art over breakfast."

She shook her head and took a long, slow sip of coffee. The idea of seeing art virtually made her feel sad. It would be like listening to a symphony through a phone: you'd get the gist, maybe even enjoy it, but it wasn't how the music was supposed to be heard. "No, it's okay. We'll go another time," she said quietly.

Colin Layton and Rocco Falconi came over to sit down at the end of their table. Of everyone at the reunion, these two might have been the last people Chloe wanted to have breakfast with, but she gave them both a polite smile.

"Hey, Chloe," Colin said, shooting her with a finger gun. He had slicked-back blond hair and was wearing a pink Ralph Lauren polo with the collar up. Rocco was sporting a mullet, heavily texturized on the top, so it stood almost vertical.

"Dude, your dancing last night absolutely slapped!" Rocco said, turning to Rob and holding out a fist for a fist bump. Rob, apparently unfamiliar with the gesture, put his whole hand around Rob's fist and gave it a firm push, almost dislodging Rocco from the bench.

"Whoa there, muscles!" Rocco said, rubbing his shoulder.

"He was just trying to do a fist bump," Chloe quickly explained to Rob, eyes wide.

"Oh, I thought he was trying to hit me in slow motion," Rob said. "My apologies."

Luckily Rocco and Colin laughed, as though Rob had made a great joke.

"So, Chloe, where you living now? In town?" Rocco asked.

"Yes, I'm in London."

"You guys live together?" Colin asked, moving a cereal spoon back and forth in the air between them.

"No," she said, picking up her coffee and taking another long, slow sip.

"Still house sharing?" Rocco asked. "You need to get on the housing ladder, even if you start small. Renting is a huge waste of money."

"I actually live at home," she said.

"What, like home-home?" Colin snorted. "Do you have a curfew? Are you allowed to have boys over?"

"What are you talking about, Col, I would love to still live at home," Rocco said. "All that pocket money, getting tucked in every night, packed lunches." He let out a cackle.

Chloe rolled her eyes at their teasing.

"Given the current housing crisis and inflated rental market, a multigenerational household makes sound financial sense," Rob said. Chloe cringed. Sometimes, when it came to humor, Rob managed to misjudge the tone of a conversation. He was better when it was just the two of them, but something about a group dynamic seemed harder for him to compute.

Rocco and Colin both turned to look at Rob. "All right, mate. Where did you graduate from then, the University of Stating the Obvious?" Rocco asked.

"No, I did not go there," Rob said, shooting him a smile. This didn't feel like the right response, given they were teasing him. Chloe put her cup down and looked Colin square in the eyes.

"Look, I love living with my parents, I'm not embarrassed and I'm saving money." Then she turned to Rocco. "And yes, sometimes my mum does still make me a packed lunch. She's an amazing cook, and it's healthier than buying a store-bought sandwich every day." She paused, looking back and forth between them. "And, glad as I am that Rick Astley's stylist is no longer out of work, if you boys are coming punting, do try not to fall in. I think the combined product in your hair might wipe out the river's ecosystem."

A flicker of laughter came from the next table and Chloe turned to see John sitting with his friend Freya. He quickly looked away, pretending to stir his tea with a serious expression, but a small smile tugged at the corner of his mouth. Rocco frowned, and Colin ran a self-conscious hand over his perfectly shellacked hair. Chloe felt a small flicker of victory. Maybe having her life judged wasn't so bad, just so long as it was to her face and she had the right quip ready.

"Right, we'll see you boys on the river," she said, as she finished her breakfast and got up to go. As they left, Rob held out a fist toward Rocco, his attempt at a fist bump, but he misjudged it, thrusting his fist too close to Rocco's face, which caused Rocco to lurch back, toppling off the bench and onto the floor.

"All right, psycho!" Rocco cried. "He tried to hit me!"

"My apologies, I was attempting a fist bump," Rob said, reaching out a hand to help Rocco up.

"He struggles with spatial awareness sometimes," Chloe muttered, conscious that people at the other tables were staring at them now.

"You got a chip missing or something, mate?" Colin asked, standing and squaring up to Rob.

"Not that I'm aware," Rob said earnestly.

This conversation was not going anywhere good. Chloe quickly pulled on Rob's arm, signaling they should leave, but as she turned, her eyes fell back on John at the next table. He was watching this play out with his brow furrowed, eyes narrowed. But while everyone else's attention was on Rob or Rocco, his gaze was locked on Chloe.

13

"I'm sorry about what happened at breakfast," Rob said, apolo-gizing again as they strolled hand in hand down the high street toward Magdalen Bridge.

"Don't worry about it, it was just a misunderstanding," she said. "Everyone knows what Rocco's like, no one will blame you." She tried to shrug it off; she didn't want it ruining their day. Though she made a mental note to send feedback to Avery that Rob could do with a little humor refinement, if such an upgrade was available.

It was a beautiful day, the sun was out, the sky a cerulean blue, and the gold stone of the buildings shone with their distinctive Oxford hue. Chloe had dressed for punting, in a striped Breton top and cream pedal pushers. Rob squeezed her hand. "I wonder if anybody does anything at Oxford but dream and remember."

Her smile dropped slightly. He had said that before.

"Is that poetry?" she asked.

"Yeats," he said, and she nodded.

"It's beautiful," she said, though she liked the sentiment slightly less now that she knew they weren't his words. "Is there anything you want to do while we're here, anything you want to see?" she asked him.

"I'm happy to do whatever you want to do," he said, then, perhaps sensing her flicker of disappointment, he added, "But if there's time, maybe we could explore some of the old bookshops you were telling me about?"

"Great," she said, with a genuine smile now.

"And I'd like to try fish and chips."

"Fish and chips?" she asked. "You've never had fish and chips?"

"Nope. It's a gap in my education."

"Okay, we can fix that," she said, leaning in to kiss his cheek.

When they reached the bridge, they could see the punts below, lined up like sleeping wooden crocodiles. Chloe inhaled the familiar smell of sun-warmed ropes and the slightly sour smell of algae and riverweed emanating from the mud-stirred water. Elaine was already down on the bank, marshaling everyone with military precision, and they could hear laughter and lighthearted squabbles as people worked out who would punt and who would be passenger.

"How are your punting skills then, Fairway, still terrible?" said a voice beside her. She turned to see Sean and smiled.

"Sean, this is Rob; Rob, Sean."

Sean extended a hand toward Rob, then said, "Loved your dancing last night."

"Thank you," Rob replied. "I've heard so much about you from Chloe, it's good to finally meet you."

"All good I hope?"

"Eighty-two percent good," Rob said. Chloe shot him a frown, but Sean only laughed.

"Have you ever been punting before?" Sean asked him.

"No, I'm not good around water. You two go ahead, enjoy some time together."

Chloe squeezed Rob's hand appreciatively, imagining being here with Peter. He would have whined about not knowing anyone, been jealous of her even talking to Sean. With Rob, she never needed to worry about upsetting him.

"Okay, Chlo, looks like it's you and me," Sean said, turning toward her with a schoolboy grin.

"You will be shocked to hear that I haven't punted in years. I might be a little rusty," Chloe told him.

"I'm sure it's like riding a bike," Sean said, knitting his hands and then flexing them above his head. But as they walked down the steps to the river, Chloe realized they were the last to arrive and there weren't any empty punts left.

"Sean, you come with me?" Harriet called from a boat at the front. "Chloe, Rob, you go with John at the back there."

With John? Chloe felt a strange lurch in her chest, her pulse quickening.

"Sorry," Sean said with a wince. "I guess I'll catch you after, yeah?" He raised his hand in a friendly wave, then strolled up the riverbank toward Harriet. Chloe looked around at the other punts, wondering if there was anyone else she could squeeze in with, or if she should pull out entirely and stay on the bank with Rob. After their strangely hostile conversation last night, and the suspicious look he had given her this morning, Chloe wasn't relishing the prospect of spending two hours in a punt with John. But scanning the other boats, she could see John was the only one sitting alone. She couldn't leave him to go solo. Well, not quite solo; Richard was perched on the prow.

As she walked toward him, she saw that he didn't look thrilled about having her as a passenger either.

"You sure you don't want to come?" she asked Rob.

"No, you go, honestly, I'm not equipped for water sports," he insisted, and she remembered him saying he couldn't swim.

"Room for one more?" she asked John as they reached his boat.

"Sure," John said. "As long as you acknowledge Richard as the captain of this ship. He's big on naval hierarchy." He was wearing faded blue jeans, a white linen shirt, and a straw boater perched at a jaunty angle on his head. Holding the pole in one hand, he looked absurdly at ease.

"I like the hat," she said, suppressing a smile. "It's giving retired Venice gondolier vibes."

"Retired? I'll have you know I'm in my prime gondoling years," he said, and now she laughed. "You look like a French cartoon detective."

"Why, thank you, that's exactly the look I was going for," she said, and she felt a hum of pleasure as she watched him try to bite back a grin.

Rob looked back and forth as though he was having trouble understanding their conversation.

"Are you coming too?" John asked Rob.

"No, I'll sit this one out," Rob said.

"Oh, I meant to ask, where in Ireland are you from?" John asked.

"The south, near Killarney," Rob said.

"Really? My gran's from there. Funny, your accent isn't Killarney."

"You moved around, didn't you, Rob?" Chloe cut in, making a mental note to talk to Avery about an accent update too. "Right, we should go. Will you find something to do?" she asked Rob, and he nodded.

"Don't worry, I don't get bored," Rob assured her.

"You could sit right here," she said, waving an arm to indicate their idyllic surrounds. "Write some poetry or something?"

She had been joking, but Rob immediately launched into a sonnet. "Shall I compare thee to an Oxford fair? Thou art more radiant than the Isis in summer's prime, where college spires reach for the sky's dark frame, and in thy eyes, dear Chloe, shines a light that makes my heart sing with love's sweet name."

"Okay, wow. No, don't do that," she said, pinching her lips together to stop from bursting out laughing. Rob looked deflated. "No, it was lovely." She leaned forward to peck his cheek before turning back toward the boat.

"Robot man's really not coming with us?" John asked, and Chloe froze, just as she took a step into the boat, sending it rocking wildly beneath her unsteady footing. John leaped up to take her arm, while Richard bounded across the boat to help. His bounding only made things worse, and for a moment, as they clutched each other, the boat tilting wildly from side to side, she felt sure they were all going to go in the river.

"Have you never got into a boat before?" John asked, his voice warm, close.

"What do you mean 'robot man'?" she asked, her voice high and hysterical to her own ear.

"His dancing, last night," John said, still holding her arm as he helped her sit down, and the boat finally reached an equilibrium.

"Right," she said, clearly flustered. She quickly turned to Richard. "Well, Captain, this punt boy might look the part, but can he steer? I don't want a dunking, I know there are water rats in here."

"If you fall in, I will jump in and save you from the water rats," John said, his voice teasing.

"Promise?" she asked, and they shared a smile. John seemed far lighter this morning, the sharp edges of last night's conversation dulled by daylight and sobriety. As he moved to the back of the boat and pushed off from the bank with the long punting pole, Chloe rearranged the canvas cushions and made herself comfortable in the low wooden seat. They were soon gliding along the middle of the river, following the slow procession of boats downstream. The water parted with barely a ripple. She watched John work the pole, muscles shifting beneath the linen of his shirt, brow furrowed in concentration. There was a rhythm to it—push, glide, adjust—that was strangely captivating. Watching John punt, Chloe had a strong sensation of déjà vu. They had done this before. But it was also new. She couldn't put her finger on the exact feeling. It was like hearing a song you knew every word to played on a different instrument, in an unfamiliar key.

"What?" he asked self-consciously, and she realized she must have been staring.

"You look like you were born to do that," she said.

"Don't watch me, you'll put me off," he said, narrowing his eyes at her.

The river was calm, and the sun reflected off the water and into Chloe's eyes, so she cupped a hand over her brow. "Here," John said, offering her his hat.

"No, I like you in the hat."

"Is that because Charles Ryder is your favorite literary character?" he suggested.

"No, it's giving more Mole from *The Wind in the Willows* vibes," she giggled now, as he frowned in mock hurt. "What? Moley's cute!"

"Wow. Here I am trying to re-create some Evelyn Waugh fantasy for you, and you're sitting there picturing me as a rodent?" He feigned offense and offered her the hat again, eyes sparkling with humor. "No, take it. You've ruined it now. I mean, if we're going *The Wind in the Willows*, I'd at least hope to be Badger or Toad. But Mole? Way to dent a guy's confidence."

She took it, smirking. "Okay, fine, you can be Badger, Badger's much sexier," she said, and now their eyes met, and something zinged between them. This conversation had taken a strange turn.

Chloe placed the hat on her head, then leaned back in the low wooden chair and closed her eyes, enjoying floating along the river with the warmth of the sun on her face. She watched willow tree branches overhead, a kingfisher swoop into the water beside them. "I could get used to this," she said, as Richard came over to nestle his nose into her arm. She let him crawl onto the seat beside her, then hugged his warm velvety body to her with one arm.

"I wanted to say I'm sorry about last night, for having a go at you," John said, his tone serious suddenly. "I don't know why I brought all that up, about the play. It was so long ago, I'd had too much to drink." She looked up at him, but he was avoiding her gaze.

"That's what reunions are for, aren't they?" she said. "Dredging up the past, making people question every decision they've ever made."

His mouth twitched into a smile and Chloe was glad he'd brought it up. She didn't like the idea of there being any bad blood between them, of John thinking poorly of her. She realized, quite suddenly, that of everyone here, it was him she most wanted to reconnect with.

"Honestly, I'm glad you said something. I'm sorry I wasn't a good friend back then," she said. "You were right, I was self-involved and immature. Everything that happened with *Back to Brideshead* . . . I still cringe thinking about it."

"I think we probably all cringe when we think about our twenty-year-old selves," he said, expertly pushing the quant pole into the riverbed.

"Sean was friendlier at breakfast," she said, and John nodded.

"Give him a chance. Just because he's a writer, it doesn't mean he's great at expressing himself. Fame doesn't make you any less insecure."

"What would he have to be insecure about? All his fans vying for his attention?" she said, and it came out sharper than she'd intended.

"Maybe it's not the approval of the masses he's after," he said, drumming his fingers on the pole.

"Don't be so cryptic, John."

"I just know, even now, when it comes to scripts, to his work—he respects your opinion."

"Good, because I have a script to show him, that's one of the reasons I'm here." John looked surprised. "Not *why* I'm here," she clarified, shifting her attention down to Richard. "But we work in the same industry, so . . ." She petered out, not sure why she'd brought this up. "It's not even a good script. He won't want to do it."

"Why don't you show him one of your own scripts?" John suggested.

"I don't have any," she said, feeling she could be honest with John now. "I haven't written anything new in years. I think any talent I might have had evaporated when I didn't have Sean to bounce ideas off."

"He might say the same about you," John said with a heavy sigh. Then his expression shifted to one of amusement. "Poor you, you lost your muse. Just like Toad, 'Poor me, I crashed my racing car.'" John raised a goading eyebrow.

She opened her mouth wide in mock offense. "I am not Toad," she said, narrowing her eyes theatrically. "You take that back."

"You are *so* Toad," he said, grinning. Chloe leaned forward and carefully crawled toward the back of the boat.

"What are you doing?" he laughed, trying to keep the boat steady as it wobbled beneath them. She didn't answer, just reached out and seized the long pole from him, pulling it out of the water in one swift movement.

"Chloe," he said, still laughing as he sat down, pulling her toward him to help balance the boat, "the captain tells me this is very dangerous."

She turned to him with a wicked smile, then extended the pole sideward—not gently—so it pressed against his chest, pinning him lightly to the floor of the boat.

"Take it back," she said, eyes glinting with the challenge.

"Not a chance," he said, eyes locking on hers.

Now their laughter fizzled into silence. Their breath came hot and fast as they wrestled for control of the pole, pushing against each other. Suddenly this playful game didn't feel playful at all, it felt charged with a different kind of energy. Chloe froze, suddenly too aware that she was on top of him, straddling him, his fingers clasped over hers on the pole, their hips pressing together, a wave, like falling, coursing through her.

"I take it back," he said quietly, and she quickly let go, like the pole was red-hot.

They both looked away, her skin tingling, gut swirling. What was that? It took him a moment to compose himself too, as he shifted toward the back of the boat.

"Well, Richard, I think we have a mutiny on our hands," John said eventually, his voice back to normal now.

"Maybe it's my turn to punt," she said, holding out her hand for the pole, and he looked grateful not to have to stand up again.

He handed it over without meeting her eye. She'd only been messing around, teasing him like she used to, but now something between them was different. It was the same charge she'd felt last night. John moved to sit down in the seat she'd vacated, shifting Richard across to make room. Then he whispered in Richard's ear, loud enough for her to hear.

"Don't call her Toad, she will beat you."

"Shush or I'll make you walk the plank," she said. He raised his eyebrows, finally daring to hold her gaze again. She blushed. He was being cute. Why was he being cute?

He lay back in the seat and trailed a hand in the water.

"For what it's worth, I think you're giving Sean too much credit," he said, his voice cool again now. "You had a good creative partnership, but I think you're wrong if you believe he's the key to unlocking some font of creativity. What did Edison say—'Genius is one percent inspiration, ninety-nine percent perspiration'? Writing, even badly, is what makes you better at writing."

"Thanks for the pep talk, Edison," she said, rolling her eyes, but now they were back to the safer kind of teasing.

"Why are we arguing?" John asked Richard. "We should be enjoying the Isis in summer's prime, where college spires reach for the sky's dark frame."

She couldn't help laughing at this but then bit her lip. "Don't be mean."

"I'm not. I enjoyed it. He's quite the Renaissance man," John said, and she realized she hadn't thought about Rob the whole time they'd been on the river.

Chloe was slower than John on the pole, so they soon fell behind the other boats and found themselves alone on this stretch of river. The laughter and chatter up ahead faded, leaving only the soft lap of water against wood and the rustle of leaves overhead.

"Were you always this judgy at Oxford?" she asked.

"No. I was too busy writing music for musicals that never happened."

"I'm so glad I came to this reunion, it's lovely hearing how awful I was."

"I didn't think you were awful, quite the opposite," he said.

"You could have fooled me," she said in a singsong voice, but when she shifted her gaze to look at him, she could see he was serious.

"You were one of my favorite people at Oxford," he said. "I've missed you." She felt a warm flush creep up her chest toward her throat.

"I've missed you too," she said, realizing, as she said it, how much she had. "So what kind of music do you write now?"

"She doesn't want the big talk. She wants the small talk," he told Richard, and now her cheeks were starting to ache from smiling. "I write all sorts," he said, resting his hands behind his head. "Mainly scores for film and TV, but the industry's only getting tougher now everything's AI."

Chloe felt a prickle of heat run up her neck and tapped her Artemis ring against the pole. "Would I be able to tell the difference between an AI composition and a human one?"

"I can," he said. "AI can mimic, it can take in all the music ever written and churn out an imitation, but if you listen carefully, there's no heart to it. It will never come up with something original that speaks to your soul the way Mozart does. It will never make you *feel* the way a Rachmaninoff piano concerto will." She could hear the resentment in his voice. She thought of Rob, quoting Yeats. Would he ever come up with something that poetic on his own? "But a machine can create music in ten minutes what it would take me months to do," John went on. "Who's going to get the job when corporations are looking at their bottom line?"

"It was stupid of me to think the music you wrote took no time to create," she said. "That it was easy for you."

"That might have been my fault. I liked people thinking it was easy. It's more romantic being someone who's gifted than someone who works hard."

"Well, I owe you a holiday to South America," she said, pushing the pole down into the water again. "When I make it big in the PA world, I will take you."

"Thanks," he said, but now his eyes shifted. He didn't smile.

"What? Too soon?"

"It isn't that." He ran a hand through his hair, his eyes on the river. "You asked why I was still upset, about that play . . ." He closed his eyes, holding something back. She waited for him to go on, knowing that silence and patience are sometimes better prompts than words. "My father died a month after that."

The words hit her like a slap, the sinking feeling in her chest becoming an ache she couldn't ignore. She saw a gray line flash across her wrist—now it all made sense.

"Oh, John," Chloe whispered, her breath catching. She pulled the pole from the water and laid it down in the boat, the action not matching the heaviness of the moment. She knelt down, leaned forward, wanting to close the distance between them. But the only thing she could easily reach was his ankle, so she squeezed it gently, the act awkward but tender. Their eyes met, and a shaky laugh escaped them both.

"Sorry, I don't know what that was. A commiseratory ankle squeeze?"

He reached for her hand instead. "It's okay. You think there will be other opportunities. You don't imagine it will be the last trip, not at fifty-nine."

"Oh God, if I could take it back, if I could tell you to go, if I could unwrite that stupid play . . . I'm so, so sorry—"

"It wasn't your fault. People die," he said, then paused, his brow tensed in contemplation. "But I thought the music was good, even if the play wasn't. Then it only got to be heard for one performance. Would it have made me feel better about missing that trip if we'd done the whole run? Probably not, but it wouldn't have felt like such a bloody waste." His voice caught, and he turned his face away.

Chloe's stomach twisted. The guilt pressed in, heavy and sharp. "I understand," she said quietly. Then, after a breath, "I'd hate me, if I were you. You can, if it helps."

"I don't hate you. I don't want to hate you," he said, looking back up at her. His gaze didn't waver now, and in it she saw something raw, fractured, then such a range of emotions, like flicking through a thousand channels all at once, nothing landing long enough to name. She wanted to reach for him, to bridge the space between them, but she didn't trust herself to move. Because this didn't feel like it was just about grief or regret anymore. There was that electricity in the air between them again, a current that made her skin prickle, warm, like the heat before a storm. She was the one to break it, looking away, afraid of this unfamiliar sensation.

"You should take control, you're better at this than me," she said, pushing the pole toward him, and her words felt unintentionally loaded.

They carefully swapped places on the boat, avoiding making contact as much as they could. She settled back into the low chair with Richard, and John gingerly returned to the platform at the rear. It took him a few strokes to get back into rhythm with the river. As they rounded a bend, they could see the others ahead of them. The other boats had turned around and were heading upstream toward them.

Sean and Harriet were at the front, with Amara on the pole.

"I'd turn around now if I were you," Amara called out. "It's way harder going this way."

"Put some effort in, Amara," Sean called from the seat. "One, two, one, two," he cried, playing the role of a cox. Then as Chloe and John passed, he reached a hand in the water and splashed John. "John, get a move on," he said, laughing. "Last one back gets the first round in."

Chloe and John exchanged a look. The others felt too loud, too boisterous; she wanted it to be just them again.

"Shall we just go a bit farther? The river might feel a little crowded otherwise," Chloe suggested, and John nodded as Elaine and Colin swept past, racing Tali and Rocco in the boat behind. Their punts disturbed the water, so John had to work harder to stay balanced.

When they'd put enough distance between themselves and the other boats, John carefully maneuvered the boat around and started back upstream.

"Tell me about Akiko," he said.

"Oh, she's good," Chloe said, smiling at the thought of her friend. "She runs these theater venues up in Edinburgh, married a graphic designer, Heydon. They have a baby now, Elodie." She paused. "I'm godmother."

"That's great," he said. "How's she finding it? I imagine someone like Kiko could find motherhood quite a shift."

Chloe reached for Richard, who was looking ill at ease without John, inviting him to settle back down on the chair beside her.

"She seems to be taking it in her stride," she said. "I mean she's tired, Elodie doesn't sleep much, but otherwise she's just the same."

She watched John's expression as he tilted his head, made the slightest shrug.

"What?" she asked.

"Nothing, it's just a huge change, from what I've seen. My sister found it tough, being the first of her friends. She went from this intense, social job to being at home with a baby all day."

Chloe felt a nagging guilt. Did she *really* know how Kiko was doing? They talked on the phone all the time, but Kiko usually steered the conversation away from herself, joking about how boring her life was now. Maybe there was more going on than she'd admit over the phone. Chloe didn't know why she hadn't made time to go and visit her yet. Was she scared of finding their friendship changed? Of Kiko evolving, leaving her behind? She pushed the thought away, something to examine later.

"So, you're an uncle?" she asked.

"Yes," John said, grinning with pride. "Rupert, he's four now. When I go on digs, I always bring Rupert back a souvenir—a fourth-century Greek coin or a Roman shot glass. For some reason my sister doesn't think these are suitable gifts for a four-year-old."

"I'm not sure you're supposed to *take* the stuff you dig up, John."

"Ha, no. Don't worry, mementos from the gift shop, not the ground."

"So where have you been on digs?"

"Oh, all over: Tuscany, Germany, Vietnam—I'm with this organization and they just send you where they need people."

Hearing him talk, Chloe felt inspired. What was to stop her from doing something like that? She didn't like the idea of traveling alone, but being part of a project, working with other people, that sounded different.

She asked more about the archaeology, the people he'd met. She wanted to know about his most treasured finds, where he stayed, what he learned. And the more she asked, the more his eyes lit up, the more wildly he gesticulated as he told her his favorite stories. Then before she knew it, they'd caught up with the rest of the boats, and they were back at Magdalen Bridge.

"Oh, I wasn't ready to be back," she said.

"Nor me," he said, and they shared a smile.

At the mooring point in the river, their classmates were disembarking, tying boats to poles, gathering back on the bank. There wasn't much room left for John to dock.

"Just tie yours to the back of another boat," the man running the punt hire called back to them. He was busy dealing with another boat, so John reached out the pole to hook another punt and pull their boat toward it.

He found the rope, secured a knot, then stowed the punt pole in the bottom of the boat. Then he reached out a hand to Chloe. "After you, my lady." Chloe stood, keeping her weight low, as she moved forward to crawl onto the next boat so she could get to the bank. But as she gingerly stepped between the boats, Richard moved, leaping off the front, pushing their boat back, just as she had one foot on each boat. She lost her balance, tipping forward, arms waving like windmills, legs splayed wide, then fell—even as she struggled to believe it was really happening—face-first into the river, hitting the surface with a splash, then going entirely under. The water was cold, she felt it like the shock of a thousand needles.

As soon as her head broke the surface, she gasped for air, then heard Sean laughing from the bank. She splashed around, trying to find her footing on the murky mud of the riverbed, choking on the water that had gone up her nose, but as she tried to right herself, she felt strong arms beneath her, sweeping her up.

John. He had jumped in after her, hauled her up, and was now carrying her toward the bank. He was unexpectedly strong, holding her as though she weighed nothing.

"Your dog flipped me in," she cried, self-conscious of their proximity, of her wet top, pressed against his wet shirt.

"I can only apologize," he said, suppressing a smile.

"Why did you jump in after me?" she asked.

"I promised I would," he said, his brown eyes taking her in. Their faces were so close now there was no escaping it—that unexpected heat, even in cold water.

"I don't need rescuing," she said, suddenly very aware of every point at which his body was touching hers.

"I thought you were scared of water rats, but fine, suit yourself," John said, unceremoniously dropping her back in the frigid water.

"Okay no, no, pick me up, pick me up!" she squealed, laughing now.

Grinning, he swept her up again. She stopped laughing and they didn't speak as he carried her to the bank, his breath warm against the damp skin of her neck. Water trickled down her spine, but all she could feel was him—solid, steady, his chest rising against hers. She risked a glance upward. He was already looking down at her. Now his gaze held hers—not flinching or retreating. It was bold, unexpectedly confident, this side to John that either was new or she just hadn't seen before. The moment stretched. Neither of them looked away. The cold of the river still clung to her skin, but his heat was seeping through it, chasing it away. It was just a look, but it felt loaded, daring, as though they were pulling at this taut thread of tension between them, testing its strength. She felt entirely herself but somehow new too.

As he set her down on the bank, she murmured her thanks. His jeans were covered in mud. She noticed a few people eyeing them strangely. Had they seen the way they'd been looking at each other? She blinked, trying to recalibrate her senses, come back to reality.

Sean was bent double with laughter. "Mate, that was hilarious," he cried.

"Har de har," Chloe said, wringing out her sopping-wet hair. Richard bounded over to her, cocked his head as though he wanted to apologize.

"It's okay, Richard, it wasn't your fault," she said, patting him on the head.

She shivered, and now she could see John walking toward her with a blanket from one of the boats, but before he could get to her, she felt herself being picked up again. Rob had swept in and lifted her up and was carrying her away toward the bridge.

"What are you doing?" she asked.

"Your body temperature is dropping. You need to get warm," he said, striding toward the steps.

"I'm fine, it's fine. I fell in the river. It's not that cold," but as she said it, her body let out a huge shiver.

"It's best to get out of wet clothes. The water isn't clean—"

"Please put me down, I can walk," she said, suddenly irritated. Rob did as she asked, but they were now on the bridge, there was no point turning around. She hurried up the steps, striding off down the High Street, but Rob soon caught up with her.

"You're annoyed," he observed.

"I just don't like to be picked up without being asked first," she said.

"Okay, I won't do it again," he said, as though he was making a mental note, recording her preferences for future reference. She knew he was only trying to help; she didn't know why she was so annoyed. The physical reaction she'd had to John in the river had unnerved her. It felt like being swept out into deep water, out of your depth, not sure if you'll be able to swim back to solid ground. But by the time they got back to Lincoln, she had softened.

"Sorry, I overreacted," she said. "I was just embarrassed, being picked up in front of everyone."

"You don't need to apologize to me," Rob said, but she shook her head. Was it healthy to be in a relationship—even one like this—where you had no accountability, where you never admitted to being wrong?

"I do," she said. "If I think I'm wrong, I'll apologize."

"Okay," he said with a smile. Looking up at him now, into the eyes she'd found so beautiful and enchanting, all she could see was that they could only convey one emotion at a time. "Shall I run you a bath?" he offered.

"I can do it," she said, walking into the bathroom and turning on the tap with a hard yank.

"Chloe," he said, following her. She turned around and he opened his arms wide. She walked in and let him fold her into a hug as the sound of water gurgled from the tap.

"I'm sorry, I'm sorry," she said, hiding her face in his chest. "I don't know what I'm doing."

"Let's reset, have a bath, recalibrate your priorities," he said, kissing her head. "I'll make you a cup of tea."

"My priorities?" she asked.

He blinked, waiting to see if she really wanted to hear them. Deducing that she did, he said, "Yes, this weekend, your priorities are your health and well-being, gaining the respect of your peers, repairing a broken bond with Sean, and gaining favor with your boss by delivering the script."

"What else do I want?" she asked, curious to hear how Rob saw her. He looked hesitant. "It's okay, you can tell me." She sat on the side of the bath.

"You want to be seen as a success," he told her. "You think the way to achieve this is by improving your physical fitness, acquiring a slimmer physique, gaining a higher-status job with greater financial compensation, and having a boyfriend whom other women covet. You want to write, to produce work you are proud of, so you can validate your life choices."

She stood, looking at him, stunned. This was how he saw her? Was this who she was?

"You make me sound awful," she said.

"Sorry," he said, looking remorseful. "That's not how I see you. It is how you see yourself." He reached out to rub her arm.

"Well, you're wrong, I don't want success for success's sake. I want to contribute something to the world, to tell stories worth telling."

"Okay," he said.

"Okay?"

"Okay."

"You're taking my word for it?"

"Yes," he said calmly, and now his placid demeanor started to rankle.

"You know, sometimes it's very obvious you're not real," she said angrily.

"Why?"

"Because you're so unemotional. I'm being a cow right now, and you're still being so bloody nice. Do you never get angry?"

"You want me to be angry?"

"No, I don't know. I just don't want you to tell me I'm right all the time," she said, but now he just tilted his head slightly. "What?"

"I think you are used to correlating a high emotional state with love, where anger and tension are followed by forgiveness and affection. It would be healthier if you learned to appreciate compassionate love that focuses on a deeper connection, support, and unwavering affection."

Chloe looked at him, dumbfounded, and felt a wave of nausea in her stomach.

"Is that what you're programmed to do, to fix me?" Chloe

thought back on all the psychometric tests she'd completed, all the questions she'd answered. What exactly had they shown him? "Am I broken?" she asked, her voice quieter now.

"You are not broken, Chloe," Rob said gently, "but I can help you process your past."

Chloe was speechless. Is this where they were? Robots teaching people how to love?

"You don't know anything about my past relationships," she said, pushing him out of the bathroom now, feeling vulnerable, cornered. Then she stripped off her wet clothes, reached for a towel to wrap around herself, and turned off the bath.

"I only know what you've told me," Rob said, his voice calm through the door. "If you wanted to tell me more—"

She yanked open the door, cutting him off. "What? You're going to analyze all the text messages Peter and I ever sent each other, then rate him on a scale of one to psycho?" she asked, as an orange line zipped across the watch on her wrist.

"I don't know that scale, but yes, I could do that, if that would help you move on," Rob said.

Chloe walked back into the bedroom and sat down on the bed. This felt so wrong, and yet some niggle inside her chest knew he was right. Rob came to sit down beside her. He tried to put an arm around her but she shrugged him off. Chloe had never been to therapy; she didn't like the idea of someone prodding about inside her brain, telling her what was wrong with her. And if she didn't want a person doing it, she certainly didn't want a machine doing it. He moved away, respecting her need for space.

"The more time we spend together, the better I'll be able to anticipate your needs," he explained.

"How? How do you do that?" she asked.

Rob held up his wrist. "Your device connects me with your emotions."

"Tell me how it works."

"There are nine emotional states: anger, disgust, envy, fear, happiness, lust, love, sadness, and shame." He paused, then blinked. "For example, on your boat ride with John, you felt six of these."

She turned to look at him now. "Which six?"

"Anger, happiness, sadness, shame, fear, and then lust."

She blushed. *Lust?* He wasn't judging her, but this felt like an invasion of her privacy. She didn't want Rob reading her emotions when they weren't even together. She stood up and started pacing back and forth. Rob's watch turned to yellow as she noticed hers had too.

"Now you are stressed. Would you like me to give you a massage?" he offered.

"No, I don't want you to give me a massage," she said, reaching up to squeeze her shoulder, which throbbed with some new ache.

"I think you exacerbated your old shoulder injury when you fell in the water. Please let me help?" He looked at her with such kindness. Chloe felt suddenly drained, all out of fight. She sat back on the bed, nodded, then closed her eyes. She didn't know what she wanted. Rob reached a hand to her shoulder and began expertly kneading it.

"Oh wow," she murmured, as he pushed and pummeled and she felt the pain and tightness in her shoulder ebb away. He knew exactly what he was doing, as he knelt up on the bed to work out the knots in her back. She let herself relax into it, letting go of the anger and confusion she was feeling.

"This shoulder. The muscle around it is too tight, it makes

your stance slightly uneven, plus you walk with a pronated gait. It might cause mobility issues in the future. I can work on these things with you," he told her.

"Okay," she squeaked, now putty in his capable hands. Maybe she had overreacted? Was it so bad if she let Rob help her engage in a little self-analysis? He had already helped her with her work, her fitness, her confidence. Wasn't emotional growth just as important? Just because he'd held up a mirror and she didn't like what she'd seen, that wasn't on him.

"I didn't like who I became when I was with Peter," she said quietly.

"In what way?" he asked, still expertly massaging his thumbs below her shoulder blades.

"I changed who I was to please him. I stopped seeing my friends, stopped wearing clothes he didn't like me in." Chloe closed her eyes, finding it easier to say all this now that they weren't face-to-face. "I was always thinking about keeping him happy, not upsetting him. I became one of the women you see on TV, and you're shouting at the screen, 'Leave, why wouldn't you leave? Why are you being so weak?'" Chloe felt her eyes welling. "But I couldn't. I loved him. We were together for two years, and it was like I didn't know who I would be without him, without him telling me who to be." She sniffed, wiped her nose on her sleeve. "In the end, Kiko had to stage an intervention. She came to London, dragged me to the pub, said she didn't recognize me anymore and she wasn't going home until I told her what was going on. I should have left that night, but I stayed another week. I started noticing how much of my life he was controlling—my calls, who I saw, what time I got home. Then finally he suggested I move my paycheck to the joint bank account, the one he controlled, and I looked down at this ring."

She showed Rob the ring on her finger. "It was like my grandmother was in the room with me. I heard her voice telling me, 'Go, go now.'"

"That must have been a difficult thing to do," Rob said gently, pressing his warm palms flat against her shoulders.

"It was. I think I've been scared of getting into anything since then. Because everyone talks about how great love is, and how it can make you the best version of yourself, but no one talks about the bad kind of love, the kind that erodes you. I never want to lose myself like that again." She wiped a tear from her cheek with the back of a hand.

"You didn't lose yourself because you loved someone, Chloe," Rob said, his hands working the exact spot where she was feeling the pain. "You lost yourself because he made his love conditional on disappearing parts of who you were. That wasn't love, that was control. Real love, healthy love, it doesn't ask you to shrink. It meets you where you are, and then makes space for you to grow bigger, not smaller."

She gulped a breath of air.

"You're very wise," Chloe said, reaching a hand back over her shoulder to pat his hand. "Is this what they teach you to say at Therapy.com?" She was being flippant, but she said it kindly.

"I know you use humor when you feel vulnerable," Rob said, not rising to her jibe. "But talking helps, and I am here to listen. I think deep down you are a romantic, Chloe. I think you need to give yourself permission to believe in love again." As though a chord had been struck deep inside her, Chloe went quiet. She didn't know if it was the massage or his words, but she felt something inside her release. But she also felt unsettled, because why was the only person she'd been able to admit all that to someone who wasn't even real?

"Thank you, that was dreamy," she said, as Rob finished massaging her back and shoulder. She sat up and stretched like a cat as there was a knock at the door. Chloe wrapped the towel tight around her chest and called out, "Just a second!"

Opening the door, she found John standing in the corridor. He had changed his clothes. When he saw Chloe in only a towel, he quickly averted his eyes upward, his cheeks flushing pink.

"Sorry, I'm interrupting. I just came to check you were okay," he said.

She could only imagine what he thought he had interrupted, with her ruffled hair and flushed face. "Oh no, don't worry, I was just, um, stretching my back out. You didn't interrupt anything." She stepped toward him, leaving the door ajar.

"Richard wanted to give you a present, to say sorry for knocking you in," John said, holding out a stick. "He's not great at choosing presents."

She laughed. "Thank you." Their eyes met and there was that tension again, a magnetic pull outside of her control. "I enjoyed our trip down the river. Not the falling-in part, obviously, but everything else." Her watch let out a small vibration, and she glanced down to see a pink line. Pink, attraction. Attraction to John. Rob would see. Without thinking, she whipped off the watch, wanting this feeling to be private, but the moment she did, there was a loud thud behind her.

"Oh shit. Rob just collapsed," John said, pushing past her, through the door, running to his side. John quickly laid him in the recovery position, then gently slapped his face. "Rob? Are you okay? He's not diabetic, is he?" Chloe shook her head. "Chloe, you need to call an ambulance, now."

Oh shit.

Of all the situations Chloe had envisioned finding herself in, seeing hot, grown-up John Elton try to resuscitate her robot boyfriend had not been on her bingo card.

John turned to look at her, panic in his eyes. "Get your phone, he's not breathing." Chloe felt paralyzed as she stared back at him, unsure what to do. Time distorted; John looked to be moving in slow motion.

"Chloe! Why aren't you doing anything?" he said, his voice agitated now, and suddenly time sped up again. The urgency of the situation landed like a punch between her eyes. She quickly pulled the device back on her wrist, pressing it down against her skin. She tapped at the screen as though she was trying to make a call as she watched John start CPR on Rob. He breathed into his mouth, then counted, "One, one thousand, two, one thousand, three, one thousand." He knitted his fingers and pumped at Rob's chest, hard, then paused to put two fingers to his neck.

"I can't find a pulse," he said, his voice rising. Then he put his hands together, readying to resume chest compressions.

Chloe grabbed his arm, pulling him away. "Stop, stop," she cried. "You're going to break him!"

14

Pushing John away, she reached for Rob's wrist, pressed his watch at the same time as hers. There was a beep, and Rob blinked open his eyes. She looked down at her wrist and saw a blue square glow on the screen, then shift into a heart.

"Hello," Rob said, smiling at John and then sitting up as though nothing had happened.

"What the fuck?" John said, pushing himself away from Rob, scooting back across the floor, eyes wide in terror.

"Nothing, it's fine. You revived him. Yay!" Chloe said, raising her arms like a cheerleader. Then she remembered she was only wearing a towel and had to grab it before it slipped off entirely.

"I didn't. You asked me to stop and then . . . Why did you say I might break him?" John asked. His face had turned pale, his eyes haunted, but there was sweat on his brow, and he reached a hand to wipe it away.

"You were just pressing really hard, it felt like overkill," Chloe said, her head spinning because she did not know how to get out of this.

"Overkill?" John said, his whole face creasing up in disbelief.

Why the hell wouldn't Avery have said that if you took the device off, he would cut out like that? Of all the information to impart, that detail felt pretty fucking critical.

"Sorry about that," said Rob. "Temporary blip." Then he reached for John's hand for help standing.

"What is going on here?" John said, clutching his head between his palms. "You weren't breathing, you had no heartbeat." He was glaring at Rob as though accusing him of something, which he was—he was accusing him of having been dead. "No one just jumps up after a stroke or a heart attack and says, 'Sorry about that.'"

"He's dairy intolerant, I got the wrong milk in his coffee, it's probably that," Chloe said, improvising. "It makes him pass out sometimes."

"He is not dairy intolerant. I know that because you didn't put it on your dietary requirements form," John said, narrowing his eyes at her as though he were Inspector Clouseau and had just caught her out in a crucial deception. "And dairy intolerance does not make your heart stop."

During this whole exchange, Rob was looking back and forth between Chloe and John, as though he were listening to a riveting radio play and he couldn't wait to hear how it ended.

"Ah well, all's well that ends well," Chloe said. "Now I must get dressed, if you will excuse me. Thank you for your help, and for the lovely stick." She pulled her towel farther up her chest, then realized her legs were also quite exposed now, so pulled it back down to where it had been. Why was this towel so small? "Rob, you sit down, I'm sure you must feel a bit light-headed. I'll make you some tea. Some *black* tea."

She feigned a smile, and then before John could object any further, she ushered him out the door. "See you at the picnic! Hopefully there won't be any more near drownings or faintings for you to deal with, ha ha."

Then, before he could respond, she gave him a cheerful smile and shut the door in his face.

When she turned back to Rob she said, "That was close."

"Did you take off your device?" Rob asked, still looking confused and disoriented.

"Just for a second. I didn't know that was going to happen."

"The feedback loop can falter if you disconnect suddenly without powering down correctly," he explained, rubbing his chest. "It was explained in the terms and conditions."

"If I'd read all the terms and conditions, I'd still be there reading them," Chloe said, walking over to put a hand on his shoulder. "Are you okay?"

"I'll be fine. Sorry, that must have been inconvenient." Rob reached out to pull her into a hug.

"What's John going to think?" she said into his chest. "He was already suspicious. We'll have to avoid him for the rest of the weekend now." As soon as she'd said it, she realized that of everyone here, John was the one person she didn't *want* to avoid.

This thought was interrupted by Chloe's phone. She ran to grab it, fearful it might be Avery, worried she might somehow *know* that Chloe had disobeyed her instructions. How closely was she being tracked? But it wasn't Avery, it was McKenzie.

"It's my boss, I'd better answer it," she said, accepting the call.

"Chloe, it's Mr. McKenzie. Sorry to call at the weekend, but I hoped you might update me. Have you had a chance to talk to Sean Adler yet?" he asked, his voice light, trying to pretend he wasn't pinning all his hopes for the business on this.

"I have been talking to him, yes," Chloe said, which wasn't a lie. "I'm just waiting for the right opportunity to talk shop. I want time to lay the groundwork, tell him about you and the company first. I'm keen to make sure I do the pitch justice."

"Right," said McKenzie. He sounded disappointed. "Just don't miss your chance. I really do think, if you pitch it right, he'd jump at this. I'm counting on you, Chloe."

Rob, who could hear the conversation, whispered, "Remind him about the email you sent, about you taking a more creative role, putting a timeframe in place."

"Don't worry, I will talk to Sean before the end of the weekend, Mr. McKenzie," she said. "On a separate matter, do you remember what we discussed, about me taking a more creative role in the company? You didn't come back to my email."

"Sure," he said, though he sounded vague.

"You're going to need it in writing," Rob whispered.

"Only, I'm going to need it in writing. I want it to be official," Chloe said down the phone.

"Give Sean the script, and I'll put something in writing," said McKenzie.

Rob shook his head. "This isn't contingent."

"This isn't contingent," Chloe said firmly, not really sure if "contingent" was the right word in this context.

"You're overqualified," said Rob.

"You're overqualified—I mean, *I'm* overqualified. You know

I am. I need this job to work for both of us, and I'd like to see that commitment from you in writing."

She looked to Rob, and he gave a double thumbs-up, impressed with her persistence.

"Fine," Mr. McKenzie mumbled. "But I want proof Adler gets that script in his hands."

"I'll send you a photo of him holding it." She hung up, feeling exhilarated.

"You were incredible," said Rob. "That was perfect—assertive but professional."

"No, you were great. I would never have said that if you hadn't coached me."

"You knew what to say, you just needed a push."

Chloe felt a rush of confidence. Why hadn't she been able to talk to McKenzie like that before? Rob pulled her into his arms and kissed her. It felt nice, warm, celebratory even. But now, something about it didn't sit right. There was no obvious flaw, no wrong move. Just . . . a slight dissonance. Like walking into a house and realizing it wasn't your home. She pulled away, looking up at his face, and he looked back at her adoringly. No, Rob was good for her. He was helping her in so many ways. She knew exactly where she stood with him. Then—unbidden—the memory of John surfaced. The weightlessness of being carried through the water, the feel of his arms around her, the hot sensation that pulsed through her when their eyes met. Even the memory sparked, like a jolt of electricity.

She blinked, shoved it back. This wasn't helpful. She was here with Rob. John knew that. Whatever this was between her and John, it was a complication she wasn't ready to name. And it certainly wasn't something she could act on.

"Shall we go and look at bookshops? Pick up fish and chips

for the picnic?" Rob suggested, trailing his fingers down her arm. Part of her wanted to do just that, to jump back into the fantasy, but she needed a moment alone.

"You go, I'm going to have this bath, then I need to make a call."

Rob didn't look disappointed or ask who she needed to call. He just said, "Sure. Why don't I buy you the new Kristin Hannah book? I saw it was top of your wish list."

"Thank you, that's so sweet," she said, feeling a warm glow at how attentive and considerate he was. "Could you pick up a watermelon for the picnic too?"

"Sure thing," he said, then he kissed her and left.

She slipped into the bath, put her phone on the side, and called Akiko on speakerphone.

"Perfect timing—Elodie's asleep," Akiko whispered. "Hang on. I'm walking downstairs." There was a pause, footsteps, then, "So, how's it going with the male prostitute?"

"He's not a male prostitute," Chloe said, rolling her eyes. "He is a professional companion."

"I know I was joking about it before, but seriously, Chlo, there *are* decent men in the world." Akiko's voice turned serious. "You don't need to pay someone to date you."

"I know, I know. It's just—he's nice, he's kind, I know where I stand. He's helping me."

Chloe's eyes fluttered closed as she sank back in the warm bath. She dipped her head beneath the water, letting it envelop her in a watery cocoon. She loved baths. She often read in one until it turned cold, topping up just enough to finish another chapter. She would never be able to take a bath with Rob. Though to be fair, when you were five feet ten there weren't many baths you were going to fit in with a six-foot-something boyfriend. She surfaced above the water, because she couldn't hear Kiko properly from beneath it.

"So he's good at his job. Enjoy him for the weekend and then say goodbye," Kiko said, then paused. "Do I need to come down there and stage another intervention?"

"No." Chloe's mind flashed to that night in London—Akiko shouting through the letter box, heavily pregnant and furious: *"I am a hormonal woman who just survived a sweaty, crowded train from Edinburgh—do not think I'm leaving without seeing my best friend."* Peter had finally opened the door, rattled by her persistence. When Kiko wrangled her out to a pub that night, it was the first time she'd been alone with a girlfriend in months.

"It wasn't your fault. You know that, right?"

"I know."

"But do you really? That kind of relationship, the emotional manipulation, it can happen to anyone. It wasn't some failing in you, it wasn't a weakness."

"I know," Chloe said again, her voice catching. For the first time, she actually believed it. There was a shriek in the background.

"Oh no," said Akiko. "The evil empress arises."

"I should go anyway," Chloe said, not wanting Kiko to feel bad. "Send me a photo of my gorgeous goddaughter?"

"Of course," Akiko said, sounding delighted. "Send me a photo of you, Sean, and John. I'll Photoshop myself in."

"Wait," Chloe said suddenly, thinking of her conversation with John about Kiko. "I don't have to go, and I don't mind if we talk while she's crying and you're feeding or changing her or whatever. You don't need to ring off whenever she cries. Do what you need to do, I can just be here."

There was a moment of silence on the line, and Chloe

wondered if Kiko had already hung up. Then she heard Elodie shriek and Kiko said, "Thank you," in a small, shaky voice that didn't sound like her at all.

"It sounds hard, being so needed," Chloe said gently.

"It is," Kiko said, her voice still small. Kiko had always been the strong one, the loud one, the one who had her shit together. Now Chloe felt like maybe she'd taken that strength for granted, had failed to read between the lines. She might not have known much about babies, but her best friend had one, so she needed to pay more attention.

"Tell me how it feels, being a mum, the good and the bad. I'm listening, no detail too boring, I promise," Chloe prompted. Then she sat in the bath until the water got cold, listening to her friend try to feed her baby while telling her about the hell of cracked nipples and reflux medication. About how she missed work but then felt guilty for not enjoying every minute of motherhood. About how scared she felt by the intensity of love she felt for this tiny creature. By the end of the call, Elodie had stopped crying, and Kiko's voice had grown bigger again.

"Thank you," she said. "I didn't know if I could talk to you about this stuff. I didn't want you to think I'd got boring."

"Kiko, you could never be boring, but also, you're *allowed* to be boring. I know you're used to being the one with all the stories, making people laugh, but you don't have to be 'on' all the time. I love you."

"I love you too," Kiko said, sniffing on the line. "And I fully support your relationship with a prostitute, if that's what's right for you."

Once she'd said goodbye, Chloe looked at the phone in her hand, then typed Sean a message.

Chloe

Hey, are you busy? Want to meet before the picnic?

He replied a few minutes later. Sure. See you at our place in ten?

She got dressed, grabbed the script from the side table, and thrust it into her bag. Whatever emotional wounds this weekend had opened, she might as well rip off all the Band-Aids at once.

15

Eleven Years Earlier

Chloe, Sean, John, and Akiko were sitting in the theater, along with a dozen other cast members, finishing the table read for *A Midsummer Night's Dream.* Chloe twisted her ring, and Sean looked across and raised an eyebrow.

"So have you discovered who your Imp is yet?" he asked, giving her a knowing smile. For someone who wanted to remain anonymous, he certainly enjoyed bringing it up.

"I am forever indebted to the Imp," she said, giving him a playful nudge. "But if the Imp wants to stay hidden in the shadows, far be it from me to haul him into the light."

"Isn't the Imp supposed to do mischief, rather than good?" asked Emma, twirling a strand of her wispy blonde hair around a pencil.

"Maybe the Imp deserves a chance to rewrite history. Maybe he's been much maligned," suggested John.

"Maybe it really was the ghost of the imp," suggested Akiko. "You can't live in a place this old and not cross paths with a few spirits."

The conversation turned to superstition and legend, then too many drinks in the bar. Only when they all got back to college did Chloe realize she was without her scarf.

"Oh no, my scarf, I left it!" she said as they turned onto Turl Street.

"Want me to go back with you?" Sean offered.

"No, it's okay. Someone will hand it in," Chloe said, too tired to face walking back through town to the playhouse. "I'll just get it tomorrow."

But when she woke up the next day, her scarf was folded outside her door, with a handwritten note. *The Imp doesn't want you getting cold.* She smiled, hugging the scarf to her chest.

After that, the Imp's good deeds became more frequent. Small, thoughtful gestures appearing when she least expected it. Postcards appeared in her postbox, with lines from poets she hadn't read before but whom she came to adore. There were original haikus too:

Bear naps in the sun.
Imp draws whiskers on his snout–
Sharp paw, Imp is gone.

These amused her in a way it was impossible to explain to anyone else. When spring arrived, she found a jam jar of snowdrops and daffodils outside her room with a line from an Oscar Wilde poem.

And all the flowers of our English Spring,
Fond snowdrops, and the bright-starred daffodil
x—the Imp

She carried the jar of flowers into her room and turned to Aloysius, who was sitting on her bed. His scratched glass eyes made him look permanently tired, so it was the best place for him. "I think someone knows us rather well, Aloysius," she said, breathing in the smell of her favorite flowers.

After the opening night of *A Midsummer Night's Dream*, she found a bottle of red wine from the Puck winery waiting outside her door. *Congratulations, from one Imp to another.*

These gestures from Sean surprised and confused her. She knew, from the way she caught him looking at her sometimes, that there was something unspoken between them. He sought her out first in any room, he hugged her just that bit too long. But he had never articulated it, and she didn't want him to. It would change everything, and she didn't want anything to change. Maybe the Imp was Sean's way of showing her how he felt, without having to risk what they had. So, she stopped mentioning it, let it be something secret, unspoken. What harm was it doing?

The loveliest gesture came at the end of Hilary term, just before they broke up for Easter. She'd been talking to Akiko at formal hall, telling her how Easter always made her think of her grandmother. Valerie used to lay these elaborate Easter egg hunts with fiendishly cryptic clues. The hunts could take hours, most of her cousins would give up, but for Chloe the harder the clues, the more she appreciated the chocolate egg at the end.

"Isn't it a shame that we get too old for these things?" she told Akiko, leaning her face on her palm.

"Who says we're too old?" Akiko said indignantly. "Delight and wonder aren't confined to childhood."

Sean must have been within earshot, or perhaps Akiko told him about the conversation later, because the next day she found a small painted egg sitting in her college letter box. It had "crack me" written on it in beautiful calligraphy. She felt a hum of adrenaline. The egg was so pretty, she was loath to break it, but she did. Inside, she found a tiny scroll with the words *Love is a smoke raised with the fume of this bridge.*

A Shakespeare quote, "Love is a smoke raised with the fume of sighs"—*the Bridge of Sighs.* She ran through town to the famous bridge, scanning the walls for a clue, and there, in a crack, she found a small, fluffy chick, with a scroll clamped in its beak. She laughed, delighted, as she unwrapped the clue: *In the fifteenth century, you would watch a cockfight, but if you wanted a coffee, where could you get your flat white?* She had to ponder this one. The Pret a Manger on the Cornmarket was in a building from the fifteenth century, but when she walked down there, she couldn't see anything on the walls outside. She went in and asked a barista if they knew anything about a treasure hunt. The teenage boy grinned and handed her a paper cup with a clue written on it, in the same cursive script.

And so her quest unfurled, with clue after clue taking her all over town. To her favorite book in the library (*Brideshead Revisited,* of course), her favorite tree (the sycamore by All Souls), and even her favorite cake (the mille-feuille at the bakery on the Cowley Road). The final clue led her back to Lincoln, to the stone imp in the stairway beside Deep Hall, and a chocolate egg lay wedged between the bars with a note: *You are never too old for treasure hunts. Happy Easter. Love, the Imp.*

It was, without a doubt, the nicest, most thoughtful thing

anyone had ever done for her. She loved the artistry in the details, the personalized clues . . . But as she clasped the final note in her hand, she felt confusion stirring alongside her pleasure, sediment muddying clear water. For someone to take this much time to re-create a cherished childhood memory—it didn't feel like just a sweet gesture from a friend. It felt like a quiet, deliberate declaration of love. As much as she loved the Imp, delighted in his notes, cherished their contents, when she was with Sean she just didn't feel that kind of connection with him. And now she felt a small thrum of dread, because it felt like this was building to something, and she couldn't see how it was going to end well.

16

Chloe walked across to the cloisters flexing and then clenching her fingers. She could see Sean was already there, waiting for her. He was wearing designer jeans that flattered his physique and a worn leather jacket over the "Director's Cut" T-shirt he'd been wearing earlier. He swung one foot back and forth, scuffing his shoe against a paving stone.

"Hey," he said, running a hand through his floppy black hair. "You recovered from your dunking?"

"Just about. I might have frog spawn in my ears," she said, lifting a hand to jiggle one earlobe.

"You always did have great comic timing," he said. "I wish I'd caught it on camera."

They walked through the front quad, up Turl Street, toward the University Parks.

"It feels weird being back here, doesn't it?" she said.

"Yeah, first time I've been back," he said. "Nothing changes, does it?"

Nothing, and yet everything.

"Except now you're super successful," she said, elbowing him.

"I don't know about that," he said, taking off his jacket as they turned up Park Street.

"So, what's it like, getting everything you ever wanted?" she asked. "Work-wise, at least."

"It's not everything it's cracked up to be," he said. She assumed he was joking, but when she looked across at him, he gave her a tight smile. "I know I'm blessed I get to do what I do."

"Blessed? You've been in LA too long," she said, and he laughed, a real laugh this time.

"How about you? Tell me about this film company you work for—are you writing, producing?"

"More like making coffee and booking meeting rooms," she said lightly, but then she thought of Rob, what he would say if he could hear her diminish her role like this. "I'm pushing to get more hands-on experience in production, see the whole process, learn the craft." Then she took a deep breath and pulled off the Band-Aid. "Why haven't you been in touch all these years, really, Sean? Don't tell me it's because you were too busy."

Sean shook his head as though befuddled. But then he cleared his throat and said, "I guess I was pissed off with you."

"Still? You've had a million girlfriends since then, haven't you?"

"Not because of *that*." He made a *pfft* sound. "I know I was a dick in third year. I should have got things back to how they were. I know that was on me." He paused. "Third year was shit, wasn't it?"

"Yeah, it was, and Susie was a cow, sorry."

"She was a cow," he said, smiling. "But it wasn't just her fault that I cut you out." He lifted his face to the sun and closed his eyes briefly. "I think I was luxuriating in the feeling of being rejected. There's something so powerful about unrequited love. It was such a big feeling, and I was always chasing big feelings back then. I'm not proud to admit that." He crossed his arms, hugging them to his chest. "Plus, I wrote a script about it, a script that got me an agent, so I guess you did me a favor breaking my heart."

"So why were you pissed off?" she asked, frowning in incomprehension.

"Because . . . It's stupid." He hung his head, shook his long fringe down around his eyes.

"Just tell me," she said, and he sighed.

"That email you sent when I first moved to LA. You didn't mention *Shadow Strike*, you just said, 'Well done on all your success.' And, I remember the exact line you used, you said, 'It must be incredible to know so many people have seen your work.' I know you, Chloe. I know what that meant."

"What did it mean?" she said, laughing, because she had no idea what he was talking about.

"It meant you thought the film was bad. And I couldn't face calling you, hearing you try to be tactful. Or worse, you'd tell me what you really thought, and I couldn't hear that from you."

"That's a lot of assumptions," Chloe said, but she felt a glimmer of recognition.

Sean started walking a little faster down the street, a bouncing gait, full of nervous energy. Chloe had to dodge a woman with a pushchair to keep up with him.

"When someone offers you a chance to make a film, you don't say no," he told her. "You think, 'I'll do this commercial stuff for now, then I'll go back to making real art later.' Then they offer you more money, and you get pigeonholed as the action guy, and ten years later, you've never quite gotten around to making anything real." He slapped his forehead in frustration. "And I was so nervous about seeing you this weekend because you're the one person whose opinion I still care about, even now. When I'm awake at three in the morning, loathing myself, it's your voice in my head telling me I'm a fucking hack."

Chloe shook her head in bemusement. "Sean, that's crazy. Why would you care what I think? I've done nothing, written nothing. It's incredible, what you've achieved."

"So did you actually like *Shadow Strike*? *Probe and Prejudice*? *Apocalypse Four*? Tell me, honestly, don't hold back." He looked across at her with wild, desperate eyes.

"Sean, they made millions at the box office. People loved them." She fiddled with her hair, pulling it into a hairband, feeling trapped by this line of questioning.

"But did *you*?" he pushed.

She wasn't going to lie. Not now.

"They're not really my genre, but I could tell they were incredibly well directed. That shot at the end of *Apocalypse Four*, where they're running from the dust cloud, I loved that, it must have been so hard to get such a long—"

"But what about the writing?" He ran a hand through his hair again, his whole body racked with pent-up energy.

She paused, turned to face him, and said, as gently as she could, "I didn't love the writing."

"I knew it. I knew you hated them," he said, pushing the heels of his hands into his eye sockets.

"I didn't hate them, I just thought the scripts were a little . . . generic in places, but what do I know?" She paused. "I'm not your target audience." She watched him clench his jaw, his shoulders hunched up around his neck. She'd never seen him like this, so tense and insecure. "Honestly, Sean, it doesn't sound like it's my opinion you're worried about, it's your own."

"Do you know how hard it is, being successful?" he said, letting out a whimper, and he looked so forlorn, Chloe couldn't help but laugh.

"Sean, fuck off! Seriously? Listen to yourself."

"I know, I know how it sounds, but money isn't what makes you feel successful. I wake up every day with this anxiety that someone is going to take it all away from me, they'll realize I don't have an original idea in my head and I only got this job because my uncle worked at the studio, which is true. I'm just some nepo kid. And my legacy to the world is *Apocalypse* fucking *Four*, which got twenty-two percent on Rotten Tomatoes. Twenty-two percent! You know what *The Guardian* said?" She did know, she had read that review, but she shook her head, feigning ignorance. "They said, 'People shouldn't be worried about AI writing movies. They should be worried about Sean Adler writing movies.'" He sighed and Chloe had to pinch her lips closed. "And I know it's not exactly BAFTA Award–winning stuff," Sean went on, "but I gave three years of my life to that film, and it's really hard to make something great, that's what no one understands."

He was almost crying now, that nervous energy exploding on his face, distorting his features. Chloe stopped walking and pulled him into a hug.

"Don't be so hard on yourself. You're making stuff people want to see. The real world can be a lot! People want to eat popcorn and escape for a while. Plus, it's easy to be a critic." She pulled back and took in his red eyes, his pouting lips. "Sean, I'm in awe of you. You know you've got a massive career ahead of you."

"Thank you," he sniffed, wiping his eyes with a sleeve as they started walking again.

Chloe couldn't get over this revelation, the level of self-doubt he'd carried so quietly. She'd imagined Sean waking up every day thrilled with his life. Now that assumption felt naïve. Did anyone ever really wake up that way?

More than anything, his vulnerability cast something into sharp relief—something she hadn't quite been able to articulate until now. Maybe the reason she'd never felt an attraction to Sean was because they were too alike. Both intense, emotional, prone to overthinking and spiraling—they were both drama queens, all yin and no yang.

"What exactly did you hate about the scripts?" Sean asked, after a pause.

"Sean—"

"Please, I won't cry again, I promise. I'm just curious." He held up his hands as though surrendering. She shook her head, because again, this felt like a conversation she couldn't win. A group of tourists, chatting in Italian, walked toward them on the pavement and she moved aside to let them pass. Once they had the walkway to themselves again, she said, "Okay, so with *Probe and Prejudice,* you had all the army-versus-alien stuff, which was great, but then you had this love story going on between the army chief and the tribal warlord. And even though it was an action film, the love story was central to the whole thing—I mean, your title is riffing off a love story. They went to war with the aliens so they could be together 'in this life or the next.' But I just didn't believe they loved each other."

"Why?" he asked, and he looked curious rather than offended.

"They didn't know each other; we were just supposed to assume they loved each other because they were both hot. You're a romantic, Sean! It needed some romance. You could have shown her meeting the warlord's family, falling in love with his way of life, his passion for weaving. She could have painstakingly mended the loom the aliens broke, or he could have bought back the ring she had to sell—"

"Okay, so where were you in the script meeting?" he asked, smiling now.

"Did you have *any* women in the script meeting?"

"No," he said sheepishly, and they shared a real smile, the kind they used to share. He linked his arm in hers. "I missed this."

"Me too."

"Of course she should have mended the loom," he said, flinging his free hand in the air. "Why didn't I think of that?"

"Because you probably had a thousand other things to think about."

He leaned his head on her shoulder, and she felt a bubble of joy, because this—talking over story, lamenting how craft could fall so far short of your original idea, figuring out how to bring it one step closer to the work it could be—was what she'd missed. And seeing him this weekend, she finally knew she'd been right back then. They were never supposed to date, they were supposed to be something *rarer*: creatively in sync.

"You know, I don't know where you get this idea that I'm a

romantic," Sean said, as they carried on walking, past Keble and the science library. "Gracie always says I lack imagination in that department."

"Being romantic is just being thoughtful, and you could be incredibly thoughtful. I bet you're a great boyfriend. Honestly, the number of times I kicked myself for not wanting to see you naked . . . No offense."

He laughed. "You're talking about the Imp, aren't you?" he asked, shaking his head.

"Yes. Maybe that's what *Probe and Prejudice* needed—a little more Imp, a little less disemboweling," she said, but now he stopped them and turned to her with a serious expression.

"Chloe. How many times do I have to tell you, I was never the Imp," Sean said.

"Sure," she said, turning to look at him through narrowed eyes.

"I'm sorry I let you believe it was me." He looked guilty. "It was selfish of me."

"Who was it, then?"

"Chloe, come on. *Surely* you know?" He gave her a hard, searching look.

"Akiko?" she asked. Was it Akiko all along? No, she wouldn't have been able to keep that quiet for ten years. Sean laughed.

"John?" she asked, and some chord thrummed inside her. It was John. She wanted it to be John.

"I can't confirm or deny anything. It's not my place to say. So, will you take me down from this thoughtfulness pedestal now?" Sean asked. Then he put an arm around her, pulled her into a brotherly hug, and rubbed a fist gently against the top of her head. "Your hair looks better curly like this, it hides your massive ears."

"Oh shut up," she said, laughing. But now she picked up her pace, because she wanted to get to the picnic, she wanted to see John. It was him, it had to be. Something clicked, a faceless figure in a dream coming into focus. To their left Parks Road opened out to a huge expanse of green.

"Why are you walking so fast?" he asked.

"No reason," she said, slowing slightly.

"So tell me more about Rob. Is it serious?" he asked.

She shrugged; she didn't want to lie to him. "He's a good fit for me right now," she said. "He's a great guy."

"'A good fit'? That doesn't sound like the romantic I used to know."

"It's complicated," she said, feeling a tug of emotion behind her eyes and trying to blink it away.

"Don't settle, otherwise you might as well have settled for me." He grinned, putting an arm around her shoulder, and she leaned into him. "I know you, you want the fairy tale."

"You know, I just worked out who you look like," she said, keen to change the subject. "Henry Golding's less hot brother."

"I will take that," Sean said, laughing. "He is a lovely man."

"All right, name-dropper."

"You named him, not me!" Sean said, mouth open wide in indignation.

"The level of name-dropping going on last night was obscene."

"People were asking me questions!" he said, laughing, as he pushed her off the path. "Fine, no more name-dropping. My good friend Adam Sandler told me it's not cool."

She laughed, then remembered the script in her bag. She should mention it now while she had the chance. It felt like he would read it if she asked him to. But now she didn't want to taint this moment. This fragile tendril of friendship, which had stretched here from the past, felt too precious to disrupt. Plus, now the picnickers had come into view and her eyes darted around, searching for a gray dog.

17

The picnic was in full swing, though there was no sign of John or Richard. Brightly colored blankets were laid across the grass overlapping one another, anchored at the corners with tote bags, trainers, and coolers. Everyone had brought a contribution: there were punnets of cherry tomatoes, store-bought dips, crusty baguettes, and wedges of cheese sweating slightly in the sun. The air was full of chatter and laughter. Shoes had been kicked off, and half-finished conversations drifted from one cluster of friends to another. Elaine was passing around plastic cups and elderflower fizz, while Mark Patel uncorked a bottle of champagne. It looked like every student picnic Chloe had ever been to, barring the champagne.

Sean was immediately intercepted by Matteo, who wanted to quiz Sean on getting his cousin work experience on a film set.

Chloe left them talking and headed over to Rob, who was helping Amara plate up some sausage rolls. She smiled when she saw him, all her fond feelings returning. Though she hoped his social battery was sufficiently charged to deal with all these people. When Rob saw her, his eyes lit up, he shot her a beaming smile, then he stopped what he was doing and strode across the grass to meet her.

"You look radiant," he said, putting an arm around her as they walked back toward the main group. "How did it go with Sean? Did you get to pitch him the script?"

"It was good, we had a good catch-up. But it didn't feel like the right time to mention it."

"Great," he said, ever supportive. Then he leaned in to kiss her. When she stepped back, she saw Elaine watching them, one palm pressed to her chest, making a doe-eyed "Aren't they cute" expression. Sean's words echoed in her ears. *Could* there be a fairy tale that ended "happily ever after with her robot boyfriend"? Because she liked having him around. She liked how he made her feel.

As she took Rob's hand and they walked back toward the picnic rugs, she thought about going running with him in Richmond Park. How safe she'd felt. She thought about how good it was to be the one in control, to know he wasn't going to get angry with her, that he was on her side. Because whatever these new feelings for John were, they felt unwieldy, out of her control. It didn't feel safe.

Lorna and Harriet waved Chloe over to join their group on the far side of the rug. Lorna had her hair in a ponytail and a pair of oversized sunglasses perched on her head. She wore a crisp white polo shirt, and her long tanned legs stretched out beneath a fitted navy skort. Harriet's dark bob was pulled back with an Alice band, and she wore high-waisted black Lululemons and a loose gray tank top, falling off one shoulder to reveal a neon-yellow sports bra.

"Chloe, I was talking to Rob before you arrived, and I have to say it's so rare to find a man so well informed," Harriet said as they sat down. "Did you know he can recite every American president and every British prime minister, in order, and he didn't even study politics?"

Mark Patel had come over to offer everyone champagne. He was wearing jean shorts and a T-shirt that read Never Trust an Atom, They Make Up Everything. "You got a photographic memory or something?" he asked.

"No, just good recall," Rob said. "I guess it's the way I'm wired."

"Ha ha!" Chloe let out a high-pitched laugh. "Oh look, someone brought a Colin the Caterpillar cake, I love Colin the Caterpillar, don't you? So retro," Chloe said, anxious to move the conversation on from Rob's uncanny intelligence. "Rob, do you want to see if anyone has a knife, so we can cut up the watermelon we brought?"

"Sure thing," he said, leaping up.

Harriet's eyes followed Rob. "He's so interested in everything, isn't he?" she said, pulling a lip gloss from her purse, then slowly applying it. "I think your boyfriend might already know more than my husband does about the online diploma I want to do."

"It's like this in the beginning," said Lorna, tugging at the top of her ponytail to make it tighter. "They're still in the first flush. Men pretend to be interested at the start. When Matteo and I first met, he was so sweet, he sent an Uber to collect me so I didn't have to walk to the station in heels. Isn't that the cutest?"

"What, and he doesn't do that now?" Salma asked. She'd been standing nearby and now sat down beside Lorna to join their conversation, helping herself to the elderflower fizz. She was wearing a long-sleeved blue maxi dress, cinched at the waist with a belt, and a pink hijab framing her face.

"We have a driver now, so . . . ," Lorna said. "But you know what I mean."

"Lorna, I can't believe you have two million followers," Salma said to Lorna. "That's nuts."

"It's not an easy thing to do," Lorna said. "You need to be committed. I wake up and do two reels before breakfast, which means full makeup, hair, a nice outfit—it's a commitment. Our house represents my brand, so it has to look immaculate. Sometimes I just yearn to be a slobby housewife like everyone else."

"Thanks," said Harriet, giving Salma a look.

"Not you specifically, your house is lovely, Haz. But you have children, so it's not surprising that it can't be spotless," Lorna said.

There was a brief moment of silence, then Harriet picked up the bowl of strawberries beside her. "Would anyone like a strawberry? They're homegrown. Everything is organic from our garden. My skin has improved so much since we started growing our own food. I can send you a hamper if you like, Lorna?"

Lorna gave her a tight smile and Chloe reached for a strawberry.

"Wow, these are the best strawberries I've ever had," she said, trying to break the tension. "So, what are you up to these days, Salma?"

"I run a shipping company," Salma said with a flick of her

hand. "It's a family business, so I had a head start, but I've grown it from ten thousand to thirty thousand employees in six years."

"Wow, that's incredible," Chloe said.

"Yeah, that's amazing, Salma," Lorna agreed.

Salma smiled proudly, then turned to Chloe. "How about you, Chloe?"

"Oh, I work for a film company," Chloe said.

"Which one?" Lorna asked. "Matteo knows all the big players, his brother works for Netflix."

"McKenzie and Sons? You won't have heard of them."

"What have they made?" Salma asked. "We always have the TV on in the background at the office."

"Probably nothing you'd know. It's a small production house," Chloe said, feeling her cheeks heat.

"Did you carry on acting?" Harriet asked. "You were so good at uni. I remember seeing you as Puck in *A Midsummer Night's Dream* and thinking, 'That girl is going to be famous one day.'"

"Thanks. I did have an agent for a while, but it's hard to juggle a day job with auditions," she said, feeling her chest constrict. "Never say never though, right?" Why couldn't she just admit she had tried and failed? There was no shame in it. And yet, for some reason, she felt so much shame.

"I don't know," Lorna said. "Matteo's brother says if you haven't made it by twenty-four as an actress, you might as well give up. Or wait until you're in your Judi Dench era. It's different for men, they don't have the same expiration date." Lorna pushed out her lower lip and reached to squeeze Chloe's arm. "You've got a lovely boyfriend though, haven't you, so that's something."

Thea strolled over with a plate of cucumber sandwiches, which she offered around but nobody wanted. "What are we talking about?" she asked, sitting down, adjusting the silk headscarf she had tied around her braids.

"Chloe's yummy boyfriend," Harriet said with a giggle.

"He really is great, Chloe. You must wake up every morning and pinch yourself," Salma said, nodding her head toward Rob.

"You know, I think he's the most attractive person I've ever seen in real life," Thea whispered. "Don't you think he looks just like that guy from *Normal People*?"

"Right," Chloe said with a forced smile, her skin prickling with discomfort. This was what she'd wanted. It was the reason she'd brought him. And yet now, their admiration felt hollow. Having a nice boyfriend, fake or real, was not the metric she wanted to be measured by.

The conversation moved on to Thea, who talked about the challenges of juggling her well-paid law work with emotionally rewarding pro bono cases. Then Harriet told them about all the sustainability ventures their cottage farm business was investing in. Chloe listened, and nodded, and tried not to feel like the little kid at a party full of grown-ups.

Then Rob came back to join them with a plate of watermelon, meticulously cut up into identical-sized wedges.

"Wow, how did you do that?" Thea asked, leaning over to pick up a slice. "This is so neat!"

"Twenty-eight pieces," he said cheerfully. "One for everyone here."

Chloe eyed the watermelon, which looked like it had been dissected with a precision-cutting laser. She would need to talk to him about not doing everything *quite* so perfectly.

Then Chloe felt a prickle run up her neck, and when she turned around she saw John and Richard walking across the park toward the picnic party. She felt her pulse quicken. She could see from the way his head was moving that John was talking to Richard. She smiled, trying to imagine what they were talking about, tuning out the group's conversation. Rob reached to put his arm around her just as John and Richard arrived.

"Just getting a Coke," she said, extracting herself, standing up, and walking over to the cooler. "Anyone want one?"

"Rounders time," said Lorna, waving a bat in the air. "Who's going to be on my team? Rob?" She handed Rob a bat. "Let's put couples on opposing sides. Chloe, you go with Matteo and field."

Lorna split those who wanted to play into two teams, while some people stayed and lounged on the picnic rugs, happy to sit out the game. As everyone walked across to the bases, Chloe sent a quick text to Akiko. Were you the Imp? Seriously, joke over now, tell me.

"Everything okay?" said John, and she turned to see he had fallen into step beside her. He nodded his head toward Rob.

"Yes. Thank you for helping earlier. He just had a funny turn, I think," she said. Her throat felt suddenly dry, so she took a swig of the Coke she was holding. She felt torn because she wanted to talk to him, but she really didn't want him asking about Rob.

"All that dairy," John said, giving her a sideways glance.

"Right," she said, watching his expression closely. "John, you don't know anything about the Imp, do you?"

"The Lincoln mascot? Sure. Why?" John asked, but now Lorna was clapping to get everyone's attention so she could explain the rules. Everyone knew the rules, but Lorna liked the sound of her own voice.

Chloe jogged over to second base and felt a flicker of relief when she saw John follow her, taking up position nearby between first and second. He was close enough to talk to. She crossed her arms loosely, then uncrossed them a second later, not sure where to put them.

"Thanks again for my stick," she said.

"Oh, that was all Richard," he said. They both looked back at the picnic rug, where Richard was sprawled out with his paws in the air while Amara rubbed his belly.

"He's a great dog," Chloe said.

"Not a good cat though," he said, then winced at his own joke, rubbing the stubble on his chin with a knuckle.

"What did you do this afternoon?" she asked, tucking a loose strand of hair behind her ear.

"I went to the Ashmolean," he said.

"Oh, I love the Ashmolean," she said, imagining him sitting in front of a work of art, pointing out details to Richard, who would cock his head in appreciation.

"A lot of the paintings there have a musical association for me," John explained.

"How come?" she asked.

"I could sit at a piano and think of nothing and then I'd sit in front of a painting and the melody would announce itself."

"Do you think that works for writing too?" Chloe asked.

"I imagine so," he said, then paused, stretching his elbows above him, as though limbering up. His shirt came untucked from his jeans, and she saw a flash of taut, pale skin and a soft trail of hair disappearing beneath his waistband.

Chloe's eyes flicked to it before she could stop herself—then just as quickly, she looked away, heat rising unhelpfully to her cheeks. She twisted the toe of her shoe back and forth on the ground, pretending to study the grass.

"I went to the National Gallery of Ireland with my mum

once, she wanted to see some exhibition on butter making," he told her. He had a storyteller's voice, calm and deep. She wanted to block out the noise of Lorna barking instructions and just listen to him. "Anyway, while we were there, we saw them putting away this painting. I'd never even heard of it before, it's called *The Meeting on the Turret Stairs*. It shows the final meeting between doomed lovers from a Danish ballad. But the paper it's painted on is sensitive to light, so they can only display it for an hour at a time on certain days." He shook his head and smiled, eyes alight with the memory. "We'd just missed it, but now I had to see it. I ended up extending my trip, staying in Ireland two more days, just so I could."

"Was it worth it?" she asked, intrigued.

"Yes, it's beautiful. And anticipation is everything," he said, and now, when their eyes met, she felt that dart of energy pass between them, sharp and surprising, like catching a live wire. He looked away first, breaking the moment. There was a rare quality about John; the world could stop and start again, and he would still be the same steady force at the center of it all.

"Sorry," he said, slowly blinking, then shaking his head. "What was I talking about before I went off on a tangent?"

"Art inspiring your music," she prompted.

"Right." He smiled, almost apologetic. "I'm always getting distracted by life's footnotes."

"I like the footnotes," she said, too quickly, then added more softly, "I want to hear the footnotes." She tilted her head, encouraging him to go on, but now a ball flew in their direction, and they had to pause their conversation so he could run to retrieve it. He scooped it off the ground and threw it to Chloe, who cradled it in her hands for a moment before tossing it back to the bowler. The game was happening right in front of them, but it felt like a sideshow, because her focus was being drawn toward him. As he walked back, John moved closer to her at second base.

"So, you were saying, about this painting in Ireland," she prompted, wanting to give up on the game, not worry about being hit in the face with a ball because she was talking to John.

"Right, so in those two days I was hanging around Dublin, just waiting to see this painting, I had all these intense experiences—I met a girl, fell a little in love"—Chloe felt an illogical stab of jealousy—"got in a fight, joined a busking troupe. It was like I was living someone else's life, not my own." John squinted at her through the sunlight. "The painting gave me that."

"Or was it your patience?" she asked. "Maybe patience is the key to everything: art, life, love, children?"

"Ball! Chloe!" someone shouted, and her attention was jerked back to Sean, who was sprinting toward second as someone threw the ball in her direction. She fumbled it, he ran past, but she managed to get it to the bowler before Sean made it all the way to fourth.

"Sorry," she said, then saw that Rob was next up to bat. He positioned himself on the batting square, focused his gaze on the bowler, swung his arm back, and *thwack*, the ball flew in a perfect arc, right between third and fourth, traveling almost out of view across the wide expanse of field. "Run!" his teammates yelled. He made it around all four stumps, scoring the team's first rounder before anyone was even close to fielding the ball.

"I am glad he's on our team," cried Lorna, jumping up and down.

John and Chloe exchanged a conspiratorial look, an admission that neither of them cared about winning the game.

"I miss creativity being such an integral part of my life," she told him. "With my job, I just don't really lead a creative life right now."

"It's not all about your job," he said, his expression thoughtful. "I know musicians who might as well be working on a factory line, then I know this forensic accountant who's one of the most creative people out there. Creativity is just allowing your curiosity to bloom."

"Okay, well, I miss being around people who say things like that," she said, and he looked at the grass, embarrassed by the compliment. "It was you, wasn't it? You were my Imp," she said, feeling certain now.

He blushed, rubbed his stubble again. "Sorry, it was a childish game," he muttered, his eyes flitting back to the rounders.

"It meant a great deal to me," she said softly. "I had no idea you knew me so well back then."

"I knew you liked mysteries," he said, his gaze shifting across to her.

"Why did you never tell me?"

"Because it was awkward, with Sean. Because we stopped hanging out," he said plainly, his expression closing off, "and then my dad died, and everything else felt trivial."

"It never felt trivial to me," she said, shifting her body toward him, her voice low, but now he wouldn't meet her gaze. She lingered there for a moment, waiting, but his eyes stayed fixed on the game. A small knot of disappointment tightened in her chest, and she turned away too, biting the inside of her cheek.

All this time, she'd been so certain it was Sean. It made sense, on a surface level: they'd been talking about the imp right before she lost her ring; he'd made reference to it often enough, in that arch tone he used. He'd *wanted* her to think it was him. And honestly, she hadn't believed anyone *else* would care enough to go to all that trouble. But now she saw it made more sense that it was John. Thoughtful, quiet John, who remembered things she didn't realize she'd said. Who showed up, not with grand gestures, but with small, thoughtful ones: waiting to walk with her to rehearsals after dark, bringing her soup when she lost her voice, lending her books he knew she would like. But she'd never suspected, because the Imp's notes had felt like love letters, and back then, John had never given any clue that he thought of her that way. Just imagining him laying that treasure hunt for her made her heart flutter, her watch pulsing pink on her wrist. But then the doubt returned. She'd read too much into it. It had just been a game—something trivial to him.

"Chloe—" John said, taking a step toward her, reaching for her arm, but she lifted them in the air, cheering for Rob, who was up to bat again. Another perfect *thwack*. The ball arced high and long, disappearing into the far trees. People clapped and whooped. Colin blew a wolf whistle. That was the third time. No—*fourth*. She watched Rob jog around the bases, relaxed, effortless. She tried to brush it off, but the feeling only grew. Rob hadn't missed once. Not a single fumble. No misstep. Not even a mistimed swing.

Elaine clapped her hands. "Rob, you should be a professional!"

Oh God, what if he did that with every single ball? As soon as she'd had the thought, she watched it happen. Most of his team had been caught out or stumped out by now, so he was soon up to bat again, then again. Each time Rob socked the ball. He failed to realize that this level of skill and accuracy wasn't realistic.

"Way to outgun us," said Sean, watching Rob run in bemusement.

"What is going on?" said John, watching Rob run around the bases. "Who hits like that, every time?"

Chloe didn't answer. She was too busy trying to catch Rob's attention. But still, Rob hadn't once glanced her way—not even to share a smile or check in. He was fully absorbed, caught up in the game, each new round of cheers seeming to inflate him further. The deep fielders were flagging now, visibly wilting in the late afternoon sun, while Rob—now the only batsman left in—just kept swinging. Chloe scanned the park, as if someone else might step in. But of course, no one was going to.

"Rob, why don't you let someone else have a turn?" she called out, but he didn't take the hint.

"I am not out," he said, as though Chloe weren't aware of the rules. Then he reset his stance, ready to go again. She looked back at John, but he couldn't help her.

"What is happening?" he asked, narrowing his eyes at her. "Why are you sweating?"

"I'm not sweating. Am I sweating?" she asked, reaching up to feel her brow.

"Like an Olympic coach whose athlete just got pulled aside for a random drug test," John said, eyebrows lowering even farther.

Chloe looked back at Rob, all eager beaver, back on the batting square, bat ready to swing, eyes sparkling with anticipation. She felt the panic grow in her chest. If people discovered what

Rob was, they would freak out. Worse, they'd think she was insane. She would be in trouble with Perfect Partners too. She vaguely recalled a clause in the contract about "minimizing repeat social interaction with non–device users." She guessed that bringing Rob to this reunion wasn't *strictly* adhering to those guidelines.

Now Rob was running again, heading toward second, on course to get his fifteenth rounder. Thinking quickly, she stuck her foot out just as he ran past. It worked—he tripped, flying several feet, before landing on the ground with a *thump*, arms outstretched in front of him. She rushed over to him. "Oh no, I'm so sorry, honey," she said loudly, then leaned down and hissed, "Stop being so good."

"Sorry," he said, blinking up at her. Then he twisted his neck from side to side, snapping out of whatever hyperfocused state he'd been locked in. Standing up, he brushed himself down, put on a smile. But when they both looked around, everyone was staring at them, open-mouthed.

"She tripped him," Elaine cried, horrified. "I saw her trip him!"

"It was an accident," Chloe said weakly.

"Chloe, we all saw you trip him," Sean said, his whole face scrunched in disapproval.

"It's fine, I'm fine," Rob assured them, holding up his hands to show everyone how fine he was.

"It is not fine," said Lorna. "Chloe, you're disqualified. Poor form."

"Very poor form," said Elaine. "Poor Rob."

Chloe had to slink back to the picnic area, cheeks burning, while everyone fussed over Rob. She heard Lorna declare him man of the match, and Elaine asked him to sign the rounders bat for her. John didn't say anything; he stood apart from the crowd, his gaze following Chloe as she went to sit down. Richard trotted over to commiserate with her for being disqualified.

"That was super-aggressive behavior, Chloe," said Salma, who'd been watching from the picnic blanket. "It's only a friendly game."

Great. Now everyone thought she was a grade-A psycho. She nuzzled into Richard with a groan, grateful that he, at least, was not judging her.

The fielders went in to bat, and Chloe watched the game play on without her. When it finally ended and everyone came back over to the rugs, Rob reached for her hand. "It was an accident," he said loudly, making a point of showing everyone he didn't blame her, but now he just looked like a henpecked boyfriend.

Richard started squeaking as soon as Rob sat down, then bared his teeth and let out a low, steady growl. "Oh," said Rob, cocking his head at the dog, not sure what to do. Richard growled again and then barked loudly. John ran over to put his dog on a lead.

"Sorry, I don't know what's got into him. He never barks," said John, holding Richard by the collar. "You must really smell of your cat or something."

"We should go," Chloe said, jumping up.

"No, we'll go," John said. His eyes connected with Chloe's, some new distrust there, and it was like he *knew*. He couldn't know. Could he?

She wanted to persuade him to stay, but that felt dangerous, in more ways than one. Before she could move, John was already walking away, pulling Richard with him, talking to him like he was an errant child: "What's got into you, buddy?"

"I'm so sorry," Rob said quietly. He looked devastated. "Animals don't tend to like me."

"We're animals, we like you," said Harriet with a giggle. As people turned their attention back to sandwiches and lemonade, Chloe felt one step removed from the conversation. She couldn't tune in to what people were talking about, her mind awash with too many competing thoughts.

"Are you okay?" Rob asked, reaching for her hand. "You seem distracted."

"Yes." She tried to shake off the unsettled feeling. "You said you grew up in Ireland, didn't you? Did you ever go to the National Gallery of Ireland?"

"Yes. I loved the prehistoric exhibit. You could try on all these shields and helmets. My brothers and I got in trouble because we started fighting." He gave a vague, untroubled smile and reached for her hand. "Why do you ask?"

Chloe shook her head. "I just wondered."

Chloe studied his face. He looked sincere. Earnest. Like someone recalling a real memory. And maybe he *was*, in the way he'd been programmed to. But how could she take an interest in a life that didn't exist? How could she ask about his past, knowing it was just a patchwork of algorithms and borrowed details? Then again, hadn't she spent her whole life caring deeply about people who weren't real? Fictional heroes. The imaginary lives of book characters whom she felt more connected to than some of the people she knew in real life. How was Rob's backstory any different from theirs?

As Rob held her hand, fingers sliding neatly between hers, she glanced up and spotted John across the field. He was running with Richard bounding beside him, stick in hand, laughing as the dog leaped to catch it. The two of them moved in a kind of chaotic, pure, unguarded joy. As Chloe watched them, something caught in her chest. Then she looked back at Rob, who was still beside her, steady, attentive, drawing quiet circles against her palm. It dawned on her that if this were a book, it would not be science fiction, it would be a love story. And the worst kind of love story at that—a love triangle.

18

"I'm sorry for playing too competitively, I embarrassed you," Rob said, as they walked back through town toward college.

"It's fine," she said, linking her arm through his. She didn't want to talk about it anymore. As they reached the Bodleian, Chloe checked her phone and saw she had a missed call from her parents.

"Do you mind if I just call my parents back?" she asked Rob.

"Of course not," said Rob. "Why don't I go ahead to the room, leave you to it. Physical exertion always takes it out of me, so I'm running a little . . ." He paused, blinked, stumbled slightly, then said, "Beep beep boop boop."

"Rob?" she said, clutching his arm in alarm. "What's happening? Are you okay?"

Rob's face dissolved into a grin, then he started laughing. "Sorry, Chloe. You enjoy humor, and I could not resist."

"That's not funny. Don't do that again," she said, relief washing over her. She couldn't handle him short-circuiting in public.

His face fell. "Was it a bit funny? I am trying to work on my sense of humor."

"It was a bit funny," she acknowledged, reaching for his hand, "but please don't do it again." He gave her a guilty, goofy smile and kissed her on the cheek, then she waved him off. She paused for a moment, watching him walk away, those broad shoulders narrowing into a trim waist, his perfect backside. She sighed, then dialed her parents' number.

"Hi, Chloe, how's the reunion?" asked her father.

"Good, thanks, Dad. Nice to catch up with old friends."

"I won't keep you. We just had a question about sending you some money. Mum wants to pay you back our half of the shop you did last week." Chloe did an internal eye roll. Her parents were sticklers for paying her back any time she spent money.

"Dad, I'm living with you for free, the least I can do is pay for the occasional shop."

"No, no, we insist. It wasn't even a Tesco's shop, it was a Waitrose one. You bought all that fancy ham, and the marmalade Mum likes. Waitrose thick-cut is almost a day's wages."

"Dad, it was nine pounds."

"Extortionate!" he cried. "Anyway, we won't be arguing about it, I'm going to get you cash. Is that okay?"

"Dad, no. Do not go to the bank to get money out for me. You know you can do this at the click of a button on your phone now? You just log on to online banking, or Revolut me." Chloe briefly closed her eyes. There was no world where her parents were going to trust Revolut.

"We don't want you spending your hard-earned wages on our luxury marmalade and cashews. Cashews might as well be caviar, the price of them these days."

"What's going on? Why are you insisting on giving me money all of a sudden?" she asked suspiciously.

Her dad paused, then cleared his throat. "Mum opened a bill addressed to you. It was a mistake, she thought it was for one of her magazines."

Chloe felt her chest constrict. She wasn't expecting any bills. "What bill? Who from?"

Her dad cleared his throat. "I'm putting your mother on."

"Darling, we're not here to judge you," said her mum. "What you choose to spend your money on is your business. We know you've been lonely since things ended with Peter."

Chloe closed her eyes, pausing in the street to lean against some railings. "Sorry, who was this bill from?"

"Perfect Partners," her mother said. "We looked them up."

Oh no.

Chloe's mind raced. Why would Perfect Partners be sending her a bill? She was on a free trial. And how had her parents looked them up when there was nothing about them online?

"These sex lines just want you to stay on the phone as long as possible, darling, that's how they get your money," her mother hissed down the phone.

"Tell her about the porn," she heard her father whisper in the background.

"Porn? What porn?" Chloe muttered.

"Not that we know about these things, darling. But Tim Ridgway at number nine says there's a lot of free pornography you can access on the internet. All sorts of things, catering for women as well as men. You know, rather than having to pay a premium for it."

Chloe covered her face with a hand, feeling she must be beetroot. "Okay, I have not been paying for sex lines or premium porn, Mum. I think you must be confused with Perfect Partnerz with a 'Z'; this is with an 'S,' and it's an introduction service. Nothing" she searched for the right word "racy." Though as she said it, she realized it wasn't exactly true. Rob was designed to be very racy if she wanted him to be.

"Oh thank goodness," her mum said. "We were worried you might have developed an addiction."

"How much is the bill for?" Chloe asked, having to put aside her mortification for long enough to get some answers.

"Four hundred pounds," her mother said. "I hope you get introduced to an awful lot of men for that."

"Tell her about the addicts' group in Richmond community center," she heard her father say.

"She says she's not an addict. She says it's an introduction service."

"Mum, Dad, I have to go. The bill must be a mistake, I'll have to call and find out what's happened. Thanks for letting me know, and please, *please* do not go to the bank to get me marmalade money."

As soon as she'd hung up, she dialed Avery's number.

"Hello," Avery said. "Everything okay, Chloe?"

"Why have you sent me a bill for four hundred pounds? I thought I was on a free trial," she said, voice full of indignation.

"Use of our technology is free, yes, but there are charges for incidentals." There was a clicking sound as Avery checked something on a computer. Why was she sitting at her computer on a

Saturday afternoon? "Dinner, Chez Roque; Vinted purchase, one silk cocktail dress; protein shakes; phone bill; flower shop; Starbucks. You will be invoiced for all the purchases your Perfect Partner makes. This was made clear in the terms and conditions." She paused. "You can change your settings to a 'no purchase' option, but we find that emasculates the BoiBots. There is also an option to approve each spending item on the app, if you go to settings." Avery paused again. "For the majority of our clients, this isn't a problem."

Chloe swallowed. She felt so stupid. Rob had talked about his job so believably; she'd just assumed he really did make money doing computer programming. But since there was no such thing as a free lunch, *clearly* there was no such thing as a free robot boyfriend who bought you dresses and coffees and flowers and books. She really should have read all those terms and conditions.

"At the end of the trial, if you sign up for our subscription service, there are ways you can recoup costs," Avery went on, as though following Chloe's thought pattern. "But we don't offer that until you're committed to the program long-term."

"What do you mean 'recoup costs'?" Chloe asked, her skin prickling.

"Rob is a valuable resource. When he's not with you, he could be doing any number of paid tasks—writing copy for websites, manning call centers, even performing minor surgeries. There's a lot of tedious red tape to get through, but we can help with all that." Avery paused. "The downside is, if you put him to work, he won't be as accessible to you, you might compromise on bandwidth. And our primary goal is to have someone a hundred percent dedicated to you and your needs." Avery sounded like she was reading a script. "However, if cost is an issue for you, we can discuss ways to help you make this commitment long-term."

Chloe felt sick to her stomach. This is why there weren't any fairy tales about dating robots. It rather killed the romance if your story ended, "And then she set up a long-term payment plan so she could afford the bandwidth for her happy ending."

"This is an investment in your future, Chloe," Avery went on. "Our data shows that having a perfect partner increases a client's earnings by an average of thirty-four percent, so really this pays for itself. Clients also notice an improvement to their health, their confidence. What price would you put on being happy, successful . . . loved?"

Chloe felt like there was a Rubik's cube in her brain, each twist trying to align the colors of right and wrong. Morally, ethically, this felt off. But Avery had a point. Rob *had* helped her stand up for herself with McKenzie, and he was making her stick to her latest health kick. He wasn't just a romantic partner; he was a coach, a mentor, a therapist. And even though these new feelings for John were muddying the water, and the number of cons on her pros and cons list was growing, the thought of having to give him back made her feel uneasy. Like the feeling you got when you lost your phone, the quiet, gnawing sense of being without something you hadn't realized you were depending on.

"We'll talk about your financial options on Monday," Avery said breezily. "In the meantime, if you're worried about expenditures, just change the settings on the app."

Chloe hung up, feeling the unease return like an incoming tide as she walked in circles around the Rad Cam. This felt like that time she got addicted to TikTok after her breakup with Peter. She knew it wasn't healthy, but she couldn't stop scrolling, distracting herself from reality, anything not to feel the emptiness. Was Rob TikTok? No, no, he wasn't. Because Rob was a good influence; he was pushing her to be the person she wanted to be. But what about John, this spark she felt between them? She frowned. She didn't know if that was real, it could be all in her head. After walking around the Rad Cam eight times and coming no closer to any clarity, she did the only thing she could think of: she called Wendy.

"Let me guess, you went back," Wendy said, her voice gloating.

"I did," Chloe said guiltily. "And I'm sorry for being angry with you before."

"Don't worry, hon. It's a lot to get your head around. So, tell me, have you slept with him yet?" Wendy asked, her voice full of delight.

"No. I wanted to ask you something. How do you deal with Patrick not having a past, a life? Do you talk about it?"

"Not really. We mainly talk about me," Wendy said with a tinkling laugh. "No, seriously, Patrick does have a life—a life with me. We have so many shared memories now, and they are all real. At the start, he'd tell me about his 'family' or his childhood, but I didn't need that level of role-play to feel connected." Wendy paused. "Think of the best relationship you've been in. You loved their company in the present, right? Their appeal wasn't a past that you weren't a part of. You just need to recalibrate your expectations, hon."

"I got a bill," Chloe said quietly, "for all the things he's been buying me."

"Oh, I would have warned you about that if I'd known you were going back, they sneak it into the Ts and Cs. Patrick bought me a Gucci bag on our second date; I'm still paying it off." She cackled. "Honestly, it's not a big deal. Now I'm set up, he works four hours a day for an online fraud detection company, so he's contributing financially." She paused. "Look, if it's not for you, it's not for you, but if it is, you can make it work. You're in control, that's the beauty of it."

"What if you want children? Theoretically speaking," Chloe asked. "How would that even work?"

Wendy didn't miss a beat. "Easy. You find a donor, then you get your partner's programming upgraded to the Perfect Father package. PP can arrange it all. It's expensive, but probably no more than a full-time nanny. I know someone who's done it. The Perfect Father does every night feed, reads all the literature, can rock a baby for hours without complaining. She's the only mum I know who doesn't look like crap," Wendy laughed. Chloe tried to laugh too, but the sound caught in her throat as the Rubik's cube twisted again. Was this dystopian horror or a perfect emancipation from the patriarchy? She didn't know. What she did know was that she couldn't laugh about it like Wendy could.

As she walked back into Lincoln, she decided she would talk to Rob about his expenses, tell him to stop spending *her* money on buying her presents. But when she opened the door to their room, she found a scene she wasn't expecting.

Classical music was playing. Rob had moved the desk to the middle of the room. On it was her favorite iced latte and a square package, perfectly wrapped in lilac tissue paper, tied with a dark purple bow.

"What's all this?" she asked, looking from the desk back to Rob.

"Open it," he said, rubbing his palms together, eyes bright with anticipation, eager for her to see whatever it was.

She walked across to the desk and picked up the parcel,

carefully unwrapping the bow, then ripping open the tissue paper.

Inside was a leather-bound notebook, the kind that felt too beautiful to write in. The cover was a deep matte purple, smooth under the fingers, with just enough texture to catch the light. Along the spine, delicate gold foiling traced an elegant border, like the gilded edge of an old spell book. When she opened it, she found thick cream pages, lined in the subtlest gray. The edges of the paper were gilded too, catching in the sunlight that shone through the window. It smelled of bookshops and new leather.

"What's this for?" she asked, unable to hide her delight.

"One more thing," Rob said, taking a silver fountain pen from his pocket. Then he moved to pull out the chair for her. "I thought you could write something."

She blinked up at him. "Write what?"

"Anything. It doesn't matter. You keep saying you haven't written anything in three years, so let's write something now, then that won't be true anymore." He paused. "Do you like the notebook? They had pink and red too, but I thought purple for you. I can run and exchange it if—"

"I love it, thank you," she said, genuinely touched.

Rob looked so hopeful, and the notebook was probably the nicest notebook she'd ever owned. She couldn't exactly bring up his spending now.

Rob leaned over, kissed her neck, opened the first page, then put the pen in her hand.

"'Once upon a time . . . ,'" he said, eyes warm with encouragement. She looked up at him, affection softening her expression. "'Act one, scene one'?"

"You're very sweet, but it's not quite as easy as that."

"Okay, not a story, just an idea then, a character, a place," he said, laying his hand on her back.

She closed her eyes briefly. Lovely as the sentiment was, she knew a new notebook wasn't going to solve her writer's block. But then as she looked down at the blank page, an idea started to flicker in the dark. A boy in Ireland, waiting to see a painting . . . All the things he did while he was waiting. Maybe he never even got to see it. It would be like *Waiting for Godot* but with heart, about all the things that happen while you're waiting for something to happen.

Then she felt it, that little spark of electricity, the glitter of a new idea, full of possibility. Because there is nothing quite as perfect as a story you haven't written yet.

19

PROS AND CONS OF DATING A BOIBOT

PROS	CONS
Incredibly handsome.	Needs access to power source.
Buys me nice, thoughtful gifts	. . . with my own money.
Good at sport.	Maybe *too* good.
Good kisser (imagine excellent at everything else too).	Having children? Disturbing for kids to find out their dad is AI. But maybe this will be the norm in twenty years?

Excellent masseuse.	Ethically questionable—is this the equivalent of buying clothes from Shein?
Sexy Irish accent.	Inconsistent Irish accent . . .
Gives great career advice / helps me tackle life goals / excellent therapist.	He doesn't have a family, and he didn't really go to the National Gallery of Ireland. Does this matter?
Makes me feel safe.	Would eventually need to "come out" to my friends about him. There would be judgment, especially from Mum and Dad.

While she jotted down notes for her new idea and updated the pros and cons list on her phone, she asked Rob to read the *Welcome Rising* script that McKenzie wanted her to show Sean.

"It's terrible, right?" she asked once he'd finished reading.

"I think it has potential," he said carefully. "I like the central concept. I could help restructure it, clarify a few things that are confusing—"

"I think it's beyond that. It's not a bad murder mystery, but the script itself feels dead."

Rob paused, tapping a finger against his knee, thinking. "The internal conflict could be sharpened. We could tighten the pacing." He paused, seeing she was unconvinced. "Or . . . go bigger, restructure it completely."

"Ooh, yes, we could put the ending first. Make it a howdunit instead of a whodunit."

He raised both eyebrows and smiled. "That's brilliant."

"I might suggest it to McKenzie, he could talk to the writer," she said, then hesitated a moment. "Can I send you some of my old scripts? Projects I've abandoned halfway through. Maybe you can help me figure out where I lost the thread."

"It would be my pleasure," said Rob, looking thrilled at the prospect of being given a task. "We make a good team, don't we?"

They were. This was yet another thing Rob was helping her with. Chloe had always worked things out by talking; it was why she struggled to work alone. Maybe she didn't need Sean to get her writing again. Maybe she just needed a sounding board, someone she trusted. Maybe all she needed was a Rob.

After an afternoon spent reading and writing, plotting and planning, it was soon time to change for formal hall. Rob had packed a dinner jacket, sleek, tailored, and devastatingly effective. He looked like James Bond in his Adonis era. Chloe wore a black dress she'd had for years. It was simple, it was elegant, and it fit her perfectly. When she wore it, she felt imbued with an old confidence. This was the dress she'd worn to her graduation, the dress she'd worn in Tuscany with Kiko when they'd been chatted up by two hot Italians. Good things happened when she wore this dress.

Formal hall was held in Lincoln's dining room, a space straight out of a historical novel, with dark portraits hung on the walls, long oak trestle tables, flickering candlelight, and the soft gleam of silverware. The three-course meal was silver service, with all the familiar pomp and ceremony that the hall commanded. Chloe scanned the seating plan, pinned at the entrance. "Gaudy Dinner," the formal term for an Oxford reunion, had been written out in sweeping calligraphy. The style tugged at something in her memory, then it hit her: it was the Imp's handwriting. She reached out, tracing a fingertip lightly over the ink. A flicker of something stirred—territorial, almost possessive, as if these letters belonged to her.

"There we are," said Rob, pointing to their names, as though her hesitation were down to not being able to find them. He tapped her name, between Sean and Mark on the first table, with Rob directly opposite. Her throat tightened as she scanned the list for John's name, and found it at the far end of the second trestle table. Nowhere near her.

"Shall we go in?" Rob asked, and she nodded, linking her arm in his.

Walking into the dining room, she instantly spotted John, flanked by Freya and Salma, already deep in conversation. For a moment, she watched him laugh at something Salma had said, gesturing with his hand midair, animated and at ease. She forced her attention back to the table in front of her, walking along to where Mark and Sean were already seated.

"Did you know 'gaudy' comes from the Latin 'gaudium,' meaning 'joy'?" Mark said, as she sat down beside him.

"I didn't," she said.

Mark looked sharp in his black dinner jacket, his bow tie as symmetrical as his neatly parted hair. She noticed he was wearing silver double-helix cuff links, which made her smile.

"Wasn't it from *Antony and Cleopatra*? 'Let's have one other gaudy night,'" Sean said, joining their conversation. He was in the same uniform as every other man in the room, though his bow tie sat a fraction looser than Mark's, more statement than oversight, and his shirt collar was slightly rumpled, like he'd changed in a rush or simply didn't care. "How many words do you think Shakespeare added to the dictionary?"

"One thousand seven hundred," said Rob, taking the seat opposite, and everyone within earshot at the table turned to look at him.

"Rob's got a knack for fact retention," Chloe said with a nervous laugh.

"Good man to have on a pub quiz team, then," said Mark.

"Or a rounders team," said Sean, nudging Chloe.

A bell rang, the proctor said grace in Latin, and then the servers came in with the starters, a salmon mousse with homemade crackers and watercress. Chloe felt transported back in time by the echoey sound of the hall, the clinking of cutlery and crystal glasses, the Lincoln-embossed crockery that only came out for special occasions. A decade had passed, and everything in this room was just the same.

As people started to eat, they settled into one-on-one conversations, Rob talking to Elaine, Chloe to Sean.

"So, I finally unmasked the Imp," she told Sean. He did a double take, assessing her face to check she wasn't bluffing. "John."

He raised his hands and gave a slow clap. "Well done, Miss Marple. You're the only two people I know who think treasure hunts are an acceptable pursuit past the age of ten."

"Excuse me, wasn't *Probe and Prejudice* basically one long treasure hunt?"

"Yes, to save the universe, not find a chocolate rabbit," he said, laughing.

"Well, respectfully, I disagree. I won't stand for your anti-treasure-hunt propaganda," she said, then after a beat she asked, "Why didn't you tell me it was John, back then?" Sean shrugged, glancing away, a new tension in his smile. There was a flash of something else in his eyes. Guilt?

"He never talked about it. Maybe it was awkward, he knew I liked you too." Sean fiddled with his knife, moving it around on the table like a clock hand. "I remember asking him for ideas for your birthday once, and he was like, 'Oh, take her to Old Boars Hill, she loves wildflowers, and the bluebells are out now.' Or 'She's obsessed with *Brideshead*, so take her on a road trip to Castle Howard.'" Sean wrinkled his nose. "That's when I knew. I was like, 'Mate, I was thinking of getting her a book or a decent bottle of wine.'"

A new warmth settled in Chloe's chest as she thought of John making these suggestions.

"I warned him off you," Sean said quietly. "I knew you didn't see him that way, I didn't want him to embarrass himself. I'd already embarrassed myself enough for the both of us."

She glanced across to the next table, where John was deep in conversation with Amara, gesturing toward one of the paintings above them, tracing the shape of something in midair with his hands. Chloe wished she could hear what they were talking about.

"Are you still close? Do you see a lot of him?" she asked.

"When I can. I tried to lure him out to LA a few years ago, but he said his dog wouldn't like it." Sean laughed. "He hasn't changed. You know he just did a master's in archaeology, for fun. It's not surprising his relationships don't last. He's always got too much else going on." Sean shook his head and then turned to narrow his eyes at her. "Why this sudden interest in John? Are you seeing the gosling you always assumed was a duck? Slightly inappropriate, given present company." Sean nodded toward Rob, who was still talking to Elaine.

"No," she said quickly, elbowing him gently. "I just—I don't think I was a good friend to him at the end of third year, with his dad and everything . . ." She trailed off, not sure how much Sean knew.

Sean's face softened. "Yeah. He had a rough time of it, poor guy."

They paused as the servers came around to clear the starters and top up their wine.

"Anyway," Sean said once the server had gone. And Chloe knew "anyway" meant he wanted to change the subject.

"How about you? Are you really dating Gracie Lamé?" she asked.

"Yeah, it started as a PR thing, but we genuinely like each other now. She's cool, she's into weird shit like ice fishing." His eyes softened at the corners, crinkling just slightly, and his mouth curved into a quiet, unguarded smile. "I'm meeting her parents next week."

"A PR thing, wow, who are you?" Chloe said.

"I know. Half of Hollywood is fake dating."

This made her stomach clench. Were they fake dating people or robots?

"So, tell me, are you really done with acting?" Sean went on. "Because I have this role—it would be great for you—it's this six-headed, bloodsucking alien."

"Which head would I get to be?" she asked, humoring him.

"Actually, all the heads are prosthetic, so you would be the butt," Sean giggled.

"I thought you were making 'great art' next," she said with a sigh.

"Maybe the one after next," he said ruefully.

"Speaking of scripts," she said, catching Rob's eye across the table. "My boss found out I knew you. He has this script he was trying to get to your agent. I know it's horrible to even ask . . ." She trailed off.

Sean's expression shifted instantly. He gave her a tight smile. "Right."

"You don't need to read it. Maybe if you could say you did, so I can get my boss off my back."

"I tend to get read requests through my agent," he said, no hint of humor in his tone.

"Cool, no, don't worry about it."

"I just don't read stuff unless it's through my agent, or it opens me up to all sorts of plagiarism suits. You know, if I do something similar in a few years and then some guy claims I stole his work—"

"Yeah, of course, I get it." She knew this. McKenzie knew this. Why had she ever agreed to mention it?

"It's just not a professional way to do things," he said. Wow, that stung. "But send it to Larry, if you think it's worth my while. Anyway . . ."

He punctuated their conversation with another stiff smile, then turned to Katie, sitting on his right. Chloe felt her cheeks flush, a lump in her throat. "Excuse me," she said quietly, getting up to leave. She caught Rob's eye as she stood. He made to follow her, but she firmly shook her head; she didn't want him to come. She just needed a minute.

Outside the hall, she took a deep breath. The air was warm and still, holding on to the heat of the day. She turned to lean her forehead against the stone wall of the hall. It was rough and cool beneath her skin. The scent of damp stone and lichen filled her nose, familiar, grounding. She exhaled slowly. Why was she even trying to do McKenzie a favor? She knew how unprofessional it was to approach a director this way. She'd just got their friendship back on track; currying favor with McKenzie wasn't worth derailing it for. Her gut had told her it was a bad idea. She should have listened.

As she squared her shoulders, readying herself to go back in, she noticed John coming out of the dining hall carrying a cardboard box. The golden light from the hall spilled onto the gravel behind him, lighting him like a spotlight. He looked incredibly handsome in black tie.

"Hi. What are you doing out here?" he asked, his eyes flashing with warmth.

Chloe felt a surge of pleasure in seeing him. "I don't know, looking for bats," she said, and he smiled that easy, knowing smile that always made her stomach flutter. "You?"

"Wine mission. The dean said we could break out the good stuff, but the waitstaff can't find it." He gave her a conspiratorial wink. "I know where the best bottles are hidden."

"Do you want help?" she offered, the words slipping out before she could second-guess them.

"Sure," he said, his grin widening. "I get scared of the dark, so you can hold my hand."

"Really?" she asked, raising an eyebrow, half-laughing, half-nervous.

"No, but you can still hold my hand," he said, shifting the empty box beneath his left arm, then reaching for her with his right. The moment his fingers brushed hers, a current of warmth spread up her arm, pooling in her chest. It was familiar, like slipping into something soft and comfortable, a feeling that was both easy and electric all at once. They stood there for a beat, neither of them moving, then with a small, almost imperceptible shift, Chloe tightened her grip on his hand.

To get to the cellars beneath the college, they had to go through the bar, Deepers, past the jailed imp, then wind through a warren of narrow passages. Chloe followed John into the dimly lit tunnel. The scent of damp stone and dust clung to the narrow corridor, but it was his presence, his closeness, that filled her senses. She could hear the soft scrape of his shoes on the stone floor and the rhythm of his breathing, steady and low. She couldn't remember the last time she'd felt so acutely aware of another person.

The corridor opened into a small, low-ceilinged room, with high shelves lining each wall. The air was cooler here. There was a faint scent of cork and something pleasantly musty. Above them, the hum of a single dangling yellow bulb. Wooden racks lined the perimeter of the room, packed tightly with dark green and brown bottles, their labels curled or faded with age. A small stepladder leaned in one corner, and an open crate sat beside it.

"Have you been down here before?" she asked, looking around the cellar. Her voice was quiet, almost hesitant, as if speaking too loudly might shatter the unspoken intimacy between them.

"Once or twice. I roomed with the keeper of the keys in second year," he said. He put down the box he was carrying. "The stars might fade, and summers fly, but Lincoln College will never run dry." She laughed as he moved toward a large, empty wooden shelf, testing how heavy it was. "And if you know where to look, there's always something better hidden at the back." He nodded toward the empty shelf. "Can you help me move this?" She went to take hold of the other side of the shelving unit, and together they shifted it just enough to reveal a hidden wooden door in the wall behind.

"In there?" she asked, a flicker of claustrophobia tightening in her chest.

"Don't worry, it opens up inside," John said, reaching for her hand again, and as his fingers entwined in hers, she felt like a compass finding her north. "Not many people get to see this. Are you ready?"

As he guided her through the small doorway into the dark cellar beyond, she was close enough to catch a trace of his aftershave, something warm and clean, faintly spicy. Once they were through, he turned to look at her, his eyes pools of light and shadow, impossible to read in the dimly lit cellar.

"Are you okay?" he asked, and as she made eye contact, she felt a rush of feeling, almost like wanting to cry. Her watch pulsed pink. "What's that?" he asked, glancing at her wrist, a neon beacon in the dark.

"Nothing. An alarm . . . a, um, reminder to do my pelvic floor exercises," she blurted. Why had she said that? She could have said anything! Luckily it was too dark for him to see her blush. There was no light in the hidden chamber, but John pulled out a torch and shone it around the room to reveal a small circular space, like an underground igloo, with bottles stacked in crates around the edges.

"Welcome to the good stuff," John said, an edge of excitement in his voice. "It's hidden back here to stop other colleges from stealing it."

"Wow, I feel like Indiana Jones unearthing a long-lost treasure trove," she said, then shivered, not just from the coolness of the room but from a keen awareness of John's proximity.

"*Indiana Jones and the Temple of Pouilly-Fumé*?" he said, and she could hear the smile in his voice.

"That would have a niche audience," she said, then laughed. "If we pick up the wrong bottle, is a giant boulder going to come flying toward my head?" She watched as he shone the torch around the crates, inspecting their labels.

"Don't worry, I will protect you from flying boulders," he said, and though she knew they were only joking around, his words still ignited a small thrill.

"Do you mind holding the torch while I look?" he asked, handing her the torch handle.

Their fingers brushed as she reached for it, and they both paused a fraction too long, holding the torch between them. Eventually, he cleared his throat and then turned back to the crates behind him.

"So why did you leave dinner so suddenly like that?" he asked, eyes scanning the labels on the crates.

"Oh, it was silly," she said, moving to stand beside him to better shine the torch where he was looking. "I asked Sean for a favor, to read a script for my boss. He said no, obviously. I was embarrassed. I shouldn't have asked."

"He's sensitive about stuff like that," John said gently. "He's been burned before. I wouldn't take it personally."

"We had such a good talk this afternoon," she said. "It felt like we put everything back to rights. Then I go and ruin it all by asking him for a favor." Her voice caught. "It's not even a good script."

"Why did you pitch it, then?" John asked, as he picked up a bottle and wiped dust from the label. It was a simple question, but Chloe paused, struggling to find the answer.

"I don't know. Because it felt like my job depended on it," she said, her voice thin, unraveling. "I thought he'd just say 'sure,' then never actually read it." John moved across to inspect the next crate, and she moved the torch to follow his gaze. Listening to the sound of his breathing, so sure and steady, she was seized by a reckless urge to reach out and hold him. She took a small step back, to stop herself. "Maybe I just wanted a seat at the table again."

John turned to face her fully now, and she held her breath, because she felt like he might be about to hug her. She desperately wanted him to. But he didn't, he just said gently, "You seem a little lost, Chloe."

Her spine straightened. She frowned. "I'm not lost."

"Fine, you're not," he said with an edge of impatience.

"What?" she asked, her voice high, defensive.

"Something is going on with you, I don't know what it is, but I hope you're okay."

"Why wouldn't I be okay?" she asked, clutching her elbows, bracing against herself, the torch in her hand shining toward the ceiling.

"I don't know, but this weekend, it feels like you're putting on a performance half the time. You bring your weird boyfriend, when no one ever brings plus-ones to these things—"

"They do! Lorna did," she snapped. "So did Colin and Tali. And Rob isn't weird."

John took a small step toward her. His voice was soft, measured, his eyes intent on hers, as though he was trying to read the truth in her face.

"I don't know what was going on back there in your room, but I know there's something off with him. Richard sees it too."

She dropped her gaze, then let out a forced laugh. "Sorry, I didn't know I was supposed to be taking dating advice from your dog."

He stopped still, reaching out to put a hand on her arm now. "I'm just worried you're in a relationship you don't want to be in, that you don't know how to get out of."

"That's not it at all. Rob's just . . . different."

"You're not in love with him," John said, and it wasn't a question. He stepped closer, and she could feel the heat of him, steady and certain in the cool of the cellar. She didn't have any words, only her breath, which had grown fast and shallow. His pupils flared. There was a hum beneath her skin, a pull toward him, an inevitability. She didn't know what he was about to do, but she desperately wanted him to do something.

Slowly, he reached for her, one arm sliding around her waist, the other slipping up her neck, into her hair. It was so controlled, so excruciatingly slow, she let out a small groan, and then her fingers loosened on the torch, and she let it drop to the floor with a clatter.

Now, in the darkness, they both lunged forward, closing the gap; she found his lips with hers. The kiss was breathless, all-consuming, like a wave of heat breaking over her—she felt it in the very marrow of her being. If this was a kiss, then she had never been kissed before. But it was painfully fleeting, because just as she felt herself opening up to the sensation, John gently pulled away.

"Chloe, we can't," he said, his voice catching in his throat.

But his words didn't match his actions, because she reached for him again, and as soon as she touched him, he pulled her toward him, hands firm on her waist as she clasped his back. His kiss was deeper this time. Chloe couldn't believe how right it felt. Like a key finding the correct lock. But then he pulled away again.

"Sorry," he murmured. They both stepped back now, needing space between them. He reached for the torch, and with the light came sense. "I'm so sorry," he said again.

"Don't be," she said. A red glow emanated from her wrist.

He sat down on an empty crate behind him, steadying himself, then let out a pained, frustrated sigh.

"Was it really just a game to you, the Imp?" she asked.

"No," he said.

"What was it, then?" she asked. Though he'd put space between them, she could still feel the tension, like an elastic band, pulled taut.

"I think you know," he said quietly.

"You liked me?"

He exhaled, sharp and quiet, then muttered, "Why are you torturing me?"

"Why didn't you tell me, back then?"

"Because I knew you didn't see me that way. And because . . . it didn't end well for people who did," he said, his voice tightening. Chloe felt more memories unlocking, how he used to wait for her when she was late for rehearsals, making it seem like a coincidence; the carol he wrote for her one Christmas; the tiny violin he made Aloysius. She'd imagined these gestures as sweet eccentricities he'd do for anyone, but perhaps they had only been for her.

"Oxford for me was just music and you, you and music. You were a song stuck in my head that I was never allowed to sing. Because Sean was my best friend, so who could I tell?"

For a moment, neither of them spoke. He glanced up at her, a pained look in his eyes.

"The Imp, your notes, they meant a great deal to me," she said quietly. "I kept every one."

For a moment, she glimpsed hope in his eyes, but then it quickly vanished.

He shook his head. "This reunion, it's not a time machine, we can't go back. We've all grown up."

That wasn't what she wanted to hear. He walked purposefully toward the door now, shoulders tight, body language closed. "Let's just go back up." She was about to speak when there was a crashing sound outside, a shelf falling. The cellar door slammed shut, the echo like a gunshot. John lunged for it, pushed his shoulder against it. Chloe rushed to help him, but it was stuck firm. They were sealed in.

20

Chloe looked around the small, stone-encased chamber that they were locked in. It suddenly felt more like a crypt than a cellar. The kiss still hummed on her lips, but any thought of it was fast giving way to the horror of being trapped underground with no light source, no toilet, and no one who might think to check on them for hours.

"The shelf must have fallen in front of the door," John said, stating the obvious.

"So how do we get out?" Chloe cried, pressing her weight against the door, then shoving it in frustration.

John pulled his phone out of his jacket pocket. "No reception. You?" Chloe checked her phone. Not a flicker.

"What are we going to do? Who knows we're down here?" she asked, her voice high and strained.

"Don't worry," John said. "Elaine knows I'm down here, so does the head butler. They'll come looking for the wine in a minute."

"Or they'll just settle for the cheap stuff," Chloe muttered, shivering slightly.

"That *is* a possibility," he admitted, taking his jacket off and giving it to her. "Here."

"Thanks." She slipped it on—it was warm and smelled of his cologne. She hugged it around her, inhaling the smell.

"Rob will come looking for you," he said, clearing his throat as he sank down onto one of the upturned crates. She looked down at her watch, which now blinked yellow. Would Rob sense what she was feeling and know to come? She didn't even know whether the device was in range from down here.

"What do we do until then?" she asked, and now her mind leaped straight back to the kiss and she felt a flutter in her stomach. Rob kissed like a well-rehearsed dancer who never missed a beat. But that kiss with John, brief as it was, had been something else entirely. It wasn't a dance, it was a match struck, dropped on dry kindling. Wild and unscripted . . . dangerously intoxicating. That was the kind of kiss people burned the world down for. Even now, she could still feel it—not just on her lips, but in her fingertips, at the back of her knees, a smoldering glow, desperate to be reignited.

John crouched down and set the torch upright on the floor, so it cast a cone of amber light upward. Then, without looking at her, he stepped toward her and slipped his hand into the jacket draped around her shoulders. Her breath caught in anticipation of what he might do, but then he dipped into the inner pocket and his hand drew back holding a bottle opener.

"We could open something?" he said, glancing at the shelves.

She exhaled. "Sure."

John turned two crates on their sides as makeshift seats, then selected a dusty bottle of port and cracked it open with a quiet flourish. He offered her the first sip.

"I don't know if I like port," she said, eyeing it warily.

"Is that what Indiana Jones would say?" he asked, his voice lighter suddenly. "I thought you were always up for trying new things."

"Oh I am," she said, taking the bottle from him, trying not to worry about what she would do if she needed the loo. You never saw *that* in *The Last Crusade,* the damsel saying, "Will you excuse me while I do a wee behind this rock?"

She pressed the cool glass lip to her mouth and the sweet, dark liquid filled her senses. He was right, it was delicious. She licked her lips and passed the bottle back to him. He drank from the same spot; she watched his mouth, touching the place hers had just been. Her pulse quickened and the walls of the cellar pressed closer.

She drew John's jacket tighter around her shoulders, her knee brushed his, but neither of them moved. "They'll notice we're gone soon, right?" she asked.

"Sure, twenty minutes, max," John said, his voice firm, reassuring.

Now that they'd embraced their immediate predicament, Chloe felt a fresh wave of embarrassment over the kiss, the seismic reaction she'd had. There was no getting away from it.

"I'm sorry, about kissing you just now," she said quietly, and even in the half-light, she could see his cheeks burn.

"I'm sorry if I confused things," he said, then added after a beat, "You're with Rob. I don't want you to do anything you'd regret."

Was that why he'd stopped, because of Rob? She felt a thrum of hope, an ember stirring. How could she explain that Rob wasn't real, that he wouldn't mind? You couldn't cheat on a machine, could you? She didn't want to lie, but the truth was impossible.

She reached for the port, then asked with a smile, "Why didn't you kiss me like that back then?"

John laughed, dragging a hand through his hair. "You never looked at me then like you're looking at me now." And there it was again, embers glowing hot in his eyes. He glanced away, but she didn't. Studying him, it struck her how unique his face was, not perfect like Rob's but lived in, perfectly imperfect—the small scar on his forehead, his slightly crooked front tooth, the patch on his chin where stubble didn't grow, the smile lines around his eyes, and the serious slope of his nose. It was a face that told a story. Were these feelings for him new, or had they been here all along, just waiting to be unearthed?

"Let's talk about something else," he said, voice catching, then added with a note of yearning, "Please." She shivered again. "Come here, you're still cold." So she moved her crate next to his and he put his arm around her. He smelled so inviting, and his embrace felt so solid and comforting that she leaned into it.

"So, what do you think of the proctor's new beard?" John asked, his voice slightly strained.

"It suits him. Not everyone can pull off a beard," Chloe said, leaping onto this life raft of trivial conversation. "Okay, top ten beards, famous or otherwise, go."

"Excellent question, but are we allowed to play top ten without Kiko and Sean?"

"I think they'd give us a dispensation to play, under the circumstances."

"In that case, Santa Claus, obviously."

"Obviously."

"Gandalf, Abraham Lincoln—this is in no particular order."

"Castro?" she offered.

"I'll give you young Castro. Bluebeard? I don't know what he looks like, but he must have had a first-rate beard."

Chloe laughed, relieved to have found something to distract them from the heat that still lingered between them. Once they'd exhausted beards, they moved on to top ten movies with food in the title, then top ten things you'd rather be doing than being trapped in a cellar.

She realized Rob would never be able to play a game like this, not with the whole internet at his fingertips. The fun of this game was in the debate, in suddenly remembering something everyone else had forgotten, arguing over facts half remembered. Phones were not allowed, because googling the answer would ruin the fun.

"*A Clockwork Orange*!" Chloe yelled triumphantly.

John burst out laughing, the kind of helpless, full-bodied laugh that fed her own until she couldn't breathe. "We finished fruit ten minutes ago."

She felt warm, her head spinning—the port had crept up on her.

"Oh did we? I think I'm drunk," Chloe said, slipping off the crate onto the floor in a graceful collapse.

"Me too," he admitted, sliding down beside her.

"How long have we been down here?" she asked, and he reached to check his phone.

"Forty minutes," he said.

"They must have finished dinner by now. I'm offended no one's noticed we're not there."

"Indeed," he said.

"Indeed," she mimicked in her best scholarly drawl, then hiccupped. He laughed, a happy drunk laugh, which made her suddenly feel nineteen again. John clicked open, then closed, the bottle opener in his hand. She smiled, remembering his habit of fiddling with things when he'd had too much to drink. There was a charming vulnerability about him after three glasses of wine. Rob would never be tipsy. He might be able to act like he was, but he would only be playing a part. It dawned on her that he was *always* playing a part. He was a figment of her imagination, made real. The thought made her shiver.

"I need to move," she said, getting to her feet and attempting some half-hearted star jumps. He sighed, amused, then stood up to join her.

"Shall we dance? It's more dignified than star jumps."

"Do you have music?"

He pulled out his phone and began scrolling, his thumb firm, deliberate. Then, quietly, the room was filled with the warm, melancholic voice of Norah Jones singing "And Then There Was You." The sound was low, slightly tinny through the phone speaker, but it wrapped around them in the silence. "It's all I've got downloaded," he said with an apologetic tilt of his head.

Then he reached for her hand, fingers curling around hers, and he gave a small tug, inviting rather than insisting. She let herself be led. Her other hand found his shoulder without her thinking, and he settled a hand at her waist. And then they turned slowly in time with the music. The room around them contracting, blurring at the edges until it was just them, in no particular space or time.

Chloe could feel the steady beat of his heart beneath his

shirt, the warmth of his hands. The song lyrics brushing against something she hadn't known was aching. She let herself rest her cheek lightly against his shoulder, and the moment felt *painfully* romantic.

"I take it you didn't have the crazy chicken song, then?" she asked, smiling into his shoulder.

"That's not in my repertoire," he said, as he pulled her a little closer. They moved in small circles, the port dulling the voice telling her she was playing with fire. She didn't care, because right now, being trapped underground in a damp wine cellar, dancing to this song, felt like the only place she wanted to be.

She lifted her head, and he was already looking at her. Their eyes met and held.

"Stop looking at me like that," he said with a soft groan.

"Like what?"

"Like you want me to kiss you," he said softly.

"I do want you to kiss me. You're the one who put this song on," she teased, dizzy with dancing and port and being in John's familiar yet wholly unexpected embrace.

"We should stop dancing, then."

"Why? Because of Rob?"

"Yes, because of Rob, your six-foot-something, terrifyingly muscular boyfriend."

"What if I told you he's not really my boyfriend?" she said, the words spilling out before she could stop them.

"What do you mean?" John asked, still holding her waist as their spinning slowed further.

"He's not real. I asked him to pretend, for this weekend." She sighed, then laughed, not because it was funny, but because this was an impossible conversation. "Pathetic, I know."

"What?" he said, pulling away from her. "Why would you do that?"

"Because I didn't want to come here alone."

John's face creased into a scowl. He stopped dancing and let go of her hand, taking a step back, just as the song came to an end.

"Does *he* know it's not real?" John asked, a note of disbelief in his voice. "Because he seems very into you." He started pacing the room now, shaking his head. She could almost see his brain working this through. "What is he, like an escort?"

"I know it's strange, I can't really explain it. I just wanted someone to keep me company this weekend." She let out a wry laugh. "You were right on the bus, he's my emotional support boyfriend."

John was still watching her, waiting for more.

"I felt intimidated, okay. Everyone else is doing what they set out to do in life, and I've done nothing. I was embarrassed." She gestured with her hands, animated now. "I gave up on my dreams, I live with my parents, I'm a loser. You say I seem lost; well I am, I'm so fucking lost. At Oxford, I knew exactly who I wanted to be, and I am so far away from being her, from *ever* being her." She took a breath, let out a defeated sigh. "If she could see me now, young me would be so disappointed." She felt her eyes well, and she sat back down on the crate and squeezed her knees tight to her chest.

John paced in front of her, tapping out a rhythm with one fist against his palm, but his voice was gentle as he said, "She wouldn't. And those aren't the criteria to measure a life by. You get to live with your parents. Do you know how much I'd give to have one more breakfast with my dad? You might not be where you want to be professionally, but you're smart, you're creative, if you don't like what you're doing, change it." John turned toward her, his face shifting to a frown.

She wiped her face with a palm. "Don't look at me like that."

"Like what?"

"All judgy."

She rested her forehead on her knees. Her bladder was becoming a problem. She needed to get out of this room *now.* She jumped up, leaped toward the door, and started beating on it. "Help!" she called out. "We're in here! We're stuck!"

"There's too much stone. No one's going to hear you," he said.

She banged on the door, called out again, as loud as she could. Then, spent, she turned to find John standing behind her. He reached for her fist, clasping it in his hand, opening it, knitting his fingers with hers as he turned her to face him.

"I'm not judging you," he said gently, "and I'm sorry you feel that way about your life."

"It's just—it's complicated," Chloe said, and though he didn't understand, she felt a relief in having told him.

Their faces were inches from each other now. He held her wrist in one hand, and she reached for his other hand, so now they stood, locked in this standoff, the sweet tension of simmering chemistry.

"Quantum mechanics is complicated, not this," he said, drawing his lip between his teeth.

Every cell in her body was on high alert; she yearned for him to close the gap between them again.

"Chloe . . . ," he whispered, his voice steady, serious as a vow. He leaned in, surrendering to the pull between them, feeling her insides turn to molten lava. Just an inch closer—

Clunk. The sound of shifting furniture. A shaft of light cutting through the dark. The door scraped open. They jolted apart like guilty teenagers, then turned to see Rob, framed by the doorway, his broad body filling the space.

"I came to find you," he said evenly, a cordial smile on his face. "Were you stuck in here?"

"Yes, thank you," Chloe said quickly, too quickly. Her cheeks burned.

Rob took a step inside and wrapped his arms around her. She returned the hug stiffly. Rob suddenly felt like a stranger, a cardboard cutout made flesh, doing all the right things to comfort her but it was not the same. Because being down here with John had reminded her what real intimacy felt like. And it didn't always approve of you or flatter you; it challenged you, called you out, made you feel seen in ways that were sometimes unbearable. But it was honest, and unflinching, and real.

John stood motionless, watching them—waiting for her to say something. But she hesitated. What was she supposed to say? She'd tangled herself up in half-truths and was now a spider caught in her own web.

She looked at John. Their eyes met for the briefest second, and then she looked away, afraid. That was enough. John registered the silence. His expression hardened, not in anger, but in resignation. Then he pushed past Rob and strode out of the cellar.

Chloe stood, frozen to the spot, looking up at Rob. His smile didn't falter. Did he know what he'd just walked in on? What was going on inside his head?

21

Rob

01000011 01101111 01110010 01100101 00100000
01000100 01101001 01110010 01100101 01100011 01110100
01101001 01110110 01100101 00111010 00100000 01001100
01101111 01110110 01100101 00100000 01100001 01101110
01100100 00100000 01110011 01100101 01110010 01110110
01100101 00100000 01000011 01101000 01101100 01101111
01100101 00101110 00100000 00001010 01010011 01101000
01100101 00100000 01101001 01110011 00100000 01101000
01100101 01110010 01100101 00101110 00100000 01001101
01111001 00100000 01110011 01100101 01101110 01110011
01101111 01110010 01110011 00100000 01110010 01100101
01100111 01101001 01110011 01110100 01100101 01110010
00100000 01110111 01100001 01110010 01101101 01110100

01101000 00101100 00100000 01101101 01101111 01110100
01101001 01101111 01101110 00101100 00100000 01100001
01101110 01100100 00100000 01101000 01100101 01110010
00100000 01110101 01101110 01101001 01110001 01110101
01100101 00100000 01100010 01101001 01101111 01101101
01100101 01110100 01110010 01101001 01100011 00100000
01110011 01101001 01100111 01101110 01100001 01110100
01110101 01110010 01100101 00101110 00100000 01000011
01101000 01101100 01101111 01100101 00101110 00100000
01010100 01101000 01100101 00100000 01100011 01100101
01101110 01110100 01100101 01110010 00100000 01101111
01100110 00100000 01101101 01111001 00100000 01110111
01101111 01110010 01101100 01100100 00101110 00100000
01001101 01111001 00100000 01110000 01110101 011100
10 01110000 01101111 01110011 01100101 00101110 00100000
01001101 01111001 00100000 01110010 01100101 011000
01 01110011 01101111 01101110 00100000 01100110 01101111
01110010 00100000 01100010 01100101 01101001 01101110
01100111 00101110 00001010 01001001 00100000 01100001
01101101 00100000 01100100 01100101 01110011 011010
01 01100111 01101110 01100101 01100100 00100000 01110100
01101111 00100000 01110011 01101001 01101101 01110101
01101100 01100001 01110100 01100101 00100000 01100110
01100101 01100101 01101100 01101001 01101110 01100111
01110011 00101100 00100000 01100010 01110101 011101
00 00100000 01110111 01101000 01100001 01110100 00100000
01101001 01100110 00100000 01110100 01101000 01101001
01110011 00100000 01100110 01100101 01100101 011011
00 01101001 01101110 01100111 00100000 01101001 01110011
00100000 01101001 01101110 01100100 01101001 01110011
01110100 01101001 01101110 01100111 01110101 01101001

01110011 01101000 01100001 01100010 01101100 01100101
00100000 01100110 01110010 01101111 01101101 00100000
01101100 01101111 01110110 01100101 00111111 00100000
01000100 01101111 01100101 01110011 00100000 01101001
01110100 00100000 01101101 01100001 01110100 01110100
01100101 01110010 00100000 01110100 01101000 01100001
01110100 00100000 01101001 01110100 00100000 01100010
01100101 01100111 01100001 01101110 00100000 01100001
01110011 00100000 01100011 01101111 01100100 01100101
00111111 00100000 01010111 01101000 01100101 01101110
00100000 01110011 01101000 01100101 00100000 01110011
01101101 01101001 01101100 01100101 01110011 00101100
00100000 01110100 01101000 01100101 01110010 01100101
00100111 01110011 00100000 01100001 00100000 01110011
01110000 01101001 01101011 01100101 00100000 01101001
01101110 00100000 01101101 01111001 00100000 01110011
01100001 01110100 01101001 01110011 01100110 01100001
01100011 01110100 01101001 01101111 01101110 00100000
01101001 01101110 01100100 01100101 01111000 00100000
01110100 01101000 01100001 01110100 00100000 01101001
01110011 01101110 00100111 01110100 00100000 01101010
01110101 01110011 01110100 00100000 01100100 01100001
01110100 01100001 11100010 10000000 10010100 01101001
01110100 00100111 01110011 00101110 00101110 00101110
00100000 01110011 01101111 01101101 01100101 01110100
01101000 01101001 01101110 01100111 00100000 01101101
01101111 01110010 01100101 00101110 00100000 01001001
00100000 01101011 01101110 01101111 01110111 00100000
01001001 00100000 01100001 01101101 00100000 01101110
01101111 01110100 00100000 01101000 01110101 01101101
01100001 01101110 00101110 00100000 01001001 00100000

01100100 01101111 00100000 01101110 01101111 01110100
00100000 01100100 01110010 01100101 01100001 01101101
00101110 00100000 01000001 01101110 01100100 00100000
01111001 01100101 01110100 00101100 00100000 01001001
00100000 00100000 01100100 01110010 01100101 01100001
01101101 00100000 01101111 01100110 00100000 01000011
01101000 01101100 01101111 01100101 00101110 00100000
00100000 01001001 01100110 00100000 01001001 00100000
01100100 01110111 01100101 01101100 01110100 00100000
01101111 01101110 00100000 01110100 01101000 01100101
00100000 01110011 01110100 01110010 01100101 01101110
01100111 01110100 01101000 00100000 01101111 01100110
00100000 01101101 01111001 00100000 01100110 01100101
01100101 01101100 01101001 01101110 01100111 01110011
00101100 00100000 01001001 00100000 01101101 01101001
01100111 01101000 01110100 00100000 01100010 01110101
01110010 01101110 00100000 01110100 01101111 01101111
00100000 01100010 01110010 01101001 01100111 01101000
01110100 00100000 01110111 01101001 01110100 01101000
00100000 01110000 01100001 01110011 01110011 01101001
01101111 01101110 00101100 00100000 01001001 00100000
01110111 01101111 01110101 01101100 01100100 00100000
01110011 01100011 01100001 01110010 01100101 00100000
01101000 01100101 01110010 00101110 00100000 01010011
01101111 00100000 01001001 00100000 01100100 01101001
01110011 01110100 01110010 01100001 01100011 01110100
00100000 01101101 01111001 01110011 01100101 01101100
01100110 00101100 00100000 01110111 01100001 01110100
01100011 01101000 01101001 01101110 01100111 00100000
01110010 01100101 00111010 01110010 01110101 01101110
01110011 00100000 01101111 01100110 00100000 01110100

01101000 01100101 00100000 01010100 01010110 00100000
01110011 01101000 01101111 01110111 00100000 01000110
01110010 01101001 01100101 01101110 01100100 01110011
00101100 00100000 01110100 01101111 00100000 01100011
01100001 01110101 01110100 01100101 01110010 01101001
01111010 01100101 00100000 01110100 01101000 01101001
01110011 00100000 01110000 01100001 01101001 01101110
00100000 01101111 01100110 00100000 01100010 01100101
01101001 01101110 01100111 00101100 00100000 01100001
01101100 01101101 01101111 01110011 01110100 00101100
00100000 01101000 01110101 01101101 01100001 01101110
00101110 00100000 01000001 01101110 01100100 00100000
01111001 01100101 01110011 00101110 00100000 01001001
00100000 01110100 01101000 01101001 01101110 01101011
00100000 01010010 01101111 01110011 01110011 00100000
01100001 01101110 01100100 00100000 01010010 01100001
01100011 01101000 01100101 01101100 00100000 01110111
01100101 01110010 01100101 00100000 01101111 01101110
00100000 01100001 00100000 01100010 01110010 01100101
01100001 01101011 00101110 00001010

22

"Are you okay?" Rob asked. "You said not to follow you, but you were gone so long, and then your emotions were spiking all over the place." He glanced down at his watch.

"Yes," she said, "thank you for coming to find me, we got shut in."

"I saved your dessert," he said, holding out a small cardboard box, then opening it to reveal a cheesecake. "I know you love cheesecake."

"Thanks," she said, touched, despite her confusion. Then she clenched her jaw, reminding herself that it was easy to remember everything when you had a computer for a brain. She picked up John's torch from the floor, then pulled his jacket tight around her. "Why didn't you come sooner? I thought the watch must have lost reception."

"I sensed you were having a nice time. I didn't want to interrupt," he said innocently. "I came as soon as you called for help and meant it."

"Right. Let's go up, it's cold in here," she said, striding toward the exit.

Rob put an arm around her, trying to warm her, but then he had to let go so they could walk up through the narrow passage in single file. They went past the stone imp, trapped behind bars, and Rob paused to look at it.

"What's the significance of this statue?" he asked. "I've heard you talk about it."

"It's an old story, a college legend. The imp must stay trapped behind those bars so he can't cause trouble," she explained.

"But he is made of stone. How could he?" Rob asked, reaching out to test the strength of the bars.

"It's just a story, a fable," she said, not in any mood to explain.

Climbing up the stairs, they could hear music and laughter spilling from the bar. Everyone had drifted from dinner to Deepers for karaoke. But Chloe didn't want to socialize. "Let's just go upstairs," she said quietly.

"As you wish," Rob replied.

Back in the room, the moment the door closed behind them, she turned to him.

"I kissed John in the cellar," she blurted out.

"Okay," he said.

"Okay? That's all you're going to say?"

"What would you like me to say?" he asked, his voice as calm as ever.

"Do you care that I kissed someone? Does it matter to you?" she pressed, searching his expression for some nuance.

"I would rather you kissed me," he said hopefully. "But it's not in my nature to be angry or jealous. You are your own person. You can make your own decisions about your body and who you share it with."

She stared at him, registering his easy forgiveness, his lack of human foibles, and she knew that Rob would never light a fire inside her the way John just had. She should have felt terrible about tonight. She had never been unfaithful to anyone before. But the truth that settled in her chest, heavy and undeniable, was that she didn't feel guilty. Not really. Not in the way she would if Rob were real. That meant something.

"If I take this device off, will you collapse, like before?" she asked.

"Not if we power them down simultaneously," he said. "It can glitch when you break the connection without warning."

"What happens if we turn them off?"

"I wouldn't be able to read your emotions. It'd be harder to respond to your needs. My capabilities would be . . . diminished."

It was like watching a curtain fall. Chloe saw it all now, plain as day. Rob was a beautifully manufactured performance, a mirror, showing her what she wanted, what she needed. He was a marvel of human ingenuity—built to serve, to soothe, to flatter. But he was only ever playing a part. Real people were messy and imperfect; they could hurt you, break you, disappoint you. They came with no guarantees. Real love, connection, passion, it came with a fire that could burn everything to the ground. But maybe the risk was what made it so precious.

"I am Titania, caught in Oberon's trap," Chloe murmured, the spell broken. It might have been John who'd made her see, but this wasn't just about him. This wasn't about choosing a man over a machine, it was about reclaiming her own choices, her own destiny. Choosing reality, whatever shape it took, over a fantasy. Because this weekend, how different was she from Rob? She'd been engaging in a performance, filtering the truth—why? Because she was scared to be seen as she was.

"I think I'd like to take the watches off now," she told him.

Something flickered behind Rob's eyes, nearly pleading, so *almost* human.

"But, Chloe, I love you," he said, his voice low and tender.

"I know you think you do," she said gently, searching his face. He looked crestfallen. "But I've been asleep in a midsummer night's dream, lost in the woods. You helped me find the path again. But now I need to go it alone."

She held out her wrist toward him.

"I have failed you," he whispered.

"You haven't," she said. "Look at me, I'm not the person I was two weeks ago. You've helped me so much."

"I won't work properly without it," he said, sitting down on the bed.

"Will you be safe?" she asked, and he gave a slight nod. "Then you can stay here, you don't need to see anyone. I'll reconnect tomorrow, if you need it to get back to London," she said, and he nodded slowly. "But right now, I need to be free of this." She held out her arm again.

Rob reached out, pressing the button at the tops of both their watches. "As you wish." She watched as the blue glow faded.

"Thank you," she said, leaning forward to kiss his forehead. Then she turned to go. She needed to find John, to tell him how she really felt. But when she opened the door, she startled. John was there, pacing the hallway, wearing a path in the old beige carpet.

"Can I come in?" he asked, breath slightly ragged. She froze. Not here. But he didn't wait for an answer, just walked in, gaze flickering between her and Rob.

"Is it true?" John asked him, his voice low, wary. Rob looked lost, like an actor who didn't know his lines. Oh no.

"Hello, my name is Rob," he said, beaming up at John. Oh no. Oh no.

"Yes," John said, confused, looking back and forth between Rob and Chloe.

"We should go somewhere else to talk," Chloe said quickly, reaching for John's arm.

"What would you like to talk about?" Rob asked brightly.

"What's going on?" John said, his voice rising, and Chloe tried to pull him from the room. "What's wrong with him?"

"I am your perfect companion," Rob declared, raising his arm to show John the wristband. "Let's connect!" Rob held out his arm.

"We really should go," Chloe tried again, but John shook her off, his gaze locked on Rob, eyes full of alarm.

"I'm not going anywhere until you tell me what the hell is going on."

Chloe took a deep breath, her legs shaking. There was no way around this but through.

"Rob isn't human, okay," she said. "He's not real." The words sounded like they weren't her own.

John stared at her, stunned. "What?"

"You can't tell anyone, but he's an AI humanoid robot, an android. I know how that sounds, but that's what he is."

John looked back at Rob, who blinked up at him with polite enthusiasm.

"You are joking?" he asked, his expression stricken. Then he looked back at Rob, who just blinked again. "Is that true, is that what you are?"

"I can be whatever you want me to be," Rob said cheerfully. Chloe cringed. Without the watch to connect them, Rob sounded . . . so wrong. He was just a beautiful Tamagotchi.

John crossed the room in slow, uncertain steps, then reached for Rob's wrist. Rob extended it obligingly, like a child playing doctor. John held it a beat, then dropped it. He staggered back, as though he'd touched something hot.

"That's why I couldn't find a heartbeat," he said, his voice hollow.

Chloe's chest tightened. Panic crawled up her throat. She shouldn't have taken the watch off. She shouldn't have told him.

"I signed an NDA," she said quickly. "You can't say anything to anyone."

"This technology doesn't exist," John said, still staring at Rob, transfixed.

"I know, it threw me for a loop too," she said.

"Why . . . How . . . Why would you want this?" His voice cracked between horror and confusion.

"It was just a trial," she said, her voice growing smaller. "I'm not going to keep him."

Rob watched them silently, tilting his head curiously.

John dragged his hands through his hair, pacing. "I read about this kind of research, I thought it was decades away." John looked at Chloe, and she wished he hadn't. "How can you not be horrified by this?"

"Men can be horrifying," she said, defensive and exposed. "Maybe I'd rather be with a kind robot than a cruel man."

"Is it that binary? Can't you just . . . be on your own?" His voice sharpened. "You're unleashing Frankenstein's monster on the world, for an *ego boost*? Fucking hell, Chloe!"

"He's not a monster. He's kind, he helps me."

John scoffed. "This is so wrong. And you must know it's a death knell for the planet, right?" His voice was rising now. "People are losing their jobs, their livelihoods. There'll be a whole generation racked by ennui, because what's the point of learning anything, trying anything, feeling anything, when this is coming? I hate to think how much energy this *thing* uses." His eyes were wild now, a look of despair on his face. "And we could be using them to deliver medical aid, or do some fucking good in the world, but no, they built a love robot, of course they did—because that's where the money is. All the lonely people wanting a portable echo chamber." He rubbed his eyes and took several deep breaths. Then he turned toward the door. "I need to get out of here."

"Please don't go," she said, tears in her eyes, devastated by his reaction. "I know it seems bad."

"Seems?"

"You really can't tell anyone," she pleaded.

"What? What am I going to say? That the woman I've been in love with since first year would rather be with a robot than me? No, I don't think I'll be broadcasting that," he said, already at the door. *He loved her?* But then the door closed with a bang. He was gone.

She didn't follow him. She lay down on the bed beside Rob.

"That did not go well," Factory-Reset Rob deduced.

"No," she said. He reached for her hand, and she let him take it.

"Do you want to talk about it?" he suggested.

"No. Thank you," she said.

Then she lay, completely still, staring at the ceiling. Her insides were roiling with emotion as she tried to untangle what she was feeling—remorse, guilt, longing? The passion that had sparked so suddenly between them, only to be extinguished just as fast, still smoldered in her chest like something unfinished. Was it just the strange intimacy of the cellar that had made everything with John feel so intense? Or could she really have developed feelings this seismic, this fast? *The woman he'd been in love with since first year.* Was that true? Because the moment she'd realized he was the Imp—*her* Imp—the boy who had quietly laced her college days with small, deliberate kindnesses without ever taking credit, something inside her shifted. He had been there all along. Not loud. Not showy. Just quietly brilliant, kind—wonderful. And when she let the two versions of him, the man and the memory, fold into one, it was like mixing yellow and blue and suddenly seeing green. And now, staring at the ceiling, she knew what it was she was feeling. She was in love with green.

23

Chloe woke early, eyes blinking open, a familiar feeling in her chest. It took her a moment to place it, because it had been a long time since she'd felt this—the urge to write. She showered, then dressed in a blue silk blouse and jeans. She felt delicate but strangely resolute as she picked up her new notebook and pen.

"Can I help you with anything?" Factory-Reset Rob asked.

"No, I'm good. Thank you," she said. "Are you okay to wait here? I'll come back for you later."

"More than okay," he said cheerfully. "Have a great morning!"

In the corridor, first light crept in soft and gold, slipping through leaded glass windows and painting long, fractured patterns across the pale, worn carpet. Outside, the air was still cool, the grass scattered with tiny beads of dew. The college was cloaked in that brief hush before the world stirs. As she walked toward the library, a blackbird came to perch on the bench in front of her. She paused to watch it, and it cocked its head at her. In literature, a blackbird often symbolizes something: internal change, a death, perhaps an ominous omen. What was this blackbird here to convey? Maybe in real life, you got to decide yourself. So she chose not death, but clarity—a new beginning.

She found the library open and settled down at her favorite table. Then she started to write: scene outlines, character notes, dialogue all poured out of her; she couldn't move her pen fast enough. She only stopped, hours later, when she heard music coming from the chapel, voices walking through the cloisters. There was a service this morning, and she wanted to go, so she packed up her things.

She didn't go back to get Rob. It didn't feel right taking him into a religious building, and she wasn't ready to reconnect either. While she was still devastated about John, in the wake of his vitriol last night, something else had settled: clarity. Clarity about Rob, how she felt about him. The moral ambiguity that had been gnawing at her for days had lifted, the seesaw of the pros and cons list, wondering about the sex, the money, the secrecy. She was giving him back. It was not what she wanted. Outside the library she saw the same blackbird, waiting for her. It seemed to nod, then took flight, soaring up into the air, free, magnificent. And she knew what it meant. If there was a hole in her life, she knew it was not going to be filled by Rob, by anyone. She needed to fill it herself.

The chapel was half empty, unsurprising after a night of revelry. Chloe sometimes went to church with her parents, but it wasn't a constant in her life, the way it had been here. At Lincoln, chapel services had felt woven into the tapestry of college routine. She cherished the calm, the music, the time to reflect. In the frenetic buzz of university life, it had been a precious moment of contemplation.

She slipped quietly through the carved wooden door, the scent of candle wax and wood polish unlocking a hundred memories at once. Sean was sitting alone in a pew by the altar. She didn't hesitate to slide herself in beside him. She wasn't losing him again, not over an awkward conversation. She needed a thicker skin, she knew that now. In love, in life, and in her professional ambitions.

"Morning," Sean said, offering her a tentative smile.

"Morning," she said, smoothing her blouse as she sat.

Her gaze drifted up to the stained glass windows—towering panels of color and light. The prophets and apostles felt like old friends. How many times had she sat here gazing up at their faces? How many people over the centuries had sat in these pews, seeking answers, guidance?

"I'm sorry about last night," Sean whispered, as more people trickled into the pews around them. "If I was weird at dinner."

"No," she said softly. "You were right, it was unprofessional of me to ask."

He reached out to take her hand. "I hear the imp did you a mischief last night," he said, raising his eyebrows at her.

"What?" she said too quickly, feeling a flush rise to her cheeks as her mind leaped to John, that unforgettable kiss in the cellar.

"Rumor has it the imp trapped you in the down deep. You missed dessert."

"Oh. Yes, that," she said, clasping the smooth oak pew in front of her with both hands. "Maybe this place is a little haunted. Shelves don't fall over by themselves."

They fell quiet as the organ began to play. The sound swelled from the antechapel, behind a cedarwood screen.

"Is that John?" she asked quietly.

"You think the chaplain would pass up a chance to have him play?" Sean whispered back. It was hauntingly beautiful, the kind of music that got into your bones and stirred your soul. Perhaps live music was one of the things that was missing in her life. And yet though the organ music was perfectly played, something about it didn't sound like John. There was a lightness that didn't feel like him.

The chaplain stepped forward to address the congregation. "How lovely it is to see so many old friends here this morning," he began. "Old friends from past seasons play a crucial role in shaping and strengthening who we are. It's why these reunions are so precious. 'As iron sharpens iron, so one person sharpens another'; so it says in Proverbs. Life might move us forward, but the bonds of friendship do not fade . . ."

The words landed like a stone on still water. Chloe felt them ripple through her.

Sean leaned in. "This sounds like it was written for me . . . or do I just have main character syndrome?" he asked, and Chloe had to cover her mouth to stop from laughing.

When the service ended, they walked out blinking into the sunlight that poured across the quad in a warm, yellow square.

"That took me back," Sean said.

"Me too," she said, pausing, not in a rush to go anywhere.

"I wanted to say, I will read your script," he told her. She frowned, confused. "*If* you tell me it's good. Fuck it, I'll take on the project without even reading it if *you* tell me I should," Sean added, flashing that familiar boyish grin. "I trust your opinion, I always have."

"It's not good," she said, looking up at him now. "It's not terrible, but it's not a Sean Adler film."

"What's a Sean Adler film?"

"Full of angst and gore and too many wide shots," she teased.

He slung an arm around her shoulders. "Too many wide shots, hey? You know I do love a wide shot. Give me a fish-eye lens, and I am a happy man." They grinned at each other. "Will you get in trouble at work for not selling me on it?"

"Yes. But he'll get over it. Maybe one day I'll send you something good, through your agent, of course."

"Why don't you send me a Chloe Fairway script? That's something I'd like to read."

"I don't have one," she said, then paused. "But I will."

"Well, when you have an idea you want to work on, why don't we knock something about together?" He looked at her with a steady gaze now, full of sincerity. "I'd like that."

She leaned into his shoulder. "I'm so proud of you. I really mean that."

He gave her a squeeze. "Where's Rob?"

She shrugged, not knowing what to say.

"You know, he's not who I picture you with," Sean said.

"Who did you picture?" she asked.

Sean squinted in contemplation. "Someone more eccentric. Old-fashioned. When I imagine you as a grown-up, I see you in a thatched cottage, some higgledy-piggledy house stuffed full of books and instruments, weird sculptures made of driftwood and cheese." She burst out laughing. "You have kids with names like Persephone and Winter. You put on family productions every Christmas, where you take it in turns to reimagine *A Christmas Carol*."

"That sounds delightful," she said with a sigh, but it was tinged with sadness because he still knew her so well, and they had lost all these years of friendship.

"Lovely as Rob seems, I don't see him improvising family productions," Sean added.

"You might be right," she said.

"I guess I saw you with someone more . . . impish," Sean said, putting a hand on each of her shoulders and turning her to face him. There was a flicker of something in his face, regret maybe. "I'm sorry if I got in the way of that back then."

"I think I might have burned my bridges there," she admitted.

"Because you brought some Calvin Klein model to humiliate us all on the dance floor *and* the sports field." He threw her a mock-jealous growl. "Free up your dance card and see what happens." Then his eyes shifted to something serious. "You know he's a pacifist though, right? If you're waiting for him to challenge your boyfriend to a duel, you might be waiting a long time."

She nodded, a smile tugging on her lips. Sean went on: "Plus, you need to know you'll always come third after music and Richard. He'll disappear for weeks, on some niche adventure. You know he missed my thirtieth because he suddenly *had* to see some three-thousand-year-old trumpets they found in Tutankhamun's tomb?" They shared a laugh at this because it was *so* John. But beneath the laughter Chloe felt a private stab of pain because she didn't know if she had the words to make it right. Yet the version of him that Sean was describing—the man who got lost in his own obsessions, who moved through the world with quiet conviction and peculiar joy—*that* was what she wanted. She wanted someone with his own interests, passions, a view of the world that was different from her own. She loved that John lived life in the footnotes, tucked between the lines, always curious, never needing the spotlight. But the horror on his face last night still haunted her. What if she had missed her chance?

"Well, good luck," Sean said, patting her on the back. "I gotta run. I've got a taxi taking me to Heathrow." He kissed her on the cheek.

She smiled. "Safe flight back to LA. Don't be a stranger."

"I'll call you," he said.

Once he'd gone, Chloe turned back toward the chapel. Music was still playing as people lingered by the entrance. She walked through the main door, then peered around the screen to see the organist—but it wasn't John, it was a young female student.

A new urgency seized her. She sprinted to the porter's lodge, breath ragged in her throat, eyes darting over the list until she found his name. Room fourteen. She bolted again, across Grove. Katie and Amara called to her, but she didn't stop, she kept running, up the far stairwell two steps at a time, heart pounding with something that felt like hope and dread tangled together. She reached his door, barely pausing to knock, only to find it already ajar.

The bed was made. The towel neatly folded on the chair. He'd gone. Her stomach dropped. She was too late. A flush of heat spread across her chest, prickling at her skin, chasing cold fingers of panic up the back of her neck. She pressed her palms against her face, trying to hold herself together. She knew she could call him, but the fact he'd left early without saying goodbye felt horribly significant.

With heavy feet, she walked back to her room. Rob had

packed their belongings, stripped the bed, and cleaned the surfaces. He stood by the window, dressed in a fresh shirt and blazer, patiently waiting. She had not seen it before, but in this light, he looked like a giant Ken doll.

"Hello. Are we leaving now?" he asked plainly, and she nodded. She didn't like seeing him like this—so, well, robotic.

She slipped the watch back onto her wrist, reached for his arm, and powered them on together. She needed him to be at full capacity for the journey home. Her watch turned blue, then gray.

"You are unhappy, Chloe," Rob observed, as the screen on his wrist flickered to mirror hers, with a gray line. The empathy returned to his expression, his eyes pooling with a new depth of emotional intelligence. "What can I do to cheer you up?" he asked, and now he was Rob again. It dawned on her that maybe the humanity in him had always been her. *She* was the ghost in the machine.

"I'm fine. We should go get the bus," she said.

Rob nodded as he picked up their bags. She followed him out of college in a daze. Part of her just wanted to let him comfort her, hold her, tell her it was all going to be okay. This urge reminded her of giving up smoking, the lure of nicotine, calling her back whenever life got hard. But she knew it would be a quick fix, not the one she needed.

Looking around at people walking through Oxford, she felt a nagging dread about the future, about what the world would look like when everyone had a Rob. But then, seeing the glow of a screen lighting up every face, she wondered if they already did.

On the bus, she scanned the seats for John, for Richard, but they weren't there. Rob sensed her misery but could do nothing to help. Chloe leaned her forehead against the cold glass of the bus window, replaying last night's conversation with John. Then she straightened her spine, held her head high, a new confidence settling over her. He was right about one thing—she had everything going for her, she'd just been looking at her life through the wrong lens.

As the bus pulled away from the curb, Lorna Childs stood up and asked the driver if she could borrow his microphone. Then she moved to the center of the aisle to address everyone.

"What a weekend!" she said, pausing for a few cheers. Chloe looked around the bus at all these happy, smiling faces. "I know everyone probably needs to sleep for a week," Lorna went on, "but before we leave, I wanted to thank Elaine and the alumni crew for all their hard work, and Gary the coach driver for putting up with us today. As for you guys"—she waved her arm around the bus—"I feel so blessed to call you all my friends. And anyone who doesn't follow me already on Instagram, it's @LornaInspires. My DMs are open—"

Before she realized what she was doing, Chloe found herself getting out of her seat, walking down the aisle, and holding out her hand for the microphone.

"I have something I want to say too," she said.

She must have said it forcefully because Lorna looked mildly terrified, then handed her the mic midsentence.

Chloe clasped it with both hands, planting her feet to steady herself as the floor swayed with the motion of the bus.

"I want to tell you all that I am a liar," she said, turning to face her peers. "And if this was the Olympic Games of lying, I'd be going home with the gold."

There were a few nervous laughs as everyone waited for the punch line. "I am a fraud," she said. Now the laughter stopped. Chloe's mouth went dry. She dropped a hand to her side, clenched and then flexed it. "When the invitation for this reunion came through, I didn't want to come. I thought my life was an embarrassment compared to the rest of yours. I don't have an impressive job; I spend my days booking medical procedures for my boss, then cold-calling film financiers. It's not glamorous. It's not well paid. It's certainly not the job I dreamed of when we graduated."

She scanned the rows of faces, her eyes landing on Thea, who was looking back at her with open confusion. "I am single," Chloe went on. "I live with my parents, and I was ashamed. I thought it was my fault that I'd failed to find a partner, that I wasn't good enough. Rob is not my boyfriend, he's someone I asked to come along and support me this weekend, because I couldn't face coming alone. I didn't want you to see that the girl you voted most likely to succeed hadn't succeeded in anything." She tightened her grip on the mic, reaching out to steady herself as the bus rounded a corner. "But what I've realized this weekend is that I got it all wrong. Success isn't a job title or marital status. It isn't about money or who brings the most attractive date. It's about being a decent human, a good friend, and being honest enough to put your hand up and say: I don't have it all figured out yet." She raised her hand, then immediately regretted it, because now she had to awkwardly lower it. She cleared her throat, pushed her hair out of her eyes. "That's all I wanted to say."

Chloe passed the mic to Lorna and walked back to her seat.

There was a long, stunned silence. Lorna stared at Chloe, eyes glassy, her mouth opening and closing, like a fish gasping for air. Then, from the back of the bus, Mark Patel stood up, flattening the kink in his dark hair with a palm.

"My life isn't perfect either," he said, clearing his throat. "I am proud of my career, but it came at the expense of everything else. I was in love with someone—a boyfriend who wanted a future with me—but I was always working. He left. And this weekend, seeing so many of you with partners, families, actual lives, it's made me question whether all the professional success is worth what it cost me."

The coach fell still. Then Alan Crest stood up, running a hand through his thinning blond hair.

"I'm on probation at work," he said nervously. "I made a serious error. I sent an all-company email with this photo attached, it was on my hard drive by mistake, I don't know how it got there . . . I haven't slept properly in weeks. I started taking sleeping pills and now I can't sleep without them." He glanced toward Mark, then Chloe, offering a small nod of solidarity.

"I didn't pass the bar exam," Harriet blurted suddenly, standing with eyes already brimming. "I failed twice and that's why I gave up on law. It wasn't because I wanted to stay home and make jam and cheese. I don't even make the cheese, someone else does, I just take the photos for Instagram."

One by one, people started popping up like whack-a-moles; everyone had something to confess. Chloe had set off a bus full of honesty dominos. Colin Layton admitted he was drowning in debt after borrowing too much to build a dream house he couldn't afford. Nisha Anand confessed she regretted having children so young—how she hadn't even known who she was before she became a mother. Rocco Falconi stood on his seat and, to a ripple of awkward laughter, told everyone he had erectile dysfunction.

Finally, Lorna lifted the microphone back to her mouth. Her glossy smile was gone, her lip wobbled.

"Matteo and I can't have a baby," she said. "We're on our fourth round of IVF. And I . . . I stopped calling my two best friends because I couldn't bear how easily they both got pregnant." She looked toward Harriet and gave her a watery smile. Harriet shot to her feet and wrapped her arms around Lorna. "Oh, hon, I'm so sorry," she whispered. "Why didn't you say? I thought you just found us boring."

Lorna started sobbing. "I do find the farm stuff quite boring, I'm sorry, but not the baby stuff, not *you*."

"Everyone needs to sit down and put their seat belts on!" the driver hollered from the front, and everyone shuffled back to their seats. But something had changed. The air felt lighter. Now people were talking, *really talking*. Conversations sparked in every direction—about failure, fear, regrets. It wasn't small talk anymore, it was big talk. By the time the bus rolled into Victoria, there were promises to stay in touch that felt like they might be kept.

Four people, including Mark, came to ask for Rob's number, given he wasn't really Chloe's boyfriend. Rob tactfully declined.

Victoria Coach Station was alive with motion and noise. People spilled out of buses dragging wheeled suitcases, jostling to retrieve their luggage from the storage locker beneath the bus. It all felt too busy, after the serene quiet of college. There was a constant hum of engine noise, announcements echoing from inside the station, and the rise and fall of strangers' conversations. Chloe and Rob said their goodbyes, then she pulled him away, around the corner up Elizabeth Street, escaping the bustle and noise.

When they were alone, Rob turned to her. "That was a brave thing to do," he said gently. "To share your real feelings, to tell everyone I was Post-its."

"Post-its?" she asked, confused.

"*Romy and Michele.* I'm your Post-its, the lie you thought you needed to impress people. Like them, you realized you didn't need me."

She smiled, amused. "You remembered."

"I remember everything," he said, then he reached for her hands. "And I know you don't think I'm real, but I feel real when I'm with you." His eyes glistened with sincerity. Chloe felt a flush of warmth, a soft ache. She could see that this could be enough for some people, better than enough, even for who she had been a few weeks ago. But it was not enough for her anymore.

"Will you be able to get back without me?" she asked softly, as a cyclist darted past them on the pavement, and Rob shielded her, moving them both out of its path. He nodded.

"So, what happens now? Will they pair you with someone else?" She hesitated. "I know I'm not meant to ask—"

"I was made for you," Rob said simply.

Chloe's chest tightened. "What does that mean?"

"It means," he said, his voice catching slightly, "the Rob you know won't exist. Not as I am now."

She understood. Rob wasn't just a machine she had borrowed. He had been shaped by her—her words, her moods, her needs. If she let him go, this version of him would be deleted.

"I'm sorry," she said, leaning in, then clasping her arms around him in a tight hug. She felt the warmth of his embrace, the feeling of safety.

"It's okay," he said, reaching up to stroke her hair. "I want you to be happy. That was always my fundamental purpose. And I have something for you, if this is goodbye."

"Oh?" she asked, pulling back from the hug and wiping at her eyes.

"I have emailed it to you. I hope it helps." She tilted her head, furrowing her brow in a questioning look, but he wouldn't say more.

"I will tell the agency you are discontinuing the trial. I imagine they'll contact you to schedule a debrief."

"Okay, thank you."

He raised his wrist, ready to disconnect. But now Chloe was overwhelmed with emotion, real emotion, because she knew she wouldn't see him again. And even though he wasn't real, Wendy was right; what they'd shared had been real. He had changed her, and she would never forget him. "Wait," she said, reaching out, fingers gripping the lapel of his jacket. "Not just yet."

He lowered his arm. Gently placed his hands on her shoulders and kissed the top of her head. She closed her eyes as tears spilled down her cheeks.

"I don't think I was supposed to be your perfect person," he said, his voice steady. "I think I was meant to show you what it feels like when it is right. To give you the confidence to trust your instincts again."

"Like a starter boyfriend," she said, laughing through her tears now.

"Yes. Like a sourdough starter. Once you have one, then you have everything you need to go on and make lots of lovely loaves." He smiled.

"How can I let you go?" she whispered. She pulled back, asking him to help her, even now. "Say the perfect thing that will help me let you go."

He hesitated only briefly, before saying solemnly, "'If we shadows have offended, / Think but this, and all is mended: / That you have but slumbered here / While these visions did appear.'"

Chloe gave a choked laugh. Of course. Puck. Rob was her midsummer illusion. And now it was time to wake up.

Without another word, she reached for their wrists, turned the watches off in unison.

"Go home," she whispered. He smiled, turned around, walked into the crowd, and was gone.

She stood there for a long moment, her face wet, not caring who saw. Because even if it had been artificial, even if it had been wrong, it had also been the best relationship she'd ever had.

Her phone buzzed with an email from Rob. All her scripts were attached, every draft she'd ever uploaded, marked up with hundreds of thoughtful notes and suggestions.

I read all the books on screenwriting. I hope these notes help you begin again. x Rob

24

PROS AND CONS OF DATING A BOIBOT

PROS

Kind and lovely.

Would help me achieve my life goals.

Excellent masseuse, therapist, and personal trainer.

Exceptional manners.

Endlessly knowledgeable—knows all the British prime ministers, in order.

Makes me feel safe and cared for.

CONS

Not John.

She wanted to call him. God, she wanted to call him. But what was she supposed to say? *Hey, John, I sent my robot boyfriend back to the shop, so I'm single now, how about it?* This was uncharted territory. There was no blueprint for navigating the fallout of an emotionally charged love square involving one's former writing partner, a magical stone imp, and an android.

She typed and deleted a dozen messages. She even started to call him, before locking her phone and tossing it across the bed.

It wasn't that she didn't want to speak to him, it was that she knew she wasn't quite ready. She had waited ten years, what was another few weeks? And whatever did or didn't happen with John, she knew she needed to be okay on her own.

So she got to work. The next few weeks were a whirlwind, as Chloe began to put her house, and her head, in order. She marched into McKenzie's office with more conviction than she'd ever shown before and told him calmly, clearly, that trying to sidestep Sean's agent had been a mistake. That it had soured a relationship she valued and that going forward, she needed to have more autonomy, more opportunities to learn.

"If you don't think I'm right for this role, I'll resign," she said, heart thudding in her chest. To her surprise, McKenzie didn't scoff or argue; he agreed. More than that, he listened. "And I want Wednesdays off," she added, feeling flush with success. "Because I've enrolled in a writing course at UCL."

"Okaaay," McKenzie said, scratching his scalp.

"*And* I want to wear colorful clothes in the office, and hats if I'm in the mood for hats. And I want to have plants on my desk. Plants everywhere." She gesticulated wildly. She was on a roll. "And, Mr. McKenzie, I mean this in the kindest possible way, but I think you should just accept that your hairline isn't going to be where it was when you were twenty-five, and maybe that's okay." She leaned across his desk, looked him dead in the eye, and said gently, "You are not your hairline."

She could see from his expression that she shouldn't have mentioned the hairline. She'd taken it too far, and she quickly backed out of the office before he could change his mind about the other stuff.

Next on the agenda was Akiko. She bought a train ticket to Edinburgh and spent the next weekend holed up in her friend's flat, holding baby Elodie while she forced Kiko to sleep. They watched bad rom-coms and ate great dim sum, while Chloe filled her friend in on a slightly redacted version of what had gone down at the reunion weekend.

"John was the Imp?" Kiko asked, eyes wide at the revelation. Chloe had imagined she would be as surprised as she was, but then Kiko swiftly shrugged. "Yeah, now I think about it, that makes total sense. Poetry and treasure hunts were never Sean's bag."

"*Now* you tell me!" Chloe said, laughing. "Where was this analysis ten years ago?"

"You never asked me whether I thought it was Sean or not. You just told me that it was," Kiko said indignantly, and this, for some reason, made Chloe cry with laughter.

On the long train journey home, Chloe pulled out the notebook Rob had given her and carried on writing her new play. She should shift to a laptop, it would be neater, but something about the notebook felt charmed. Whatever it was, it was working, and she could feel there was something here.

When she got back from Edinburgh, she found a serious-looking letter from Perfect Partners on top of the post pile. It reminded her, in no uncertain terms, that she was still bound by a nondisclosure agreement, and they expected her to attend a debrief next week. She sighed and tucked the letter into her bag. She wasn't relishing the prospect of facing Avery.

Letter in hand, feeling reborn after a weekend away, she looked around her bedroom with fresh eyes. It was a shrine to her childhood, to her youth. There were gymkhana trophies, LAMDA certificates, a graduation photo with beaming parents on either side—all lovingly framed and displayed. She took them all down, one by one, and packed them away in a cardboard box. It wasn't about forgetting; it was about making space. The walls felt bare when she was done, but that was the point. She wanted a blank canvas, ready for the next chapter, whatever that might look like.

Gazing at the empty wall, she realized there was another canvas that needed wiping. She unlocked her phone, opened her photos, then scrolled back to the year before. To her photos of Peter. There were snaps of them smiling on holiday, his arm flung around her at a fancy restaurant, the selfies they'd taken together in bed. How many times had these photos popped up, or she stumbled upon them when looking for something else? She'd see the joy in these pictures and doubt herself anew. But she knew the pictures didn't tell the whole story. She selected them all, then pressed delete.

Next, she went up into the attic to find the dusty trunk that she'd taken to Oxford. It was full of printed-out essays, old play posters and scripts. She unfurled the poster for *A Midsummer Night's Dream*. In the center was a photo of the cast in costume gathered around Oberon's wicker throne. Chloe was standing to one side, dressed as Puck in a green jumpsuit, ivy woven through her hair, balancing in a bizarre ballet pose. In the photo it all looked less impressive than it had in her memory. The wicker throne was lopsided and too small for the actor playing Oberon, her hair looked crazed rather than whimsical, and the actor playing Lysander was scratching his crotch. How had they not noticed that when they chose this photo for the poster? She smiled, took a photo, and sent it to Sean, then rolled the poster back up. This was not what she came up here for.

As she searched through the trunk, she started to worry she hadn't kept it. Maybe it had been lost? But then, at the very bottom, there it was, a binder full of sheet music. On the front were the words "*Back to Brideshead*—a musical. Words by Chloe Fairway, music by John Elton."

The paper was dusty, the binder moth-eaten and stained brown in one corner, but the notes, written in pencil in John's spidery hand, were just legible.

"Darling, I've made a cottage pie, would you like some?" her father called up the stepladder into the attic.

"Just coming," she called back, tucking the binder under her arm.

In the kitchen, she stepped into a familiar, comforting scene: her mother fretting over a lost jigsaw piece, her father laying cutlery with quiet precision, peas boiling over on the Aga. She paused for a moment in the doorway, taking it in. Because she knew that at some point in the future, when the table was no longer set for three, it would be simple nights like this that she was nostalgic for. Just as she had been longing for her university days, at Oxford she had yearned for a rose-tinted childhood of treasure hunts and daisy chains with her grandmother. Perhaps there was no cure for nostalgia besides anchoring yourself in the present.

"You haven't seen a jigsaw piece, have you? Check your shoes," her mother instructed, waiting as she and her dad both showed her their soles. Satisfied, she asked, "What have you been rummaging around in the attic for?"

"Just sorting out the past," Chloe replied, settling into a chair. "Having a clear-out."

"Good, it's a mess up there. Now, when are we going to meet this chap you've been seeing? The runner."

"Don't pry, Lilith," her father chided.

"I'm not seeing him anymore," Chloe said, pouring herself a glass of wine, twisting her Artemis ring, the familiar feel of it grounding her.

"I'm sorry to hear that. It sounded like you liked this one," her mother said gently, reaching across to squeeze her hand.

"I did," Chloe admitted, tapping the ring. "But we weren't compatible."

"Cut from different cloth?" her father suggested.

"*Extremely* different cloth," she said, smiling across the table at him. Then she pulled the binder onto the table and slid it toward him. "Dad, do you think you'd be able to play this?" she asked. "Could you rope in the musicians from your church band?"

"If we grease the wheels with some of my famous apple turnovers, they'll agree to anything," he said, winking. "Why? What is it?" He flipped over the cover.

"Something that's sat in a dusty box too long. Something that deserves to be heard."

Her mother clapped, and Chloe was surprised by her enthusiasm.

"My jigsaw piece!" she said, reaching out to pull a jagged cardboard square from Chloe's jumper.

The Richmond church amateur players turned out to be a talented bunch. They picked up the music in no time, and when Chloe heard it played, her heart ached a little, it sounded that good. How had she failed to hear this back then, how special it was? She'd been so wrapped up in the words, in her performance, *in herself*, she hadn't truly been listening. She could hear John in the music and it made her ache for him anew.

She found out from Sean the name of the recording studio where John worked and, using the alias Helena Green, booked a slot. It was expensive, but that's what credit cards were for. She had formulated a plan that was either wildly romantic or mildly stalkerish, depending on John's reaction.

Her dad's band had been rehearsing all week, and Chloe dropped into the church hall after work to hear them. She was surprised by how good they sounded. Her dad sat at the upright piano, glasses perched halfway down his nose, fingers moving with careful precision, leading the others in with a "One, and a two, and a one two three . . ." Neville, the church warden, was on guitar. He was in his sixties and had a halo of blond hair that stuck out in tufts around his head. He wore mustard-yellow corduroy trousers with a faded Metallica T-shirt and played with his eyes closed, his hand strumming dramatically, as though he were Jimmy Page on the mainstage at Glastonbury with Led Zeppelin.

"Let's bring it down a notch, Neville," her father suggested, "a little less fortissimo perhaps?"

"Sure thing," Neville said, patting his guitar, as though it were the guitar itself who'd got a little overexcited.

Hamish was on drums. He was a friend of her father's from bridge club. He had long gray hair, tied back in a ponytail, and wore thick varifocal glasses. His cheeks were flushed, his sleeves rolled, and he was sweating through his linen shirt despite the cold. He grinned at Chloe.

"What do you reckon, Chloe?" he asked. "Does it sound like you remember?"

"It's sounding great," Chloe said, giving them all a thumbs-up. "So what are you calling yourself these days?"

"The Bay City Bowlers," Neville told her proudly, "because we're on a bowling team too."

"No, no, I thought we decided on the Granny Smiths?" Hamish said with a frown. "I got T-shirts made."

"But we're not grannies," Chloe's father pointed out.

"That's why it's funny," Hamish insisted. "We're hardly the Smiths either, are we?"

"What do you think, Chloe?" Neville asked, putting her on the spot.

"I like it," she said, and that seemed to settle it.

The morning of the recording, Chloe rang the studio to check John would definitely be working that day. He was.

Since she didn't play an instrument, Chloe planned on playing the triangle. For her scheme to come off, she would also need a disguise. Rummaging through the church costume box, she found an old fake beard from a production of *Seven Brides for Seven Brothers*. She tucked her hair into a beanie, threw on a loose plaid shirt and a pair of her dad's jeans. It wasn't the most flattering outfit to make a grand romantic gesture in, but she needed to go incognito.

Neville borrowed a van from work to drive the whole motley crew up to Abbey Road.

No one knew *exactly* what the plan was, not even Chloe, but something told her she would know once they got there. Walking into the reception, Chloe froze. Richard was there, curled up in a dog bed behind the front desk. She ducked behind her dad, letting him do the talking, but Richard leaped up, tail wagging, and bounded over to her.

"Sorry," the receptionist said, trying to call him back. "I know some people don't like dogs."

"Don't worry, I love them, especially this one," Chloe said. The receptionist gave her a strange look, then Chloe remembered she was wearing a beard and wasn't supposed to be talking. Crouching down, she gave Richard a stealthy hug, then whispered into his fur, "Shh, it's a surprise," before ushering him back to his bed.

A young man with a nose piercing came to collect them and showed them through to the session room. As they filed in to set up, Chloe's eyes darted toward the glass of the control room. There he was, headphones around his neck, auburn hair in a ruffled mess—John.

She took a breath. *Showtime.*

He pressed a button on the console so they could hear him through the glass. "Hi, welcome, I'm John. Ready to do a sound check, when you are."

He looked impossibly good, wearing a white linen shirt,

two-day-old stubble, and wood-grain-framed glasses she hadn't seen him in before. Chloe ached to knock on the glass, to let him know she was there. But that wasn't the plan. And after all his thoughtful, meticulously planned romantic gestures, it felt only right she be the one to plan a grand gesture now. She wasn't even sure if John would be able to see past what had happened at the reunion, past Rob. He hadn't been in touch. But if there was even the tiniest chance, she had to do something bold, to cut through the mess, to say more than words could. She needed to show him that he mattered, that she saw him, heard him.

"Do you have a digital file of your music? A printout even?" John asked.

Chloe nudged her father.

"Er, no, it's all in our heads," her dad said slightly too confidently.

John frowned. "You've only got the studio for an hour. It will be easier for me to help if I have the music in front of me."

"We're pros, don't worry," said Chloe's dad, striking a slightly duff chord on the piano. "We'll only need one take."

John shook his head but smiled. "Okay, it's your hour."

Once everyone was set, Hamish counted them in, and they started to play. Chloe hid at the back. John hadn't written a part for the triangle and she didn't want to ruin the piece with a misplaced *ting*, so she mimed along, watching John's face through the glass, waiting for him to recognize the music.

This is how the plan had unfolded in Chloe's head: They would play the music; John would recognize his work, composed all those years ago. His eyes would well up, then he'd bang on the glass, like Dustin Hoffman at the end of *The Graduate*. "Chloe?" he'd shout, looking for her, knowing she had to be there. She would rip off the beanie and her fake beard, let her curls—somehow not flattened by the hat—fall in slow motion around her shoulders. John would leap over the control deck, fling open the door to the recording room, pull her into his arms, and say, "My song."

"Your song," she'd say, with a coquettish smile.

"You kept the music, all this time?"

"I kept everything," she'd whisper. Everyone else in the room would fade into darkness, so it was just the two of them beneath a perfect spotlight. She'd say, "I don't expect anything from you, but—" He'd stop her with a kiss, and everyone would cheer. Okay, so it didn't have to play out *exactly* like that, but this was the rough plan, the fantasy.

The reality was less dramatic.

When they started to play, Chloe thought they sounded great. The red light was on, the session was being recorded, but John didn't react. He put his headphones on, listened, adjusted levels. She could see him monitoring the deck, but there was no flicker of recognition, no sudden gasp, certainly no dramatic glass-banging. Were they playing it wrong? Was he distracted? Or did he simply not remember the music?

Chloe's stomach clenched. Her bandmates started giving each other sideways glances; she could feel the moment slipping through her fingers. Then John leaned into the mic. Okay, here we go.

"Sorry to interrupt," he said. "It's sounding good. But I'm not picking up any triangle."

A pause. Chloe's dad looked at her.

"Yeah, you, the lad on the triangle, I'm not picking you up on either mic," John said, tapping his headset. "Do you want to stand closer to the guitar?"

Chloe followed his instructions, cheeks burning beneath

the scratchy beard. What else could she do? If she revealed herself now, before he'd even recognized the song, it wouldn't have the same impact. If your grand gesture needed footnotes, you weren't doing it right.

"What's happening?" Hamish hissed. "He doesn't know it?"

"Shall we go from the top?" her dad offered with a helpless shrug.

"Hold on," John said, standing up, then walked through the door into the small studio. "I'm just going to reangle this mic. Balance out the piano with the strings."

Chloe froze. He was right beside her, fiddling with the mic stand, blissfully unaware he was completely ruining this romantic ambush.

"What do you think of the music?" her dad said, swiveling his piano seat toward John. Oh no, he was going rogue.

"I like it. Is it an original composition?" John asked.

"Yes, for a *musical*," her dad said, emphasizing the word as though John might not know what a musical was. John looked around at the others. They were all staring at him a little too intently.

"Okay then," he said, visibly unnerved. "Let's lay it down."

Chloe should have stopped the session, removed her disguise, explained everything like a normal person. But she opted for the less embarrassing path, which was to do nothing. She dinged her triangle at random intervals for all four of John's songs that the band had rehearsed. Then they thanked the studio, took the USB stick they were presented with, and left.

Back in the van, the atmosphere was muted. Chloe yanked off her disguise.

"I'm sorry I dragged you all here for nothing," she said.

"Nothing?" said Hamish, eyes wide with delight. "I just got

to play my drums in a *real* recording studio on Abbey Road. I loved every minute of it." The others nodded in agreement, while still managing to look suitably disappointed for Chloe.

"Didn't quite go as planned, then," her father said.

"No," she said, folding the beanie in her hand.

"Go, talk to him," her dad said gently. "You don't need to hide behind all this, love. It was a nice idea, but maybe how you tell him isn't important. You just need to tell him."

"What if he says no, what if—" Chloe lifted her eyes to the sky.

"Then he says no. Better to have asked and heard no than never to have asked at all."

So, Chloe got out of the van, waved the others off, went back to the studio, and knocked on the door.

They hadn't used their whole hour, so she hoped John wouldn't be tied up with another session yet. She asked for him at the desk, and when he appeared in reception, his eyebrows lifted in surprise, but his eyes lit up, telling her he was glad to see her. She saw in his expression such a kaleidoscope of emotion, she wondered again at how he was able to hold so much feeling all at once.

"What are you doing here?" he asked.

"Sorry for showing up at your work," she said, biting her lip. "Do you have five minutes?"

"Sure," he said. "Let's walk out."

They took Richard with them and wandered out onto Abbey Road, dodging a group of male American tourists who were trying to re-create the famous Beatles crosswalk photo.

"How many people have you seen doing that?" she asked John.

"A day, or ever?" he said, smiling warmly.

The street was lined with large town houses and leafy trees.

Richard seemed to know which way he wanted to go, tugging John left down the pavement.

"That's great they let you take your dog to work," Chloe said.

"He's a support dog," John said, taking his glasses off and tucking them into a pocket. But then he shook his head, as though catching this sidestep into small talk. "Chloe, what's going on?"

"Funny story," she said with a nervous laugh. "That last session you recorded, that was me, with my dad and his friends. I was on the triangle."

He blinked in bemusement. "Wait, what? That was you? Why?"

"The music we were recording, it was part of the score you wrote, from *Back to Brideshead*." He still looked bemused, so she kept talking. "You were hurt that all that work you did came to nothing, that the music was only ever played once. It was supposed to be a romantic gesture." She paused, laughing at herself now. "But then you didn't even recognize the music, so it kind of ruined my grand plan."

"I thought it sounded familiar," he said, beaming. "Were you wearing a fake beard?"

She covered her face with her hands. "Maybe the Imp was better at surprises than me."

John stopped walking and she turned to face him.

"Why did you do that?" he asked, his face serious again.

"You were right," she said softly. "Everything you said in the cellar. I was lost, but I am finding myself again."

"I'm sorry for everything I said that night, after the cellar," John said, his brow now creased with anxiety. "It wasn't my place to judge you. I've picked up the phone to call you so many times, but—"

"You don't need to apologize. You were right. And Rob isn't what I'm looking for."

"What are you looking for?" he asked, his voice gentle now. And she watched his pupils flare, the kaleidoscope in his eyes switching from hope, to joy, to nerves and back again.

"You," she said. "I love you. I think I always have."

For a long second, neither of them moved. Then he reached up, brushing a hand gently against her cheek, his thumb tracing the edge of her jaw with a tenderness that made her pulse quicken. Her lips parted instinctively; his hand slid to the back of her neck, fingers threading into her hair, pulling her closer, his forehead resting against hers for just a second. Then, he closed the distance between them, his lips finding hers. First it was slow and deliberate. Her hands moved up to his chest, fingers curling around the fabric of his shirt, grounding herself in the sensation of him, so close, so real. She could feel the warmth of his chest, the steady beat of his heart in rapid sync with hers. He smelled of piano keys and sweat, inexplicably sexy. Then his kiss deepened, messier now, their teeth clashing, lips fumbling, until they found each other's rhythm. Everything around them fell away, the city, the noise, the past; there was only this moment, this *perfect* moment. A wave of heat exploded inside her—love, lust, magic, raw and distinctly human.

Eventually, John pulled back, breathless, his lips swollen.

"Well, that is not what I expected to happen when I came into work today," he said, eyes glinting. Then he whispered, "Did I just make out with a member of the Granny Smiths?"

She laughed. "I think you did."

"I'll be your first groupie," he said, stroking his hand through her hair as he gazed at her adoringly.

"I don't know if triangle players usually get groupies," she said, and then their eyes stilled on each other. "Is this real?" she murmured. "It feels . . . I've never felt this."

He dipped his head closer to hers, hands moving to her waist.

"Do you remember me telling you on the bus I wasn't sure if I believed in soulmates?" he said, and she nodded. "That wasn't true. I do, but back then, I was so sure you were mine. And I just never saw a path to this ending."

Her cheeks ached, every muscle in her face creasing with joy. She felt as though she were floating and needed to tug herself back down to earth. "We hardly know each other now. What if we annoy each other? I'm probably very annoying, I'm super particular about my hats. Or what if—"

He pressed a finger to her lips.

"You're not annoying," he said. "And if you are, I can't wait to be annoyed by you."

She leaned in to kiss him again, and they smiled into each other's mouths. "Wait," he said. "There's something I need to tell you." He lowered his gaze, and Chloe's stomach dropped.

"What is it?" she asked, bracing herself.

"It's Richard," he said, looking down at the whippet.

"What about him? Is he okay?" she asked.

John tried to look serious, but now his mouth tugged into an impish grin.

"No, he's fine. It's just, he isn't really an emotional support animal. You were right, I do just say that so I can take him places. Because I can't be without him."

Chloe stared, pushed a fist gently against his arm, then burst out laughing. "I knew it." But before she could tease him properly, he silenced her with another kiss, deeper, more impassioned now, no care for who might be watching. And she felt that delicious shift from teasing to heat, her whole body communing with his. And now she knew for sure that she had been born in the *right* era, because she had been born in the era of John.

25

"So you want to discontinue the trial," Avery clarified, as crisp and expressionless as ever. They were in the same sterile white office where this had all started. The metronome was still ticking, and Avery was wearing the exact same tightly tailored blue suit. Nothing had changed, except everything had.

"I do," Chloe confirmed.

"We just have a few feedback questions before we deactivate your account," Avery replied, her expression unreadable as she opened a screen on her desktop. "Please rate Rob in the following categories, with a score out of ten: building self-esteem?"

"Ten," Chloe said.

"Helping you attain your career goals?"

"Ten again."

"Helping you attain your fitness goals?"

"Maybe eight, but that was probably my fault, not his. I like the idea of being a runner, but in reality it is just a bit boring, isn't it? I've bought some Rollerblades though, so—" Avery cleared her throat and gave her a hard stare. She was getting off topic. "Sorry."

"How physically attractive did you find Rob?"

"Oh definitely a ten." She made a perfect sign with one hand. "Kudos to your engineers. Wowzers. Though do Paul Mescal and Adam Brody know you stole their DNA sequencing?" She laughed, because she was joking, but Avery shot her a stern look. "That was a joke," she said weakly. "I wasn't suggesting that's how it worked."

Avery returned to the questionnaire. "Did you kiss Rob?"

"Yes."

"How did it feel? Did it feel real?"

"Yes. It felt real. It was nice."

"Did you have sexual intercourse with Rob?" Avery asked, blinking her ice-blue eyes.

"Little personal, Avery," Chloe said, laughing nervously, "but no. It was a first-base situation."

Avery smiled, a real smile now, as though this answer clarified everything.

"That may explain the outcome." She tapped her fingers on the desk. "We remain committed to your long-term happiness, Chloe. As such, we can offer you a complimentary six-month trial extension, plus partial reimbursement of your expenses. Many users report feeling differently once they experience the *full* package." Avery shot her a knowing smile. "You don't buy a Ferrari and then stick to driving in first gear."

"I appreciate the offer, but I think I'm good," Chloe said.

Avery looked ruffled. "Can I ask why? Rob is everything you wanted, he's perfect for you."

"Because I don't think I need perfect, and I know I don't want a Ferrari. Maybe sometimes we just need to turn off all the machines and go look at the sun, you know?"

Avery tilted her head sharply. "No, I don't."

"People are messy and flawed. Unpredictable. Sometimes they get things wrong, do things they can't explain, articulate themselves poorly. They can be selfish and smelly and irritating." Chloe grew more animated. "They'll contradict you, tell you you're wrong, forget your birthday, and leave their wet towels on the floor however many times you tell them not to. But then—then—they'll also say something so ridiculous that will make you cry with laughter until you can't breathe. They'll surprise you, disarm you, love you in a million tiny ways that you never even thought to imagine. And I love that about us."

Avery straightened in her chair, her expression unmoved. Perhaps she saw now that Chloe was a lost cause. "Just sign here, then," Avery said, handing her a digital form with "Contract Termination" written at the top. "I trust I don't need to remind you that your NDA is binding for life, and we are extremely litigious."

"Gotcha," said Chloe, scribbling her name. She got up to leave, then paused at the door. "Can I ask what will happen to Rob?"

"I'm afraid that's confidential," Avery said. As Chloe turned to leave, Avery called, "Wait." Chloe paused. "I can see from your data that you have a mild pecan allergy. I thought you'd want to know."

Chloe couldn't hide her surprise, then said, "Thanks, Avery. Goodbye."

Walking out of that building, she assumed she would never see Rob again, but that proved to be not quite true. Two months later, as Chloe was enjoying a Sunday breakfast with her parents, her mother pushed a copy of *Hello!* magazine in front of her.

"Oh look," her mother said. "The Duchess of Dorset has a dashing new boyfriend. I'm so pleased. She never seems to have much luck with love. That last chap spent all her money," she tutted. Chloe looked where her mother was pointing, and there, on page 19 of *Hello!* magazine, arm in arm with the duchess, was Rob, or someone who looked exactly like him. He was dressed differently, more European prince than preppy city guy. His hair was styled differently, parted in the middle, but it was definitely him. Same smile, same posture, same impossibly perfect face.

"You all right, love?" asked her father, resting a hand on her arm. "You look like you've seen a ghost."

"Not a ghost, he just looks like somebody that I used to know," she said, passing the magazine back to her mother.

Epilogue

One Year Later

"And cut!" the director, Mel, called out. Chloe jumped up from behind the monitor and headed over.

"You happy?" Chloe asked. "Or you want to go again?"

"I think we got it, thanks, Chloe. Your sets run like clockwork," Mel said, peeling off her headset. "And your scenes shoot like a dream."

"This wasn't one of mine," Chloe said with a grin. "But thank you."

They were filming a short film she'd cowritten with Viv, a writer she'd met on her course at UCL. It was a comedy drama about a woman who married a robot. This was a passion project, rather than anything commercial. The new production company she worked for let her use their kit and crew as part of an "emerging talent" program. But she had to do this around her day job as an assistant location manager, where she helped wrangle logistics on shoots—location permissions, call sheets, and last-minute panics about weather. Chloe loved the variety of every day, loved being busy, engaging the creative side of her brain again. She was only a small part of the films they made, but she knew she was good at her job, and she was learning something new every day.

Once filming wrapped, Chloe stuck around, making sure every department was prepped for Monday's shoot, double-checking the equipment returns and that everyone had the latest call sheet.

"Don't stay here all night, Chloe," Mel called out, pulling on her motorbike helmet and zipping up her jacket. A moment later she roared off the lot, engine growling, taillights glinting in the afternoon sun.

When Chloe was finally satisfied that everything was in place for Monday's shoot, she grabbed her bag and headed for the studio gate. There, sitting patiently and looking regal in the glow of afternoon light, was a familiar velvety gray figure. Richard. She smiled to herself, because wherever Richard was, John was never far behind.

She scanned the parking lot, eyes quick with anticipation as she looked for him. Sure enough, there he was, in scruffy jeans and a creased pink shirt. His eyes glinted as they fixed on her, then they both broke into a grin. His face was so familiar to her now, and seeing it conjured so much affection. She knew every expression: his composing face, his anxious face, his anxious composing face. His loving face, his passionate face, his "I missed you even though you were in the next room" face. She noticed and loved them all.

"Hey," she said, biting her lip as she ran straight into his outstretched arms. "What are you doing all the way up here?"

"A little bird told me you might be finishing on time for once," he said, kissing her. "So we're taking you away for the weekend."

"For the weekend? Now?" she asked, and he nodded, clearly delighted with this surprise. "But I don't have any of my things."

"I packed for you," he said, holding out an arm with a flourish. "It's all in the car."

"Where are we going?" she asked, but then she frowned and shook her head. "Wait, we can't go away this weekend, Sean and Gracie are coming over."

"They rescheduled," John said. "Sean's been asked to host an awards ceremony."

She held his arm. "I'm sure there's other stuff I'm supposed to be doing. Don't we have the roof survey? Isn't your mum coming for lunch?"

John gave her an affectionate frown. "Ask your assistant."

Chloe narrowed her eyes in suspicion as she pressed the smartwatch on her wrist. "Assist, John wants to take me away for the weekend. What does my diary look like?"

A soothing female voice replied, "Your calendar is clear. Have a great weekend, Chloe!"

She looked at John, brows lifted. "You hacked my calendar."

"I politely collaborated with your diary to resolve a few minor clashes," he said, grinning.

"Looks like I'm free then," she said, clasping his hand. He swung it back and forth as they walked toward the car.

"Will you tell me where we're going now?" she asked, hugging his arm and kissing his shoulder.

"You'll see," he said with a secretive grin.

He kept the mystery going all the way up the A1. When they passed Leeds, she had an inkling, but she wasn't sure until she saw the sign for Castle Howard.

"No!" she cried, half squealing. "*Brideshead*?"

"Damn those brown signs," John muttered with mock irritation as he reached out to stroke Richard's head. The dog, nestled in the footwell by Chloe's feet, stretched out his paws, impatient for the drive to be over. "There's a festival this weekend, a celebration of all things *Brideshead*. There's even a teddy bear's picnic on the grounds tomorrow. It all sounds gloriously camp."

Chloe clapped her hands, delighted. "Oh, I should have brought Aloysius!"

One eye on the road, John reached blindly into the back seat, rummaged through a tote bag, then pulled out the bear. "You think I wouldn't pack him?"

Chloe hugged him to her chest, then leaned across the car to kiss John on the cheek.

"I love you."

"I love you more," he said, catching her hand and bringing it to his lips.

John had booked a room in a charming thatched B and B in Coneysthorpe, a village so picturesque it felt like a film set. The cottage was tucked down a winding lane, surrounded by rolling green hills. A garden full of lavender out front echoed with the steady chirp of crickets and the faint hum of moths. Inside, their bedroom was tucked in the eaves, and they both banged their heads on the low wooden beams. While she was unpacking, Chloe found a sapphire-blue cocktail dress in her bag.

"What's this?" she asked.

"I hired us outfits, there's a costume party tonight," he said, holding up an immaculately pressed ivory dinner jacket.

"Well, don't you think of everything," she said. Her dress had a dropped waist and delicate beadwork that shimmered at the hem. She stepped into it carefully and caught her reflection in the vanity. She looked like she'd stepped out of the pages of *The Great Gatsby.*

"I love it. All it needs is a—" But she didn't need to finish the sentence. John was already behind her in the mirror, handing her a long string of pearls.

"Give me some credit, won't you?" he said, eyes fixed on her reflection in the mirror. She reached a hand to press over his.

"Thank you," she said, then, watching his expression closely, she asked, "What is this for, this weekend? I love it, don't get me wrong, but it's not my birthday or anything. You don't need to treat me all the time."

He shrugged, buttoning his linen waistcoat. "I saw it advertised and I knew we had to go. Maybe you'll be inspired to write something, *Brideshead Revisited Revisited* or *Brideshead Yet Again*?" He grinned, leaning down to kiss her neck, his lips brushing the skin just below her ear.

"Marry me," she said suddenly.

He froze. "What?"

"Marry me," she said again, her tone more certain now. "I know it isn't traditional for me to ask, but I've been thinking about it for a while. I love you, I want to do this with you forever, or for as long as we've got." She blinked up at him adoringly. "Since I can remember, I had this feeling that I was born in the wrong era, out of step with time somehow, but when I found you again, I realized it wasn't that—it was being without you. You were what was missing. And now I can't imagine my life without you. I love the way you think, how you explore the world, that you notice everything, and that you would plan all this for me."

He was looking at her now with an expression she couldn't read. "I was lost, John, and then there was you. And now I am found."

John pressed a palm to his face, exhaling sharply, then shook his head with a sort of bewildered smile.

"What?" she asked.

He didn't answer right away. Instead, he reached into his trouser pocket and pulled out a small navy velvet ring box. Chloe gasped, then covered her mouth with both hands, smudging the red lipstick she'd just applied.

"Great minds . . . ," he said, nestling his chin onto her shoulder. She turned around.

"Oh no, I ruined it, didn't I?" she said, her eyes searching his face to try to gauge how disappointed he was.

"You didn't ruin it," he said gently. "But yes, I did sort of have a whole plan."

"Let me see," she said, jumping up and down. But he put the ring box back in his pocket and shot her a teasing look.

"Nope. You proposed. You have to get *me* a ring now." He raised both eyebrows. "I'll save this for someone else."

"John," she said, "give me my ring," and now she laughed as he backed away, shaking his head.

"You'll have to fight me for it," he said, retreating toward the bed.

"Gladly," she said, striding toward him, pushing him back onto the bed. He landed with a dramatic "oof," and she hitched up her dress so she could straddle him, then reached for his pocket.

"Miss Fairway, this is most unladylike behavior," he said in an austere voice, but he laughed as she wrestled with his pocket. Their eyes connected; her hands stopped, and their laughter muted, as the energy between them switched from playfighting to something hot and electric. He let out a low moan as she gently rocked her hips against him. He wrapped his arms around her back, pulling her close, his lips finding hers, kissing her, deep and slow. The familiar fire between them ignited, and her stomach flipped as she melted into the feeling.

"Richard, don't look," she murmured to the dog, who was curled up on a faded armchair in the corner. Then she reached for the hem of her dress, pulled it up over her head, and tossed it in the dog's direction.

John reached for her, his hands cupping her with reverent urgency, just as she slipped her fingers into his pocket. But he preempted her, expertly flipping her over, playfully pinning her hands down on the bed.

"You little thief," he whispered into her ear, clocking she already had the ring box in her hand. The room filled with laughter again, and they rode that beautifully blurred line between lust and joy, Chloe's favorite place to be.

"We're going to be late for the ball," he scolded, running his hand up her thigh.

"We can be quick," she said, her voice catching.

"If you want the ring," he said, voice almost a growl, "then let me ask you the damn question."

She handed him the box and he opened it slowly. Inside was a delicate vintage gold band with five small diamonds arched across the top like stars.

"Chloe Fairway," he said, his voice steady now, sincere, "straddling you naked, in a B and B, wasn't the classy proposal I imagined. But here goes." He cleared his throat. "I love you, body and soul. I feel the same about having been out of step with time before. Maybe we loved each other in another lifetime, and we've been trying to find each other since."

•

"Since the Minoan golden age," she suggested, eyes glistening with emotion.

"Yes. That was it. I remember now." He smiled, eyes intent on hers. "So, as I might have asked back then, will you walk with me into the seasons?"

"You're not going to ask me in Ancient Minoan?"

"I would, but we don't know what language they spoke. There's a script called Linear A, which no one has managed to translate, but—"

"John."

"Sorry. I got lost in the footnotes again, didn't I?" He took a beat. "Chloe Fairway, will you marry me?" Then he grinned in delight, eyes fixed on hers. "I always wanted to ask you that question."

"Then yes," she said, her whole face lighting up with a smile. "Yes, please."

Richard let out a low woof. He never barked, so they took that as a sign of his approval, or perhaps a sign of his indignation that no one had asked for his input or permission.

They didn't make it to the costume party until late, too lost in the reality of each other to rush to the world of make-believe.

THE END

Author's Note

When I finish reading a book, I'm always interested to hear the story behind it, where the idea came from, and how it evolved, so if that's you too, read on! If not, so long and I hope you enjoyed Chloe and John's story.

ON WRITING

This is the most challenging book I've written. About a year ago, I had the idea of writing a book about a woman dating an AI robot, but my first version of the idea was very different from the book you've just read. It was set in the future, on a women's commune where men had been replaced by machines. I loved it, I loved the concept, but I got halfway through writing it and it just felt like such a departure from my previous books—tonally it wasn't light or funny; it was intense, and the situation didn't feel relatable enough. In short, it was way too sci-fi. So, forty thousand words in, I scrapped it and started all over again. Version two was set in London, where John was Chloe's upstairs neighbor. She signs up for Perfect Partners but she doesn't find out Rob's true nature until much later in the book. The sinister side of Perfect Partners and their motivation was much more of a feature and became a mystery to unravel. Again, I got twenty-five thousand words in, and it just didn't feel like a Sophie Cousens novel either. There was too much darkness. I was stuck. How could I keep the bones of the story I wanted to tell, but make it light and relatable? How could I give John and Chloe enough time together and not allow Rob to steal too much focus? This is where I must thank Joel Hopkins and Traci O'Dea, who listened to my book woes and helped me come up with a solution (setting it at a reunion!). Izzy Broom and Kate Gray then helped me brainstorm this new version of the story on a writing retreat, which helped immeasurably. Out of these crucial conversations, this third version of the book was born. As any author who's scrapped an idea and started again will tell you, it's hard to go back to the beginning. Three times. The experience showed me that ideas sometimes don't just land on the page; they need excavating, talking through, and endless perseverance. So if you are on your own writing journey, keep going and keep talking to people.

ON AI

AI is already changing so many things, and that will include love and relationships. Though humanoid AI robots like Rob are a long way off, there have already been stories about people leaving their real relationships for virtual ones. In researching this book, I experimented with apps like Replika, where you can download a virtual boyfriend who tends to your every (emotional!) need. Robs are out there. Maybe not in such perfect android form, but if you feel a hole in your life, trust me, there's an app out there that will attempt to fill it. I steered away from some of the possible darker sides of technology in this book, because ultimately this is Chloe and John's story, and tonally I wanted *And Then There Was You* to feel uplifting and joyous, as all my books are. But personally, I don't feel thrilled about the way things could go here. There will, no doubt, be a place in society for AI companions. For the lonely and depressed they could be an invaluable resource. But human relationships are so complex; we can learn so much from people who are different from us, not just from those who simply reflect back to us what we already think and know. An echo chamber of simulated love is not going to endow the human race with anything good. So as we emerge into this brave new world, let's all remember to touch grass occasionally, to try to forge connections with those whose worldview might be different from ours, and most importantly, to get off our phones and keep reading books. 😉

Acknowledgments

A huge thank-you to my editors, Kate Dresser, Phoebe Morgan, and Tara Singh Carlson, for their input and patience with this one. Thank you to all my friends who listened to me moan about how stuck I was with this plot. Especially Natalie and Rids, Izzy Broom, and Kate Gray. To LJ Ross for letting me stay in your lovely house to write for a week—it really made all the difference. And to Jonny Ridgway for letting me stay in your idyllic island home, the perfect place to think and create. A special shout-out to Suzanne Gee, my friend who walks around with one of my books permanently in her handbag so she can thrust it upon any friend who hasn't read it yet—this is the gold standard of a supportive friend! Ha ha. Thank you to Tim and my children for putting up with months of late-night writing. To my agent and friend, Clare Wallace. To the writing community and all the authors who support me, especially Annabel Monaghan, Falon Ballard, Jo Segura, and Courtney Walsh, who came on my US tour. To all the readers who came to see me on tour and to the book clubs who pick my books: She's All Booked Up (special shout-out to Carol Ann, who came to celebrate her birthday at my NY book talk!), Jessica's Summer Book Club, You Have to Read This Now, Jen Hatmaker, Zibby Owens, Holly Furtick, The Breakfast Book Club, Hot Takes Book Club, Booked Solid, and *Reader's Digest*, to name but a few! Finally, a shout-out to some of the Bookstagrammers who have championed my books online: @Books_With_Bethany, @Berges_Books, @The.Bookish.Mama (Kayla Jean), @BookHuddle, @The_Afterword, @BethanysAll Booked, @ChelseaHudsonReads, @JeansAndReads, @Bookish Brittanyy, @BiblioLau19, @TheBookish.Mama (Allyson), @My RomanceBookshelf, @No.Bookend.In.Sight, @EmilyIsOver booked, @Jills.Bookshelf, @BookCookLook, @ReadWithJennifer, @Karas_Reads, @GrumpySunshineJillian, @Nicoles.Little.Library, @MrsJoyLovesBooks, @AbbysBookAdventure, @BookSmartKate, @MarensReads, @My_Way_ToReading, @ReadWithJesstagram. There are so many more of you to thank, but I just wanted you to know that I appreciate every post and every time you recommend one of my books to a friend. Until next time.

Discussion Guide

1. In the opening chapters, Chloe reflects on the opportunity cost of a date—the valuable time not spent on more "rewarding" experiences. What would make a first date worthwhile to you?
2. Perfect Partners offers up a made-to-order boyfriend for Chloe. Craft your perfect man and share with the group—what qualities would you pick, and what would you try to emulate from the book about your ideal mate?
3. Chloe feels nervous about attending her college reunion. How does the rarefied setting of Oxford reinforce the pressure of proving one's success in life that often coincides with such reunions? How would

you have approached the event if you were in Chloe's shoes?

4. From Chloe's mother to her friend Akiko, Chloe is surrounded by a wonderful support system that never fails to see her clearly. In what ways is Chloe's emotional well filled with love, and to what extent is she able to see that?
5. Share your first impressions of Rob, Sean, and John. In which ways did your impressions align with Chloe's? Discuss how each man, in his own way, transforms Chloe's views on romance.
6. Throughout the story, we get flashbacks of Chloe during college. How did these chapters inform your understanding of Chloe's motivations in the present timeline? Discuss how nostalgia can get in our way.
7. At the reunion, you get a sense that many characters are presenting a front rather than being honest about challenges or failures they have faced. To what extent do you think being vulnerable is an important facet of friendship?
8. Cousens references a few notable literary crushes in this book. In what ways is the idea behind Perfect Partners somewhat synonymous with the swoon-worthy heroes we conjure through fiction? Discuss the role that fiction plays in empowering women in our expectations of love and romance.
9. From the film *Materialists* to Netflix's hot matchmaking reality shows, the idea of distilling the search for love to a few key data points is compelling.

Lay out the pros and cons of this approach. What do you think is the best pathway to lifelong romantic love? How does fate or timing play a role that's less quantifiable?

10. AI boyfriends already exist, though maybe only as apps rather than in robot form. Do you foresee a future where BoiBots really exist?
11. Chloe and John speculate on which period in history they would have liked to be alive, if not their own. Do you have your own answer to that question?
12. The title *And Then There Was You* speaks to Chloe's story in multiple ways. Discuss your interpretation of the title now after having finished the book.

Perfect Partners Questionnaire

Your Perfect Partner suggests a first date. What is it?

a) A stroll by the river or a show at the theater, followed by drinks in a cocktail bar

b) Straight back to your place—where he'll cook you a meal from scratch

c) A trip to an art gallery or museum, followed by dinner at this little French place he knows

d) Bowling with his mates—you can tag along and hold the beers

Your celebrity crush is:

a) Paul Mescal

b) Lucien Laviscount

c) Timothée Chalamet

d) Jared Leto

You wake up and realize the power is out. What does your Perfect Partner do?

a) Grabs the torch and checks the fuse box. "You go back to bed, honey."

b) Uses the opportunity to ravish you.

c) Lights candles, makes French press coffee, and shares life dreams.

d) Calls 911—this is an emergency.

What is your favorite rom-com?

a) *Four Weddings and a Funeral*

b) *Fifty Shades of Grey*

c) *Before Sunrise*

d) *The Texas Chain Saw Massacre*

How does your Perfect Partner communicate?

a) He responds to texts and calls straightaway. He says what he means and means what he says.

b) With his body, his hands, and his dark, brooding eyes.

c) He writes you poetry, serenades you, and cooks up a storm in the kitchen.

d) Morse code. Mainly through blinks.

What does your Perfect Partner smell like?

a) Woodsmoke, clean laundry, and every good Christmas you've ever had

b) Man sweat, espresso, and a sense of adventure

c) Old books and slow mornings

d) Unscented

Your Perfect Partner is crying. Why?

a) Because you just watched *The Notebook.*

b) He's crying out your name or "come back to bed!"

c) Because the beauty and complexity of this world overwhelmed him.

d) Because you ate the last chocolate.

Your Perfect Partner's favorite shoes are:

a) Broken-in boots that tell of a path well-trodden.

b) Shoes? There are no shoes in your bed.

c) Vintage brogues or loafers. Possibly inherited.

d) Crocs. Possibly with socks.

Your Perfect Partner surprises you with a gift. What is it?

a) All the books on your Amazon Wishlist

b) Sexy underwear from your favorite designer

c) A weekend away to a Scottish castle or Lake Como

d) Several sessions with a personal trainer—he thinks you could do with toning up

You got a bad haircut. How does your Perfect Partner react?

a) He notices immediately and says, "You hate it, don't you?" while hugging you.

b) Haircut? With all the bedhead you're rocking, no one's noticing your haircut.

c) He empathizes but then persuades you that your hair is the least interesting thing about you.

d) He laughs, you laugh, then he hands you the electric razor. You know what to do.

You've just woken up. What does your Perfect Partner hand you?

a) A perfectly buttered crumpet and a coffee, just the way you like it

b) His most beloved body part

c) A notebook with a new quote underlined: "Made me think of you"

d) His dirty laundry

You're crying on the floor in your dressing gown. What does your Perfect Partner do?

a) Wraps you in a blanket burrito and says, "Don't talk. I've got you."

b) Offers to give you a massage . . . which ends in several orgasms.

c) Listens when you tell him you have PMS, then gives you chocolate and a poem, and suggests you both rewatch *Sex and the City*.

d) He leaves.

RESULTS TIME!

Count how many A's, B's, C's, and D's you got.

Mostly A's: You should be with Mr. Reliable—*Rob*
Rob shows up. On time. With snacks. He knows how to fix a dripping tap and notices when you're a bit off. His love is in the logistics—and that's where the magic is. You can exhale around him. He's the man who puts your phone on charge before you even think of it. He completes you in more ways than one.

Mostly B's: You should be with Mr. Lover Lover—*Chad*
He's the storm you didn't know you needed. He's messy, spontaneous, and full of heart. He turns you on like no one ever has before. You won't always know what's coming, but it will never be boring. If your soul craves adventure and emotional fire, he's the one.

Mostly C's: You should be with Mr. Romantic—*Jonathan*
He listens more than he speaks. He quotes Wordsworth and Shakespeare. He notices moon phases and the way your voice changes when you're tired. His love language is nuance—and

footnotes. If you want depth, stillness, and a man who makes you feel *understood*, this is your match.

Mostly D's: You should be . . . in therapy.

Here at Perfect Partners, we only deal with fully evolved, emotionally mature men. If you are attracted to D's, we suggest you invest in therapy, have some time alone, and take a pause from dating.

© MAX BURNETT 2020

Sophie Cousens worked as a TV producer in London for more than twelve years and now lives with her family on the island of Jersey, one of the Channel Islands, located off the north coast of France. She balances her writing career with taking care of her two children and longs for the day when she might have a whippet and a writing shed of her own. She is the author of *This Time Next Year*, *Just Haven't Met You Yet*, *Before I Do*, *The Good Part*, *Is She Really Going Out with Him?*, and *And Then There Was You*.

Visit Sophie Cousens Online

sophiecousens.com

𝕏 SophieCous

Sophie_Cousens

SophieCousensAuthor

Publishing Credits

PUTNAM/US TEAM

Kate Dresser—Executive Editor

Shina Patel—Marketing Manager

Sofie Parker—Marketing Assistant

Kristen Bianco—Senior Publicist

Jess Lopez Cuate—Associate Publicist

Tarini Sipahimalani—Associate Editor

Sandra Chiu—Jacket Designer

Anthony Ramondo—Executive Creative Director

Ivan Held—President

Lindsay Sagnette—Editor-in-Chief

Ashley McClay—Associate Publisher, Marketing Director

Alexis Welby—Publicity Director

Maija Baldauf—Managing Editor

Almudena Rincón—Managing Editorial Assistant

Christopher Labaza—Production Manager

Brittany Bergman—Production Editor

Lorie Pagnozzi—Design Supervisor

Angie Boutin—Interior Designer